PENGUIN

TO WHOM

Ruth Prawer Jhabvala was born in
to England at the age of twelve. She was edu
London University, and began writing after graduation and marriage.
Her published work includes four collections of short stories, *Like Birds, Like Fishes*, *How I Became a Holy Mother*, *A Stronger Climate* and *An Experience of India*; and the novels *The Nature of Passion*, *Esmond in India*, *The Householder*, *Get Ready for Battle*, *A Backward Place*, *A New Dominion*, *Heat and Dust*, winner of the 1975 Booker Prize, and *In Search of Love and Beauty*.

She has also collaborated on several film scripts, among them *Shakespeare Wallah*, *Autobiography of a Princess*, *Quartet* and *The Europeans*. She has written several plays for television and the film script for the film of *Heat and Dust*, which had its world première at the beginning of 1983. Ruth Prawer Jhabvala won the Neil Gunn International Fellowship in 1978.

Her writing has won widespread acclaim: C. P. Snow said of her, 'Someone once said that the definition of the highest art is that one should feel that life is this and not otherwise. I do not know of a writer living who gives that feeling with more unqualified certainty than Mrs Jhabvala' and the *Sunday Times* called her 'a writer of genius ... of world class – a master story-teller'.

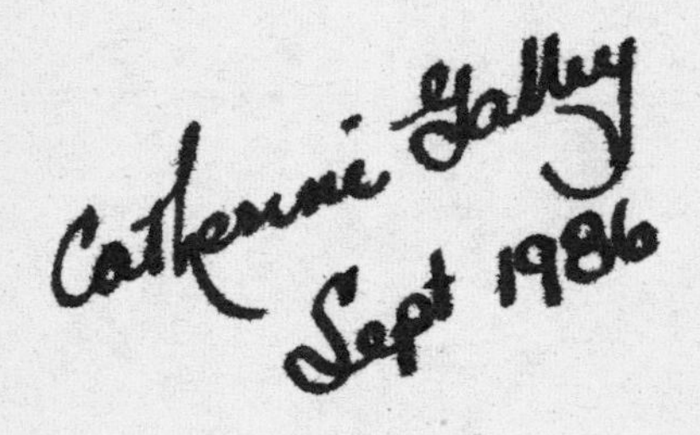

TO WHOM SHE WILL

RUTH PRAWER JHABVALA

PENGUIN BOOKS

Penguin Books Ltd, Harmondsworth, Middlesex, England
Viking Penguin Inc., 40 West 23rd Street, New York, New York 10010, U.S.A.
Penguin Books Australia Ltd, Ringwood, Victoria, Australia
Penguin Books Canada Ltd, 2801 John Street, Markham, Ontario, Canada L3R 1B4
Penguin Books (N.Z.) Ltd, 182–190 Wairau Road, Auckland 10, New Zealand

First published by Allen and Unwin 1955
Published in Penguin Books 1985

Made and printed in Great Britain by
Richard Clay (The Chaucer Press) Ltd,
Bungay, Suffolk

Filmset in Monophoto Times by
Northumberland Press Ltd, Gateshead,
Tyne and Wear

1

Mrs Radha Chakravarty and her daughter Amrita sat in a tonga. Two ladies unmoving and passive, yet jerking up and down, backward and forward, with grave faces, as the carriage rattled over the street. Amrita, slim and pale, wore a yellow sari of chiffon as fine as a dried leaf; her small head with the very black hair piled and coiled on top swayed on her neck. But Radha was stout and darkened by age and the sun; large authoritative thighs pushed against her grey silk sari and her black umbrella was laid across her lap. Behind them hooted a car; Radha looked keenly at its occupants, while Amrita looked through them. The tonga moved aside and the car passed them, hooting loudly. Radha was annoyed: 'When they have a big car, they think they have to make a lot of noise.' Every time she rode in a tonga she felt annoyed in this way; this was because out of three sisters she was the only one who owned no motor car.

The tonga turned without warning into a side street. A car behind had to brake suddenly and painfully, and nearly ran into a coolie who was staidly crossing the road with a basket of oranges on his head. The driver of the car stuck his head out of the window and swore at the tongawala, who swore at the coolie, who gaped. Another turning, and the stalls and shops and cars and cries were left behind; another, and now there were tall yellow houses, heavy with respectability. Radha took a deep breath; here at last was the air she had been born to breathe. They stopped outside a house taller and more respectable than all the rest. Radha fumbled with her large worn bag and dropped it.

'Now see what you have done!' she cried at the tongawala, who promptly asked for three times the normal fare.

Inside the house two servants who stood at the bottom of the stairs beamed with delight and salaamed. Radha gave them a quick practised scrutiny, found all correct, and nodded a brief acknowledgement.

'Are you well?' the older servant asked, while the younger one grinned and grinned.

'Well,' Radha answered over her shoulder as she walked upstairs.

The two servants looked at one another, nodding, while the older said, 'There she goes,' and the younger repeated, 'Yes, there she goes,' and then they both laughed and looked pleased.

The two ladies entered the study. It was dark inside and musty with old age. At a large desk with pigeon-holes and carved clusters of grapes sat Rai Bahadur Tara Chand; he had a massive head with thin lips and an impressive brow, and he wore a white shirt and a dhoti which fell like sculpture over his broad knees.

'Good morning, Pappaji,' Radha said with exaggerated deference. She put all the filial respect she could into the tone of her voice; this she did partly because she always felt nervous before her father and in a need to placate him; and partly as an example to Amrita, to demonstrate to her how much respect a daughter owed to a parent.

The Rai Bahadur looked sternly at her over his steel-rimmed spectacles. He had always looked stern but since his retirement even more so: facial and vocal expression were all that were left to him with which to impose his dignity on the world.

'Your sisters are in the drawing-room,' he told Radha, who turned to Amrita.

'I think your grandfather wants to speak with you about something,' she said coyly. The old man tapped his foot with the big broad toes lying flat on the sandal. Radha threw a significant glance at her daughter, who looked the other way.

'You may sit down,' the old man told Amrita when they were alone. She sat facing him across the desk, on the very edge of the massive oak chair, which had corkscrew legs and a leather seat studded with brass tacks round the edge. She felt very young and naughty.

'I think you know what I want to speak about,' the old man said. His voice was precise, the accent pure English. The voice and the accent of the distinguished barrister who had had so many English friends; friends who had said about him, 'He is like one of us.'

Amrita said, 'I think so,' in a very low voice.

'You think so,' he repeated. And then: 'I suppose your mother has already spoken to you.'

'Oh,' Amrita said, her large eyes larger with distress, 'Mamma never stops speaking to me about it.'

'It is indeed a serious business,' he said sternly. She felt very miserable, remembering how serious it was, and looked at the floor. 'I have inquired into the young man's family,' he said, and left a pause of which she was not intended to take advantage. 'The result,' pause, 'was not satisfactory.'

'But Grandfather –' she said, looking up at him, appealing.

He held up a hand of authority which silenced her. 'I agree that in this country an exaggerated stress is laid on such matters. But you know that I myself am not hidebound in this way; that indeed I have allowed two of my own daughters to marry outside their immediate community, and in one case quite distinctly beneath her own level of, shall we say, breeding and fortune.'

Again a pause; and this time Amrita said, 'You mean Mamma?'

'Let us remain to the point.'

'Yes, Grandfather.'

'Well then. It is apparent that I am one who is willing to leave a generous margin in these matters; that I do not insist on the exact parallel. But in your case' – and he looked at her searchingly – 'in your case, the margin, the discrepancy between the two families, the young man's and yours, is too wide. It is a gulf that I cannot find it in my conscience to allow you to bridge.' He let the last sentence put the full stop; it seemed to him a fitting and a conclusive metaphor. The phrase echoed in her ears. She wondered if the interview was over.

Not quite.

'I have also,' he went on, 'spoken to the young man himself, and I may mention that I was not impressed either by his personality or by his capabilities. However,' he said, 'that is a point on which I do not wish to insist. If the family background had been satisfactory, I would not have unduly concerned myself over the young man's deficiencies. They are, after all, your affair.'

She felt sick with misery. This was the hardest: why should Grandfather have found Hari so wanting? The only thing she could tell herself was that he had not understood him; and this she did.

The old man nodded at her. 'It is nearly time for lunch,' he said. She got up and noiselessly left the room.

She would have liked to be alone, but she had to go and join her mother and her aunts. They were sitting in the drawing-room, shut in by pieces of heavy English furniture and a clutter of tastelessly chosen objets d'art. The curtains were tightly drawn and there was the same musty smell as in the study.

'You are not looking well, Amrita. What is the matter?' Tarla auntie said severely. She was sitting on the edge of a red plush arm-chair, thin and dried up with her hair cut short and permanently waved into precise folds.

'What is the matter!' Radha repeated contemptuously. 'How can she look well when she does not lead a good life?'

'She is a working girl,' Mira auntie said with a kind smile, throwing two cashew nuts into her mouth. She was very fat and very soft, and wore a sari patterned all over with enormous yellow sunflowers.

'Working girl!' Radha snorted. 'It is a sickness.' She looked keenly at her daughter, trying to read her reaction to the talk with the grandfather. But Amrita was on her guard. She pretended to be engrossed in a little sandstone ornament standing on the occasional table next to her. There were many such ornaments in the room: little china figurines, a lacquered musical box, symbolic marble statues – a lady with a lyre, lovers sprawled on a rock – two cuckoo-clocks, an oil painting representing a goddess sitting on a cloud. They had all been brought back by the grandfather from his travels round Europe, and were matters of great family pride: 'This comes from Vienna, this from Florence in Italy, this from Baden-Baden in Switzerland.' There was also a portrait of the grandfather looking extremely dignified in his barrister's robes; and a yellowing photograph in a silver frame of the dead grandmother, small and gentle and old even in middle age, with her hands folded and the sari covering her head.

'Girls nowadays must work,' Tarla auntie said, 'they must be independent.'

'Please do not try to impress us,' Radha said. 'We know very well already how modern you are.'

Tarla auntie disdained to reply.

'But it is only a few hours a week,' Mira auntie said. 'And it is so nice. Always I turn on my radio when I know our Amrita is announcing, and I sit and listen and if anybody comes I say, "this is my niece Amrita whom you hear".'

Radha let out a snort of disgust. She did not remember how proud she too had been when Amrita had first become a part-time announcer on the radio. Not possessing a set herself, she had gone in to her neighbour's whenever Amrita was announcing, and she had sat there in their best arm-chair and looked proud. But the novelty had worn off quickly; she could just as well hear her daughter at home and in the flesh.

Tarla auntie made a come-back: 'Perhaps you want the poor girl only to sit at home and wait to be married.'

'What other duty has she in life,' Radha promptly answered, 'than to be married and give me grandchildren?'

Amrita tried hard not to listen. She was thinking that of course Grand-father had quite failed to understand Hari. But her mother was intent on drawing her in: 'And these terrible people she meets there at the radio, they are all not fit to speak with a girl of good family.' Amrita still made no response, but played with the tassels of the lamp-shade in orange silk.

'It is good for a girl to mix with other classes of society,' Tarla auntie said. 'It broadens the outlook.'

'There are the servants,' Radha replied. Amrita dropped the tassels and turned now to her mother, touched after all.

'Why do you speak like that, Mamma,' she said. 'We were not so proud when Pappa was alive.'

'Those times were quite different,' Radha said unperturbed. 'Then it was an honour to be poor and have nothing.' And she looked, out of habit, defiantly at her sisters: it was a relic of those times when she had had to make a virtue out of cotton saris and a husband who was often in prison.

'How hot it is,' Mira auntie said, fanning herself with a little handkerchief, and hoping to give a more pleasant turn to the conversation.

'But today a girl of good family must be very careful,' Radha went on. 'She must always be a lady and speak only with people who are fit to speak with ladies. And the people you meet at the radio station,' she concluded decisively, 'are not fit to speak with ladies.'

Tarla auntie drummed on the side of her armchair with skinny fingers. 'Your ideas,' she said with emphasis, 'are feudal.'

'Such words,' Radha took her up immediately, 'may sound very good on your Committees, but here we do not like them. Feudal!' she repeated with disgust, 'what does it mean, feudal-peudal, why can you not speak like other people?'

Tarla shrugged her shoulders and replied, 'I am not very much used to speaking with ignorant people.'

'It *is* hot,' Mira auntie said hastily.

Radha drew a long breath in order to answer Tarla with sufficient emphasis, but just then the butler came in to announce that lunch was ready. This effectively changed her train of thought. She let out her breath again and, out of habit rather than conviction, almost absent-mindedly, scolded the butler for delaying too long.

The dining-room was also furnished in oppressive Victorian style. The dark curtains were drawn to shut out the sun. The silver shone dully. The broad heavy dining-table, with the legs carved into lions' heads, was spread with a gleaming white cloth and laid with initialled cutlery. The servants moved noiselessly over the marble floor, filling up the water glasses and holding the trays with food for the diners to serve themselves. They ate curried vegetables with cutlets and curds and chapatis, followed by a mountain of very white rice and chicken-curry. There was little talk because the Rai Bahadur did not feel inclined to encourage conversation. He sat at the head of the table and dominated his family, which was all that was left to him to dominate. From time to time he spoke, pronounced upon the weather or the quality of rationed rice with ringing authority. He addressed himself solely to Tarla auntie, who answered him precisely and in a clear, rather loud voice, though he was not at all deaf.

After lunch the Rai Bahadur retired back to his study, there to sit very upright, though with eyes shut, in a leather arm-chair with ear-flaps; asleep, he looked monumental and immovable. The ladies went back to the drawing-room. In spite of the drawn curtains and the fan turning with a low whirr from the ceiling, the room was heavy with noonday heat. This heat, together with their lunch, acted as a pleasant and irresistible soporific. Mira auntie went unashamedly to sleep in her arm-chair; she snored with a happy liquid sound. Radha clicked her tongue and said that Mira had no self-control. But after a while she herself began to yawn; yawned and yawned and finally retired to the bedroom which, before their marriage, she had shared with her sister Mira, and lay down on the counterpane of pink silk.

'So, Amrita,' Tarla auntie said when they were left alone. But what Amrita wanted less than anything now was another confidential talk.

She answered with a feigned yawn and an apologetic smile, said, 'I think I will go and lie down,' and went to the bedroom where her mother was lying with her hair straggling loose and her sari crumpled about her; sleep had swollen up her face, and she looked dissipated.

Tarla auntie too got up after a while and retired to the bedroom which had been hers before marriage. She took off her sari and folded it very neatly before stretching herself, thin and rigid, on the bed.

The drawing-room was left to the snoring of Mira auntie and the ticking of the two cuckoo-clocks. Silently and eternally the goddess sat on her cloud, the lady played her lyre, the lovers sprawled on their rock. The musical box had been broken long ago.

2

Hari Sahni was a pleasant-looking young man. He wore a neat little moustache and his hair was always shiny and oiled. He was also the eldest son in the family, so it was no wonder that they all thought very highly of him. He lived with his mother, his younger sister, her husband and three children, and his younger brother in the downstairs part of a one-storey house in one of the new colonies. They had three rooms and, leading off the courtyard, a very small kitchen and an even smaller lavatory-bathroom. There was a door in the courtyard wall but instead of leading into the street, this now led into a little shed made of wooden planks, where their cow lived.

Hari sat in the courtyard on a charpoy, eating his dinner. He ate gram and vegetables and curds out of little brass bowls on a tray, and his mother kept bringing him freshly made chapatis with which he shovelled up his food. She watched him, saying 'Eat, son, eat.' She was a short, healthy old woman, dressed in a white cotton sari which she wore pulled over her head. The younger brother sat on another charpoy, eating a banana and looking discontent. He was a sturdy boy, almost fat, with a face like a potato, quite unlike Hari who was slim and sleek.

It was evening and very noisy. The three children were bouncing a ball against the courtyard wall and quarrelling as to whose turn it was next, while their mother, milking the cow in the shed, stuck her head out from time to time and threatened to tear them to pieces. The people living on the upper floor were having their usual fight on the stairs. Out in the street a man with huge coloured balloons bobbing on a stick was blowing a little tin horn to advertise himself. A car, trying to pass, hooted incessantly, while three women stood in the middle of the road and loudly abused the panwala who sold betel-leaves and Coca-Cola in the little three-sided hut with a straw roof. A few houses away, the inevitable wedding was being celebrated; familiar and sentimental film songs came wailing unendingly through a loudspeaker.

When he had finished eating, Hari poured the water from his drinking-glass over his hands to wash them and stretched himself out on the charpoy. He stared up into the sky and thought vaguely pleasant thoughts about Amrita. These became clouded every time he remembered his interview with the grandfather, so he did his best not to remember. Instead he hummed loudly in tune with the music from the wedding.

Mohini, his younger sister, came out of the shed with a jug of frothy milk, which she set down in order to slap her children, one two three, very fairly and equally. Then she put her hand to her throat and made vomiting noises. The old mother clicked her tongue – 'You are sick again?' Mohini nodded and made more noises in her throat, and her mother cursed, in a general way, all husbands who, though they earned not above Rupees 250 a month and had to live with their wives' mothers, still thought of nothing but their own pleasure.

Under cover of this, the younger brother appealed to Hari, 'Give us two annas.' Without stopping to think nice thoughts about Amrita, Hari put his hand in his pocket. The mother saw him and shouted, 'Do not give that Satan any money!' but too late, for the boy had already disappeared with his prize and was on his way for a cone of gram.

'I will tear his eyes out,' the mother said, 'a hundred times I have told him, do not dare ask your elder brother for money!'

Hari murmured, 'Let him be,' and continued to dwell on the thoughts of a lover, swaying his head in time with the sweet-sad song that came oozing out of the loudspeaker.

'Ah, you are too good,' the mother said, looking down at him fondly as he lay stretched out on the charpoy, one arm under his head, his eyes melting in dreams. Mohini was being sick in the bathroom, loudly and with relish, while her children listened to her outside the door. The little servant-boy, aged nine and with a perpetually worried expression on his face, was on his hands and knees in the kitchen, wiping a wet cloth over the floor.

'Too good,' the mother repeated, and when Mohini came out of the bathroom, announcing that she was feeling better now, she told her, 'He is too good, again he has given money to that Babla, he will spoil him.'

'The good-for-nothing,' Mohini said, shaking her fist in the direction of the door through which the younger brother had disappeared, 'what for does he want money, he gets enough at home with which to stuff his stomach.'

The mother was still looking down at Hari and shaking her head over his goodness. 'Too good,' she was murmuring, and at length, with a deep sigh, 'How happy will be the woman whom our Kaka takes to wife'; Kaka being the name by which Hari was known to his elder family-members.

Mohini slapped a hand in front of her mouth, and her eyes brimmed over with laughter. She spluttered from behind her hand, 'How is your Memsahib, brother?' and went into a fit of giggling.

'That is only talk,' the mother reproved her, and stroked Hari's hair. 'He is a good son, he will marry a nice girl, you will see; one of our own girls whom his family will choose for him.' She shouted at the little servant-boy who sat gaping at them from the kitchen threshold, 'Get in, you, do your work!' though not in an unkindly manner.

'And his Memsahib?' Mohini laughed. 'How she will cry when we make a wedding for him!'

Hari got up slowly and said, 'I will go for a walk.'

'You are going to your Memsahib?' his sister teased, and then hid her face in her hands and rocked herself backwards and forwards with silent laughter.

Hari was a little sad because there was no one at home who could understand about his feelings for Amrita; so he went to his sister's house in search of sympathy.

He walked down to the end of the road and then turned the corner. In his own street, the houses still looked yellow, the plaster crumbling off only in places, and the road still relatively clean; but in the street around the corner, though it had been constructed at the same time, respectability had already degenerated. The houses oozed brown wounds and bulged out of doors and windows with children and washing and jutting ends of furniture. Banana-peels, tomato-skins and rotting bits of vegetable lay squashed in the dust, sniffed by skinny pariah-dogs. On a waste patch, tiny low huts made of mud and old planks of wood had sprung up, stuffed with too many women and too many children, old rags, newspapers, worn-out blankets and discarded tins. Privately owned cows walked slowly up and down the road or sat with spread haunches, flicking their tails. A grey bullock, belonging to no one, grazed hopefully among the huts.

But when Hari turned the corner again, respectability came back in a road of privately built houses. They were fairly large houses, detached from one another and incorporating all the favourite whims of the owners – rashes of fantastically curved jalis, red drainpipes, pillars like snakes. The tiny gardens in front were smothered in indiscriminately planted bushes, and flowerless creepers climbed thickly up the walls. Many doctors lived here; there were big boards printed over with degrees and qualifications. There was also an advocate, an income-tax adviser and a private maternity home. In this street lived Hari's eldest sister Prema.

She was, as usual, lying on the bed eating sweets. The house had five rooms, all very expensively furnished with three-piece suites and coffee-tables and silver vases, but Prema and her husband lived mostly in the bedroom. When Hari appeared in the doorway, his sister said 'Come' and sniffed unhappily. Tears were rolling down her cheeks on to the luridly illustrated magazine open before her.

'What is it?' Hari asked apprehensively. He hoped he would not have to listen to her sorrows; he had come to talk about his own.

She wiped her knuckles over her cheeks and smiled. 'This story,' she said, tapping the magazine in front of her.

'The story?'

'You will laugh at me,' she said.

'But why do you have to cry over a story?'

New tears came rolling down her cheeks. 'You must not laugh at me. You do not know how I feel it. It is such a wonderful story, so sad: and it is my life, my life exactly.'

'Your life?' he said, and took a sweet. He hoped she would not be too long over this.

'Take, take,' she said, pushing the bowl of sweets nearer to him. 'It is fresh barfi, six rupees a seer. The woman in this story, she is married.'

'So?'

'Unhappily married,' she went on, glancing at him significantly. 'Her husband – he is bad. He treats her badly. He – he goes to other women.' And then the tears began to flow more quickly and her voice sobbed: 'My life,' she cried, 'my life exactly!'

'But why?' Hari said, 'Suri does not.'

'He does!' she wailed. 'I am sure he does!'

'No, no,' he soothed, 'you are mistaken.'

'I am not a child,' she said, wiping her tears away with her net duppata. 'I know the world. I have read much and I have thought much and I know all about it. A man like he – always away from home – every night he comes home later and later – and I here alone, waiting for him – just like the woman in the story – O it is terrible, terrible!'

'But because the man in the story ...' Hari protested, 'that does not mean that Suri also ...'

'You do not understand!' she cried. 'You are a man but I am older than you are, and I have read a lot and I know. This story, I tell you, it is *my* story. The woman always alone at home: it is a big home, luxurious, elegant, but how can she be happy? She sits in the middle of all this expensive furniture, carpets, silver, many servants, but her heart is breaking inside her. O how sad, how sad,' she sobbed, 'and how *true*!'

'Poor sister,' Hari murmured, genuinely sympathetic. He did not like to see anyone unhappy.

'Listen to this,' she said, swallowing down more tears and running her finger along the page. 'Here. Listen: "for the heart is like a fruit which can only prosper in the warm sunshine of love, without love, the heart, like the fruit without the sun, must wither and die".' She looked up, her eyes shining with tears. 'Is it not beautiful? "The heart is like a fruit..." Kaka, I tell you, this is Truth. I know. I have felt this truth in my own life.'

Hari sighed. 'I too ...' he suggested.

'You are also unhappy?' she said, a trifle grudgingly.

'You know. I have told you.'

'Ah, yes yes. This girl Amrita.'

'You are the only one with whom I can talk,' he said. He knew this would make her listen.

She sighed. 'Only those who are unhappy themselves can feel the unhappiness of others.'

'At home they laugh,' he complained. 'Just now, Mataji and Mohini ... they will never understand how I feel about Amrita. They think it is impossible for me to love a girl from a different community.'

She nodded wisely.

'As if love knew any boundaries.'

'And her family too.' The memory of his interview with the grandfather made him feel acutely uncomfortable all over again. The old man looking over his steel spectacles, his precise voice, the large imposing desk – how it had all flustered him; and, as always when he was ill at ease, his English had deserted him. Usually he spoke English quite fluently, but under such circumstances he could somehow only speak in broken and incorrect sentences. And the old man waiting for him while he groped around for, and could not find, the English word, waiting with such exaggerated, such sardonic patience – Hari shuddered and quickly slurred over the memory.

'I know,' Prema said. 'You have told me: this terrible old man.'

He had not told her everything, only as much as he could bear to tell about that interview.

'Such conceited people,' Prema said, and indignantly ate a piece of barfi. 'Do they think they are better than we are because they live in a big house and have been to England? I also live in a big house and if I wanted to I also could go to England. And we have a big car brought specially from America, and I have clothes fine enough for the finest lady in Delhi, one salwar-kamiz I have it cost Rs. 250, I do not know if the ladies in that family have such clothes. Why did you not tell him that?'

He could not imagine himself telling the old man that his sister had an American car and a salwar-kamiz worth Rs. 250. Besides, the point had not arisen, at least, not explicitly.

'You should have let me speak with him,' Prema said. 'Shall I go to him? Do you want me to? I shall show him the worth of our family.'

'No,' Hari said instinctively, 'O no.'

'But why,' she asked, not for the first time, 'do you not bring this girl to us?'

This was a matter he knew he would have to settle now. He had evaded it as long as he could, evaded pressure not only from Prema's side but also, and more so, from Amrita's.

'Perhaps,' she said, 'you would not like to bring her to our mother's house. It is small, and things are perhaps not as the girl is used to. And there are too many people, Mataji and Mohini and the children and Babla, there are too many. The girl would feel shy.'

'Yes,' Hari said, 'and if I brought her, then everybody else would come to see, the Varmas and the Puris and the Chaddhas and the Bhasins. They would make my poor Amrita feel so shy.'

'So you must bring her to me,' Prema said.

Again he felt unhappy. It was true, Prema lived in a big house with expensive furniture and, though she hardly ever wore them, she had a lot of very good clothes; it was also true that her husband had a big American car. But still he felt reluctant to bring Amrita here; this he could not or would not explain to himself, so how could he explain to Prema.

'Why not?' she pressed him.

'Yes,' he echoed, 'why not.'

'So you will bring her?'

'I do not know ...'

'But why not?'

There was no answer to this that he could think of.

'You are right,' he had to say; 'why not.'

'You will bring her then?'

He hesitated; but he was trapped.

'All right,' he said, miserably, 'I will bring her.'

She pressed his hand. 'It will be all right,' she said. 'You will see. I will make everything nice.' And she pressed his hand again.

3

Amrita, humming lightly under her breath, stood by the window in the sitting-room at home and looked out into the garden. It was still early in the morning but already the sun was white and hot, flooding the lawn and cutting sharp shadows out of the plantain and papaya trees. The gardener, dressed only in a loin-cloth and a turban, was trimming a jasmine-bush; the shears snipped sharply and blended with the liquid cries of the swallows; in the distance a crow cawed. Amrita leant her head against the anti-burglar bars and felt happy, because today she was going to see Hari. She could hear her mother shouting at the servant in the kitchen and Krishna Sen Gupta in the bathroom singing under the shower. Today, she thought, I shall see him, another three, four, hours and I shall see him, and she hummed in tune with Krishna Sen Gupta. Then she moved about the room, arranging the ornaments, the wooden birds, yellow with blue stripes, tigers and plaster-of-paris elephants, two bullocks pulling a plough, little bowls of imitation fruit.

Amrita was very fond of bright colours; she painted a bit herself, and her one attempt in oils – Women at the Village Well – was hung over the sofa. It was the only painting in the room; otherwise the walls were covered with photographs. In the place of honour, on the wall facing Amrita's painting, was a coloured one of Gandhiji, smiling in blue; beside, above, and beneath it were photographs of Amrita's father, Nirad Chakravarty: Nirad Chakravarty as a young lawyer, very thin and earnest in a tight-fitting European suit with a high collar and a book under his arm; Nirad Chakravarty, still thinner and more earnest but now wearing only white khadi clothes, on the outskirts of a group of prominent Congress personalities; Nirad Chakravarty on a platform, addressing a meeting; Nirad Chakravarty one of a group around Gandhiji himself; and the last picture taken in 1944 just after he came out of jail at the expiration of his last sentence, alone in a garden chair, a little dim, death foreshadowed in the blurred photograph.

Radha came slopping down the passage in her old slippers, and when she came into the room, eating a banana, she said in a preoccupied manner, 'Ah Amrita, it is good you are already dressed. Today I want you to come out with me. I have promised a visit this morning to Lady Ram Prashad.' She knew very well that Amrita had to go to the radio station, that was why she said it. Amrita knew that she knew, and did not bother to reply.

Radha lovingly straightened the photographs of her husband. She did this every morning and dusted them too, with her own hands. They were her greatest pride and possession. She had had them framed and had hung them up only after her husband's death and after Independence, which had come three months before his death (he had been by that time already too ill and too remote for the event to stir his interest). They were her compensation for the years of deprivation for the sake of a cause to which she had paid lip-service – yes, very ardently – but which in her heart of hearts she resented because it would not allow her to wear fine saris and possess, like her sisters, a diamond necklace and a motor-car. But today these pictures were worth more than a diamond necklace and a motor-car. She would look at them, shake her head over them, and sigh, 'If he had lived, today he would have been a Minister.' This was not true: he would have been at most an M.P., and an Independent at that; his idealism was of too rigid, too literary, too quixotic a nature to have allowed him to ally himself with any party actually in power.

'I do not like this sari you are wearing,' Radha said to reopen the offensive. 'To go to Lady Ram Prashad you will please wear the green one of chiffon which I bought for you.' Having finished her banana, she looked round for somewhere to deposit the peel, and not finding anywhere, she called the servant from the kitchen and gave it to him.

'I must go now,' Amrita said, twisting a garland of jasmine into the coil of hair at the back of her head.

'Go where?' Radha inquired innocently, and then, 'A hundred times I have told you, why do you not change your hair-style, modern girls cut their hair short, it is very fashionable.'

The bathroom door banged and Krishna Sen Gupta came out, still singing. Radha shouted at him, 'Do not make such noises in my house!' and to Amrita she said, 'Lady Ram Prashad said specially, please bring your Amrita, I have not seen her for a long time.'

'You know very well I have to go to the radio this morning,' Amrita said at last, 'how can I go with you?'

'You are not going to that radio! Never again!' Radha shouted, so loud that even the gardener was startled and for a moment stopped clipping the bush.

Amrita sighed. This happened almost every time she set off; she had got into the habit of expecting it now.

'You are not going!' Radha was shouting. 'I, your mother, forbid it!'

'And I, your lodger, forbid it!' cried Krishna Sen Gupta, fresh from his bath. He really was the lodger, though Radha hated the word. Finding that the bungalow was too big for only the two of them, and that it was rather dull having no one but Amrita and the cook to quarrel with, Radha had decided to take in what she had heard called a paying guest. She had made discreet inquiries to find a suitable person, which in the end had brought her Krishna Sen Gupta, who had come to Delhi to take up a teaching post at the University. He was a Bengali, which made it all right, for Nirad Chakravarty had been a Bengali; his father was a well-known lawyer in Calcutta, which made it even more all right; and later it was discovered that his father had, from 1933–5, shared a prison sentence with Nirad Chakravarty in Meerut jail: this, of course, made Krishna quite one of the family.

'You will please be quiet and go away!' Radha turned on him. 'We do not want you here, we are speaking in private. Also I do not like to see your face so early in the morning, why do you not go to your work?'

He grinned amiably and made his morning salutations to the ladies; neither of whom returned them.

Amrita said, 'Now I must go or I shall be late.'

But her mother blocked the doorway crying, 'You are not leaving this house; if I have to lock you up in a trunk, you will not go!'

Amrita clicked her tongue in exasperation and said, 'Please Mamma, let me pass, it is getting late and you know I have to go.'

'Did you not hear what your mother said?' Krishna said sternly and added to Radha, 'She is unmanageable; a very badly brought-up girl.'

'I shall not be home for lunch,' Amrita said.

'You want to starve yourself too?' Radha demanded, moving out of the doorway.

Amrita, already in the passage, explained over her shoulder, 'I can get something to eat in the radio canteen.'

'Spending money uselessly when you have good food at home,' Radha grumbled, following her. 'I am not a zamindar that you can spend my money as you like.' And seeing the gardener contemplating the plantain tree, she shouted, 'To drink my tea and eat up my food, then you are first-class, but to do a little work, that is too difficult for you!'

'I earn my own money,' Amrita said proudly from the garden gate.

'Pah!' Radha cried, looking after her from the veranda steps, 'you call those miserable few rupees money?' Then she ran to the garden gate and called into the street, 'At least see that you eat something properly!'

Amrita was so embarrassed that she hurried down the street as fast as she could without looking conspicuous. Krishna, some books under his arm, came running after her. When he drew level, he said, 'I will escort you to your bus.'

She walked a little faster and said, 'Please leave me alone.' But he drew level with her again and kept beside her. They were almost the same height, for he was short; he was also very thin and walked with a stoop. He wore large hornrimmed spectacles and had a shock of hair which stood perpetually on end.

'I have offended you?' he asked.

She did not reply but walked on staring straight in front of her. 'But what have I done?' he persisted.

The sun was already very hot, so she put up her parasol, Burmese and leaf-brown; it also shielded her face from him.

'I fail to understand your attitude,' he said with dignity, and peered under the parasol, which she promptly tilted sideways. 'Go away,' she said, but could not help laughing a little although she was very cross.

'You are unreasonable,' he said in a hurt tone. 'Why do you reject my friendship?'

'Why must you always,' her grievance finally came out, 'come and talk nonsense when Mamma is shouting at me? You know it makes her more cross.'

'But I only try to make peace.'

'Go away,' she said, and crossed the road to the bus stop.

Two women in Punjabi dress were already standing there; they scrutinized Amrita from top to toe.

'I am the neutral power,' Krishna said. 'I am India the peace-maker.' The two women looked him up and down.

'There is no need for you to wait,' Amrita said.

'It is all right, I am not in a hurry.'

Then the bus came; but just before it set off again, Krishna stuck his head in and called, 'Please do not forget to eat something properly!' Now the whole bus looked at Amrita.

4

That morning she had two programmes to announce. By the time she came off duty it was one o'clock, and she walked straight up to the canteen. Hari of course was not there yet, and she sat down by herself at one of the tables and told the bearer that she was waiting for someone. She was used to waiting for Hari, for he had no very exact ideas about time. One o'clock to him meant any time between one and two. It became rather embarrassing sometimes to have to sit and wait for him so long, all alone with the bearers looking at her sideways and the other tables full of people laughing and talking together; but usually she was so happy just expecting him, knowing that he would soon be with her, that she did not mind at all. Certainly she never blamed him; his unpunctuality was for her part of his charm. He was delightfully unpractical, so truly Indian, so unworldly, that he could not think of hard-set European things like time and clocks. But today she was lucky, for he came in at twenty past one; and as soon as she saw him walking towards her, very neat and clean in his white shirt and white trousers, with his smooth oiled hair and his trim little moustache, as soon as she saw him, the now familiar surge of happiness came over her again and she told herself, how I love him.

He broke into a wide smile of pleasure, so frank and undisguised and generous, and then sat down opposite her saying, 'How hungry I am, I have had nothing to eat since my breakfast, and then I had only a little gram.'

She said nothing, and did not even dare look at him. She was afraid that if she looked at him she would not be able to bear it, but would have to jump up and do something ridiculous and unsuitable. So she gazed down at her hands, with a very faint, irrepressible smile of pleasure on her lips, and she thought, how I love him.

'What shall we eat?' he said, and studied the menu, though he knew it by heart. The bearer waited behind him while he concentrated very hard, thinking what to order. At last he decided, and then he explained to the bearer, very meticulously, exactly what he wanted.

'O Hari,' she said, as soon as they were alone, and she dared look at him.

'It was all right?' he said anxiously.

'What, my Hari?'

'What I ordered. I was not sure. I thought would she like seekh kebab or shami, but then I decided seekh because last time we were here we had shami.'

'Whatever you want, I want,' she said. Sitting like this, opposite him, looking at him, was the greatest pleasure she knew. She forgot everything then: her mother's nagging, her grandfather's displeasure, her own instinctive unease at thus loving a young man of her own accord and against her family's wishes. She gazed at him and she said, 'You are so sweet, Hari.'

'No you,' he said with enthusiasm, looking back at her, his eyes large and dark and full of love, 'it is you who are so sweet.' Then he warmed to his subject, and with his elbows on the table, he leant towards her a little and he spoke to her about love, about his heart and how soft and tender it felt towards her and how sometimes he thought it would melt. But his words made little impact on her. They were too vague and abstract, they seemed unreal and rather remote to her, as if they came from a different context and had no connection with their love for one another at all. But nevertheless, she was very happy because all the time he was talking to her, she was thinking about how much she loved him.

'All day my soul sings and dances for you,' he was saying, and then someone slapped him on the back and he turned round and said, 'Hallo-hallo-hallo.' Amrita was used to such interruptions, for Hari was very popular and had many friends. He greeted everyone with the same rapture, as if everyone he saw was just the person he wanted most to see.

When they were alone again, and Hari was about to carry on from where he had left off, Amrita prevented him with, 'Yesterday Grandfather spoke to me.'

At once Hari took his elbows off the table and leant back again and looked very sad. So she said quickly, 'But I do not care what Grandfather says; believe me, Hari, I do not care what any of them say.' And when he still looked sad, she went on, 'Please believe me. Please. What does my family matter? You know I would give up everyone and everything for you. Nothing matters. Only you.'

He put his elbows back on the table and looked at her with adoring eyes. 'I am unworthy,' he said. 'You are a goddess and I am unworthy of you.'

She pleaded, 'Please do not say such things, my Hari. I cannot bear it.'

'A goddess,' he insisted. 'You are a goddess; I worship you.'

Their lunch arrived and Hari at once began to eat. Amrita was not hungry; and anyway, it was enough for her to watch him eat. She always liked to watch him over his meals; he ate with such relish and with such unselfconscious enjoyment. He handled knife and fork rather awkwardly, which was another thing she found charming about him. He was simple and unspoilt, and his ways the traditional, truly Indian ways which had been lost in her family. She now rather despised her family's sophisticated, highly westernized way of living and thought of it as being false and unreal and quite unsuitable. Some time ago, shortly after she had first met Hari, she had tried to revolt against this way of living and had started to eat with her fingers at home. But her mother had become so indignant, and Krishna Sen Gupta so amused, that she had had to give it up. Once, also, she had asked Hari, why he did not always eat with his hands when he was with her, as he was accustomed to do; but this too had not been a success. Hari had been shocked and rather hurt; to him it had seemed as if she were suggesting he did not know how a gentleman should behave.

He waved to someone on the other side of the room, turned back to help himself to more pickle, and announced, 'I am on duty at 2.15.'

'O no!' she cried, her eyes widening with the disappointment of it. 'O Hari, always it is the same, always we meet and then at once we have to part again. It is terrible. I cannot bear it.'

'I too cannot bear it,' he said very sadly and with his mouth full. And because he was sad, she felt she had to cheer him up again; he must never be unhappy. So she looked at him fondly and said, 'Never mind, my Hari, one day it will be different, because we shall always be together and nothing will ever be able to part us.'

Then he remembered, and he blurted it out: 'Please will you come and see my elder sister.'

'At last!' she cried, radiant. For a long time now she had been urging him to let her meet his family, and always he had evaded her. And she wanted so much to meet them: she thought they must be wonderful people, simple and true and unostentatious; already she admired them tremendously. She only hoped that they would accept her as one of themselves and not despise her for having been bred to false, foreign ways.

'I hope you will like my sister,' Hari said.

'Can I do anything but love her when she is your sister!' she cried. Nevertheless, he did not feel reassured. Prema of course had promised that she would make everything nice and see to it that things were as

Amrita was used to, but all the same he felt uneasy; though he did not exactly know why.

'She is my sister too,' Amrita said. 'Only I am afraid that she will not like me ...' And when Hari was about to protest, she added hastily, 'or even if she likes me, she will perhaps not like the sort of girl I am. She may think I am very spoilt and westernized and affected; because my family have made me like that, I know it. I am afraid that your sister will despise that, and so she will not be able to like me. O Hari, often I worry about it, and then I am so grateful to you for not despising me for using knife and fork and speaking a lot in English and having been educated in a convent and at Lady Wilmot College.'

Hari did not understand. The things for which she thanked him for not despising her were perhaps the things for which he loved and admired her most; and those for which he knew his sister would admire her the most. So, not understanding, he took refuge in murmuring, 'My love for you is so great, surely it will break me.'

She did not listen to this, but went on, 'But, O Hari, even if your sister does not like me, if your whole family do not like me, what will it matter? They cannot come between us. They are no more important than my family. They will never be able to separate us.'

He looked very dubious at this. It was not a point he cared to consider; but fortunately it was not a point that needed considering, not just yet. So he could answer with a free conscience and a look of love, 'Who can ever separate us? Who can come between us? We are as one.'

5

Radha liked visiting her sister Tarla; she often felt that she derived spiritual benefit from these visits. For Tarla lived in a huge house, pale yellow, with balconies and verandas, a terrace and an imposing porch. There were three full-time gardeners to tend the trees and lawns and flower-beds, and grow more flowers in pots all round the terrace. There were garages for the two cars and even a stable, for Tarla's husband kept a sleek brown horse on which he would go, correctly attired, riding down the bicycle tracks. Inside the house, too, it was very luxurious; the rooms were air-conditioned, cool as the smell of ice-cream. Radha always thought that she herself should have been mistress of such a home, rather than her austere sister Tarla. She felt it was better suited to her personality.

But she would not have been prepared to take on Vazir Dayal, Tarla's husband. When she came in, he was sitting far back in an arm-chair, dressed in a long dazzling white coat and white leggings; he held a whisky glass, and a large ring shone on his middle finger. He did not get up when Radha came into the room. He had cultivated exquisite manners, but they were not meant for his sisters-in-law.

'Where is Tarla?' Radha demanded briskly. But he only shrugged and murmured something rude. She settled herself comfortably among the cushions and asked, 'Are you ill?' to which he replied wearily 'No more than usual.'

A fan turned softly from the ceiling, not really necessary in that cool room but providing a sweet titillating breeze. An enormous Persian carpet covered the marble floor; it was patterned all over with tiny flowers in pink and green and blue, dainty and fresh and poignantly artificial. The divans were almost at floor level and matched the brocaded silk of the curtains; green and crimson horsemen glittering against a sombre background. There was a long low cabinet, with bronze grillwork twisting behind the glass front, and on it a tea-set, red and gold, fine as breath, curved shallow cups with long handles pointing upwards. Vazir Dayal himself was responsible for the furnishing and decorating of the house. It was the only outlet for what he considered irresistible artistic instincts; instincts which also led him to patronize, sporadically, when he was in a good mood and not too indolent, some of the innumerable young artists who went on painting-trips to Kashmir and came back to hold exhibitions in hired halls in Delhi.

'Is Tarla not at home?' Radha asked again, though she did not much care whether she was or not. She was comfortable here and intended to stay. There was sure to be a good lunch, for Vazir Dayal's artistic instincts also expressed themselves in the kitchen; and he himself could always be ignored.

He took a sip of whisky and said, 'Leave me alone, I am thinking.'

'How rude you are,' Radha remarked placidly. She did not really mind; she knew it was part of his personality. Vazir Dayal Mathur was a landowner with vast inherited riches which had, all his life, allowed him to do nothing except cultivate his personality. In his youth he had affected a romantic Byronic temperament, had roamed about in Calcutta, Paris, London, New York. For years he and Tarla had been separated while he was being Byronic abroad. But with middle age had come fatigue, and he had been content then to come back to India and to his wife and peacefully contemplate his personality at home.

Tarla came in with short, precise steps, wearing an emerald sari with a faded gold border. She held a file in her hand and was murmuring some figures over to herself, 'Lucknow, Rupees 500, Allahabad, 350; not good enough.' Then she saw Radha and said, rather displeased, 'O you are here.'

'And what else am I to do,' Radha replied with spirit, 'now that my daughter has no more use for her mother? Am I to sit at home and eat my two, three, chapatis alone and talk to myself like an old woman?'

Tarla went on murmuring '350 not good enough' and sat down and fluttered through her file in a preoccupied manner.

'Leave this alone,' Radha said, 'I have come here specially to speak with you. I wish to speak with you about Amrita.'

Tarla shook her head over the file, looking very much the busy committee-woman. Which she was: ladies' committees were her passion, her rich compensation for an unsatisfactory husband.

'I do not know what to do with her,' Radha said. 'The girl is eating my life up. Why must I be so punished? I never gave my parents one moment's anxiety even.' This was not true: her marriage with Nirad Chakravarty had always been considered as something of a calamity. But it was all so long ago that she had chosen to forget.

'Why do you not leave the poor girl alone,' Tarla said, regretfully laying her file aside, 'she must live her own life. What is it you want her to do?'

'I want her to behave respectably, as is fitting for a girl of good family,' Radha replied with dignity.

Vazir Dayal stirred slightly in his arm-chair, contemplated his whisky glass, and said, 'Is this little what-is-her-name not behaving respectably?'

'Her name is Amrita,' Radha said, 'you know very well it is Amrita so why do you pretend you do not know?'

'We are expecting visitors for lunch,' Tarla said pointedly.

'Then I think I will stay,' Radha decided. She was pleased, for visitors ensured a specially good lunch. 'But tell me – you always pride yourself on how much sense you have got – why then do you not tell me what I am to do with Amrita? Do you know she really wants to marry this man? I have never heard such talk!'

'How bourgeois,' Vazir Dayal said and slightly raised his glass, which made the bearer hurry over to refill it.

'Nonsense,' Tarla said, 'it is all only talk. When you stop talking to her about it, then she will forget.'

'She will forget when she stops going to this radio station. It is there that she learns all these bad things and forgets the good manners and education I have given her. But now I will put an end to this, she must never go there again, I have told her.'

'She must do something,' Tarla said.

'Why?' Radha challenged, 'what did we do before marriage, what do other girls of good family do before marriage? Nothing: they stay at home and learn perhaps to play the sitar.'

Tarla looked disgusted, but she was prevented from making a suitable reply by the entry of Professor Hoch. He came sweeping in, a short rotund German with long grey hair and a little red beard, wearing a frequently-washed white linen suit which was a trifle too short in the legs and the arms. He ardently kissed first Tarla's hand, then Radha's, and made a mock, though very deep, bow to Vazir Dayal.

'And how is your health, please?' he said in Hindustani. He had lived in India for twenty-five years and prided himself on his Hindustani; though he had never yet realized that his German accent rendered it unintelligible.

'Guten Tag, Herr Professor,' said Vazir Dayal, 'Wie geht es Ihnen?' which was about as far as his German accent would take him.

'Danke danke,' the Professor murmured, and added in English, 'You are an accomplished linguist. You speak German quite free from accent.' He smiled at the two sisters; being charming to ladies was his speciality. That, and Indian Art. He was a very voluble expert on the subject, and a most enthusiastic exponent of 5,000 years of Cultural Heritage.

'Voudriez-vous quelque chose à boire?' Vazir Dayal said, and the Professor replied, 'Merci, vous êtes très bien, un petit whisky, ça va,' and mopped his brow with a big checked handkerchief.

Radha cried, 'Now please, Professor Hoch, speak in English, you know we want to hear all that you say, such clever talk we cannot hear every day!'

He gave a little bow of acknowledgement in her direction, while taking his glass of whisky from the bearer. 'And how is your charming daughter?' he asked.

'Why do you not come to my house,' Radha said, 'then you will see with your own eyes. How you will like to see her paintings! Such beautiful pictures she makes for me! One I have framed and it hangs on the wall in the drawing-room, with the pictures of her father and Gandhiji. Everybody who comes to my house, they look at this picture which my Amrita painted and they think it is made by some famous artist!'

Just then Lady Ram Prashad Khanna and Dr Mukherji came in. The Professor leapt to his feet; even Vazir Dayal got up slowly and reluctantly on to his long legs in their brilliant white leggings. Looking around for somewhere to put his whisky glass – Tarla relieved him of it – the Professor seized Lady Ram Prashad's hand and planted a long, deep kiss on it. She smiled on him, her hand stretched out: he was a great favourite with her. Dr Mukherji, though, would not let her hand be kissed. She snatched it away and he kissed the air.

The ladies sipped pineapple juice, the two gentlemen whisky. Professor Hoch was so excited, he could hardly sit still but kept bouncing up and down on his round little buttocks, making himself agreeable. Lady Ram Prashad smiled and smiled all round, showing large and beautiful teeth which were slightly askew; this was the only indication that they were not her own. She was a tall woman with grey hair and a stately bosom, and she wore an expensive sari of a deep purple Mysore silk. She was a lady out to please, who always, on all occasions and under all circumstances, made a point of being charming. Not so Dr Mukherji; for whereas Lady Ram Prashad smiled almost all the time, Dr Mukherji looked mostly morose. Everybody knew her to be a brilliant economist; and since everybody knew it, she saw no point in putting herself out to prove it. She kept almost completely silent and took no interest in any conversation. She was aggressively plain and always dressed in cotton saris, which sagged on her shapeless figure.

Lady Ram Prashad smiled upon Professor Hoch and said, 'I wanted so to speak with you, Professor, about our Pageant. We do need your help.'

'Command me!' cried the Professor, in Hindustani.

Tarla leaned forward keenly and said, 'O yes, the Garden Party of the Ladies' Council.'

'We must have a Pageant,' Lady Ram Prashad said. 'We must arrange something very symbolical. There will be many people from the Embassies, and we want to show them our beautiful Culture.'

Professor Hoch nodded, knowingly. He was always being called upon to show beautiful Culture to the Embassies. 'Let me see now,' he pondered, and put one hand over his eyes for greater concentration.

'I thought perhaps,' Lady Ram Prashad said, 'we could show some aspects of all our old Cultures – Mohenjodaro and Harappa,' she said glibly, and then a little more slowly, 'the Gupta period, and the Moghuls and – the Moghuls, that would be very charming. And then we could show modern times; for instance, the Five-Year Plan and all the wonderful scientific things that are being done nowadays. Last year the Ladies' Committee for the Advancement of Literacy arranged such a Pageant, and it was a great success. I remember we had a letter from the Minister of Scientific Development to congratulate us.'

Professor Hoch, his hand still on his eyes, murmured 'The Five-Year Plan. An excellent idea.'

'Did I tell you, Lady Ram Prashad,' Tarla said, 'Mrs Dass has kindly consented to send some of the little girls from her school to dance and sing for us.'

'Such sweet children she has at her school,' Lady Ram Prashad said, sipping pineapple juice, 'such nicely brought up little girls. Really, Mrs Dass is a very capable lady; all the Ministers and Secretaries and Deputy Secretaries send their daughters to her for education.'

'It is a pity,' said Radha, 'that I could not also send my Amrita to her. But now, of course, she has finished her education. She is B.A. now, a graduate from Lady Wilmot College.' Nobody was ever quite sure what Amrita had studied at Lady Wilmot College. But it was enough to know that she had gone there and mixed with the daughters of the best families.

'Such a clever, charming girl,' Lady Ram Prashad acknowledged.

Professor Hoch took his hand from his eyes and said, 'Our Pageant must show the beauty and simplicity of Indian village life.' Lady Ram

Prashad beamed upon him. 'We must show our women at the village well, the simple grace of their movements as they draw up the water or go about their household tasks, their unself-conscious dignity, the sublime rhythm of their gait.'

'And also,' Dr Mukherji dropped in, speaking in a very low voice, not caring whether anyone heard her or not, 'village women in labour, with the female scavenger standing by with a piece of glass to cut the navel cord.'

Professor Hoch continued, 'And we must show the villagers gathering together after the day's work to sing their traditional songs and dance their traditional dances. For it is in these songs and dances' – he got up and started pacing up and down on the Persian carpet: he was a practised lecturer, indeed that very evening he was to give a lecture to the International Study Circle on the Ancient Culture of Mohenjodaro and Harappa – 'it is in these simple village songs and dances,' he said, pacing thus, one hand behind his back, 'that the heritage of India is preserved in its purest and most traditional forms.'

'How true,' Lady Ram Prashad gravely nodded; and daintily she wiped pineapple juice from her upper lip.

'If we want to show to our foreign guests the real, the true spirit of India,' the Professor continued, 'we must show them not degenerate city life with its evil western influences, but life as it is lived in the village, unchanged for generations, unruffled by the comings and goings of conquerors. Pure as water drawn from the clear sparkling well' – a phrase which he hoped to be able to fit in the evening's lecture – 'the Indian village reflects the very soul of India, for ever still and at peace, oblivious of Time, lost in its contemplation of the Infinite.' And then it was time for lunch.

The meal had been ordered and arranged by Vazir Dayal, and today he had expressed himself in cream of almond soup, ragout fin, pimento slices, chicken mayonnaise, mushrooms in cream and a mocha souffle. Dr Mukherji, who was so strict a vegetarian that she did not even eat eggs, was served with boiled vegetables and chapatis. She was the only one who ate with her fingers. Professor Hoch and Lady Ram Prashad were voluble in their praises of the food, though only the Professor could really do justice to it. Lady Ram Prashad had to think of her figure; since she often had to appear on public platforms to address meetings or inaugurate new ventures, she did want to look at least dignified.

Professor Hoch was kept very busy. Besides eating, he had to talk Art with Vazir Dayal, Amrita with Radha, Social Work with Lady Ram

Prashad and Tarla, and admire Dr Mukherji's simple ways. The last was the most thankless task, for Dr Mukherji did not even glance at him, although he very ardently commended the beauty of cotton saris and boiled vegetables.

Vazir Dayal was saying, 'Who is this artist who is holding an exhibition at the Freemason Hall?'

The Professor, who had been exchanging smiles with Lady Ram Prashad, became instantly grave, to give his artistic opinion: 'A very talented boy, very talented. He left the Delhi Polytechnic School of Art last year and has just come back from a painting tour of Kashmir. He showed me some very interesting canvases and I myself advised him to hold an exhibition. He has distilled all the beauty and the colour of the Valley; his use of green for trees is especially remarkable.'

Vazir Dayal speared a mushroom on to his fork and idly remarked that perhaps he might buy a painting or two.

The Professor expressed himself delighted. 'I will bring the artist to you,' he said. 'He may learn much from your experience and let himself be guided by your taste. Our kind host,' he said, turning to the others, 'is a truly great patron, such as, alas, there are few in this modern world of ours. He is, as every great patron should be, not only a man of taste but also, in his sensibility, an artist himself. He brings back to my mind the age of our great Moghul Emperors, of Akbar, Jehangir, of – ah! Shahjehan, when aesthetic sensibility and a cultivated taste for the arts were the hallmark of every noble and courtier. Age of splendour,' he sighed, 'age of greatness,' and helped himself to more chicken mayonnaise.

Vazir Dayal frowned over his plate, to hide his pleasure. To hear himself compared to a Moghul noble and courtier was very agreeable to him. He always thought of himself as having been born in the wrong age. He kept, in a special drawer in his dressing-room, a costume of the Moghul period, a long coat of cloth of gold, pale pink silk leggings, a turban studded with pearls. He even had a pair of ear-rings. Sometimes he dressed himself up in these things, sat on a carpet in front of his full-length mirror and read Urdu poetry aloud to himself.

'We have a great History,' said Lady Ram Prashad. She had heard much about it from Professor Hoch and always read the historical feature articles in the *Sunday Statesman* and the *Illustrated Weekly*.

'Thank God,' said Radha, 'that it is being kept alive in the minds of our children. My Amrita studied much history when she was at the Lady Wilmot College, and often I saw her read books about the Moghul Emperors and all those olden times.'

'Education!' said Lady Ram Prashad. 'It is the greatest gift we can make to our children. And what a fine thing it is to see our daughters educated side by side with our sons! The emancipation of women is one of the greatest achievements of our modern age.'

'And Indian womanhood,' said Professor Hoch, raising a dessert-spoon heaped with mocha souffle by way of toast, 'is the greatest justification of feminine emancipation. A modern Indian lady is one of the rarest, finest flowers civilization has yet brought forth.'

All the ladies, except Dr Mukherji, looked modest.

'Of course,' said Tarla, in her best platform manner, 'the greatest step forward was the abandonment of the idea of early marriage. We must be grateful that today Society is sufficiently advanced to think of women as something more than a mere marriageable commodity.'

Dr Mukherji made her second contribution to the conversation. 'Last week,' she said, 'my sweeper's daughter was married. She is twelve.'

Coffee was served in the drawing-room. They sipped from the tiny black and gold cups which they held with their little fingers daintily curved. Only Dr Mukherji grasped her cup fully in her fist and emptied it in two gulps, while Vazir Dayal squeamishly looked the other way. Radha was beginning to feel herself irresistibly sleepy. She was in the habit of lying down after her lunch, and the habit was getting hold of her now. That was the worst about these modern luncheon-parties, one was expected to make conversation after food as well as before. She tried to listen to Professor Hoch expounding on the relevance of Buddhist sculpture to modern architecture, but his voice kept getting farther and farther away from her. She found herself idly wondering whether his red beard, wagging up and down in front of her as he talked, was dyed; she decided that it must be, since his hair was quite grey. And she thought, why does he not cut his hair, it must feel very hot around his neck. The only thing that kept her awake was exchanging charming smiles, from time to time, with Lady Ram Prashad.

And now, over her second cup of coffee, Lady Ram Prashad got down to business. In between conversation about Art, Culture and the Ladies' Council Garden Party, she edged in a reference to the forthcoming election of the Ladies' Committee for the Teaching of Handicrafts, which made Tarla lean forward with an intense expression on her face.

'I have heard it said,' Lady Ram Prashad mentioned casually, in between sips of coffee, 'that Mrs Kartar Singh is to be put forward for nomination as President.'

'Quite out of the question,' Tarla said promptly, giving a little slap to her knee.

'Who is this?' said Radha. 'Mrs Kartar Singh, the wife of Dr Kartar Singh the M.P., who lives on the Asoka Road, Number 59A?'

Tarla gave her a withering look, for she did not like her sister to meddle in these committee matters which were none of her business.

'A charming lady,' murmured Professor Hoch, 'though perhaps not as educated or quite as intelligent as some of our other ladies.'

'She is a fool,' Radha said decisively, undeterred by Tarla's disapproval. 'If her husband was not M.P., nobody would ever think of electing her on any Committee.' Lady Ram Prashad sipped more coffee, seemingly unconcerned.

'Of course such a nomination is quite out of the question,' Tarla said again. 'I will see to it myself that only your name is put forward for nomination, Lady Ram Prashad. We can allow no one else to stand as President of our Society.'

'If a mere man may meddle in these matters of high politics,' said Professor Hoch, with a bow first at Lady Ram Prashad, then at Tarla and Radha and finally, a little hopelessly, at Dr Mukherji, 'it does seem reasonable to allow only a lady as experienced, as diplomatic and influential as Lady Ram Prashad Khanna to guide so important a Society.'

Lady Ram Prashad modestly lowered her head to study the bottom of her coffee-cup.

6

Hari Sahni's family was a large and widespread one. They were Punjabi Hindus who in 1947, at the time of the Partition, had to leave their native Lahore, which they incorporated into Pakistan, and fly to Delhi. They had lost almost everything; their houses, their business, many of their valuables, all had to be left behind. It was complete disaster, absolute ruin: if it had happened to one man alone it would have been unbearable. But there is consolation in numbers, and there were hundreds of thousands of them. Their relatives, their friends, their neighbours, all were ruined with them, all had to start life afresh: there was no individual disgrace attached to this ruin; it was spiritually bearable. And like almost all Punjabis, they were resourceful, courageous, intensely practical people who faced their situation squarely: there was no help for it, and they had to earn their living; so they started again. They did not care how small or humble were their beginnings, and they worked hard. Within three or four years they were almost where they had been before, and some of them had even bettered themselves.

Fortunately for them, they had not been landowners – except in a very small way – but tradespeople, who depended for their success on their wits and their contacts: and wits as well as many of their contacts they had been able to bring with them. They were owners of small workshops, car-brokers, small-time contractors, insurance salesmen, never really prospering, never really poor, always just managing to keep themselves within the middle classes. From time to time one of them did make money, and the sense of glory as well as the sense of security inherent in his wealth was then shared by the whole family.

Though many of them lived not in Delhi itself but in small towns and large villages within a few hundred miles' radius of Delhi, family reunions were very frequent. A funeral, a wedding, a betrothal, a name-giving, an initiation, would bring them all together: they believed in celebrating these things thoroughly and, above all, in full strength.

Now it was a name-giving that had called them together. In the house of one of them – a rather distant branch from Hari's – a child had been born, and great preparations were being made for the ceremony of giving it a name. For days beforehand the relations had been streaming in from their outlying towns and villages; and on the night before the actual ceremony, those members of the family who lived in Delhi came to the house of the celebrant to greet the new arrivals and partake of the general spirit of festivity.

The house was in the heart of the city, in a lane so crowded and narrow that Suri found it difficult to get his car through (his wife Prema wrinkled her nose and wondered how people could bear to live in such districts). But inside, in the big paved courtyard, the noise of the streets came only as a faint echo; here all was privacy.

But not a quiet privacy: that was not the kind they cared for. The courtyard, big as it was, was overflowing with relations. There seemed to be a predominance of women and children, especially children; sharp old women with mumbling lips, square, healthy young women, children with huge black eyes. The old women wore white cotton saris pulled over their heads, the young ones wide pyjama trousers with coloured shirts over them; the little girls had gold earrings and wore silver bangles round their arms.

Most of the young women were busy cooking; some of them were far advanced in pregnancy – huge unashamed stomachs shook before them and pushed out their shirts – but that did not prevent them from working as hard as the others. They squatted on their haunches and vigorously shook sieves in the air and patted flat cakes and stirred in black cauldrons; the bangles on their healthy round arms jangled up and down.

One old woman, squatting on the end of a charpoy, mumbled continuous prayers to herself while three children, lying on the charpoy, stared at her wide-eyed and silently. Another sat cross-legged on the ground, holding a baby across her knees while she kneaded its head and crooned. 'Sleep baby, sleep; you have eaten bread and sugar, now sleep.' The charpoys were mostly crowded with sleeping children, three or four, even five, to each charpoy; the grown-ups sat on old strips of carpet or on brightly coloured grass mats, men on one side, women on the other, observing an instinctive segregation. After the men had eaten, the old women were served and whatever children were still awake. Last of all the young women sat down, huddling together in a corner and quickly gobbling down the remains.

The night was very warm and languid, the sky sparkling with stars and a silver piece of moon. The food was rich and good; it made them sigh and stretch themselves and look up into the sky and think about Life. Someone brought out a dholak and sat down there, on a strip of carpet, fingers idly, invitingly, ambling over the drum. One of the women began to hum, softly at first, under her breath almost, till a few more joined her and then her voice rose, still softly, above theirs; she sang of how weary she was of this world and she pleaded, 'Lord, call me, take me to you.' They all nodded their heads and when she had finished they said, 'Good, good, well done!'

Almost unconsciously they moved together into two semi-circles, one of men, one of women, and then there were more songs. They sang of women waiting for their husbands to gather the harvest; of a lover about to marry his beloved, his heart bursting with joy; of little sisters welcoming their elder brother's newly married wife. All happy songs, but all with an undertone, intangible and ineluctable, of plaintiveness. One of the younger men brought out a flute, and their hearts leapt as his music coiled and danced around the songs.

Prema's husband, Suri, was the happiest and the loudest; he clapped his hands, he slapped his thighs, he called, 'Good, good, O very good!' He was a big, stout man with thighs bulging in tight trousers; he wore a cream-coloured silk shirt and a gold wrist-watch; he was the rich man of the family, he glittered and shone among them. When the songs were of love, Prema looked reproachfully towards him but he only sang and clapped and loudly laughed; and remained quite unaware of his wife. They were singing, 'Oh, surely he will not forget, night and day I think only of him, how can he forget?' and Prema's eyes were full of tears. She was thinking of the happiness of other women, and also of her own happiness before marriage; she looked at Suri and she sighed, loudly enough for her neighbours to hear. But no one noticed; she let the tears flow freely down her cheeks.

Now one of the young girls was singing. She sang a popular film song, more plaintive, more suggestive, more full of love and longing than anything that had gone before. Hari watched her and listened in fascination. He had seen the girl before at various family functions, he even knew that her name was Sushila and that she was one of the Anands who lived in Subzimandi, in the vegetable-market district of Delhi. But he had never before realized that she was so pretty. She looks like a film star, he thought.

She was big boned and big bosomed, with broad healthy features and a lot of wavy black hair rippling round her shoulders. He stared at her and even forgot to think about Amrita, although the song was one of love.

He knew it very well, he had seen the film in which it had first appeared; as a matter of fact he had seen the film three times, he had liked it so much. But only now that Sushila was singing the song did he realize how beautiful it was, how full of human truth. She is better, he thought, much better than the singer in the film. She did not have a very good voice; it was high-pitched, a little shrill even, and unmistakably untrained. But she sang with so much expression, knew how to let her voice rise and fall so skilfully, burdened with love and longing and the ache of the heart, that she stirred Hari profoundly and brought out all that he thought was best in him. He felt tears behind his eyes: he thought he had never before truly understood how sad Life was, Love was, and how beautiful.

Hari's mother was also looking at Sushila. 'A lovely girl, lovely,' she commented to an old aunt squatting next to her. 'Lovely,' the aunt echoed; 'a real Punjabi beauty,' and her eyes stole towards Hari. Then she looked at the mother.

'As the Lord wills it,' said Hari's mother, having followed the other's glance.

'We are all in His hands,' the aunt assented piously.

And now they sang for the newborn baby who tomorrow was to be given a name. Rhythm leapt and danced out of the dholak, the flute swung, coiled, went mad almost with joy; they clapped their hands and sang, 'Let our baby's mother dance!'

The mother of the child, a short square woman with broad hips and a pigtail down her back, snatched the baby from its grandmother and began to dance with it a few rhythmical steps from side to side, shaking her hips, one hand in the air. They applauded more than ever. 'Wah, wah!' they cried and laughed and nudged one another; some of the women had tears in their eyes, they were laughing so much as they pointed at the mother dancing there, her mouth trembling with laughter. The baby slept, fists clenched, an expression of intense concentration on its shrivelled little monkey-face.

And then they cried, 'Let the mother's sister dance!' But she was shy and would not get up till they pushed her and pulled her, and the mother thrust the baby into her arms, saying, 'Go on then.' She tried to do a few steps, but was overcome with shyness and buried her face in the baby's satin gown and smothered it with kisses.

Still they clapped and roared, 'Dance, dance,' and the mother's younger sister leapt up and took the baby and she danced vigorously, turning and turning with tiny steps, while drum and flute and voices mounted to a crescendo. Some of the children woke, sat up on their charpoys and looked out with sleepy eyes; a few of them began to blubber, but no one noticed.

Suri was up on his feet, too excited to stay still, and letting out a wild sustained cry, he began to turn himself, with his fat buttocks stuck out, one hand on his hip, one finger shaking in the air. The baby's grandfather, broad and rough and vigorous, threw a handkerchief over his head and began to dance with Suri, the two of them turning about one another, each performing his individual dance, each wild with his own abandonment.

Hari bobbed up and down on the ground, laughing out loud, clapping his hands, the dancing and the singing possessing him and pitching him into such enthusiasm that he could stand it no longer, but had to leap up and begin to dance, his excitement bursting out in a loud cry, which he warbled by shaking his finger in his mouth.

So they danced and cried, the incessant rhythm of dholak and clapping hands thrilling beneath their noise, till they fell to the ground, one after the other, laughing and gasping with exhaustion, and wiping their wet faces with handkerchiefs.

The circle began to break up. The women soothed the children back to sleep, the men yawned and scratched themselves. The old woman who had been squatting on the end of the charpoy, mumbling prayers, was fast asleep, still upright, her mouth a little open, a painful whistling sound coming from the toothless cavern.

But Suri was wide awake, humming snatches of song and trying to rouse the flute-player to start again. 'It is still early,' he said, 'we have only just begun.' It was by this time about one o'clock in the morning.

'I am so tired,' Prema complained. 'Take me home.'

Her husband did not even hear.

She sighed audibly, then yawned. 'I shall go alone,' she announced.

Hari did not feel tired. He was too full of noble sentiments to think of going to bed yet, he wanted to laugh and talk, he wanted to share his emotion with another, sympathetic soul. He looked towards Sushila, the girl who had sung so beautifully. She was sitting alone, a little apart from the others, her hands clasped over her knees, her head flung back. He could see her fine large eyes gleaming in the dark. Buoyed up by his excitement and lifted by the lateness of the hour above everyday sentiments and considerations, he dared to sit himself down at a little distance from her and say, smiling, 'You have a beautiful voice.'

She turned her head towards him. The night and the darkness, the music still tingling inside her and the applause she had met with, lifted her too above her own shyness; she smiled back at him and looked straight into his eyes. 'O no,' she said, and laughed out loud, perhaps with pleasure at the compliment, perhaps only because the night's singing had made her happy, 'I do not sing very well: I have never been taught.'

'You sing better than anyone on the films,' he said earnestly. 'With such a beautiful voice you do not need any other teaching.'

Suddenly she said with passion, 'It is what I want most in the world.'

'What?'

'To sing on the films,' she said, looking at him with large, longing eyes as if her ambition depended on him. 'To be a film star.'

He nodded. He understood her ambition and honoured it. It made him more than ever want to share his mood with her, to talk to her of – he did not quite know what – but at any rate of something profound and something at the same time intensely joyful. Perhaps even of Love, though not of course in any particular manner: of Love only in the abstract.

And then her mother's voice came between them. Sushila got up at once when she heard her and shook her head as if to shake thoughts out of it; she looked a little guilty. But Mrs Anand smiled a tolerant little smile and adjusted her daughter's dupatta. 'Tonight you are not thinking of sleep?' she said, almost tenderly. Hari had also got up, looking sheepish. He felt shy before Sushila's mother, she was such a big, bold, handsome woman; but for him too Mrs Anand had a kind word.

'You young people have too much energy,' she said, and stared at him with undisguised penetration, weighing him up as he stood before her, shuffling his feet and giving a foolish little laugh.

Then his mother came and joined them. She smiled at Mrs Anand, who smiled back. She patted Sushila's cheek, murmuring. 'You are a beautiful girl,' and measured her, as Mrs Anand had measured Hari, from head to foot.

Suri, who was still trying to persuade people to sing, though the dholak had already been carried indoors and the strips of carpet were being dragged end to end ready for sleeping on, called to Sushila, 'Come, daughter, sing for us!'

Mrs Anand called back in her loud bold voice, 'Is this the time for singing?' But Suri came walking towards them, saying, 'She has the voice of an angel.'

'She has already sung too much,' Mrs Anand said, letting her eyes flash at him, well aware that Suri's look was fixed on herself rather than on her daughter.

'We can never hear too much of the voices of angels,' Suri said, staring back at her.

'Very fine talk,' Mrs Anand said, smiling white teeth and brilliant eyes at him; and then Prema joined them, sleepy and very cross. She peered at Mrs Anand suspiciously and did not like what she saw.

'Take me home,' she said to Suri, querulously. 'A hundred times already I have told you.'

'It is very late,' Mrs Anand said, 'why do you not stay here? We are all sleeping here.' And indeed already the strips of carpet and the grass mats were crowded with sleeping figures bundled together.

Prema said proudly, 'It is not difficult for us to get home, we have our own car,' and having played that trump card, felt a little less tired.

But Mrs Anand was unperturbed. She was too conscious of Suri's admiration for her, and Hari's mother's admiration for her daughter, to be rocked from smiling self-confidence.

Hari said, 'Yes, let us go home,' for he felt suddenly very tired. The effects of the party were draining out of him, and he felt awkward because Mrs Anand had surprised him talking with her daughter. He no longer wanted to talk with her: she was a pretty girl, yes, and she could sing, but he was too tired now to feel romantic. He only wanted to go home, away from the smiling Mrs Anand, to lie down on his charpoy and think, just before going to sleep, of Amrita, as he had trained himself to do.

7

'Let us go to *The Cavalier*,' suggested Hari, 'and have tea.'

Vaidya agreed, 'Good idea!'

Amrita was annoyed. She wished Vaidya would leave them alone, but he seemed to be unaware that he was in the way. He was some assistant in the External Services department of the radio. He was a Maharasthian, a tall, thin, gangling young man who talked too much; his teeth protruded and he seemed to have an excess of saliva. His presence and his incessant chatter irritated Amrita but seemed to amuse Hari, which irritated her all the more.

'I do not want to go,' she said. This was true not only because of Vaidya, but also because she disliked being seen in a public restaurant alone with two young men.

'I am so hungry,' Hari said, and laid a hand on his stomach. 'Please let us go.'

'If you are hungry we can go up to the Canteen,' she said.

'That is a very mundane suggestion,' Vaidya spluttered. 'Do you not understand that not only his body is hungering, but also his soul is hungering for the music and the gaiety of *The Cavalier*? And may I add, for the beautiful, beautiful women?'

'Yes,' Hari said; and when Amrita gave him a shocked look, went on hastily, 'I mean I want to hear the music there. Every day I go to the Canteen and it is so dull. Please Amrita,' he added, looking at her so pitifully that she could not help herself, but had to say, 'Oh, very well then,' though not very graciously.

Outside *The Cavalier*, small boys were jumping up and down, begging them to buy the evening newspaper – 'Only one anna,' they urged, 'only one.'

A tired doorman opened the over-elaborate swing-door for them. Inside it was air-conditioned, exquisitely cool although the place was crowded. The headwaiter found them a table, rather too small for the three of them, in the middle of the room. Amrita felt very much embarrassed. She did not dare to look up, for she knew she was being scrutinized from all sides; as was every woman tolerably young and pretty. Hari did not notice the offensive stares that afflicted her; he had been born into a society unused to disguising its interest for the sake of politeness, and considered staring at young women a perfectly natural reflex action. He did it himself without the slightest reticence.

The three-man band was playing a potpourri of westernized Indian tunes. The place was too small for all the noise they were making, and the total effect was that of an embodied headache. The violinist was a middle-aged European; he was starred as Rudolf, the Well-known Artiste from Vienna. He had receding hair and prosaic spectacles; he played listlessly though with determination, as if he were adding up an unending column of figures. There were a lot of waiters in dazzling white, busily threading their way between the tables with silver trays and napkins. A cigarette-boy, dressed up in blue with red braidings and a little round hat held with elastic under his chin, walked slowly round and round with his tray slung before him. A sweeper in a khaki uniform crouched on the floor and surreptitiously swept the crumbs from under the tables.

Hari and Vaidya stared at girls, sucked iced coffee through straws, and enjoyed themselves. Amrita kept her eyes lowered, and listlessly crumbled a small cream cake on her plate. She was acutely conscious of the noise Vaidya made as he sucked his straw; she did not notice that Hari was making the same noise and with the same relish.

Most of the patrons were men with gold wrist-watches and rings and oiled hair who ate a lot, drank a lot, stared a lot and talked hardly at all. There was one isolated group of skinny intellectuals who had nothing but black coffee; they gesticulated wildly and never stopped talking in high-pitched voices. Some – though very few – of the men had brought their families; the women – always several of them together – sat silent, fat and placid, while the children, also fat, bit into one cake after the other, spilt ice-cream and emptied the ashtrays on to the table-cloths. There were several young girls, mostly two or three together, accompanied by a number of young men. They were very well-dressed girls with their hair cut short and fashionably styled and a lot of make-up on their faces; several of them wore European clothes and smoked cigarettes with a self-consciously smart air.

'Of course,' Vaidya said, sitting half-turned in his chair to get a better view of the girls behind, 'all this is only an imitation.'

'An imitation,' Hari said, as if he were not quite sure what the word meant.

'An imitation,' Vaidya said, 'of western ways. Do you think it comes natural to our people to sit like this on chairs and at tables, pretending to use knives and forks?'

Hari laughed, though he was not quite sure what Vaidya meant. He had a charming laugh, expressing real enjoyment; it encouraged the other to carry on in the same strain.

'Look at those girls,' he said, and Hari looked. 'They do not exactly express chaste Indian womanhood, is it? They have modelled themselves on what they think is the style of European women. And listen to that music: almost completely westernized. And see these cakes – not Indian cakes. And knives, forks, spoons. All imitation. We are a nation of imitators.'

'What nonsense,' Amrita said.

'You cannot really blame us,' he went on, unperturbed. 'Our own ways are so crude, so uncivilized, it is no wonder we try to imitate better ways when we see them.'

'I do not think this is so very wonderful,' Amrita said, meaning the restaurant and the band and the patrons. At the next table sat a fat Sikh in a pink turban; he stuffed one cake after the other into his beard and stared at Amrita.

'Of course it is a very bad imitation,' Vaidya said. 'They do these things better in London and in Paris.'

'Have you been there?' Hari asked, with genuine interest, not because he wanted to disconcert the other.

Vaidya had to admit that he had not. But the confession did not put him out: 'One knows these things,' he said.

'Yes,' Amrita said, 'from the American films.'

Vaidya swallowed an iced cake and said, with his mouth full, 'This is a pitiful country.'

The band stopped, and one or two people listlessly applauded. In the comparative silence the manager could be heard threatening a waiter with dismissal.

'It must be very nice in Europe and America,' Hari said. 'I should like to go there.'

'You would be unhappy,' Vaidya told him. 'You would be a misfit.'

'And you?' Hari said. 'Do you not want to go?'

'I shall go there one day. But I shall know how to adapt myself.'

'And Hari,' Amrita said indignantly, 'would not know? Is that what you are saying?'

The band started to play again, this time in Russian style. 'Ruski!' cried

Vaidya and drummed his feet. Then he answered Amrita, 'Hari is a dear boy,' he said and stroked Hari's hair with chocolate-covered fingers. 'I love Hari very much.' Hari grinned and looked sweet. 'But we cannot deny that he is a true son of India.'

'What is wrong with that?' Amrita challenged. She was very angry; she could not bear to see Vaidya patronizing Hari, and Hari taking it all in such good part. He is too good, she thought, too humble, and felt urged to spring to his defence.

'There is nothing wrong with it,' Vaidya said, stuffing the chocolate éclair into his mouth. 'Only Europe is no place for such as he.'

Hari laughed heartily. 'And what about Amrita?' he said. 'Do you think she will be happy there?'

Vaidya considered Amrita with his head on one side. 'She is what is known as a lady in our society,' he said. 'That is to say, she has been brought up to a sheltered and idle existence and taught never to think for herself. Spiritually she is still in purdah.'

The sweeper, silently and as unobtrusively as possible, swept some crumbs from under Vaidya's feet.

'Do you hear that?' Hari laughed, and looked at Amrita.

'I am not listening,' she said.

'You should listen,' Vaidya said. 'We should all listen to the truth about ourselves.'

She gave him a short, fierce glance and wished somebody would make him listen to the truth about himself. Especially about the saliva which foamed constantly at his mouth as he talked.

A large glass of ice-cream topped by a wafer and a glacé cherry was now placed before the fat Sikh at the next table. He popped the cherry into his mouth and continued to scrutinize Amrita. Much embarrassed, she turned her head and looked the other way, towards the door; and found herself looking straight into the face of Krishna Sen Gupta. She was so startled she looked away again immediately and missed the nod of recognition which he was surprised into giving her.

'Will you have another coffee?' Hari asked her. 'Or perhaps another milk-shake?'

She shook her head, too agitated to be able to speak. She wondered if Krishna was still standing there, but did not dare look up again. All she wanted now was to get out, quickly.

The band stopped playing again and Vaidya, tipping his chair backwards, applauded loudly and cried, 'Encore!' Everybody now looked at their table.

Amrita whispered, 'Let us go home, please, Hari.' But he did not hear her; he was intent on admiring Vaidya.

'What are you shouting?' he asked him, and Vaidya replied, 'Encore. It is French. It means once more. Encore!' he shouted. 'Encore!'

The band ignored his applause; Rudolf held his violin between two fingers and wiped his face with a stiffly laundered handkerchief.

'Please let us go now,' Amrita said again to Hari.

Vaidya struck the table with the flat of his hand and shouted for more cakes.

'If you are not coming, I shall go alone,' Amrita told Hari. The fat Sikh, ice-cream dribbled on his beard, watched her with bovine concentration.

'But why do you want to go already?' Hari asked her. 'It is so nice here.' He was truly happy. He loved the music, the smartly dressed girls, the waiters hurrying past with trays of coffee and ice-cream; this, he felt, was Society.

'Sit, sit, woman,' Vaidya said loudly. Having once by his loud applause gained public attention, he meant to keep it. 'Enjoy the good things of Life.'

'Even if they are only imitation,' said Hari, laughing gently.

Vaidya slapped him on the back: 'You are learning!' he cried, and Hari looked delighted.

'I am going,' Amrita said and resolutely got up, thus giving the fat Sikh the opportunity to see the rest of her. She looked sideways towards the door and was almost surprised that Krishna was no longer there; she had been so sure that she could feel his disapproving spectacles gleaming upon her.

Hari sadly called for the bill. He did not resent Amrita's insistence, though he felt very disappointed: he had been looking forward to another pleasant hour or two here amid these elegant surroundings. He cast a lingering look around; his eyes dwelt for a moment on a Eurasian girl in a black and white checked dress, smoking a cigarette.

'Please come, Hari,' Amrita said quietly. She also would have liked to look round to find out whether Krishna had gone or stayed; but she did not dare for fear of looking straight into his face again.

'Women!' said Vaidya, throwing his hands up in the air and a despairing look at Amrita. A few people at the adjoining tables laughed.

8

Krishna Sen Gupta had been back in India for four years now and was getting used to it again. Before that he had spent five years in England as a student. In spite of twinges of homesickness – regrets for his curry and rice, for the warm idle nights spent lounging in the open, for the intimacy and individual wit of his native language – in spite of that, he had enjoyed England. So much so that he had not really wanted to come back. But he knew he had to. Not only because he had to start off on a career; not only because he was an Indian and his place in India – this feeling was with him intermittent only and, he thought, merely the result of sentimental convention – but chiefly because of his parents. They put no pressure on him, they tried to make him feel he could do as he liked; but he knew it was not as simple as that. Both his parents had been prominent members of the Congress movement, both had suffered long spells of imprisonment. But by the time Krishna had grown up, the fight was finished; there was nothing left for him to do. He often thought that if he could have taken an active part in the Independence movement, it might have been easier for him afterwards to stay out of India: he could have rejected, had he wished, the fruits of his own sacrifice. But it was much harder to reject that of theirs.

So he had come back. And he had hated it at first. He had no work for several months, and had nothing to do but dwell on, indulge and intensify this hatred. He hated the uncomplaining poverty, the apathy he saw all around him, in the streets, the bazaars, on the steps of the temples. He hated the servants who took it for granted that he was the master, and that it was their life's duty to do his menial work for him. He hated the beggars and the insolence with which they made it clear that they belonged to this society, had every right to exist in it. He hated – perhaps most of all, because it hemmed him in all the time and threatened to engulf him – the complacency of his own class, the civil-servant mind, the stolid satisfaction with routine work, with salary and position for ever fixed, with yawning pleasures in once-English clubs. He hated the policy of intimidation on which the whole system seemed to rest – the instinctive subservience to superiors and instinctive bullying of social inferiors. He hated the frank immorality of business and the unashamed dishonesty of shopkeepers. He hated the women because they were ignorant and innocent and submissive. He hated the heat which undermined and insulted his vigour. He hated – hated everything; even his parents, because it was they who had made him come back to this.

They knew very well what the matter was. In their youth they had also been sent to Europe for their studies and on their return had experienced the same difficulties. But in time there had been something definite, something concrete, for them to revolt and fight against: their newly acquired European liberal principles had found an outlet and a Cause. But their son's could only be reconciled and finally perhaps rubbed away by time and habit.

'It will take time,' the father comforted the mother at night; 'it will take time, but he will get used to it again.'

Krishna thought he could never get used to it again. He spent his time sitting in coffee-houses and impressing young men who had not been to England. He talked cynically and bitterly. Then a little work started to drift his way, a newspaper article here, an occasional lecture there, a book to be translated from Bengali into English. He began not to notice the services done for him by the servants, to accept the beggars at their own valuation, to regard young girls as members of another species. By the time he got his appointment at the Delhi University, he had almost got used to the heat.

To see Amrita sitting in a restaurant with two young men, one of whom was making a spectacle of himself, had annoyed him. That night at dinner he refused to talk either to her or to her mother. Afterwards he wandered moodily around the garden, tried to sit and read in his room, but found it too hot, and finally settled himself in a deck-chair on the lawn at the back of the house.

Amrita was sitting on the front lawn with her mother. She too was silent and moody. She felt – though she did not admit this to herself – rather ashamed before Krishna. And she was distinctly nervous: there was always the fear that he might say something to her mother. She did not think he would; but he was so unpredictable – to her anyway – one never knew what he was going to do. He might make some facetious remark which would raise her mother's suspicions; and once Radha's suspicions were roused, she was not the woman to rest until she had satisfied them. True, Krishna was obviously in no mood to make facetious remarks; but then he might drop a hint some other way, by some sarcastic comment which his irritation might force out of him. He was not, Amrita knew, very good at hiding his feelings.

Radha was shifting about restlessly in her cane arm-chair. She yawned, and wished she had gone to a cinema. Amrita's silence began to irritate her intensely.

'Why are you sitting there quiet like a dead fish?'

'What?' said Amrita, not having heard.

This irritated her mother more than ever. 'What?' she mimicked. 'You have not even the manners to listen to what I say. I am nothing. You can treat me like I was a wall.'

'I was thinking.'

'Thinking! You are a very rude girl.'

'What is rude about thinking?' Amrita not unreasonably asked.

'Have you nothing to say to your mother?' Radha demanded. 'Is she nothing to you that you sit beside her and do not hear her or see her? Other daughters are happy when they can be together with their mother, they sit and they talk and they tell their mother everything. But you do not even speak to me. You are no company for me at all. Strangers are better to me than my own daughter.'

Amrita made no comment. She was not really listening, she was thinking of what she could say to Krishna Sen Gupta. But Radha was warming to her subject and took her audience for granted.

'You no longer know how to speak with educated polite people,' she was saying. 'You have forgotten all the manners I have taught you, because now you speak only with people who have no manners. But I knew how it would be. As soon as you went to that radio station. I knew how it would end.'

'Yes, Mamma,' Amrita said patiently. She had known that sooner or later it would come to this: all her mother's conversation nowadays turned about this point.

'When a girl of good family falls in with low people, this is what happens. She does not even know any longer how to treat her own mother with respect. The mother does not count, she is a piece of wood.'

Amrita let her talk on. She decided that she really must go and speak to Krishna, so she abruptly got up and walked away. Radha stopped still in the middle of a sentence and shrilled after her, 'Where are you going?' But Amrita walked straight through the house into the rear garden.

There was a full moon and the lawn was like a dull mirror. Krishna's deck-chair stood in the middle; she could see only his legs stretching out of it. He gave no sign of seeing or wanting to see her. She sat down on the grass near his chair. She plucked a blade of grass and sucked it.

'Did you eat too much at *The Cavalier*, so now you have indigestion?' she finally asked him, for she had to get to the point and could think of no better way.

He made no answer. She waited. He said nothing. She knew she would have to be more direct.

'Were you shocked to see me there?' she asked; and when he still said nothing, she took this for an affirmative and went on to defend herself. 'Everybody is always telling us to be emancipated, to be like European women, but, when we try to be, they are shocked and say we are behaving badly.'

Krishna stirred; she was appealing to his reason, and that was an appeal which he had learnt in England to find irresistible.

'But you yourself feel guilty,' he pointed out.

'Only because it is you who make me feel guilty. If everybody thinks it is bad that I go to a restaurant with two young men, then of course I feel guilty.'

He felt that his anger had quite evaporated and that he was suddenly in rather a good mood. Perhaps he was flattered that she should have chosen to come and justify herself before him: but he did not probe into the reason for his change of mood; he was content just to feel pleased.

'And I feel so embarrassed,' she went on; she rather liked confiding to him. 'When everybody stares so, all the men, it is terrible. Krishna . . . will men always stare at us like that?'

'Until we are used to seeing you move freely among us.'

She nodded, plucked another blade of grass, and after chewing it for a while, wondered if she would have enough courage to ask. She had.

'Did you see the people I was with?'

'I heard them.'

'That was Vaidya,' she said hastily. 'He is not a nice man, I do not like him at all. He is always talking, and such nonsense too, and he is always showing off.'

'Why then did you go with him?' Krishna asked. Really, he was feeling ridiculously happy and light-hearted. He looked up into the sky and wondered if he started to count the stars, how far he would get. He had wondered about this since he was a small boy; but he had given up counting long ago.

'We could not get rid of him,' Amrita said. 'He is one of those people who do not know when they are not wanted. Krishna . . . why did you not come and speak with us?'

'Because I am not like your friend who does not know when he is not wanted.'

'I wish you had come,' she said.

He recognized a very pleasing symbolism in the fact that he had given up counting the stars. He began to compose a verse in Bengali: 'In youth I counted the stars; now I am old and my eyes look down into the rice-bowl. Ah youth! Ah age, and death of dreams.' When he had first come back from England, he had sneered at such verses: he had explained that they were facile and sentimental, and only demonstrated how shallow and tinselled was the Indian soul that took delight in them. But now, after four years back in India, he felt himself once again moved by them, and sometimes, when he heard a good one, tears came into his eyes. 'In youth . . .' he repeated to himself, and aloud he said, 'Amrita, do you ever count the stars?'

'I used to,' she replied, 'when I was a small girl. But I never got very far, there were so many, and always I forgot which I had counted and which not.'

Her answer pleased him and he wanted to recite his verse to her. But before he could do so she said, 'I wish you had come to speak with us in *The Cavalier*. Because the other one was Hari.'

Then he was happy no longer. 'Now I am old . . .' he jerked the verse out of his mind; facile, sentimental, he told himself, and was angry.

'If you had come you would have met him,' she was saying. Why does she not leave me alone, he thought, but she went obliviously on, 'I wish you had met Hari.' There was a short pause during which he wished her away and she summoned up enough courage finally to ask: 'Please, Krishna . . . will you come and meet Hari some time?'

'Why?' he asked angrily; all the evening's irritation had come back to him.

'Because I should like it so,' she innocently answered.

'Amrita!' Radha called. She stood on the back veranda. She saw the deck-chair in the middle of the moon-flooded lawn and Krishna's legs sticking out of it, and Amrita sitting on the grass beside him. 'There you are,' she said, 'both of you.'

'Please Krishna?' Amrita pleaded.

Radha came walking towards them. 'It would be as well for me to live like a sadhu at the bottom of a deep pit,' she said, 'as live together with you two.'

9

Prema had everything ready, and she sat waiting on one of the flowered divans in the drawing-room. There were three of these divans ranged round the wall at regular intervals; between them were armchairs, also flowered, and small tables. The pattern was divan, small table, arm-chair, divan ... and so on in admirable symmetry. On each small table stood one silver ashtray. Precisely in the middle of the room, on a wildly patterned square of carpet, was another small table; on this stood a polished and unused silver tea-set. A large coloured full-length photograph of Prema dressed up in her best clothes hung on one wall; on the opposite wall was a coloured full-length photograph, equally large, of Suri. A vase bulged waist-high in the imitation fireplace; in this were stuck eight artificial flowers which looked as if they had been starched.

Prema gazed round with satisfaction. Everything, she saw, looked new and expensive. She herself looked new and expensive. She was wearing a three-quarter-sleeved leaf-green kamiz with a pattern of lilac parrots and a leaf-green silk salwar; a leaf-green duppata was decorously arranged over her bosom. She wore four gold bangles on her right arm and three on her left and long gold ear-rings set with green stones. She was strongly scented. This girl of Hari's, she thought, should see what sort of a family Hari belonged to. She was to be received in the drawing-room; afterwards they would have tea in the dining-room, just the two of them, at the big dining-table which Prema herself had already laid, very carefully, because she did not trust the servant to put the right cutlery in the right place.

But Amrita was a little disappointed. She had expected a supreme simplicity and was rather taken aback by the flowered divans and the silver tea-set. And she had not expected Hari's sister to be so – she groped for the polite expression – so *lavishly* dressed.

'Please sit,' Prema said with dignity, indicating one of the divans. She looked Amrita up and down and decided at once: too thin. She was also rather surprised that Amrita should be wearing such a plain sari: it was a pale yellow chiffon with no embroidery, no spangles, no decoration at all, not even on the pallu. Though she supposed it must be pure chiffon, at Rs 10/6 a yard, since Amrita came from such a good family.

Amrita sat down, and Prema wondered whether she should sit on the next divan or on the same one; she decided on the same one because the next was too far away. She folded her hands, sparkling with rings, in her lap and began to make polite conversation.

'How hot it is,' she said. And no jewellery, she was thinking; not even bangles; she was shocked. 'If I had known that it would be so hot in Delhi, even in September, I would not have come back from Simla.'

She had gone to Simla in May. Suri had an uncle there and she had gone to stay at his house; but there had been so many others of Suri's relatives that she had been glad to come back to Delhi after three weeks, hot as it was.

'Of course,' she said, 'we always go to the hills in the summer. Usually to Simla. It is a very interesting place and always there is so much to do. There are picnics and dances and tea at *Nirula's*.'

In fact, she had spent most of the time at home, quarrelling with Suri's relatives and helping with the cooking – and wishing she could go back to Delhi.

'It is a very elegant place. Of course it is rather expensive but that is only right because it is meant only for better-class people and it keeps the others away.'

'Yes,' said Amrita, gazing intently down at her hands lying folded in her lap.

Prema continued to make polite conversation. 'Do you care for reading? I am always reading. I have all the new magazines. I will lend them to you.'

Surreptitiously she compared the colour of her arm with Amrita's. She had to admit that Amrita was slightly fairer but comforted herself with the thought that she did not care for that type of complexion; it was too yellow for her liking. And Amrita wore no bangles.

'Some of the stories in these magazines are very good. They are so true to life. I have learnt much from them and also they give me comfort.' She sighed. 'One can forget one's sorrows when one is reading,' she said, and sighed again.

Amrita remembered that her father used to say the same thing, but she thought that he had meant it in a different way. So she kept quiet.

'And when one has many sorrows,' Prema said with a third sigh, deeper than all the rest, 'it is good sometimes to forget.'

Amrita felt embarrassed. She also felt hot and a little sick from Prema's strong perfume and hair-oil. She said, for she felt she had to make some answer, 'I am afraid I have not many books.'

Prema decided that this girl was not very interesting to talk to. She probably did not have any deep feelings; and Prema did not like people who had no deep feelings. So she said, 'Shall we have tea now?' and led the way into the dining-room.

The furniture in the dining-room was also new and shining with spirit-polish. Prema had covered the large, long table with a white cloth. The tea-things laid out for the two of them looked rather isolated, like rabbits lost in the snow.

'Bearer!' Prema shrilled; and when no bearer came, shrilled louder, 'Bearer!'

Still no one came.

'These servants,' Prema said to Amrita, one lady to another.

At length she cried, 'O Pritam!' and the boy appeared instantly with the teapot. He had been nursing it on the fire for two hours and had been eagerly looking forward to this moment. He dumped it on the table and scrutinized Amrita.

'Go away, owl,' Prema whispered to him fiercely. She would have liked him to hand round the plates but she was afraid he might make some unmannerly mistake.

'You will please help yourself,' she told Amrita. 'No ceremony. This is your own home.'

There were plates heaped with sweets, huge yellow ladoos, white barfi with breath-thin silver paper, brown gulab jamuns oozing syrup, golden rings of jalebi. Another plate was filled with cashew-nuts and pistachios; another with samusas; and there was one of little iced cakes in green and pink.

'You have made too much trouble for yourself,' Amrita said.

'It is no trouble. I get all sweets and cakes ready made. I always go to *Ragho Mull's*. They are so good; a little more expensive, of course, but it is worth it. O Pritam!' she called. Pritam had been listening behind the door. 'A spoon for the sugar.'

'You have a very nice home,' Amrita said.

'Everything is new. My husband does not like old things. When he sees something old, he says, "Out with it, buy new."'

Pritam came in with a cardboard-box. He opened it and revealed brand new spoons wrapped in tissue-paper.

'One spoon, I said,' Prema hissed at him. She took off the tissue-paper and stuck a spoon into the sugar. Another little servant-boy who had crept in behind Pritam peered open-mouthed at Amrita.

'These servants, it is so difficult to train them,' Prema said. 'Please eat.'

Amrita was still struggling with an enormous yellow ladoo. She was crumbling it with her fingers, but Prema used a teaspoon.

'What can you expect?' Prema said. 'They have always been used to working in ordinary Indian households and they do not know how things should be done. I think in your house also you must be having this difficulty?'

'No,' Amrita said, 'we have only one servant and he has been in the family a long time.'

Only *one* servant, Prema thought. But she said kindly, 'I always think it is better to have less servants; they give so much trouble.' It was her duty as hostess to set her guest at ease.

Amrita had not expected that she would talk servants with Hari's sister. It was all so different from what she had imagined. She had to admit that Prema was not after all so truly Indian as she had thought she would be. And all the time she kept wondering, when are we going to start talking about what matters; but she felt that they were getting further and further away from any chance of approach to the intimate subject of Hari.

'Running a household,' Prema was saying, 'is not easy. You will find out when you are married.' And Amrita wondered whether this, at last, was the opening. 'Marriage,' Prema said, staring into the distance over the plates of sweets and cakes and samusas, 'is not an easy thing.'

'No,' Amrita murmured. She waited a little breathlessly for Prema to go on.

'One has many sorrows,' Prema said. 'One tries to hide them from the world but they gnaw at the heart. You see me here in my home,' she said; 'you see expensive furniture, silver knives and forks, servants, and also we have a big car which my husband had sent from America. You probably think this woman must be happy; but if you could see into my heart ...'

Again Amrita felt embarrassed; and also deeply disappointed. She said, for want of anything better, and to cover up both embarrassment and disappointment, 'What make is your car?' and felt idiotic.

Prema shut her eyes. The girl is a fool, she thought. She opened her eyes again and said, 'Please eat'; though the ladoo on Amrita's plate did not seem to be getting any smaller. 'Please take,' Prema said. 'Or there will be so much left and who is to eat it all?'

It was Hari who ate a lot of it. He came in the evening after Amrita had gone, and was very excited.

'Is she not pretty?' he asked at once.

Drawing and dining-rooms had been shut up again and Prema was lying on the bed. She felt very tired and had changed back into her old clothes. She was nibbling at a piece of barfi; the radio was playing, a woman wailing a love song.

'Quite pretty,' she said coldly.

'What was she wearing?' asked Hari eagerly.

'A very plain sari. It was yellow. I do not think it was even real chiffon; I think she bought it at one of the refugee-stalls and paid only Rs 2/8 a yard.'

'And did you like her? Is she not beautiful?'

Prema said nothing. She left the piece of barfi and started on an iced cake instead. The radio sang, 'How my heart laughs when you come.'

'What did you talk about?' Hari asked. 'What did she say? What did you say? Did you talk much about me?'

'No.'

He was taken aback, but only for a moment. 'She is so pretty,' he said. 'Did you not find her very pretty?'

'She did not eat much. See how much there is left.'

'But what did you talk about? Please tell me everything.'

'She did not say much,' Prema said.

'No, she is rather quiet. How sweet she is! She is so shy.'

'I did not think her shy.'

'No?'

'Not shy.'

'What then? Please speak, sister.'

Prema looked at the cake she was holding. The radio sang, 'My tears are calling you.' After a while Prema said, 'Kaka,' and paused while he looked at her expectantly; then she put the cake down, for this was almost a solemn moment. 'Kaka,' she said, 'this girl is not the girl for you.'

He was astonished; he did not understand. 'Do you mean you did not like her?'

'Shall I say the truth? No, I did not like her.'

'Oh,' he said, quite crestfallen, and sank down on the edge of the bed.

'At once I read her character,' Prema said. 'She is proud and conceited; and rather stupid. And also she has no feelings.'

'Oh, no, no, no.'

'You asked me to tell you the truth; and I am telling you.'

'Oh, no,' Hari said. 'You did not understand her.'

Prema turned her face away from him and laughed bitterly. 'When you have lived and suffered and read as much as I have, then please come and speak with me about understanding.' And after a while she added more gently, 'I have spoken for your good only, Kaka. I am your elder sister; I always think of your good. There are things you are too young to understand; you have not lived enough in the world and you cannot understand people's characters. But I know; I can read people's characters like I can read a book. And I tell you, all my experience of the world tells you, this girl is not the girl for you.'

Hari was terribly unhappy. He could not contradict his elder sister, but her words made him so unhappy.

Suri came home. He saw all the sweets piled up on the table next to Prema's bed and said, 'Who has been having a feast?' He selected a ladoo, opened his mouth very wide and popped it in.

'How late you are,' Prema said. 'Every night you come home later and later, and here I sit waiting for you and your food is cold.'

Suri's mouth was very full with the ladoo. He turned the knob of the radio. They had not noticed that the singing had stopped and that they were hearing a talk on agricultural development. Suri twiddled the knob till he got more music; swallowing the last crumbs of the ladoo, he swayed his head and joined in with the singing.

'Be quiet,' Prema said. 'You will give me a headache; already I feel very bad.' Indeed she was very tired; making polite conversation to Amrita had exhausted her.

Suri sat down on the bed and eased off his shoes. Then he stepped out of his trousers and wrapped himself into a lungi instead.

'Where have you been all this time?' Prema said.

He shouted to the servant and sat down on the bed; his legs were tucked under him and he played with his toes. His big toe waggled: this seemed to give him pleasure. When the servant came with his food on a brass tray, he at once began to eat, tearing off large strips of chapati; afterwards he wiped his mouth with the back of his hand, burped, and called for a toothpick. His head swayed in time with the music. Smiling with pleasure at the recollection, he said, 'That girl the other night, what a beautiful voice,' and his head swayed and he said, 'Wah, wah!'

'Shall I go home now?' Hari asked.

'Stay,' said Prema. 'Eat more sweets.'

He took a ladoo and began to eat it; he looked disconsolate.

'And what a beautiful face,' Suri said, 'Kaka, no?'

'You mean Sushila Anand?' asked Prema. 'She is a very nice girl.' She was not jealous of Suri's praise; she knew that any respectable girl was sacred to him. 'I like her.'

'She is one of our girls,' Suri said. 'A real Punjabi beauty.'

'Not really beautiful,' Prema said, 'but a very nice girl. Our own girls are the best, who can deny it?' She looked meaningfully at Hari, who was not listening.

'Strong and healthy,' Suri said. 'She is what I call a beauty.'

'I want the car tomorrow,' said Prema.

'I need it,' answered Suri, throwing his toothpick on the floor.

'Always you need it,' she said. 'Whenever I want the car, always it is "I need it".'

Suri scratched the sole of his foot and yawned. Hari sadly ate a piece of barfi.

10

After dinner at the grandfather's house, they all sat out in the garden: the grandfather, Tarla and Vazir Dayal, Radha and Mira auntie. Amrita had stayed at home; she had pleaded a headache. Radha was quite glad of her absence because she wanted to make the occasion a family council over Amrita.

The night was very hot. They sat in their deck-chairs, and all of them felt their age. The heat clung to them, exhausted them. Mira auntie languidly fanned herself with an enormous fan decorated with yellow peacocks. It was very quiet. Not a breath of wind stirred in the trees. A sickening scent of night-flowers rose from the bushes and spread itself like a pall. The summers of centuries seemed to be brooding over the old garden.

Vazir Dayal, sagging in a deck-chair with his long hands dangling limply over the sides, groaned softly, 'This heat . . .'

The grandfather said crisply, 'It is only a matter of making up one's mind to it.' He sat upright, with his hands planted on his knees, as if in defiance of the heat.

'My mind fails and falters,' Vazir Dayal said. His wife gave him a warning look, but it only goaded him into adding, 'But then I am what you would call a decadent.'

The fact was, Vazir Dayal and his father-in-law heartily disliked one another. The Rai Bahadur disapproved of everything about his son-in-law; every word spoken by Vazir Dayal sent him into a state of chronic irritation. Vazir Dayal knew this and did his best to aggravate it.

'And September too,' Mira auntie said. 'It should not be like this in September.'

'We will not talk about it,' said the Rai Bahadur.

'No,' Tarla backed him up, 'talking about it only makes it worse.'

'Perhaps,' Mira said. 'But I feel it so because I am fatter than any of you.' Nobody could deny this. Mira was indeed very fat. She spread in large soft folds over the sides of her deck-chair.

'When I was in family way it was worse than this,' Radha said. 'I remember April, May, June, it was terrible with a weight like a bullock inside me.'

Vazir Dayal limply flapped his hand at her and protested, 'Please do not be so sordid. You make me feel quite ill.'

'It is worst for women in family way,' Radha went on unperturbed. They had all learnt to ignore his little utterances. 'Yesterday, I saw Nimmi Kathuria, Ratna Sharma's second daughter, the one that married Phool Chand Kathuria of Kathuria and Co., the chemical firm, and the poor girl was well advanced, she must have been in seventh or eighth month. How she was suffering with the heat, poor girl, I pity her.'

'I remember when I was carrying Harish how hot I felt, O it was very bad,' Mira said. She was a widow and had one son, a dentist, as large and fat and placid as herself.

'It is a pity, Tarla,' the Rai Bahadur said, 'that you cannot also regale us with your experiences in pregnancy.'

'For this you may thank me,' said Vazir Dayal.

'Often I envy you, Tarla,' Radha said. 'One's children can be so difficult. When we are young they break our arms, when we are old they break our hearts.'

'My Harish has never broken my heart,' Mira said.

'God bless him,' Radha added automatically.

'Harish is a fool,' said the Rai Bahadur. He had never disguised his opinion of his only grandson.

'He is not very clever,' Mira agreed placidly. 'I think he takes after me. And of course his poor father was a little slow, too.' She sighed, and waved her fan.

'Often I wish,' Radha said, 'my Amrita was more like your Harish.'

'She has at least some spirit,' the Rai Bahadur said.

'She is a very obstinate, headstrong girl,' said her mother.

'It is your own fault,' Tarla said. 'Why can you not leave the poor girl alone? It is not good always to watch and push a young girl; that is a very old-fashioned idea. You must stop nagging her, then she will be all right.'

'I do my duty as a mother by her,' Radha flared up. 'Nagging her, what do you mean? You have never had any children, Tarla, so you have no right to talk.'

'If I had, I hope I would have known better than you how to deal with them,' Tarla answered. 'I saw Amrita the other day and she looked so ill and upset.'

'Is that my fault!' Radha cried. 'God knows I do everything for her,

I cook her the best dishes, with my own hands sometimes I prepare them, I wait on her like a servant, I buy her clothes, only last week I gave her a sari – pure georgette, I got it at Varma Brothers at the Sale, I paid twenty five rupees and it would have been sixty rupees if it had not been the Clearance Sale – only the stupid girl said she did not like the colour.'

'What colour was it?' Mira asked.

'I would not be at all surprised,' Tarla said, 'if the girl had a nervous breakdown.'

'God forbid!' Radha cried.

'She seemed so nervous and run-down when I met her.'

'But what can I do?' Radha wailed. 'It is all this talk about the boy she met at the radio. I have reasoned with her, I have argued with her, I have wept before her; what more can I do? I wish you would speak with her again, Pappaji. She will listen to you.'

'I have spoken to her once,' the Rai Bahadur said. 'I have told her that she cannot marry this boy. She must regard that as final.'

'The word of God,' Vazir Dayal audibly murmured.

'But still she refuses to give him up!' Radha cried. 'May his eyes drop out, has he bewitched my girl?'

'The girl needs distracting perhaps,' Tarla suggested, more to her father than to her sister. 'She leads a rather dull life, I think we should put some new interests in her way.'

'How often I have said,' Radha protested, '"Amrita come to the cinema", "Amrita come with me to see this person, that person", but always – no, "I am tired, Mamma" or "I do not feel like it, Mamma." Do you want me to drag her out of the house by her hair perhaps?'

'I did not mean we should send her to cinemas or on useless visits,' Tarla said. 'I meant we should give her an interest in life, let her do some constructive work.'

'Such as drinking tea on committees,' said Vazir Dayal.

'I am willing,' Tarla went on, 'to take her to some of my Meetings. There is so much work to be done, and always we need new helpers. And once Amrita has begun to be interested in Social Work, she will forget all about this affair.'

'It would be a good thing perhaps for her,' Radha said. 'You do not speak quite without sense, Tarla.'

Then the Rai Bahadur spoke, 'I have been pondering along a different line.'

'Yes Pappaji?' Tarla said deferentially.

'I have been thinking,' her father delivered himself, 'that we ought to send her abroad. To Europe, to England perhaps.'

'Europe!' Radha cried. 'England! My poor little bird alone in England!'

The Rai Bahadur uttered a brief sound of irritation. 'Why do you excite yourself so,' he said. 'Can you think about nothing calmly and with deliberation like a responsible adult?'

'It was the shock,' Radha explained. 'How can I think of my child in England?'

'It is so far away,' Mira said, 'and I hear they do not get enough to eat there.' She clicked her tongue in gentle commiseration.

'But what do you intend she should do there, Pappaji?' Tarla asked, to show that at least one of his daughters was a responsible adult.

'She could pursue her studies,' the Rai Bahadur said. 'She could enter one of the Universities.'

'But already she is such a studied girl,' Radha said. 'Already she is B.A., a graduate, the clever child.'

'Let her go to Paris,' Vazir Dayal said with a dreamy air. 'She will learn much there.' Actually he had been very bored in Paris, but he had never admitted this to anybody.

'If you have no sensible suggestion to bring forward,' the Rai Bahadur turned on him, 'then kindly spare us your idle flippancies.'

'My dear sir,' said his son-in-law, 'what cause have you to throw reflection on the University of Paris?'

'What do you propose she should study, Pappaji?' Tarla asked.

'Surely you can see for yourself that is quite irrelevant,' her father said. 'The main purpose is that she should get away from here into completely different surroundings, among different people leading a different life, and at the same time have her mind trained and disciplined by application to some course of study.'

'Could we not perhaps send her to Bombay?' Radha suggested. 'It is not so far away and she could stay with Shakuntala. I also would enjoy a trip to Bombay,' she went on, warming to the idea. 'I have not seen Shakuntala for many years, and also there is Parbati and the children, and old Shantidevi auntie, and the Rai Bahadurs and the Ram Kumars, and so many others. Yes, Pappaji, I think a visit to Bombay would do Amrita much good, she would forget everything.'

'And I also will come,' Mira said. 'Only last week I was thinking how I would like to go to Bombay and eat ice-cream at Midi's.'

'We are not speaking of eating ice-cream at Midi's,' the Rai Bahadur said sharply. 'We are speaking of sending Amrita to study in England.'

'I have always thought England a very dull place,' said Vazir Dayal. 'It is one of my prejudices.'

'She could live in a hostel,' Tarla said. 'I believe there are hostels specially for Indian students.'

'Hostel, nothing!' Radha cried. 'She will live with me, with her mother as a daughter should. We will rent a house; only a small house, four-five rooms that will be enough for us. Perhaps even we will take a flat, but I do not like to be without a garden. I will take Gian with us, because it is so difficult to train a new servant, and also I hear servants are hard to find in England.'

'Please do not forget also to take Krishna Sen Gupta,' Tarla said.

'Idiot,' Radha answered, but Mira asked, 'Why must Krishna Sen Gupta go with them?'

The Rai Bahadur struck his knee with the flat of his hand and said curtly, 'Amrita will go alone.'

'Oh no, Pappaji!' Radha cried. 'We cannot send her alone to England, who will look after her? And how are we to know she will not get into bad company there? She might even want to, God forbid, marry an English and such a thing I will never survive. Think of it – in our family – a mixed marriage! First you can make my funeral rites.'

'Sometimes I feel,' said the Rai Bahadur, 'that we have a touch of insanity in the family. I believe some distant relative of your mother's – was it an uncle? an aunt? – thought he was a jackal and had to be taken to Poona.'

'Oh,' said Mira, and the shock made her stop fanning, 'how terrible. I never heard Mamma speak about it.'

'But how can I stay alone without my daughter,' Radha said. 'How am I to live? Perhaps I could take another paying guest, if someone suitable can be found, but no paying guest, however good his family, can take the place of a daughter.'

'Amrita will go alone,' the Rai Bahadur said; his foot was tapping.

'Of course,' Tarla said.

'It is easy to see, Tarla,' Radha told her, 'that you are not a Mother.'

11

The children were chasing one another in and out of the three rooms, screaming; now and again Mohini, their mother, shouted and stamped her foot at them, and sometimes caught one and smacked the back of his neck. The small square of courtyard was completely filled with sun and burned like an oven. There was no redeeming fleck of shade anywhere. The little servant-boy was scouring pots in the kitchen; his hair lay matted on his forehead and perspiration ran into his eyes.

Inside the house it was a little cooler. The three rooms were almost completely filled by charpoys, small ones for the children, big ones for the adults. Some of the charpoys were set upright against the wall, and articles of clothing hung over the protruding legs. In one room stood two armchairs and a cane-bottomed chair; the two armchairs had soiled yellow dust-covers and broken springs, but the chair had lately been recaned. There were also two cane-hammocks, once coloured but now faded, and a mat on the floor. Big tin trunks stood pushed against the wall; they contained all the family belongings, clothes and blankets, ornaments and wedding-photographs and silver pieces.

Hari's mother was sitting on the mat and saying her prayers. She let out a stream of indistinct syllables in a low voice, rising from time to time to a higher note which acted like a punctuation-mark, and then subsiding again into the stream of muttering. The children danced all round and took no notice of her. She herself seemed in a hurry; for she was rattling on faster and faster till at last, with an air of satisfaction, she pronounced the final word on a high note. Then she hoisted herself painfully to her feet and groaned, 'O Lord, Lord.'

'Naniji, Naniji!' the smallest child shouted, and tried to spring on the old woman's back. The bigger boy wiped his hand on the dangling sari-end that hung over her shoulder.

'Get away!' their grandmother said, raising a threatening hand at them. They danced round her, shouting, 'Nani, our Naniji!' She hit out at them and then laughed out loud. 'The little ones,' she said, 'and when they grow up they will be big and rich and they will look after their Nani and let her lie on her bed and eat mangoes all day long.'

Mohini shouted from the next room that she would peel every shred of skin from the children's bodies if they did not keep quiet. 'With my own nails!' she cried.

She came in with a big earthenware pot full of curds and sat down on the mat and vigorously began to churn the curds with a long stick. The children fled, pretending to be trains, puff-puff-puff and whistling shrilly. 'Tonight I tear your tongues out!' Mohini shouted after them. The old woman lowered herself down on the mat again and watched the churning; she nodded her head up and down.

'The servant has not yet brought the vegetables,' Mohini said.

'He stinks with laziness, may his eyes drop out,' the mother said.

Mohini poured some of the churned curds into a huge drinking-glass and liberally flavoured it with pepper and salt; the milk was bubbling with froth and all the butter had come to the top. The old woman lifted the glass and drained it in a few gulps; when she had finished she had a white moustache which she did not bother to wipe off. She said, 'It is a hard life, O Lord.'

Just then Prema came in. She left her shoes at the threshold; her feet were broad and thick, Mohini's broader and thicker; the old woman had huge hard toenails which seemed to bend upwards.

'I wanted the car,' Prema said, as she sat herself cross-legged on the floor, 'and he would not let me have it. Everything I want he says no. But if any of his relations want the car, then it is different, then it is of course with great pleasure, please keep it all day and also tomorrow if you wish. Only his own wife must go down to his feet and beg, and still she is answered with no. Give me some buttermilk.'

'And I,' Mohini said, as she poured the milk in a white stream, 'again it is the same, sick sick sick all day, but what does he care?'

The mother sighed and said, 'It is a blessing from the Lord.'

'It is a crime,' Prema said, wagging her head and clicking her tongue, 'already there are three and now another, and still the husband is earning only Rupees 250. Why do you allow him?'

'What can I do?' Mohini said. 'He is like all husbands, he thinks only of his own pleasure.'

'Like all husbands,' Prema echoed with feeling.

'It is a woman's fate to suffer,' the mother said, and both her daughters nodded. 'Only our Kaka's wife, she will be the lucky one.'

Mohini giggled and looked at Prema out of the corner of her eye. 'You have not told us about his Memsahib,' she said and giggled again.

'Memsahib,' Prema said contemptuously. 'She came on the bus and she told me herself they had only one servant.'

The mother burst into a short and passionate prayer.

'She is not even very pretty,' Prema went on.

The mother groaned and prayed afresh.

'And I think she is stupid. She has nothing to say.'

Mohini laughed and churned the curds with renewed vigour. Prema absent-mindedly looked at her own plump smooth hand and then back again at her sister's broad and chapped one. 'But you need not worry yourself, Mataji,' she said, 'as long as I live, Kaka will not marry this girl.'

'It is good for a boy to have an elder sister,' the mother acknowledged.

'Who is at home?' a voice cried from outside.

'Please come!' the mother and Mohini called aloud. 'It is not Bhuaji?' they asked one another.

'You have milk on your lip,' Prema told her mother. The old woman tried to wipe it off with the back of her hand but it had already dried.

It was Mrs Anand, Sushila's mother, who came in. She stood in the doorway, shuffling off her shoes and smiling at them. She looked big and insolently healthy. Prema arranged her dupatta more becomingly, and they all got up to do the visitor honour.

'No ceremony,' Mrs Anand said. 'Please sit. This is my own home.' She too sat herself down on the floor and wiped the perspiration from her face with her dupatta.

'It is good to see you here,' the mother said.

They did not know her very well. She was a member of a very distant branch of the family with which they did not have much contact. They knew that her husband was a car-broker and that they had three good-looking daughters, the eldest of whom, Sushila, had reached a marriageable age. There were rumours that Mrs Anand herself was a shrewish, loud-mouthed woman, and once or twice there had been some very strange whispers about her; though these may only have been due to the fact that she behaved in a rather more free and more outspoken manner with the menfolk than was the general rule among the women of the family. At any rate, nobody could point to anything definite and her respectability was quite secure.

She sat now, drinking her glass of buttermilk and looking at them with smiling eyes. They waited, wondered, and were polite.

'It is very hot outside,' Mrs Anand informed them. 'But in your house it is cool.'

'Please rest yourself,' the mother said. 'It is a very small house but it is yours. We are only your servants.'

'My house also is small,' she said. 'I hope you will come and honour me.'

'Your house is a palace,' the mother said politely; she had of course never seen it.

Prema examined Mrs Anand's clothes. Her kamiz and salwar were, she saw, of a not very superior material, but they were well-cut and looked quite stylish. Prema wondered who her tailor was. She had to admit that Mrs Anand was remarkably well-preserved for her age. Her eyes still shone large and bright, her broad hips curved provocatively, her breasts – which were not very carefully covered by her dupatta – stood round and erect. Of course, Prema told herself, the bloom of youth was gone, but what was left was not bad, not bad at all, for the mother of three grown daughters.

'And how are your daughters?' she said.

Mrs Anand turned her head quickly towards Prema, and after a while smiled. Prema did not like her smile.

'They are growing into women,' Mrs Anand said.

The old woman nodded: 'It is a fine sight for a mother.'

'And sometimes also a sad one,' Mrs Anand sighed, not very convincingly. 'To know that soon one must part with them and send them to a husband's house, that is very sad for a mother. Though of course,' she added hastily, 'we are not yet thinking of that, they are very young.'

The other three now understood the purpose of the visit. They grew rather excited and at the same time wary.

'My eldest, Sushila, is only sixteen,' Mrs Anand said. Prema thought that Sushila must be at least eighteen.

'Sixteen,' the old woman said, 'it is a fine age. I was sixteen when I had my first child, my boy, who died.'

'Ah,' Mrs Anand said, 'in those days marriage came early. I myself was betrothed when I was eight and married at sixteen. But it is too young.'

'Too young,' the old woman agreed. 'A girl's sorrows will come upon her early enough. Mohini, a pan.'

Mohini got up and prepared four betel-leaves, which she handed round on a little brass tray. Now they all sat chewing and placidly shifting the leaf from one corner of their mouths to the other. Mrs Anand waited for them to make the next move and they waited for her. Meanwhile they talked, very pleasantly and politely, about the heat, about common acquaintances, the sufferings of pregnancy and the price of vegetables. There was no hurry. Outside in the kitchen the servant-boy was clattering some pots, and in the next room the children were still playing at being trains. From time to time hawkers looked in at the window to offer them, through the anti-burglar bars, fish or vegetables or lampshades from Kashmir. They chewed their pan and sometimes wiped the perspiration from their faces with their dupattas.

At last Mrs Anand worked the conversation round to the subject of sons. She told of the son of an acquaintance of hers, who was a very lazy good-for-nothing boy; all day he lay on his charpoy and even smoked cigarettes in his own home before his mother and sisters, and once he had run away to Bombay because he wanted to meet film stars. Mrs Anand opined that such sons were a source of great sorrow to their families, especially since it was very difficult to marry them off, for who would give his daughter to such a husband? But she thanked God that there was no sorrow like that in Hari's mother's house; that on the contrary her son brought her only joy and consolation. 'It is good for a mother to have such a son to lean upon,' she suggested.

'He is a pearl,' his mother said; 'a jewel among sons.'

Mrs Anand sucked the juice which the pan had collected in her mouth.

'He is twenty-two years old now,' the mother went on. 'He was born on Holi day the year his father bought the big brown cow. He is young, but already he is earning very good salary.'

'And as long as I live,' Prema added, 'he shall want for nothing.'

'Every day people come to my house with offers for him,' the mother said. 'Such big dowries they offer for him – one lakh, two lakhs – it is a story we hear every day. But what need is there for us for such big dowries? It is the girl we value, not the money. We will wait for a beautiful, fair, hard-working girl from good family and then, even if the dowry is not so very good, we shall be happy.'

Mrs Anand nodded, smiled and chewed her pan. They were all very satisfied; they had said and heard all they wanted to say and hear, and now they again turned the conversation to more general matters. They talked, smoothly, placidly and in perfect harmony, of indifferent things, covering up the significant part with a layer of small talk to give the visit the appearance of just an ordinary polite social call. After a decent interval, Mrs Anand got up and took her leave, and the farewell she was accorded was even more cordial than her welcome had been.

12

Cars, long-bodied monsters, glistened in the drive of Tarla's house, and overflowed into the hot street, rows of them. Their drivers crouched in whatever shade they could find; some slept, some read tattered little Urdu newspapers, one little group was playing four-on-ace. The city lay gaunt and parched in a shroud of white heat. But the trim lawns, the well-kept flowers of Tarla's garden blossomed and flourished like racketeers in a famine.

And inside the house it was cool. The fans stirred up silent breezes. The marble floors shone like polished ice. Bearers in crisp snow-white uniforms glided backwards and forwards with silver trays and frosted glasses. The ladies, in their fine silk saris in softest shades of blue and green and turquoise, rustled and rippled like flowers in the cool of evening. All the curtains were drawn, shutting out the sun, shutting out the life of the exhausted city. There were Punjabi ladies, Maharasthian ladies, Parsi ladies, Madrasi ladies, Bengali ladies, old and young, slim and fat, but all ladies. They sipped iced lime-water and waved slim hands in the air. Their talk penetrated the house like the chirping of birds. Somewhere upstairs a piano tinkled. The ladies formed and reformed themselves into groups, they nodded, they smiled, gentle as a minuet they swayed.

Amrita stood a little apart, feeling awkward and out of it. Tarla auntie was so busy, gliding from group to group, greeting with respectfully joined hands here, with an affectionate pat there, threading the various groups together, rallying the shy, toning conversations up or down. From time to time she drew Amrita into the midst of it, absent-mindedly smiling, 'My niece, Amrita Chakravarty,' and Amrita stood for a moment answering futile questions with futile answers and then helplessly dropped out. Lady Ram Prashad Khanna bore down on her, was charming and disappeared again. Unknown ladies inquired after her mother and sent polite greetings. She had already out of desperation drunk three glasses of iced lime-water.

Then they were all shepherded into the long reception-room. Little gilt-

and-white chairs with damask seats had been arranged in rows to face the table that stood at one end. Behind this table were three more chairs and on it three glasses of water and a bell. Amrita shyly sat down in the middle of the last row but two. It appeared that she was thus splitting up a group of ladies who sat on either side and talked across her. She stared straight in front of her and wondered whether she ought to offer to move. Tarla auntie, Lady Ram Prashad and one other lady with big fat arms which she kept folded in front of her sat behind the table. Tarla auntie spoke first.

'We all know why we are here today,' she said, and briskly proceeded to read out a list of names and figures. These apparently were donors and their donations. All the ladies listened avidly, and from time to time some of the less polite ones murmured. When she had finished, Tarla auntie said that it was good but not yet good enough. She called for renewed effort. She spoke of duty and responsibility. The ladies nodded. The fans turned. Co-operation, Tarla auntie said, perseverance. Vigour and determination. Sacrifice and selflessness. Our country, our people, our heritage. She sat down and drank water. Some of the ladies applauded.

Then Lady Ram Prashad got up. She said how good everybody was and how hard they worked; how their efforts were appreciated; how this Minister had said to her only yesterday and that Minister had told her only last week; how pleasing it all was and how commendable; and then, with a flourish and the air of one giving a treat long held in store, she read out a message from the Prime Minister.

Amrita examined the hair of the lady sitting in front of her. She counted the number of coils into which it was wound and longed to push back a pin which was sticking out. Little white jasmine flowers decorated the coils, and she pretended they grew there in the hair, and that the lady watered them every morning and pulled out the weeds.

Now the lady with the big arms was speaking. She kept sweeping a huge fist over the table and shouting 'Action! Action!' Her sari was bundled together on the shoulder and fastened with a large pin. She spoke very sternly; the ladies listened politely. The longer she talked, the more excited she got. Her hair began to fall down. Perspiration glistened on her face. She was very angry. She talked of slackness and apathy, of torpor and selfishness. Amrita imagined her taking the pin from her shoulder and running it through the body of the stout lady sitting in the front row. She imagined the pandemonium, the shrieks of the injured lady, Tarla auntie ringing the bell. 'Action!' the speaker shouted.

Amrita was now sorry that she had drunk three glasses of lime-water.

She felt she had to go to the bathroom quickly, but she did not dare get up and walk out while she was being harangued so sternly. She tried to take her mind off it. She looked at Lady Ram Prashad listening with her head on one side and a sweet smile fading on her lips. She counted the crimson dragons on the curtains. She mentally unwound the coils of hair on the head in front of her and wound them up again the other way. She listened to the speaker – carelessness, neglect, indolence – and felt genuinely sorry that she had not done more to help. She wished she were sitting at the end of the row. She imagined she had been to the bathroom and had come back relieved. Finally she got up and murmured, 'Excuse me'; the ladies shifted their knees to let her pass; she stumbled over a bag on the floor, felt several heads turning round, murmured she was sorry. 'Action!' she heard, and then she was outside.

Even when she had finished in the bathroom, she did not feel like going back again to the meeting. She combed her hair before the mirror, smiled at herself a bit, and was glad that her teeth were so white. This particular bathroom was done out in a very faint green marble; there were three others in the house, one in shell-pink, one in pale yellow and one in eau-de-nil. Amrita washed her hands and hoped Tarla auntie would not notice that she had left the meeting. She thought she would go down into the lounge and look at the art magazines which her uncle always kept in a pile on a little coffee table. But then she heard the piano upstairs and she went towards the music-room instead.

There she found Vazir Dayal sitting at the piano in an emerald-green dressing-gown, a whisky-glass beside him. He did not play well but with great style. When he saw Amrita, he nodded at her absently and went on playing, swaying over the piano and back again and sideways with a pained expression on his face. One lock of hair had fallen over his forehead and had been allowed to lie there. He finished with a great flourish, starting right down in the bass somewhere, running up to the top notes and back again with a final bang; then he sank his head on to his breast and shut his eyes and let his hands hover high up over the keys before letting them sink, like dead birds, into his lap.

'Please go on, Uncle,' Amrita said. 'I like so much to hear you.'

'Enough,' he said, and got up and drank his whisky. He pushed his hair back from his face and walked up and down in his golden slippers.

'So,' he said at last and planted himself before Amrita, all five foot ten of him, and there was enough left to admire even though he was beginning to run to fat. But she did not like to look up at him; she looked down at her lap and, as always when she was with him, felt badly-dressed.

'I was in the meeting downstairs,' she explained, 'but I came out.'

'You must forgive your aunt,' he said. 'It is her consolation for me.' He flung himself down on the rose-covered chaise-longue and lit one of his long black cigarettes. Its smell made Amrita think of incense and morocco leather. 'So,' he said, 'they are sending you to Europe.'

'But I do not want to go,' she said.

He looked at the smoke curling from his cigarette and said, 'Then of course you must not go'; and when she failed to react to this, added, 'You must always do only what you want.'

This, she knew, was one of those provocative generalities which he was fond of throwing out and then leaving, untended, unsupported, to fall where they would.

'Mamma told me that you had all decided that I must go.'

'Decided decided,' he said, waving one long hand in the air. 'Who can decide the fate of another? Your grandfather, of course, as usual, pontificated ...' He waited for her to take him up on this. But she would not; she liked her grandfather better than she liked her uncle. And besides, she did not know what pontificated meant.

'You must not let them force you,' he said.

She would have liked to answer, 'But what can I do?' but saw no point in it. She knew he was not interested in her, and she did not want to talk about what concerned her so deeply in order to trifle away a half-hour for him.

'They tell me,' he said, 'that you are having what is called an affair of the heart. And of course, your family, like all families, are doing their best to break it. The affair I mean, as well as your heart.

'You must stand up to them,' he languidly advised. 'You must defy them. That will be very good for them, especially for your grandfather.'

'What do you advise me to do, Uncle?' she said, more for the form of it than because she wanted to know.

'I have told you,' he answered. 'You must do what you want, you must defy your family. They will always try to hinder you from anything you wish to do, and that is why you must defy them. Look at me,' he said, and turned himself fully towards her, so that she could look at him. 'I have always done what I wanted. I have defied everybody.'

'For you it was different.'

'Because I am a man? Because I am rich? Because I am I?'

'Because you are a man,' she chose tactlessly.

'Nonsense,' he said. 'Do you not all call yourselves emancipated nowadays? Please listen to your aunt making speeches downstairs.'

'I must go back to the meeting,' she murmured, remembering.

'Marry him!' Vazir Dayal said decisively. 'If you wish to, marry him.'

Here was the first support she had had; here the words she had wanted to hear. But she did not value them. She knew they were spoken not out of interest for her welfare but out of a mixture of spite against her grandfather and a desire to show himself magnanimous and free-thinking. Vazir Dayal's thoughts were not on her but, as usual, on himself.

'Thank you, Uncle,' she said nevertheless, out of politeness.

13

'They want to send me to England,' Amrita said.

Hari did not hear. He was looking through the glass which separated the control-room from the studio at the singer standing before the microphone. She was an American lady on a short visit to India, and she was singing Schubert songs. She stood dead straight before the microphone; one hand was laid on her bosom, the other held a sensible leather handbag. Her calves bulged above a pair of court shoes. It was these calves that fascinated Hari; they looked so solid, so reliable.

'Did you hear what I said?' Amrita asked him.

'Yes,' he lied.

'And still you have nothing to say?'

'Of course,' he replied, wishing he knew what she had said. He was surprised at the rigid stance of the American lady. She had not moved once since she had started singing; the hand on the bosom and the handbag seemed fixed for all time. Only her mouth opened and shut; Hari supposed it was those large calves that gave her such firmness.

'You were not listening,' Amrita accused him.

He had to admit it. 'I was listening to the song,' he explained. 'It is so strange. Do you like it?'

'Of course,' she said impatiently. 'It is very beautiful. Only she sings badly.'

Hari did not think it was beautiful at all. It had no feeling, he thought. He could not make out the words very well, red rose on a heath. Red roses of course were beautiful, but he did not think them a fit subject for a song. Unless they stood for something else: for a bleeding heart, for instance. Bleeding hearts could be sung about, for they meant love and sorrow; and love and sorrow were the stuff of music.

'If you were not listening,' Amrita said, 'why do you say you were?'

Fortunately he did not have to answer, because she pressed the knob which put them on the air in order to announce the next song. The lady remained in the same attitude waiting for the announcement to finish;

then straight away she started to sing again. Hari had quite a shock, the way she started so abruptly. And on such a merry note too. He had not thought her capable of such gaiety; and certainly, looking at her, one could not imagine that the body and the voice were connected.

'She has no expression,' Hari said. And he thought of Sushila Anand; now there was a voice, such feeling, such expression. And she sang beautiful songs too. Sad songs; and songs, he thought, should be sad. They should express all the deep feelings in the heart. Not like this quick, merry song the American lady was warbling. Something about a wanderer. Who wanted to hear about a wanderer unless he suffered and was sorrowful?

'I said,' Amrita repeated, 'that they want to send me to England.'

'England!' he cried; but at this point the next announcement was due.

'But how wonderful,' he said as soon as they were safely off the air again.

'Wonderful!' she cried.

'I mean for you,' he said hastily. 'It is so wonderful to travel.'

'Do you really think that I would rather travel than be with you?'

'No, no –'

'If you were in my place, you would go? You would rather be in England than stay with me?'

'I would wish to stay with you,' he said dutifully.

'And do you think I love you any less?'

'Amrita,' he said, quite touched.

'But you said "wonderful".'

'You give up England for me,' he said. 'Your love for me is so great. I am unworthy.'

'Please do not speak like that!'

'I am,' he repeated sadly. 'Who am I? Hari Sahni, an announcer in Hindi section. I draw only Rupees 300 a month. I live in a rented house, paying Rupees 50 rent. I am nobody. I am nothing.'

'You are my life,' she said, and then had to announce the end of the programme.

They lingered down in the studios, in the air-conditioned corridor. People hurried up and down with scripts under their arms. Hari knew practically everybody and greeted them with rapture. The door of one studio opened and strains of classical Indian music came wailing out.

'Let us go in and listen,' Hari suggested. 'They are only rehearsing.'

'But I want to talk with you,' she said.

'We can talk in there. It is only rehearsal.'

The musicians sat on the floor, cross-legged on a brightly coloured grass mat, their old, fantastic, and exquisitely carved and painted instruments before them. They looked a ragged and rather sinister lot, with their flapping shirts and their naked toes sticking up into the air; some of them were unshaven and all of them needed a hair-cut. They played with placid expressions on their faces; only the tabla-player smiled, smiled and smiled as his fingers scrabbled with the quickness of mice over the surface of his drums. The conductor squatted on a chair, one leg tucked under him; he was not conducting so much as dancing, his shoulder-blades going up and down and his head wagging. He too was smiling, and from time to time he shouted 'Wah!' in triumph.

Amrita listened to the winding, plaintive strains of the music, so old, so far away in time and spirit, and yet still with the power to melt and possess her. It made her feel very tender and exalted. She wanted to hold Hari's hand and would have done so if they had not been in public. But she felt she must speak to him, must share her ecstasy with him. She felt so good and so pure, and everything – life, everything – was suddenly very simple.

'Hari,' she whispered, 'it is all very simple.'

'No, no,' he whispered back, 'it is very difficult. You do not know how much hard work and study they have to do to play this music.'

The musicians looked as if they were in a trance, and the conductor gave out pained little shrieks of ecstasy. The music reached up and up, into an ever more rarefied purity, straining to touch eternity.

Amrita whispered, 'It is that I love you. And you love me. What else matters?'

It was a sentiment after Hari's own heart. 'What else matters,' he whispered enthusiastically. They were both then very, very happy, and stood side by side swaying their heads to the music.

Then the rehearsal was over and the musicians left; Hari smiled at all of them and congratulated them on their performance. He and Amrita were left alone in the big studio, bare except for the grass mat glowing in red and purple on the floor, and the instruments scattered about, and a slender silver microphone.

'Let us go,' Hari said. 'I must speak with a man in the Pushtu section.'

'One minute please, Hari,' she said, made gentle by the music, 'I want so to talk with you.'

'My Amrita,' he murmured. 'The man in the Pushtu section can wait.'

'Hari,' she said, 'I know now it is all very simple. I will not go to England. I will stay here with you, for we belong together.'

'You are so brave,' he said, 'so noble; you have so much feeling.'

The door opened and Vaidya came in. 'So here you are,' he said to Hari. 'There is a new film at the Palace, you will come?'

'Now? You want, Amrita?'

'No,' she said abruptly; the effect of the music was banished.

'This lady always says no,' Vaidya said. 'But she never means it. She will come.'

Amrita gave him an angry look which was lost on him.

'It is a strange thing, Vaidya,' Hari said. 'Only a few days ago we were talking about going to England, and now Amrita's family are going to send her there.'

'So you are going to England,' Vaidya spluttered patronizingly at Amrita.

'I am not going,' she answered shortly.

'Again she says no,' Vaidya said. 'She has a very negative spirit.'

And then Amrita became really angry. She had been feeling so tender and exalted, and in that mood had wanted to talk with Hari and deliciously plan their future together: and now here again was this man, whom she disliked, interfering between them with ridiculous suggestions of going to the Palace and making personal remarks about herself. She could stand it no longer.

'Go away!' she cried quite suddenly. 'Please, why can you not go away, why must you always pester us?' She had never in her life before spoken to anyone except her mother in this fashion.

Vaidya was so surprised, his glasses slipped off his nose. He stared at Amrita; his mouth hung a little open. Hari also was surprised: he had never seen Amrita angry, and he could not understand why she should be angry now.

She turned round abruptly and walked out of the studio and along the corridor. Hari exchanged a puzzled look with Vaidya and then went running after her crying, 'Please wait for me!' and 'Hallo-hallo-hallo', with an absent-minded, though delighted, smile at someone who came walking past him.

'Why are you angry?' he asked when he had drawn level with her; and when she did not answer, did not even look at him, he pressed her, 'Was Vaidya not polite to you? Perhaps he said something to you when I was not there? Please tell me and I will speak with him.'

She stopped still and looked at him searchingly. It seemed strange to her that he should not understand.

'Please tell me,' he said again, looking searchingly back at her. 'I will speak with him.'

She turned away from him and walked on again, rather quickly so that he had to run to catch up with her. She pushed the swing-door and walked out of the air-conditioned studios into the hot corridor. The swing-door flew to in Hari's face and he stopped still for a moment with the surprise of it. She did not even look back. She walked straight across the deserted entrance-hall, and the man behind the desk looked at her strangely.

'Amrita!' called Hari, as he emerged from the studio and ran after her.

'Go away, Hari,' she said.

'Now you are angry with me too,' he complained, as they both stood still facing one another, watched by the man behind the desk, who had nothing else to do.

'Please do not be angry with me,' Hari appealed.

'No, I am not angry with you; but please go now.'

'Why do you want me to go, Amrita? Have I offended you? If I have, I will never forgive myself. I will kill myself. I will pluck my own heart out.'

'Yes Hari,' she said. 'But you have to speak first with a man in the Pushtu section.'

'Yes,' he agreed sadly. 'Please tell me, Amrita, you are angry with me?'

She looked away from him. She was afraid that at any moment she might burst into tears.

'No,' she said very quietly, 'I am not angry with you. If you do not hurry, the man in the Pushtu section will go away.'

'That is true. It is nearly five-thirty. But really you are not angry with me?'

She shook her head; she did not trust herself to speak.

'Then I am happy again,' he said, and broke into a pleased smile.

'Hurry,' she said, with an irony that was quite lost on him, 'or he will go away.'

He gave her a last affectionate smile and gaily walked off, humming a little tune. He was very glad that she was not angry with him.

14

In the evening Amrita went shopping with her mother. They went to Connaught Place, the fashionable shopping-centre in New Delhi, a pillared arcade forming a large circle with a park in the centre. Radha loved shopping, especially in the evenings when everyone else went shopping too and there were so many acquaintances with whom to exchange greetings and the latest news. And she loved the shops, glittering one beside the other, bulging out of their doorways – ivory and carpets and draped saris with silver stars; cotton vests at reduced price and ladies' sandals with high platform soles; embroidered handbags and carved bookends, sewing-machines and Japanese tea-sets, suits dry-cleaned, with tickets, and blue ice-boxes and a grey fur coat on a hanger – Radha enjoyed everything. She would walk into a sari-shop, because she was so fond of looking at nice silks, make the shopman unfurl roll after roll of material till the counter billowed with them and then tell him she would be back tomorrow.

'Come child,' she said to Amrita trailing beside her, and she pushed through the crowds in the arcade, her head turning from side to side, her eyes alert, waving away the hawkers who stepped forward from between the pillars to offer her Turkish towels, very cheap.

Boys walked up and down with trays of hairpins and combs and safety-pins and thin plastic toys. An old blind beggar shuffled forward rattling a tin pot like a bell and shouting 'Ram Ram Ram' without stop. A smiling fortune-teller in a beard promised good fortune to foreigners, and showed browned and tattered letters of recommendation. A sadhu strode in his orange robe. Policemen lingered in shorts. Ladies, perfumed, powdered, painted, rustled by in elegant saris.

'How crowded it is,' Radha said happily: 'really one should not come in the evenings.' And 'Oh, there is Mrs Prem Chand! How fat she has become.'

But Amrita did not enjoy herself. As a matter of fact she hardly noticed where she was, she was so busy with her thoughts. These were very miserable, since all the time they were fixed on that afternoon's scene with Hari. She had been unjust to him, she had been rude to him, she had hurt him terribly, and it was only his goodness that had caused him to walk off smiling; his goodness which would not let him hurt her – as she rhetorically put it to herself – by showing her his hurt. She now wanted only to see him and beg his forgiveness. She felt she must see him, now, at once, tonight.

Radha stopped to speak with acquaintances – but how nice to see them, how wonderful they looked and had they heard about poor Mrs Agarwal, and O this heat and yes, thank God, Amrita was a pretty girl and very soon now she would be going to England.

Amrita was only just polite enough to greet and smile, and when they passed on she merely said, 'I am not going, you know that.'

'Keep quiet, you are a stupid girl,' Radha told her, and she really did keep quiet, because all she wanted to do was to think of Hari and how she had wronged him.

By the time they were on their way home, sitting in a tonga, it had become a necessity for her to see him that evening. But how could this be managed? If I could send a note, she thought, as they rattled through the old part of the town, hemmed in on all sides by motor-cars and placid bullocks and pedestrians who would not get out of the way. But who would take a note for me, she thought, and the tonga-walla in his stained turban cursed and muttered and whipped his horse. She did not dare trust their own servant with it, for he was sure to blab to Radha during one of those long confidential conversations they held together, in between their fights over the curry and the ghee and the sugar. Next door's servant perhaps? He would be glad to earn a few annas. Here she was nearly jolted out of the tonga as the driver pulled off the tram lines because a tram came creaking and jingling towards them, swaying like a pregnant mare, the passengers bursting out from all sides. But he was sure to confide to their own servant at some time or other, and then again it would get round to her mother. No, she could not trust any servant; Radha had the knack of getting anything she liked, not only out of her own servant, but out of other people's too. A procession protesting against cow-slaughter held up their progress, young men with banners and a cow with orange flower-garlands.

There was really no one, she reflected sadly, whom she could confide in and trust. She had to rely on herself: but how could she – and she flushed at the thought – go herself to Hari's house? Be calm, she told herself, for her heart was fluttering wildly; let us start at the beginning.

Supposing it were possible for me to go – and of course it is not possible – how for one thing could I get away from home?

Just then Radha said, 'Tonight after dinner I am going to the Raos. I have not seen Aruna Rao for too long. You can come with me, Amrita.'

So there was that problem solved.

'I do not want to,' she said. 'I am too tired.'

'They have recently been to England and they will be able to answer all your questions.'

'I have none to ask,' Amrita said shortly. While Radha was gone to the Raos, she herself would be able to slip out of the house and make her way to Hari's. But once there, what could she do? She could not explain herself to his relations; they would be amazed to see a strange girl walking in and inquiring after Hari. She herself was amazed at her audacity in even thinking of such a thing.

They reached home, they had their dinner; but still she had not thought of a solution. She had considered and rejected all the possibilities that occurred to her. She felt exhausted with thinking about it. But with exhaustion came desperation, and she was more firmly, more desperately, fixed than ever: I must see him tonight.

'Now we will go to the Raos,' declared Radha after dinner.

'Why can you never understand one no, Mamma?' asked Amrita; and she sounded so weary that even Radha did not want to insist. Besides, she was eager to be off.

She contented herself with, 'You are a very inconsiderate daughter with no love for your mother in your heart,' and sailed out with her umbrella under one arm and her old handbag under the other.

Amrita paced up and down the veranda; her thoughts ran round in a circle, round the only thing that mattered: I must see him tonight. She felt she could not spend the night, nor let him spend the night, without reassuring him of her love. It was really very simple, and it seemed strange to her that there should be so many obstacles in the way of two people who merely wanted to see one another for a few brief moments, and reassure one another that they loved. Her feelings battered against the convention which forbade her to go herself to Hari's house; but she had not the courage to override it, and too much modesty; her training, her tradition, being too strong for her.

Krishna Sen Gupta called from the lawn: 'Come out here: it is quite cool,' but she did not even hear him. She was leaning over the balustrade with her chin cupped in her hand and her eyes fixed into space. The night was dark and moonless and heavy with the scent of night-flowers.

'What are you thinking about so hard?' Krishna asked her. She heard his voice this time though she did not take in the words. And his voice raised a new thought: Krishna. Perhaps Krishna.

'Full of interesting conversation as usual,' he said, when she did not answer him.

It was impossible of course. Unthinkable. But there was no one else. And she had to see him.

She walked out into the garden. Krishna stood on the lawn and watched her walking towards him. She was lithe and slim and her sari enveloped her in folds like sculpture. She looked unreal in the blue-black night, as if on coming nearer she must melt away and linger only as a fragrance, an unseen flower.

'Come,' he said. 'It is cooler here.' And he wanted to stretch out his hand and hold her, to make sure she was real and there beside him.

'O Krishna,' she said, and now he could see her face shadowed by darkness; but a real face with large anxious eyes fixed on him.

He did not dare speak. His heart beat loudly and he kept his hands clenched in his pockets.

'O Krishna,' she said, 'I am so unhappy.'

He had to swallow before he could speak: 'What is it?' And to himself his voice sounded hoarse and cracked, but to her it came gently, almost tenderly.

'I must see him,' she said in her desperation.

'Whom?'

'Hari.' His hands unclenched and came out of his pockets.

He turned away from her: he did not want her to see his face.

But she was too intent on her own feelings to notice his. 'Please, Krishna,' she said, 'help me.'

He gave a little laugh in what was meant to be self-mockery; but it only sounded false and melodramatic. He was terribly ashamed of himself and did not know how to cover it up. He said roughly, 'You are asking me to play pimp for you?' hating her for having caught him unawares.

'What?' she said: fortunately she did not understand. 'Krishna, I am asking you, I am begging you, go to him, tell him I must see him, here, tonight, Krishna!'

He began to pace up and down, still shaking with anger and humiliation. After a while: 'And you really think I shall go?'

'Yes,' she said, desperation making her bold. 'You will go because I beg of you so humbly.'

And yes, he thought, I shall go. He stood still, but he did not look towards her. He had no reason to refuse her request, no reason except, he told himself, vindictiveness; and he could not be vindictive towards her when she knew nothing of the humiliation to which she had put him. She was so ignorant; so innocent; and of that at least he was glad.

'All right,' he said drily, 'I will go.'

15

Mr and Mrs Anand were received with great honour. The cow, who had been sitting at her ease in the middle of the courtyard, was banished into her shed, all the chairs and footstools in the house were brought out, sherbets were offered and the little servant-boy despatched immediately to fetch Suri and Prema. The two visitors offered courtesy for courtesy, protesting hard that this was their own home, so what need was there for ceremony. Nevertheless Mohini, Hari's younger sister, hastily put on a clean dupatta while Babla, the younger brother, was pushed into the bathroom to wash his hands and change his shirt. The mother looked nervously towards Hari, but there was no need for anxiety there: he was fresh from a bath and scrupulously clean in the fine white kurta and pyjama he always wore at home; his hair shone like a mirror. But he was rather surprised at all the fuss; he had not thought that the Anands were such important people. He felt Mrs Anand's sharp black eyes boring into him, and thought that she must still be bearing a grudge against him because he had talked to her daughter on the night of the party. He wished now he had never talked to her, even though she was pretty and could sing with great feeling.

It was some time before Suri and Prema arrived because, having heard who had come, Prema had to change her clothes. She was very fine now in a pink silk kamiz with blue roses on it and a pink salwar; the dupatta was also pink, to match. Mrs Anand was dressed up in a vividly flowered salwar-kamiz and a dupatta of green net. The two of them greeted each other with great cordiality and scrutinized one another's clothes.

When they had all settled down again, Prema and her mother exchanged significant looks and then glanced towards Hari.

'Brother,' said Prema, 'yesterday we heard our Bhuaji is not well in her health, perhaps you will go and see how she is feeling today.'

'What, now I am to go?' asked Hari; he wanted to sit and listen to the conversation and also drink sherbet.

'Yes now,' Prema said a trifle sharply, and to the younger brother, 'You too will go,' pinching his arm to forestall objection.

After the two brothers had reluctantly gone, more sherbet was served and also several bowls of sweets (hastily sent over from Prema's house where they were kept in her refrigerator). Mr Anand, a dried-up, rather dark little man, kept looking at Suri with adoring eyes, and enthusiastically greeted every remark he made. For Suri was his ideal; a man who did well in business. Mrs Anand mostly smiled at Prema and pretended not to notice that Suri could not keep his eyes off herself. Her magnificent bosom was decorously covered by the green net dupatta and from time to time she arranged it even more decorously.

For the first half hour conversation was general, discreet and exquisitely polite. Then at last the mother said, 'What a beautiful girl is your eldest daughter,' and Suri said, 'And what a voice,' and Prema, 'A jewel of a girl.'

Mr Anand, who was of a rather excitable nature, giggled and rubbed his hands; but his wife said calmly, 'She is a good daughter to us.'

'Such a daughter I would like to see in my house,' said the mother; and Prema, 'Such a sister it would be good to have.' Mohini also wished to say something but felt too shy; so she contented herself with throwing a fierce look towards her children, who were quietly playing together in the corner by the cowshed.

'She is very young,' said Mrs Anand.

Suri slapped the palm of his foot which he was holding under him, 'It is her youth we value.'

'The younger the wife, the better it is for the husband,' said Mr Anand, and would have giggled if his wife had not glanced at him; he scratched his thigh instead.

The mother sighed and said, 'Our children are always young for us. My Hari, he is twenty-two years old, but for me what is he but a child.'

Mrs Anand also sighed, though not very convincingly, thinking of her three daughters growing into women.

'Last month,' the mother said, 'Brahma Shankar the marriage-broker came with a very fine offer for our Hari. It was such a chance for him: the dowry, you would not believe if I told you the figure. But how could I part with my boy?'

'You have heard of Seth Ram Kishore Chaudhury, the mill-owner?' Mrs Anand said, not to be outdone. 'He has a son, a beautiful boy. Well, I will say nothing . . .'

Her husband looked at her in surprise.

'Hari has very good prospects,' Suri said decisively.

'You will take him perhaps into your business?' Mr Anand said, and got very excited.

From very close by came a loud burst of gramophone-music, a sudden frenzy of canned joy. For the season of weddings was well under way, and every day young couples were joined together to the accompaniment of bands and gramophones and clattering crates of Coca-Cola.

Prema shook her head and clicked her tongue and said, 'They are very ordinary people and they make such a big wedding for their daughter. I do not know where they get so much money from, the father is only a grade 3 clerk, he cannot be drawing more than one-fifty. And the girl is not at all pretty, she has a very dark complexion. And I have heard said that the bridegroom also draws only one hundred a month, he is a steno-typist in a private office and he comes from a very poor family from Karnal. Why do such people try to imitate better people and make a big wedding when they have not enough to fill their own stomachs even?'

But still the music droned and echoed and filled their courtyard, startling the cow, who mooed.

'That is how it is in the world,' Mrs Anand said. 'Even poor people want to make a show and deceive others as to their earnings. But what is the use? When everybody knows that for the rest of their lives the parents will have to pinch and starve, and the youngest daughter will perhaps have only one small trunk-full for her dowry.'

'That is true,' said the mother, 'but also it is fitting that a girl's wedding should be celebrated well. It is a great day, and the taste of it should stay sweet in her mouth for the rest of her life.'

'How much money was spent on my wedding!' said Prema: and Mohini looked a little sad, because there had been only one very small band at her wedding, and her dowry had filled only three trunks while Prema's had filled twelve.

'A special house was taken for the bridegroom's party,' Prema went on, 'and we had three bands and we used up one hundred seers of ghee for the ladoos alone, and there were more than five hundred guests eating and drinking for four days.'

The mother sighed and said, 'We have not so much joy in life that we can forget that day.' And they all nodded and thought back upon it, Prema with tears in her eyes because she had been happy then and did not know what was in store for her.

Mrs Anand said with dignity, 'We shall see to it that the day on which our eldest daughter is given to a husband shall also be remembered for many years.' She stretched out her foot and waggled the toes: the nails were painted bright red. Suri looked at them.

'Yes,' said Prema, 'it is our duty to make a girl's wedding happy for her. The Lord knows what is to come after'; for she had seen Suri looking.

'Bearing children is also no joke,' Mohini contributed.

And then Krishna Sen Gupta came walking through the house into the courtyard, with his big horn-rimmed spectacles and his hair standing on end. After he had introduced himself and declared that he was a friend of Hari's, they made him very welcome. He had to sit down among them and accept a sherbet and a little plateful of sweets; he hated both sherbet and sweets but – 'a friend of Hari's and to take nothing in our house!' so he had to submit. His presence put an end to their conversation, but they did not mind this; they had already said all that was necessary and had come as near to an understanding as they had meant to.

'Sen Gupta?' Suri said. 'Ah, you are a Bengali. All my life I have admired you Bengalis. The whole brain of India is in your heads.'

'The whole brain of India!' cried Mr Anand, delighted, and he pushed Suri's knee, saying roguishly, 'Ah but Suri Sahib, a little of it has also got into the heads of us Punjabis, eh eh?' And Suri laughed, slapping Mr Anand heartily on the back.

'Put a Bengali next to a Punjabi in business,' Mr Anand said, 'and then we will see.' He himself worked very hard buying and selling other people's cars without any prospect of ever owning one himself.

Prema found Krishna Sen Gupta very agreeable. He is a gentleman, she thought, and was glad that her brother Hari had the sense to choose such friends for himself.

'You will be very welcome in my house,' she told him. 'A friend of my brother's is also my brother. And you will like to sit in my house. Of course it is a little too big for only husband and wife, but it is very comfortable.'

Krishna thanked her and tried to take another gulp of sherbet; it was very sweet and made him feel a little sick. The music from the wedding drummed in his head. He was also rather nervous because he did not know how Hari would react to his presence. Since he had posed as such a good friend, it would be embarrassing if Hari revealed that they had never set eyes on one another before.

When Hari did come the first thing he said was, 'But Bhuaji was not sick at all, she was very surprised when I told her yesterday she was sick.'

Mohini could not help letting out a loud giggle, but she at once clapped her hand before her mouth and looked threats at the children.

'Do you not see who is here?' Prema said, and Hari greeted Mr and Mrs Anand with joined hands and a sweet smile, though he had already greeted them on their arrival.

'No, here,' said Prema, pointing at Krishna Sen Gupta, 'do you not see your friend Mr Sen Gupta?'

Hari stared at Krishna, who said, 'Hallo, Hari.'

'Hallo-hallo-hallo,' Hari greeted him with a rapturous smile, 'you are here? If I had known, I would have come sooner,' and he wished he had a better memory for faces.

Krishna liked him immediately. There was nothing strange about that, for most people liked Hari immediately. His smile was irresistible; a smile of such pure delight, such frank and undisguised pleasure at seeing his friend, that Krishna really began to doubt whether they were not, after all, old friends. Hari put both his hands on Krishna's shoulders and squeezed them, and then they held one another's arms and shook hands long and warmly, while the others watched them, smiling, for it is always good to see the meeting of friends.

'I am very happy,' Hari told Krishna, 'very happy,' pumping his hand up and down and affectionately squeezing his elbow, 'it is so long,' he hazarded, 'since I have seen you.'

Krishna smiled, pumped and squeezed back, and then said, still with the same wide grin of pleasure, though in a very low voice so that only Hari could hear. 'You have never seen me.'

'Ha-ha.' Hari answered, 'you have not changed,' and he pinched Krishna's cheek, 'not changed at all.'

Krishna affectionately put his arm round Hari's shoulder and drew him aside.

'Amrita has sent me to you,' he said.

'Amrita?' Hari said and looked worried.

Krishna threw a warning look over his shoulder in the direction of the others.

'She wants to see you,' he said softly.

'When?'

'Now.'

'But I have not had my dinner,' Hari said in great distress.

'She said it was very important.'

'But what is the matter? She is ill?'

'No, she is not ill. She only said that it is very important that she should see you now.'

'How can I come now?' Hari appealed. 'It is very late and I have not had my dinner and look, I am not properly dressed, see I am wearing kurta-pyjama, I cannot go and see Amrita in kurta-pyjama ...'

Krishna made Hari wait at a little distance from the house, while he himself went in. Amrita was standing waiting on the front veranda, and as soon as she saw him she came running to meet him.

'How long you have been!' she ungratefully said. 'Where is he? You have brought him?'

'He is outside. Is your mother still away?'

'Yes, yes, she has not yet come home. Why do you make him wait outside?'

Krishna went to the gate and whistled. That whistle especially pleased him: it was such an integral part of the whole situation.

'Now please be careful,' he warned Amrita. 'Do not take too long. You know your mother will soon be home.'

But she did not hear him: she had run towards Hari and then could do nothing but look at him out there in the darkness.

'This is where you live,' Hari said, looking with interest towards the house, a dim white shape beyond the lawn.

'Hari,' she said. 'Hari. Hari. Hari. At last you are here.'

They walked towards the house. She felt drained and emptied with the relief of it.

'I had to see you,' she said breathlessly. 'I had to see you to beg your forgiveness.'

'Please?' he said. They had arrived on the front veranda now: Hari looked round and made out the bougainvillia climbing over the balustrade, the white cane settee and cane armchairs with cushions. Krishna Sen Gupta had withdrawn; he considered that his duties had come to an end.

'Please forgive me, Hari,' Amrita said. 'If you knew how much I have suffered all evening, you would forgive me.'

He looked lost. Everything had moved a little too fast for him, and he still could not quite make out how he had got there, and why indeed he had had to come at all. Also he felt distinctly hungry; and here was Amrita complicating everything by talking about forgiveness and suffering. He wished he were home.

'I do not understand,' he said pathetically. 'What has happened?'

'Please, Hari, forgive me.'

'But what for must I forgive you?'

'O you are so good!' she cried. 'You pretend you have forgotten.'

Hari kept quiet. If she said he was good to have forgotten, it was not for him to contradict her.

'And I was so very bad to you,' she said. 'I was so angry.'

Now he remembered how she had shouted at Vaidya that afternoon. Yes, he remembered. She had been angry with Vaidya, but why then should she beg his, Hari's, forgiveness? She had not been angry with him: he had asked her – he remembered very distinctly – and she had said, No, Hari, I am not angry with you. It was all very puzzling, and he so hungry.

'That was why I had to see you,' she was saying. 'I could not have lived without seeing you.'

Being in love of course was wonderful; not only wonderful but also necessary. It was what he had always thought of all through adolescence, what all the films he had seen and all the songs he had heard and all the conversations he had held with his friends had taught him to expect of himself. But he had not thought that it would be so complicated.

'And now you have forgiven me?' Amrita asked.

Love should remain a feeling, something charming and romantic connected with flowers and moonlight and music in lotus-bowers. It should have nothing to do with things like being called for by strangers in the night, and being whisked away before one could have one's dinner, and being brought to strange houses to hear the object of one's love talking in riddles. That was so unsettling; and one could not love with the right feeling if one was unsettled.

But because something like that seemed expected of him, he said, 'My heart belongs only to you, how can you speak of forgiveness when every word you say is music to me,' and Amrita was just going to pour out her gratitude, when a voice said, 'Amrita? Who is it?' and there was Radha stern and square on the veranda steps.

Now who is this, Hari thought, and felt put out. He was tired, he was hungry, and he did not want to meet any of her relations. Still, one had to be polite, so he joined his hands under his chin and sweetly smiled at Radha.

'Mamma,' Amrita said faintly, and because there was nothing else left to say, 'this is Hari.'

16

Prema's interview with Sushila Anand went off very well. She had made no such elaborate arrangements to receive her as she had done for Amrita: after all, Sushila was one of us, so it was all right to receive her in the bedroom with the odd shoes lying about and the shirt Suri had worn yesterday and a half-empty cup of tea left over from the morning.

Sushila made herself at home at once and they both sprawled over the bed and ate sweets and talked about life. They had the radio on and every now and again Sushila joined in with the singer, and she had such a lovely voice, so sad and full of deep feeling that one could not help realizing the sadness of life in general and of one's own life in particular. Prema nodded her head as Sushila sang and they pressed hands and understood one another perfectly. They were Women together.

Prema told her everything: about the complexities of a woman's life and the deep silent suffering that was her lot; and men's selfishness and their brutality; about the aching heart in the midst of splendour; about the cost of the dining-room furniture; and Suri, a lot about Suri; and then, above all, about Prema. Sushila was such a sympathetic listener. She understood and she appreciated, she sighed, she said, It is Life, she said, O poor, poor Prema, and sometimes she wept and then Prema wept too, and it was as if their two souls mingled in one sorrow. And it turned out that Sushila was also very widely read, even though she was so young, and she liked the same magazines as Prema, she had such a fine literary taste, one could talk and comment with her for hours about one's favourite stories. The servants kept coming in and out, bringing them tea and sherbet and more sweets, and sometimes they stayed to listen and also nodded their heads and said, It is Life. Prema had not felt so melancholy for a long time, she could not remember when she had spent a more pleasant evening. Time glided away under their talk and soon it was dark, and they lay there on the bed, sweet and drugged with sadness, murmuring confidences to one another and not putting on the light.

Hari came, and asked why were they in the dark, and then they sat up and Sushila arranged her hair. Hari was pleased to see her, though a little surprised because he had not thought that she and Prema were friends. The servants spread rugs in the courtyard, and they all went to sit out and ate freshly made pakoras. Prema and Sushila held hands and from time to time one of them pressed and then the other one pressed back in perfect understanding. Hari asked Sushila how was her film career getting on and she smiled, and Prema said perhaps Sushila had other plans now, and Sushila smiled again.

Hari wished she would go because he had come to talk to Prema very particularly. He wanted to tell her about what had happened the night before at Amrita's house. The memory was very unpleasant to him: never had he seen a lady so angry. And then in the morning, at the radio station, a very superior servant in white uniform and huge turban had handed him a note; a note which informed him that Amrita's grandfather expected to see him at his house that evening at eight o'clock sharp. It was now eight-thirty, but Hari had still not made up his mind to go. Or rather, he told himself that he had not yet made up his mind, that he wanted to talk to Prema first, but really it looked as if he had quite made up his mind not to go. From time to time he had an uncomfortable vision of the old man sitting waiting behind his desk, looking at the clock and tapping his foot.

And he could not get away from the thought of Amrita's angry mother; he could still see her looming vast and threatening on the veranda steps, could still hear her – 'At once I will call the police and they will take you to prison, and then we will see how you come to respectable houses in the middle of the night to corrupt respectable girls.'

Police and prison, these were terrible words to him; no wonder his nerves were all on edge. He gave quite a start when Suri came in from behind him and clapped him on the shoulder in brotherly fashion. Suri laughed uproariously when Hari gave such a jump, and asked him what was the matter, was his mind far away and lost in thoughts of love. Whereupon Sushila blushed and looked shyly at Prema who pressed her hand, and Suri laughed still more. Hari also laughed, though a little uncertainly and only out of politeness; and Sushila blushed more than ever.

Then Mrs Anand came to call for her; she had a good look at Hari and let Suri have a good look at herself, while she absently pulled her dupatta a little higher above her bosom. Prema let go of Sushila's hand and asked Suri, did he not think it would be polite to take Mrs Anand and Sushila home in the car.

They all went out and the visitors drove off. Prema made sure that Mrs Anand was sitting comfortably with Sushila at the back.

Hari was very glad to be alone with Prema at last. 'I must talk with you,' he said. 'It is very important.'

'And I,' she said, 'must talk with you. It is also very important.'

That was the worst about Prema: if one came to confide in her, she invariably had something to confide as well, and she always managed to get hers in first.

'It is about Amrita,' Hari said.

Prema made a sound of impatience and swept some crumbs off the pakora plate to lick them from her finger-tips. 'Again that girl,' she said. 'I thought it was all finished.'

'All finished!'

'I told you: she is not the girl for you. You must forget her.'

'But I love her.'

'Love, love,' Prema said, 'you do not even know what love is.' And she called to the servant to bring some more pakoras.

'I am not hungry,' Hari said.

'They are for me,' she said. 'You are only a boy, there are things you do not understand.'

'I know that I love,' he persisted with quite unwonted obstinacy.

'Perhaps you do not know whom it is you love,' she suggested, and then shouted at the servant: 'You put spinach in these, how many times have I told you not spinach!'

'I do not mind spinach pakoras,' Hari said, and took one. 'Of course I know: it is Amrita, who else.'

'You know nothing,' Prema said. 'You do not even know yourself or you would never think that this girl is good enough for you. You do not love her, she has only made you believe so.'

He had faced the grandfather; he had faced the mother (he grew hot at the thought); he was risking police and prison; and now here was Prema telling him that he did not love at all.

'You cannot read a woman's heart,' Prema said, 'so how can you tell when you love?'

And then the tempting thought came creeping in: how would it be if he did not love? He could ignore the note in his pocket; he could forget all about the grandfather and the mother; he need have no fears of police and prison. Life would become simple once more. He would be able to think of love calmly, abstractly and without anxiety, and look at girls in streets and restaurants with something more than detached curiosity.

'That is why you must listen to me,' Prema was saying. 'I am a woman, and I understand these things.'

'I love her,' he said again, almost firmly: he would not be tempted.

'Hari!' she cried, quite angry. 'How are you speaking to your elder sister! Is this the respect you show, by contradicting every word I say?' And she called to the servant to take away the pakoras. 'And do not let me see you putting spinach in again,' she said. 'No one can eat them like that.'

Hari was very sorry to have annoyed her, but he could not help feeling that she was being unreasonable. What was it she wanted him to say? He could not say he did not love, when he was sure he did love. And of course he was sure; just see how much easier it would have been not to love – did not that prove his sincerity? He would have liked to explain that to her but did not quite know how to.

'Her grandfather,' he began, but Prema interrupted him immediately.

'I have no time to listen to that now. I have something really important to speak with you about.'

'And is not love important?' Hari said: he thought that appeal would surely strike an echo in her heart.

But it was the wrong echo. 'Yes,' she said, 'that is what I want to speak with you about.'

Just then Suri came back.

'Where have you been so long?' asked Prema.

'You yourself told me to take them home in the car,' he said.

'Yes, but you did not have to stay so long. Did you go into the house?'

'How could I refuse when she asked me.'

'Yes,' she said bitterly, 'she asked you.'

Suri turned to Hari and said, 'You are happy now?'

'I have not yet told him,' Prema said.

'What?' Hari asked.

Prema took his hand and said, quite gently now, 'Kaka, do you not think Sushila is a beautiful girl?'

'Yes,' Hari said, 'she is very nice.'

Suri burst out laughing: 'How slow he is!' But Prema clapped her hands in the air, crying 'There is nothing to laugh about!' Hari looked from one to the other.

Prema took his hand again. 'Kaka,' she said, in the same gentle tone as before, 'we have all been thinking that it is time now for you to be married.'

'You have been happy long enough,' Suri said.

'Why do you not keep quiet!' Prema turned on him. 'Why must you spoil one of the most serious moments of my brother's life?'

Hari was quite amazed. 'You mean,' he said, 'you are arranging ...'

Here the servant appeared and asked, could he bring the Sahib's dinner now.

'Go away!' Prema shouted. 'This is not the time to speak of dinner!'

'But I am hungry,' Suri said. 'Let him bring my food.'

'All that is noble in life, all that is fine, you do not understand,' his wife told him.

'I did not know,' Hari said. 'You are arranging ...'

'Yes Kaka,' Prema said. 'You and Sushila. We think it is best for you: she will give you happiness.'

Hari nodded. He had always known that sooner or later this would come, sooner or later his family would decide that it was time for him to be married. He had always accepted the prospect with equanimity: what must be must be, and anyway it had to happen to everybody: it was life.

'Like all wives, she will give you happiness,' Suri chuckled.

'Yes,' Prema said fiercely, 'like all wives, when they are treated right by their husbands.'

And Sushila Anand: they had chosen well for him, he had no cause to complain. She was pretty, very pretty – prettier than Amrita even, though he did not care to admit this too openly to himself – she had a beautiful voice, she was very intelligent and very soulful, and he had no doubt that she was skilled in household affairs. A man could not ask for a better wife.

'Are you content, Kaka?' Prema asked him.

'Of course he is content,' Suri said. 'She is a beautiful girl, and young and fresh.'

Then too, Sushila was a girl from his own community, she had been reared against the same background and to the same habits and traditions as he himself had been. He would not have to feel any constraint in her or her family's presence: his ways were also their ways. He would be able to eat with his fingers and burp when he wanted to (many a time had he suffered discomfort in Amrita's presence because he had not wished to offend her with a noise which was probably not taken as much for granted in her family circle as it was in his). He would be able to speak his native, racy, colloquial Punjabi and feel no embarrassment because his English was not as good as it might be. Her family would accept him as he was, and his family would accept her. Life could flow on as it always had done, practically without any readjustments. It was a smooth, sweet, honeyed path they were laying for him.

'She is very different from her mother,' Prema remarked, but Suri did not take her up on this. 'She is modest,' Prema added, 'as is fitting in a woman.'

'And a wife is always a wife,' Suri told Hari. 'Whatever she may be, we get used to her. It is every man's lot to take a woman into his house, and we have to accept it.'

'Enough of such talk!' Prema cried. 'Do you think my brother is like you? He at least has a heart and will know how to treasure the wife God has given him.'

'What do you understand of this,' Suri told her. 'You do not know the feelings of a man when first they talk to him about taking a wife.'

And there was that note in Hari's pocket and all the complications behind it. If he took Sushila, there would be no more complications; the sweet clang of the wedding music would drown them all.

'I know my brother's feelings,' Prema said, and laid her hand on his arm. He felt it hot and sticky. 'He is content with the choice his family have made for him and happy that he can give so much joy to his mother and his sisters.'

'Yes,' Hari said, 'but I cannot marry when I love another.'

'What is this?' Suri asked.

'Stupid boy!' Prema cried, and took her hand from his arm. 'I have told you, what you feel is not love!'

Hari looked down at his feet and did not answer. The temptation to agree with her had to be resisted.

'I had not thought you would be so obstinate,' she said. 'Is this how you repay our love for you? Have you no shame that you break your mother's heart, and your elder sister's, by your obstinacy?'

Hari, looking very miserable, protested that, no no, he did not wish to hurt them, but how could he help his feelings? 'I love Amrita, it is not right for me to marry Sushila.'

Suri put his arm round Hari's shoulder and said, 'It is only a game and we all play it. After marriage you will forget and you will laugh at yourself for taking it seriously.'

Pritam, the servant-boy, aged 18, married and with two children, nodded and said wisely, 'Yes, Sahib, that is how it will be.' He had been following the conversation with great interest.

'Love is not a game,' Hari protested somewhat weakly. At the moment he could not help wishing that it were.

'Only a game, what else,' Suri reasserted. 'There is no harm in playing it but we must not take it seriously.'

'How dare you,' Prema cried, 'teach my brother your loose morals! We all know what you are, but must you spoil him too with such talk?'

Hari murmured, 'It is not right. Not right.'

'What,' Prema took him up, 'it is not right to do as your mother and your elder sister and all your family wish you to do? That is not right? It is right then perhaps to put strangers above your own kin and to bring sorrow into the house.'

'No,' Hari said, 'no no no.' He was so perplexed: he knew he must not displease his family and he also knew that he must not betray his love for Amrita. Even though that love was at present beset with, and entangled in, so many difficulties, the grandfather, the mother, thoughts of police and prison: and now, worst of all, the displeasure of his own family.

Prema took his hand again. 'I know,' she said, fondling it, 'my brother will do as his family wish him to do, because he loves us.'

Suri said, 'He has sense in his head. He knows it is a good marriage we are arranging for him.'

Hari hung his head, let Pema fondle his hand – and said nothing.

17

Rai Bahadur Tara Chand sat in his study, with a huge tome of a law book open before him. He read, and from time to time made notes. It was what he did all day and every day, and had done for the past ten years, ever since his retirement. There was nothing else left for him to do, and he had never been interested in other books besides law books. The drawers of his desk and cabinet were filled with the notes he had made; he would never be called upon to make use of them, but he did not admit this to himself; perhaps he did not even realize it. His name was still sometimes mentioned in legal circles, but there were few who knew him or cared for him personally. Young lawyers no longer came to consult him. His former colleagues were either dead or lived in a retirement as obscure as his own. Many of his closest associates had been Englishmen, and with those who were still alive he kept up a correspondence which was eager enough on both sides, since it recalled their days of activity and importance.

The house was always silent. All the servants had been in the family a long time, and they were used to moving about quietly for fear of disturbing the Sahib at work in his study. They padded silently over the marble floor with its pattern of brown roses and, once out of the cook-house quarter, spoke to one another only in hushed voices. Their life, like their master's, was a succession of long empty hours. There was not much work now that the Memsahib was dead and the daughters married and gone. The only time the cook got a chance to practise his art – he prided himself especially on his pilaus – was when some member of the family came to visit. The Rai Bahadur himself lived mostly on salads and vegetables simply cooked.

The coachman had nothing to do except to groom the pony into elegance and polish the brass-work of the carriage till it glittered in the sun. His horse and carriage were a pride to look on, but he rarely got the chance to show them off, for nowadays his master seldom went out. The coachman felt so frustrated that sometimes, in the evenings as he sat bubbling over his hookah, he spoke of taking another place somewhere.

But who would want a coachman in these vulgar days of motor-cars, when at most a half-dozen old families kept their own carriages? And they all had their own coachmen, as old as himself and as proud of their horses and their brasswork. So he spent most of his time sitting outside the cookhouse, drinking as much tea as the cook felt inclined to give him, and thinking up new ways of getting that musty dusty smell out of the carriage cushions.

The butler also sat mostly outside the cookhouse, drinking tea and feeling superfluous. He as much as the coachman was a member of an extinct species, for there were few households now who kept a butler to manage their domestic affairs. And there was nothing left for him to manage in the Rai Bahadur's house. The cook, the bearer, the coachman, the gardener and the sweepers had been as long in the old man's service as he himself and hardly needed his supervision any more. There were practically no visitors to announce, and he was tired of counting the silver, since no single tea-spoon had been missing for the past twenty-five years. Twice already he had returned to his native village and then come back again. Boredom was even worse there, amid those surroundings which had grown strange to him; and his sons and daughters and grandchildren and great-grandchildren and great-great-grandchildren were too busy to do him anything but perfunctory honour. So he had come back to serve in the house: his life belonged to the Sahib now.

They all, all the servants, looked forward to the days when the daughters came to visit the house. Radha was the greatest favourite. She always had more orders and more complaints than anyone else, and she set all the servants bustling about to fulfil commands which she forgot two minutes after she had given them. She was ever ready to point out the smallest specks on their uniforms and scold them heartily for all their illnesses. Mohan Lal the butler had been scolded by her for every single tooth he had lost, and he had only two left now which he cherished for her further displeasure. She could scent the smell of a bidi an hour after it had been smoked, and her first words on coming to the cookhouse quarter – and she came more often than anyone else – were always, 'Mohan Lal, you have been smoking bidis here again, how filthy.' If a dispute arose between them, she settled it by out-shouting them all. She regularly accused the cook of using the ghee for his own cooking and drinking up the eggs (she had once caught him licking out an egg-shell). She knew all their family histories, how many surviving children and grandchildren they had, how much dowry they had received with their wives, how much dowry they had given with their daughters. She had found places for many of their relations and knew their exact degrees of kinship, whether from the mother's side or the father's. She kept a track of all new births and marriages and funerals. Once she had found fault with the way they treated their wives or brought up their children, now she found fault with the way their sons and grandsons treated their wives or brought up their children. They all enjoyed her very much.

But lately she never seemed to have time for them. She came sailing into the house, gave them a quick look-over ('Is this how you keep your clothes? You think you are in a banya's family?') and then went straight into the drawing-room or the study, there to argue long and loud about Amrita.

Today she was in such a flurry she did not even notice them, although Mohan Lal had kept a button loose on purpose. She made for the study, saying, 'Now we shall see' to Amrita, who came trailing despondently behind her.

'Good morning, Pappaji,' she said in that special honeyed voice which she kept only for her father. The old man looked up from his book with his pen poised in the air.

'Sit down,' he ordered them, and they obediently sat. He carried on writing his notes.

Radha was bursting with impatience; she could hardly sit still, but kept sliding backwards and forwards on the edge of her chair. But she did not dare ask anything because she knew the old man liked to take his time. Amrita sat looking down at her hands folded in her lap, quite placid, as if she were prepared to wait for ever.

At last the old man shut his book, straightened his notes and neatly screwed the top on his pen. Radha kept hopping about on her chair and watching her father's minute, precise actions with vulture eyes. But it was to Amrita he spoke.

'I summoned the young man,' he said, 'but he did not choose to appear.'

'What!' Radha cried, 'you called him and he did not come?'

Amrita gave no indication of interest or concern. It was all, her silence said, nothing to do with her.

'May we take it as an indication,' her grandfather said, 'that he wishes to renounce all his pretensions to connection with our family?'

Love and despair made Amrita bold, even before her grandfather.

'Perhaps, Grandfather,' she said, 'but I do not think it means he wishes to renounce me.' She spoke quietly and respectfully.

The old man shut his eyes and said, 'We will now regard the whole affair as a closed chapter. You will go to England –'

'No! No England for her!' Radha burst in. 'How can I trust her there when she deceives me here even, when she is living with me in my own house? We will make a marriage for her, now, at once, that is the only way.'

'You will go to England,' the Rai Bahadur repeated, ignoring the interruption, 'and there you will enter one of the Universities to continue your education.'

Amrita raised her eyes to him and said quietly, 'Please, Grandfather, I would rather not study any more. I am not very clever and I do not learn very easily. If I go to England, it will only be a waste of money.'

'Everything we have spent on you is a waste of money!' Radha cried. 'We see now the result of your expensive education. With girls like you the only way is to marry you off at fifteen, quickly, to any respectable man who will take you. B.A.-P.A., it is all only a waste.'

The Rai Bahadur continued to look only at Amrita. 'The question of expense is one that does not concern you,' he said. 'I have decided to send you to England to study, and there the matter ends. I can see no point in further argument.'

Amrita did not argue further. But her silence was not the silence of assent.

'You understand me?' her grandfather felt forced to add.

Again she kept silent.

'Have you no answer to make to your grandfather, you rude, disrespectful girl?' Radha prodded her.

But Amrita saw no point in any answer she could make: she knew they would listen to no words except words of submission. And she was not prepared to submit: things had gone too far for that, her resolution had been hammered down too firmly.

The Rai Bahadur was a man who demanded and got respect. His outward personality – his bearing, his speech – demanded it, as well as his status as head of the family. But if this respect, this unquestioning obedience, was denied him, if the force of his personality and of his status made no effect, what means had he then to enforce it? He worked like a symbol, very powerful if its content and significance are accepted, meaningless if they are not. Amrita, by her silence, seemed to challenge him to prove the existence of power behind the symbol of his personality: and he, being wise, recognized that he had nothing with which to meet that challenge.

Radha, being less wise, did not recognize it.

'Pappaji,' she cried, 'do not be so lenient with her! Make the wicked girl speak and tell us she will do her duty as is fitting in a daughter!'

But the Rai Bahadur knew that blustering and threatening would do nothing except lower his dignity.

'You will go to England and we will hear no more of this distasteful affair,' he said, his voice as forceful and commanding as ever. 'That is all.' They were dismissed.

But Radha was not content. She wanted to see and hear Amrita submit to their wishes, beg their forgiveness, show herself once again a dutiful and respectful daughter. For weeks now she had been striving for this end, and she could not rest till she, or the grandfather for her, achieved it.

'Pappaji,' she urged him, 'you are too good. You do not treat the girl as she deserves. Why do you not teach her what her duty is?'

'That is all,' the Rai Bahadur said again. He felt old and weak, and wanted only to get back to his law books.

'Come, Mamma,' Amrita said and got up.

'You are giving me orders now!' Radha cried. 'Pappaji, why do you not help me? Show this daughter of hell what is the respect due to her mother and her family.'

'Go, go, go,' the old man said.

'Pappaji . . .' But there was nothing for it but to go.

Outside by the stairs the servants were waiting for Radha, nodding and smiling and looking forward to her words of rebuke. But none came; she was too busy telling Amrita what happened to disobedient daughters to heed anyone else who might need her exhortation.

'What!' the cook cried, when he saw her making for the entrance door. 'Finished? Is that all? You are not staying to eat in our house?'

She turned round and said, almost perfunctorily, 'Villain, rogue, I can see you are fat and smooth with our ghee.' And although Mohan Lal furiously swirled the button which he had specially kept loose for her, she took no further notice of them.

'Your own daughters will be black with sin,' she was busy telling Amrita, 'and they will break your heart up into little pieces for you. Now we will see what your Tarla auntie has to say to you.'

Tarla auntie had already been told of Hari's secret visit. Radha now lost no time in informing her of the latest development.

'And you will not believe me when I tell you,' she said as soon as she came in, 'but the villain did not go when Pappaji called him. Just did not go! And now Pappaji says Amrita must go to England, but I am not happy about it, Tarla, not at all happy, I tell you.'

She sank down on the divan and said, 'Ah, how cool it is in here, you do not know how fortunate you are to have an air-conditioner, give me some pineapple juice.'

Tarla auntie, in a sari of grey silk, slightly faded, was busy at the cabinet-cum-writing desk; she was writing out the minutes of her latest Committee meeting very slowly and carefully in fine stylized letters. Obviously she did not care to be interrupted, but her sister was not sensitive to the preoccupations of others, especially when she herself had come with such important business to be discussed.

'I am not happy about it, Tarla,' she said again. 'I do not like to differ from Pappaji but I really feel I cannot let her go. Are you listening to me, Tarla?' for Tarla was continuing to write out her minutes.

'Yes,' she answered, 'I am listening.' And regretfully she laid aside her pen, gave a last lingering look over the paper and then turned to Radha. 'You are not happy about it: so?'

Amrita sat, as she had sat at the grandfather's, quietly with her hands folded in her lap, perfectly aloof, perfectly detached.

'How can I be?' Radha said. 'When I cannot trust that wicked girl out of my sight for one little half hour even.' Suddenly she shouted at Amrita, 'You go away, we do not wish to see you here!'

'Now what is this?' said Tarla auntie.

'She is no daughter of mine!' Radha cried. 'Go away, my eyes hurt when they look at you. Go, go, I have to speak with your aunt.'

Amrita looked at Tarla auntie who said, 'Go if you want to, Amrita, your uncle is in the music-room.'

'Yes, go!' Radha cried, and then added to Tarla, 'We are staying for lunch, what have you cooked?'

Tarla resigned herself and said, 'Mira also is coming.' Amrita quietly slipped out of the room.

'Mira coming here for lunch?' Radha said. 'You are always inviting her and you never ask me. You love her more than you love me,' she accused.

'But you never need to be invited,' Tarla pointed out.

'It is not right to love one sister better than the other,' Radha told her. 'Now I love you and Mira both the same. You are both stars of the same radiance shining in my heart.'

Tarla said, 'You wanted to speak with me about Amrita and England.'

'Not one night's, what am I saying, not one minute's rest would I have if she went to England! All day I would sit and all night I would lie and see her marrying Englishmen.'

A long cream-coloured car drew up outside and the next moment Mira came in, wearing a very pale lilac sari and blouse to match, and perspiring a lot. She sat down on the divan next to Radha, saying 'whew' in relief, a balloon hissing air, and waved her fan – lilac to match her sari – in front of her face.

Radha looked her up and down and said critically, 'Another new sari.'

'You like it?' Mira asked, exhibiting herself.

'It must have cost too much,' Radha said. 'You spend too much money on clothes, Mira. It is very unsuitable at your age; you are not a young girl any more.'

'I know,' Mira sighed. 'But I do so like new clothes, they always make me feel young again, and then also I forget all this,' and laughing, she heaved up the folds of fat around her hips.

'Eat less,' Radha said severely, 'and then you will not need new clothes to make you feel thinner. Tarla,' she said, getting back to serious business, 'you will please talk with Pappaji. You are the eldest, that is why he will listen more to you. You will tell him that it is not safe for Amrita to go to London: I cannot allow it.'

'It is so far away,' Mira agreed.

'It is marriage we must think of now, not England,' Radha said. 'There is no rest for me until I see her taken away to a husband's house.'

'It is women like you who retard our progress,' said Tarla.

'Oh,' Radha bridled up, 'so you think you are the only one who is emancipated? I will tell you that I am just as emancipated as you are: only I am also a mother.'

'I too am a mother,' Mira said irrelevantly, 'but I do not think I am very much emancipated.'

'I believe just as much as you do in women's freedom and the Hindu Code Bill and everything,' Radha said, 'but it is quite different when one thinks of one's own daughter. You would know that if you had one.'

'You mean,' Tarla said with that sarcastic little smile which both her sisters had hated ever since they were children, 'that one's daughter should not be free?'

'That is not what I said!' Radha cried. 'You are so busy thinking about yourself that you never listen to what others say. Bring me some more,' she told the bearer, holding out her empty glass: Tarla's pineapple juice was always freshly made and ice-cold. 'What I meant was that a mother's heart cannot endure to see her daughter's reputation in danger. I want to save her from unhappiness. She is only young, poor child, she does not know what she is doing. That satan can do anything he likes with her, she is so innocent. I must save her from such people, their heads should be struck from their shoulders, it is my duty as a mother.'

'With a son one does not have such trouble,' Mira said. 'I know with my Harish –'

'If we could hear of a good family with a nice educated boy,' Radha said, 'that is what we want. He must be well-educated of course, England-returned I would like, and he must have a good position, an I.C.S. or a gazetted officer with a good salary and pension. Such a beautiful fair girl like my Amrita, I would not let her go to just anybody.'

Tarla said, hard and practical, 'You have anyone in mind?'

'Oh, oh,' said Mira, 'and only yesterday she was a little small girl in a short frock and plaits, and always she liked my gulab jamuns so much, always she came to me and said "Mira auntie, give a gulab jamun, you have the best gulab jamuns I have ever eaten".'

'Why do you think I am talking with you?' Radha asked Tarla. 'You with all your Committee-Shommittees, you must know somebody.'

'I am not a broker,' replied Tarla.

'Your own sister's daughter: she is also your daughter,' Radha pointed out.

'It is a pity,' Mira sighed, 'she cannot marry my Harish. That would be so ideal for all of us.'

'You use too much scent,' Radha told her and wrinkled her nose. 'It smells so strong, it is making me quite ill.'

'But it is only eau-de-cologne.'

'It is horrible. It would be better to wash than to use so much eau-de-cologne.'

'Lady Ram Prashad . . .' Tarla said musingly.

'I wash too,' Mira said.

'What about Lady Ram Prashad?' asked Radha.

'She has a son. He is in America.'

'What use is he to me if he is in America? Shall I travel there all the way to look at him? You always pride yourself on how much sense you have, Tarla, but you speak quite without sense.'

'She mentioned,' Tarla said with slow patience, 'that he will be coming home in October.'

'That is different. Could you not have said that at the beginning instead of confusing us all with talk of America.'

'My Harish,' Mira said, 'always calls it the States. It is so confusing, often I do not know what States, is it Uttar Pradesh or Himachal Pradesh, then he laughs at me and says it is of course the United States.'

'You have met him?' Radha asked. 'He is a good-looking boy? He is fair complexioned?'

'The United States of America,' Mira explained.

'No,' said Tarla, 'I have not met him.'

'They are a good family,' Radha reflected.

'He was studying in America,' Tarla went on. 'Lady Ram Prashad said he is a very intelligent boy. He will of course want an educated girl.'

'And my Amrita is perhaps not educated! Where will he find a more educated girl? She is a B.A., he cannot ask for more.'

'Too much education in a girl,' Mira opined, 'is also not good. I would not like my Harish to marry a very learned girl.'

'And a very learned girl,' Radha said, 'would not like to marry your Harish. Oh,' she mused, 'but Lady Ram Prashad's son, how his mouth will gape when he sees my Amrita. In America they do not have such girls. American girls have very large teeth.'

'But they have healthy teeth,' said Mira, who took a professional interest in these things, since Harish was a dentist. 'It is English women who have bad teeth. When they are thirty they have not one tooth left in their mouths.'

'And American women have no chests,' Radha said, complacently patting her own luxurious one.

'What is a woman without a chest,' Mira said, and she too squinted down at hers, large round cupolas blown up to bursting-point within the tight lilac blouse.

Tarla, thin and rigid and very flat, looked disdainful and wondered, as she often did, how these two came to be her sisters.

'I hope he is not dark-complexioned,' Radha said. 'Lady Ram Prashad is rather too dark, she has not a nice complexion at all. I hope he does not take after his mother.'

'It does not matter in a man,' Mira said. 'Harish's father was also dark, but what a handsome man he was.'

'A man does not have to be as fair as a woman,' Radha agreed. 'But I would not like my Amrita's husband to be too dark, because of the children. How would I look, with a horde of black grandchildren? Like Mrs B. S. Bali, the wife of the Session Judge. She has a little granddaughter who is quite black, a very ugly child, she does not like to show her at all.'

Mira clicked her tongue in pity for Mrs B. S. Bali and said, 'Is it not time for lunch?'

Meanwhile, upstairs in the music-room, Vazir Dayal played patience at a little rosewood table and talked to Amrita.

'I will help you,' he said.

'How can you help me please, Uncle?' she asked, not very interested. Nothing interested her much just now: she kept herself aloof to maintain her attitude of resistance.

'With money,' he answered. 'Money money money,' he said under his breath while he shifted a card; he was very pleased because the game was working out.

'But I do not need any money, Uncle.'

He laughed, feeling exceptionally good-humoured: for here was the 10 to go under the jack, and the 9 and the 8 to follow it, what a skilful patience player he was.

'She does not need money,' he said, and laughed again. 'Her family want to send her to England. There is a young man, and if only he had the money he would go to England with her, for there one is free and can marry or not as one wishes. But she does not need money.'

Amrita looked at him, quite startled. This was something which had really never occurred to her. Vazir Dayal was pleased with the effect he had made.

'It is good to have a rich uncle,' he said.

Amrita thought of herself and Hari in England. They would be quite free and independent; there would be nobody to come between them; no Radha to disapprove of him, no Prema to disapprove of her, no Vaidyas to burst into their intimate moments. All day and every day they would have only one another: he would be with her at breakfast, at lunch, at – and then she paused, remembering the necessity of breakfast, lunch and dinner.

'O but Uncle, what can we do once we are married, over there in a strange country so far away? How could we live?'

Vazir Dayal was looking for a red 7 and could not find one; this irritated him.

'We hear so much of the adventurous spirit of youth,' he remarked, 'and all you can say is, "How could we live, Uncle, what could we do, Uncle?" I am paying for your fare, is not that enough, must I also find you employment and a house to live in?' and he furiously shuffled his cards.

Amrita thought it over. Even supposing she could accept this money from her uncle – and she was by no means sure she could – the question remained whether Hari would consent to come. He was rather timid – like a little child, she thought tenderly, who feels lost and unhappy when he is taken out of his familiar surroundings. He would of course want to be with her and, quite incidentally, he would also be very excited at the thought of going to England; but when once he came to consider the concrete possibility of it, he might begin to hesitate and to draw back, just because he was so childlike, so sweetly timid. And then too, the thought of having to find work and to fend for himself alone in a strange, far-off country would be terrible to him; he was used to having all his relations at the back of him, and existence without that support and security might seem almost impossible to him. She herself would, of course, do all she could to help earn a living for the two of them, but she felt rather sceptical about her abilities.

Vazir Dayal was still looking for his red 7.

'You cannot expect me to do more. Can you not recognize a good opportunity when it is offered to you?'

Of course she could: and most especially because it was an opportunity, a possibility, she had never even thought of. She had her doubts whether she had the right to accept money from Vazir Dayal and put herself under such an obligation to him, when she knew that he did not care very much what happened to her. But then, was he not her uncle, her close relation, her own mother's own sister's husband? Besides, there was no one else to whom she could turn. She was not in a position to scruple over accepting help when it was offered to her, whatever might be the motive, or the indifference, behind the offer.

'It is so kind of you, Uncle,' she said.

'Kind kind,' he waved her aside, 'what has kind to do with it: you need the money and I have it, finished.' And just at that moment there came into his hand what he was looking for – a red 7, and yes, a 6 and a 5 and a 4 to go with it, and he added, as he placed the cards into their position, 'And I will also help you once you are over there, what is it to me. I will give you enough money to settle you for a while, you will be able to go and see Europe, see Paris, Rome, Berlin, see' – and he waved a card – 'Life. I will give you the money.'

After a pause, Amrita asked, 'Why are you doing this for me please, Uncle?'

He laughed and shrugged his shoulders. 'It is my fancy,' he said grandiosely.

It was not a motive to make her any happier about accepting his money. Nor was she sure that there was not worse behind it, that the cause of his generosity towards her was not very largely a desire to spite her mother's family. But again she felt that she was in no position to pry into motives.

'Go,' he said, 'go to your dear Mamma and tell her that you are very happy to obey her like a good daughter and to go to England.' He shuffled his completed cards together with a complacent deftness. He felt very pleased with himself, though probably even he was not sure what pleased him most, to be helping Amrita, to be annoying his wife's family or to have completed his patience so successfully.

'Where have you been, child?' said Radha. 'Why do you not come and sit with your mother and your aunts?'

'It was you yourself who told her to go,' Tarla pointed out.

But Radha had forgotten all that. She stroked Amrita's cheek and looked at her tenderly. 'My little one,' she said.

Mira auntie also looked at her, with her head on one side and an expression of love on her face.

Amrita was too busy with her own new scheme to be surprised at her mother's change of attitude. She let her cheek be stroked and smiled at Mira auntie, who smiled back and gave a deep rueful sigh.

'Only yesterday,' she murmured, and Radha sighed too.

'Mamma,' Amrita said, for she could not hold it much longer, 'I will do as Grandfather says. I will go to England.'

Tarla auntie alone showed any surprise.

'This is new,' she said in her matter-of-fact way. Radha just went on stroking Amrita's cheek and looking at her tenderly.

'I will go to England,' Amrita repeated, a little more loudly.

'Such a brave girl,' said Mira auntie.

'Are you not pleased with me, Mamma?' Amrita asked.

'You are my own dear daughter,' said Radha.

Tarla auntie smiled sceptically. 'Please remember that nothing is settled. I must speak with Lady Ram Prashad first, and I am by no means sure that she will be agreeable.'

'Why should she not be?' Radha said, dreamily studying her daughter's face. 'How pretty you are, my little one.'

'I will go whenever you want,' Amrita said.

'My darling,' Radha said, 'you need not worry your sweet mind over England. We have other plans now.'

Mira auntie blew her nose on a lilac chiffon handkerchief drenched in eau-de-cologne and said, 'How old it makes me feel.'

'What other plans?' Amrita asked, very suspicious now, but her mother only smiled and began to stroke her cheek again.

18

It would not be true to say that Krishna Sen Gupta had never thought of Amrita in terms of woman and love. In a society in which there was not much opportunity for social intercourse between the sexes, it came naturally to a young man to think of every young woman of his own class in such terms. From the first moment he had seen her – or rather, even before that, when he had first learnt of her existence – he had considered her possibilities. But he had quickly summed them up as practically nil. Abroad he had got used to a freer type of woman, more experienced, more outspoken, more conscious of the effects of her sex and more deliberate in her use of them; Amrita's reticence, her complete mental innocence, what he called her prudery, repelled him. There were very few other young women for him to meet, and they too were almost all cast in the same mould as Amrita. His female fellow-lecturers, his women students, Amrita's friends – they all had that same shy disregard of his own sex. For them there were only fathers, brothers and husbands, and they themselves only overtly recognized their womanhood in so far as it made them, or was going to make them, wives and mothers. Krishna could find nothing to say to them, nor had they anything to say to him. He was neither father, brother nor husband, and there was no other kind of relationship they knew of to establish with him. After he had lived in Radha's house for some time, Amrita began to accept him as a brother, so that at least they had some basis on which to meet. But beyond that brother-sister relationship neither he nor she ever consciously looked.

However, he had been back in India for four years now, and the memory of the kind of woman he had learnt to like was fading. Perhaps even he was beginning to find that, like many other ideas and memories he had brought with him, she was an anomaly in these surroundings: certainly whenever he saw an Indian or Eurasian woman behaving with the freedom of a European one, he experienced a feeling of distaste. But Amrita's shy smile, her soft voice, her hands fluttering from out of her sari, these belonged; and what formerly he had characterized as prudery, he now thought of as a natural, a very fitting, reticence. Perhaps he first became aware of his change of attitude to women in general, and Amrita in particular, on that night when she had sent him to fetch Hari. The time was unfortunate; for he felt himself rejected and humiliated before he had even formulated his attraction towards her to himself, let alone shown it to her. He was a very proud young man and his sense of shame was no less acute because she knew nothing of his new feeling for her.

To make matters worse, she now regarded him as her confidant. She had no other and she greatly felt the need of one. So it was to him that she first carried the news of her uncle's offer. It startled him, but he scrupulously kept up the attitude of helpful impartiality on which he had resolved. He considered the proposition as fairly as he could, while she pressed him for advice.

'But why is he doing this?' he asked. He did not like Vazir Dayal, and doubted his motives as much as Amrita had.

She gave him the same answer as she had given herself: 'What does it matter why?'

He agreed to this and concentrated on the main question. 'Do you want to do it? Are you sure? Do not let yourself be forced into it by some idle whim of your uncle's.'

'There is nothing else for me to do,' she said miserably.

He had to agree to this too. It was a drastic step, but if she was really determined to go through with it and marry Hari, then it was the only one. He felt almost relieved at the thought that here was the final solution to her problem, and to his too.

'And Hari?' he asked.

'I have not spoken with him yet.'

He kept quiet. He remembered how reluctant Hari had been to leave his home and come to Amrita that night when he had gone to fetch him. Amrita would have to do some very persuasive talking to get him to England.

'Krishna . . .' Amrita began, looking down at the floor and playing with her fingers.

He was on the alert immediately. He knew from the tone of her voice that she wanted him to do something for her, and he was reluctant to do it, whatever it might be. He wished she would leave him alone and not involve him in an affair about which he wanted to know nothing. His peace of mind depended on his aloofness from her and Hari.

'Krishna,' she said, 'please, I would so like you to do something for me.'

'You want me to speak to Hari?'

She nodded and looked at him shyly. 'You will?'

If his feelings towards her had been negative, he could have refused. But as it was, he had to establish his impartiality in his own eyes. She would have ascribed his refusal to indifference; but he himself to vindictiveness.

'I shall not be seeing him tomorrow nor the day after, not till Friday. And I do so want him to know. Please, will you go to him?'

Moreover, he felt sorry for her. He knew very well, perhaps better than she did herself, what efforts it cost her not only to be thus having to take the initiative in the affair, but also in the first place to be loving Hari at all. He knew it was a constant struggle with her innate modesty, with all she believed and felt and had been taught to believe and feel. But within him was the constant nagging hurt that she was making this struggle for somebody else, and had not been prompted to make it for him.

'He may be in the *Bombay Coffee-House*. Often he goes there in the evening.'

So Krishna, driven more by his own conscience than by her asking, went off to find Hari.

19

The *Bombay Coffee-House* was the favourite haunt of disillusioned young men. They sat there for hours on end, drinking black coffee or lime-water with pepper and salt and talking bitterly about the social system. Most of them were graduates who had left the University and did not know what to do with themselves or their degrees; so they spent their time hating first their families and secondly Society in general. Some of them were already hanging on to the fringes of journalism or got occasional small jobs on the radio, of which they talked as much and as often as possible. When they became more successful, they no longer frequented the *Bombay Coffee-House*; but there were always plenty of others to replace them, for many new graduates left the Universities every year.

Hari was happy there. He talked a lot, laughed a lot, sometimes smoked, and listened to his friends. Often he did not understand what was being said, for he read only the local news and the advertisements in the newspaper, and had no opinion about the Government. What especially puzzled him was why they should all speak so bitterly about Society and what they called the Social Set-Up; for him Society meant photographs of parties at the Gymkhana Club which he saw in illustrated weeklies at his sister's house, and these did not seem to him bad but, on the contrary, very nice and desirable. But he liked to listen to his friends talking, and when he did not understand he always leant forward a little and listened all the more eagerly.

It was very hot in the coffee-house, although the doors and windows had been flung wide open to let in the evening air and the flies, and four huge fans turned in a row from the ceiling. A smell of long-since-eaten potato-chips and vegetable samusas crept about the room and clung to the waiters in their dubious white uniforms and napkins wilting over one shoulder. Though there were long blue menu-cards, with many rich and expensive dishes printed on them, practically the only food items ever served were chips and samusas, for these were the only ones the clientele could afford; if they had been able to afford anything more expensive, they would not have come to the *Bombay Coffee-House*. Perhaps this accounted for the expression of cynical disillusionment on the faces of the waiters; or perhaps they were only imitating the clients. There was a dusty notice behind the cashier which said 'Silence Please'; it was a source of never-failing amusement.

This evening Hari was particularly happy because they were not condemning Society; instead, one of them was relating the exploits of a cousin of his. This cousin had inserted an advertisement in a popular newspaper, styling himself Doctor Meher Chand, famous in Europe and consulted by all Ministers and Gentry. Doctor Meher Chand offered a potion, made after an old-time recipe received from a holy man in Allahabad and guaranteed to cure bile, impotency, chronic headaches and all women's disorders. An overwhelming number of applications was received in response to this advertisement; and Doctor Meher Chand, having established his headquarters in a tiny little room, rented at Rs 10 a month and leading off from a shoemaker's shop near Kashmere Gate, spent his time pouring green coloured water into little bottles and sending them off by registered post. In return he received, besides Rs 1/8 a bottle, many letters of thanks and appreciation. He was doing very well indeed, until his father found out and packed him off to an old uncle's in Cawnpore.

This story was received with great laughter; Hari laughed too, though he felt a little doubtful. He had always thought these advertisements were genuine, and he knew that many of his relations answered them and relied on them. Not so long ago his sister Mohini had written, and a little box of pills had come back, neatly packed; and he had heard her say that she had had good results and had written off for more. He was pondering about this when he looked up and saw Krishna Sen Gupta. Police and prison broke rudely into his reflections, he heard Radha's angry voice, could feel again the terrible leap of his heart, and then pictured the grandfather sitting behind his large desk, waiting, tapping his foot, the clock ticking. He half rose in his chair and looked at Krishna with anxious eyes.

'Hallo,' Krishna smiled pleasantly and led the way to a separate table.

Before they had time to sit down, Hari burst out: 'My sister was not very well in her health last night, I had to fetch the Doctor, that is the reason why I did not come.' And when Krishna made no comment, he went on explaining desperately, 'I was ready to go at eight o'clock. I had eaten my dinner specially early, but then she had such fever, how could I refuse to fetch the Doctor?'

Krishna said: 'Amrita sent me.'

'Not her grandfather?' Hari asked, hopefully leaning forward in his chair.

'No,' said Krishna, 'he has other messengers'; and Hari heaved a great sigh of relief.

Krishna laughed and thought how gratified the Rai Bahadur would be if he knew in what awe Hari held him. He himself had never had much respect for the old man: the Rai Bahadur's heavy authoritative manner had jarred on him from the very beginning, and prejudiced him against attempting to find out if any more solid qualities lay behind the – as it seemed to him – pretentious manner. He was, moreover, influenced by his father's contemptuous reference to the old man as a time-server who had only attained a distinguished position because other men, of greater abilities than his own, had refused to serve in the English courts.

'Why do you laugh?' Hari asked, somewhat hurt.

Krishna only shook his head, laughed again and called for two iced coffees. He felt quite at home in the coffee-house; not that he had ever been there before, but it was exactly the sort of place in which he had spent his time in Calcutta, when he had first come back from England and was out of a job. The moment he had come in, the smell had brought those times back to him; and at the first sip he took from his iced coffee the memory was sharpened, and he was filled with a pleasantly painful nostalgia. The restlessness and discontent of four years ago seemed to him now a fine and noble thing, though at the time he had thought himself very miserable.

'They are very angry with me?' Hari asked.

'Who?' Krishna was thinking of Calcutta and the particular smell of his favourite coffee-house and the way the waiters used to shout the bill to the cashier when the customer was leaving; and he wondered what had happened to all the other young men with whom he had sat and talked and mourned the bitterness of life, and whether they were still sitting there.

'Amrita's grandfather and her mother,' Hari said. 'How angry her mother was with me! She has a very strong temper. Was she very bad to Amrita afterwards, after I had gone?'

'Amrita does not mind much any more. She has heard her mother very often.'

Hari shook his head in pity for Amrita and called for a spoon with which to scoop the cream from the bottom of his coffee glass. 'They should always give one a spoon,' he told Krishna. 'How else is one to eat the cream? It is too difficult with the straw.'

And Krishna, looking round at all the discontented, disillusioned young men, felt a little ashamed of having a job with a good salary and almost accepting things as they were.

'You come here often?' he asked Hari, and thought of himself as rolling smoothly into middle age.

'Usually in the evenings and sometimes in the morning too,' Hari answered. 'I meet my friends here. I always drink coffee and sometimes I eat potato-chips.'

So Krishna ordered a plate of chips. He liked Hari very much, but he could not understand how Amrita had come to like him so much.

'You know they want to send her to England?' he said.

Hari nodded: 'I do not know how I shall live without her.'

But Krishna knew how: Hari would come here to the coffee-house in the mornings and in the evenings, drink coffee, talk with his friends, from time to time sigh deeply to show he had a sorrow, then expatiate upon sorrow in general, upon women, upon love, heave another sigh and then confide to whoever was nearest to him about Amrita, how he loved her and how her family had cruelly sent her away because of him. It would not be an altogether unpleasant life.

'She wants you to go with her,' Krishna said.

Hari smiled sorrowfully. 'And I, how much I want to go with her. But how can I? I have no money.'

'If you had the money, you would go?'

'What else, I would not wait one moment even.'

'Amrita has the money for you.'

Hari stopped scooping cream and looked up.

'You can both go to England now and be married there.'

'You are making a joke of me,' Hari said uncertainly.

'Why should I be?'

'But Amrita has no money.'

'Her uncle is giving it to her,' Krishna said. 'He wants her to go away and marry you.'

'Her uncle? But her uncle does not know me.'

'All the same, he wants her to marry you and he is giving you the money.'

Hari took a handful of potato-chips, dipped them in red chutney and chewed, while he pondered over this sudden proposition. He had not yet quite realized it and was floundering about trying to assimilate it. 'It is fantastic,' he said. Krishna shrugged his shoulders and waited for the next reaction.

'Why should her uncle do this?' Hari asked, and shook his head. One of the young men with whom he had been sitting suddenly called over: 'O Hari, do not forget Silence Please!' and pointed at the notice behind the cashier; this brought a great burst of laughter.

'Ha-ha,' Hari said absent-mindedly; and then he turned to Krishna and politely explained the joke: 'There is a notice saying Silence Please.'

'I see it,' Krishna said. 'It is very funny.'

'Is her uncle so rich?' Hari asked with sudden awe.

'Immensely.'

Hari nodded, much impressed. 'It is a wonderful thing to have so much money.'

Krishna agreed and undid another button of his shirt. It was very hot, and flies kept settling on the chips and on the rim of his coffee glass.

'If I had so much money –' Hari began.

'You would go to England with Amrita,' Krishna took him up.

'Yes,' Hari had to agree.

'Well then,' Krishna said, 'you have the money now and you can do as you wish. Both of you can do as you wish.'

Hari tried to scoop some more cream out of his glass but there was nothing left. 'If only it were so easy,' he said, licking the empty spoon. 'But how can I leave Delhi? My whole family is here, my mother, my sisters, my brothers, how can I leave them?'

'Why not?'

The question surprised Hari. He gave Krishna a puzzled look and said, 'They are my family,' for that explained everything.

'But you want to marry Amrita.'

'Yes.' But he did not sound very certain of himself.

Krishna tensely tried to catch a fly and waited.

'How can I go to England with her?' Hari appealed. 'My family will never let me go.'

'Then go without asking them,' Krishna said, and opening his fist, discovered that he had not caught the fly after all.

Hari did not even try to find an answer to this proposition. It was impossible, simply that, and could not even be thought about. His mind was not conditioned to thinking about it.

Krishna realized this very well but he persisted: 'What is to stop you?'

'You do not understand,' Hari murmured. It was no use trying to argue with someone who did not even understand the simple fact that it was impossible to leave one's family and go to England without first consulting them and getting their consent.

'No, I do not understand,' Krishna went on ruthlessly. 'First you say that you want to marry Amrita and that if only you could, you would go to England with her, and then when it is made possible for you to go, you say that you cannot go because you cannot leave your family. How can I understand that?'

'Put yourself in my position,' Hari pleaded.

'I am putting myself in your position, and still I do not see what can stop you from going. Unless of course,' he added maliciously, 'you care more for your family than you care for Amrita.'

To that Hari did not dare reply. He eluded the question. 'Please, it is not like that at all.'

'How is it then?'

'You do not understand,' he said again. 'There is another matter too . . .' He sighed and passed both his hands over his smooth, oiled hair.

Krishna showed no curiosity; he concentrated on catching flies. But the urge to confide was welling up inside Hari till he could feel it tickling behind his lips. He could stand it no longer. He watched Krishna ineffectively catch flies, and his lips burst open.

'It is this: my family are arranging a marriage for me, this is why I cannot go.' And having confessed, he hung his head, and felt an awful silence lapping about him.

He heard Krishna say, 'Oh I see,' quite quietly and reasonably, and he looked up and saw the waiters still rushing up and down with trays of coffee on their shoulders, and the young man at the next table tossing a dead matchstick over his shoulder.

But then a new fear came upon him, and putting out his hand, he laid it on Krishna's and pleaded with eyes as large and soft as a girl's, 'Please, you will not tell Amrita, it is not good that she should know.'

Krishna raised his eyebrows, and his spectacles rose too. 'Why not?' he said. 'Unless you intend to marry as your family want you to.'

'Oh no!' Hari cried, a bit too loudly, 'no, no, please do not believe that. It is not that at all.' And when Krishna kept quiet, he got more flustered and felt he had to say something further: 'I do not want her to know because,' he tried desperately to think of a because; and having found it, rushed on with new energy, 'because it will upset her. That is the only reason. I am thinking only of her.'

Again Krishna kept quiet and again Hari was goaded into continuing: 'Of course; how could there be another reason? I cannot marry anybody else when I love Amrita. It is impossible. I love her.'

'And your family?'

'They cannot,' Hari said bravely, 'stop me from loving Amrita. They cannot open my heart' – he laid his hand on that spot – 'and pluck her out from there'; and he began to stroke the place under which he thought his heart lay.

'So you have told them that you cannot marry the girl they have chosen for you?'

Hari passed the question over by repeating, 'I cannot marry her when I love Amrita.'

'You will go to England then?'

'How can I go? My family –'

'But if you stay here, they will make you marry the other girl.'

Hari buried his head in his hands and moaned. 'Love,' he said; 'what does not the heart suffer for love.'

Krishna undid all the buttons of his shirt and fanned himself with the menu. It was intolerably hot. Hari kept his head buried in his hands and moaned a bit more.

'Can we go?' Krishna said. 'It is too hot in here.'

Hari nodded without raising his head; Krishna called for, and paid the bill.

Outside the coffee-house, a panwala sat crouching against a pillar, a little tray in front of him with coloured powder, red and yellow, laid in pools on the green leaves. While he mixed pans for Krishna and Hari, he talked with the man perched on a high stool outside the coffee-house; this man was employed to open and shut the door for customers but he did not often remember to do so, as he found it more interesting to talk with the panwala. Nobody ever tipped him anyway.

'So,' Krishna said, as they walked on, chewing their pan, 'what can I tell Amrita?'

Two girls passed them, in coloured kamiz and salwar, with pigtails swinging down their backs. Hari looked them up and down and turned to watch them from behind. He did this instinctively and at the same time as he pondered a reply to Krishna's question.

'I can tell her,' Krishna said, 'that you will go to England with her?'

'I beg you,' Hari said, 'try and understand my position.'

Krishna affected irritation: 'What am I to tell her then?' he said, quite sharply, and Hari gave him an anxious look and said, 'You are angry with me?'

'What does it matter,' Krishna cried, 'if I am angry or not! Who am I that you should trouble yourself about my feelings? It is Amrita's feelings you should be thinking about.'

'Oh I do, I do,' Hari said quickly, 'every moment of the day I think of her, she is the nightingale of my heart, the stars of my eyes, the juice of my liver, tell her that.'

'And that means you will go to England with her?'

'If only I could,' he said, 'I would follow her to the ends of the earth.'

'It is only to England you need go.'

Hari looked at him appealingly. 'My family,' he said, and just then he saw some friends of his and broke into a wide smile saying, 'Hallo-hallo-hallo.' His friends, four healthy youths in American bush-shirts strolling round the arcade and looking at women, stopped and grinned, and one of them said in English, 'How are you?'

Hari seemed delighted to see them and showed himself quite ready for a long talk. 'Where are you going?' he said.

'We have just come from the cinema.'

'It was a good film?' Hari asked.

Krishna took his arm, said, 'Forgive me,' and walked on with him. The four youths stared after them, and Hari looked back with helpless eyes.

'Am I to tell her then,' Krishna said, 'that you cannot come with her because your family are arranging a marriage for you here?'

Hari gave a little cry of horror. 'No, no, no, you must never tell her that.'

'What else then?'

But Hari kept a miserable silence.

'Please tell me what I am to say. That you are going to England with her, or that you are marrying somebody else here, which?' and when Hari still kept quiet, he repeated: 'Which?'

'How can I marry somebody else? I love Amrita.'

'Then you have decided that you will go to England?'

Hari kept quiet again; he was content now to let Krishna settle everything for him, as long as he did not have to voice any definite decision for himself.

'All right,' Krishna said, 'I will tell her then that you will go with her.' And they parted at the bus-stand, both with heavy hearts.

20

The Anands, father, mother, three daughters and an old grandmother, lived in three rooms in the vegetable-market district. It was a very close and crowded district with a warren of narrow by-lanes, and stalls jutting out on to the pavements piled high with fruit and vegetables and mounds of fly-soiled sweets. There was always a lot of noise and children playing and ragged little bands passing through with lurid cinema posters to advertise the latest film. At a corner three or four men sat continually playing dice on a board, watched sometimes by only one man, sometimes by a whole group standing by, chewing pan and scratching under their armpits. Adolescent boys played badminton over a rope strung between a lamp-post and a milk-and-ghee shop. At night, though, it was very quiet; charpoys were brought out into the street and people slept in rows.

The Anands lived over a tailor's shop. A door, always open, led from the side of the shop up a very dark and narrow flight of winding stairs. They had two rooms on the first floor, leading off from a veranda at the back of the house which they shared with another tenant; their third room was on the floor above, and over that they had a square open space on the roof on which they lived and slept all through the summer nights. It was here that they entertained their guests – Hari and his family, his mother, Prema and Suri, Mohini with her husband and children, and the younger brother. It was a very happy occasion for all of them, even for Hari, who chose to forget its significance and just enjoyed himself.

Sushila was the eldest of the three Anand girls but the other two were very close to her in age. They were all of them just in their first bloom and they promised a rich flowering. They had inherited their mother's large shining eyes and abundant bosom, though in them these features were as yet less consciously provocative. They were softer, sweeter than the mother, with smiling mouths, moist and pink; only Sushila wore lipstick, but it was very discreetly applied, not, as with the mother, in a hard red line. The two younger ones giggled continually and nudged one another, and from time to time tugged teasingly at Sushila's kamiz.

Sushila herself was very quiet today; she kept her eyes lowered most of the time and blushed and feigned annoyance when her sisters teased her. She wore a very fine white silk salwar, and her dupatta was pulled over her head; whenever it slipped off from her thick wavy hair, her mother said something sharp in an undertone which made Sushila blush and hastily pull it back again. Then everybody smiled and the sisters nudged one another and tittered.

The Anand grandmother, a very thin, harsh old woman, showed herself only after the guests had arrived. Hari's mother and his sisters greeted her with great deference but she refused to put herself to any courtesy for them. She glared at them and nodded fiercely to herself with tight lips, as if to say I thought as much. She mumbled some rebuke to her daughter-in-law but Mrs Anand only shrugged her shoulders and took no notice. 'Sin,' the old woman audibly muttered; 'to expose the girl to the eyes of the man she is to marry, that is a sin.' Everybody pretended not to hear and after a while she took herself off, distinctly cursing them all, to purify herself with prayer in the room downstairs.

Hari could not keep his eyes off the three girls. He thought them all very pretty but Sushila the prettiest. He wanted to talk to her as he had talked to her that night after the party when he had first become aware of her, but today she was no longer as free and easy with him as she had been then; she kept at a distance from him and never once looked in his direction. He tried not to notice how the others continually looked from him to her and smiled. But when she went for a moment to stand by the parapet overlooking the courtyard, he strolled over to stand beside her. She did not turn to look at him; he could see only the round outline of her cheek with the dupatta falling over it. Her well-developed bosom rose and fell more quickly as he stood beside her. They did not speak for a while but kept looking down into the courtyard where two men were washing themselves in the dark by the pump. Hari was unpleasantly aware of sharp smiling eyes watching him from behind. He shifted his feet, cleared his throat and said: 'So what progress is there in your film career?'

He saw her cheek flush and the corner of her mouth twitch slightly. Her head sank lower till her chin rested on her chest and she murmured, 'Please do not make a joke of me.'

He protested, 'Why should I make a joke of you?' She did not answer, only shook her head deprecatingly, so he went on, 'I think you have great chances with your beautiful voice. There are not many girls in India today with such a voice.'

Again she shook her head, and the dupatta slipped to the back of her hair. Hari stood very close beside her, so close that he could smell the scent of her fresh young body; her hair shone in the evening light. 'Really it is so,' he said, but he was thinking of other things. He pictured to himself her smooth body, strong and brown and stark naked, bending in the shadowed light of the moon and her hair springing out like a black flame. 'You must come,' he said weakly, 'to the radio station for an audition.'

She turned then suddenly and looked up at him. Her eyes shone out large and liquid. He wanted to say something more, about films, radio, audition, his mouth moved and framed the words but his voice would not come. While he stood there looking at her, trying, but unable, to talk, she swung away from him and almost ran to rejoin the others. He stared after her, even wanted to stretch out his hand to detain her, but she was detained by another, firmer hand. Her mother grasped her elbow, pulled the dupatta over her hair and led her back to Hari.

'What are you two young people talking about?' Mrs Anand said with a smile of hard white teeth. 'Is she entertaining you well? You must do him honour,' she told Sushila, 'he is our guest.'

Sushila kept her eyes lowered. Hari shifted from one foot to the other and weakly smiled; he felt all the others looking at them, and he now wished that Mrs Anand had not brought her daughter back to him.

'Yes,' Suri laughed out loud, 'it is right to honour a guest!' and Mr Anand laughed too, tee-hee; the two Anand sisters giggled.

Prema came up and took Sushila's hand on the other side from Mrs Anand. She pressed the limp shy hand and looked up at Hari; he was surprised to see her eyes full of tears. His mother too was wiping her eyes with a corner of her sari.

Mr Anand planted himself before Suri, and with an air of great importance put his hand in his pocket and brought out two ten-rupee notes and one one-rupee note. 'Well, Suri Sahib,' he said, 'your boy is ours, we book him, here is our money,' and he counted it out, ten rupees, twenty rupees, twenty-one rupees, into Suri's hand. Suri held the money. 'He is booked,' he said and laughed. Hari's mother let out a loud sob, while Hari desperately pretended not to notice what was going on.

At a nod from their mother, the two younger Anand girls began to move round with large dishes full of yellow ladoos, which they had made in the house the day before. 'Good, good,' Suri said as he took one, 'it is a happy occasion,' and Mr Anand echoed, 'A happy occasion.' Prema noticed at once that Mrs Anand had not used pure ghee for the ladoos and looked forward to pointing this out to her husband on the way home. Hari's mother sobbed, 'His father should be alive and with us on this day,' and then choked and coughed and coughed while Mohini jumped up and thumped her heartily on the back.

Suddenly from the veranda two floors below came an uproar of voices. Women shrilled and children howled and men boomed with anger. It was one of those family quarrels, sister-in-law against sister, wife against brother-in-law, grandmother against everybody, the tension of community living bursting into a sudden climax which had to rage itself out before it could sink back into the calm of everyday subdued resentment. They all knew it well, this kind of quarrel, it happened from time to time in every family circle; and usually they took no more than a mild good-humoured interest when it concerned other people. But for some reason Mrs Anand was very angry. Her lips drew in tight and her eyes flashed – her daughters watched her apprehensively – and then she cried, 'Again those people! Always they must scream and shout, how can we live in one house with such people!'

Everybody looked at her in surprise and her husband said mildly, 'It is not so bad. We ourselves also have these little quarrels sometimes,' and that made her more furious than ever.

'Have you no pride,' she shouted, 'to compare us with those wild mountain-tribes? All day they scream and shout, they burst our heads with their voices! I would like to throw them out of the house and their miserable little trunks after them! They cook their filthy food, and the smell of it is enough to make me sick like a pregnant woman, and their children run wild like savages with no shoes on their feet. How can we live with people like that?' Anger made her look ugly and much older than usual. Prema stole a triumphant little look at Suri and noted with satisfaction that he was watching Mrs Anand in amazement.

'We have to share veranda with them,' Mrs Anand went on turning to Prema, whose face at once assumed an expression of sympathy, 'and always they make it full of their washing. You have never seen such clothes as they hang up, all rags and tatters, I am ashamed when anybody sees them, they might think it is our washing! My servant wears better clothes than the master of their house.'

Prema clicked her tongue in disapproval of such washing. Sushila began to cry; her mouth turned downwards like a little girl's and the tears crept down her cheeks; but nobody noticed her.

'And all day their old mother is taking a bath, whatever she does, whatever she touches, always she must take a bath! And still she smells! And whenever they have the water on, ours only comes in a little trickle and then what can we do? And in the middle of the night she starts to say her prayers, she cannot say them silently like other people, no she must shout and sing and wake us all from our sleep, can such prayers be pleasing to God?'

'Neighbours,' Prema opined, 'can become very difficult.'

'They are animals!' Mrs Anand shouted. 'They do not know how to live and they make our lives bitter to us.'

'It is always best,' Prema said sweetly, 'to live in one's own house.'

Mrs Anand pulled herself together at that to answer vaguely but with dignity, 'Such people are fortunate.'

The old grandmother, attracted by the sound of her daughter-in-law's angry voice, came sniffing to see if there were any part for her in the quarrel. She looked round with disapproval and said, 'You shout so loud. How can I say my prayers when you shout enough to bring up devils from hell?'

'We are not shouting,' said Mrs Anand. 'It is those satans down there.'

'They are bad people,' the grandmother said. 'The old woman pretends to pray but she does not know the meaning of prayer. God does not hear her.' And she quickly mumbled a prayer to show that at any rate God heard her.

'It is what I was saying,' Mrs Anand agreed. This made the old woman very suspicious, for she was not used to hearing her daughter-in-law agree with her. She said sharply, 'You are not a fit person to judge the prayers of others. First please God yourself, then look to others.'

Hari's mother sighed and said, 'You are right, Mataji, we are all sinners.'

Suri said, 'We leave it to the women, they pray for us,' and laughing uproariously slapped Mr Anand on the back. Mr Anand also laughed very heartily and repeated, 'The women will pray for us.'

'That is why one marries, Kaka,' Suri told Hari. 'So that a wife can pray and get our sins forgiven.'

'Sins forgiven!' Mr Anand shouted, but his mother said severely, 'What talk is this, have you no shame before God?' so that he tittered only behind his hand.

Prema looked at her husband very sternly, but as usual he was not looking in her direction. Mrs Anand smiled and tugged at her dupatta and said, 'Suri Sahib will always have a joke about everything.' But Suri did not look at her either.

'With such jokes,' the grandmother said, 'the tongue will become black in the mouth.' Only Prema audibly agreed with her.

Hari was the first to notice that Sushila was crying. He saw her wiping her eyes with her dupatta and at once felt very sorry for her; but he was too shy, before his family and hers, to ask her what the matter was.

'And that is the only reason for marrying, Suri Sahib?' Mrs Anand tried again, very archly. Suri did not seem to hear; at any rate he did not answer, though she stuck out her bosom very provocatively in his direction.

'Sushila is crying!' one of the Anand sisters suddenly shouted. Sushila lowered her head and tried to pull her dupatta further down. Everybody stared at her, except Hari, who hastily looked the other way.

'I am not,' she whispered, but they all saw the tear-marks on her face and Suri said, 'Why do you cry now? You can cry for the rest of your life but now it is a happy day for you.'

'Tee-hee,' Mr Anand said, 'cry for the rest of her life, it is true.'

'And is it any wonder that she is crying,' Prema demanded while she stroked the girl's hand, 'when unfeeling people make jokes and laugh about sacred things?'

'If she had done her duty by God,' the grandmother pointed out, 'there would be no need for tears now.'

Suri put his arm round Hari's shoulders and said, 'No no, there is no need for tears. Look this way, daughter, and see if there is any need for tears.'

'Look at him!' Mr Anand cried. 'He is a fine boy!' His other two daughters looked at Hari and tittered.

Sushila blushed and kept her eyes lowered; but her mouth-corners irresistibly twitched into a smile. Prema pressed her hand and whispered, 'Do not be afraid. My heart feels for you.'

'Look up!' Mrs Anand commanded and pinched the girl's arm.

'My boy!' wailed Hari's mother.

Sushila slowly raised her eyes to Hari and she smiled and blushed, smiled and blushed.

'Wah!' Suri cried, clapping his hands, and the others joined in, especially Mr Anand, and there was great rejoicing.

Only Hari stood silent and with a sheepish smile on his face. For some reason he was thinking of Krishna Sen Gupta, and the thought made him feel very uncomfortable.

21

Two bearers glided to and fro over the Persian carpet, bending over the guests with a caressing air to offer them, from trays, cheese pakoras and cucumber sandwiches and triangles of buttered toast; while Tarla sat enthroned at a table in the middle of the room efficiently pouring tea into Limoges cups, by her knee a three-tier cake-stand with doilies bearing French pastries and lemon tartlets and a magnificent chocolate layer-cake. The curtains were drawn, the air was softly, artificially cooled. The ladies wore their finest saris, Tarla in a fawn silk, Radha in deep crimson, Mira in pale rose chiffon, Lady Ram Prashad in dark lilac, Amrita in a light-green georgette. Mira and Amrita wore jasmine wound around their hair, and there was a smell of bodies perfumed and powdered and eau-de-cologned. Vazir Dayal, drinking whisky, dazzled in white.

Amrita was rather surprised by all the elaborateness, the sumptuous tea and the elegant saris. There had been a struggle at home between herself and her mother because, as she had said, she did not see why she had to put on her best sari, the pale green one of finest French georgette, only to go to tea with Tarla auntie; Radha had answered that Lady Ram Prashad would be there, but Amrita had said that even so, they did not usually dress up in their best for Lady Ram Prashad. In the end, though, she had given way, following her policy of letting her mother win on the less important points. Krishna Sen Gupta had not been at home; which rather disappointed Amrita, because she always liked him to see her when she was nicely dressed.

Lady Ram Prashad, drinking tea with her little finger poised in the air, radiated charm and kindness. She praised everything, the air-conditioning, the cheese pakoras, the Limoges cups; but most of her charm was concentrated on Amrita. What a delightful sari, she said, smiling her beautiful, large, slightly askew teeth at Amrita, such an exquisite colour; and she liked nothing so much, she said, as to see flowers in a young girl's hair. Whereupon Mira auntie fingered the jasmine wound around her bun. Lady Ram Prashad inquired very sweetly about Amrita's work at the radio and her education at the Lady Wilmot College. Radha listened tensely, and was furious with Amrita for not being more forthcoming. Sometimes she could stand it no longer but had to rush in and colour her daughter's brief, embarrassed replies. As for Amrita herself, she was both puzzled and uncomfortable at being the centre of their interest, and heartily wished they would shift it on to some other topic. But there was little chance of that; for whenever the conversation threatened for a moment to get on to more general matters, Radha took good care to direct it back again to Amrita.

Tarla auntie also did what she could to bring her niece out, but she was handicapped by the necessity of keeping a watchful eye on her husband. Vazir Dayal had already drunk four neat whiskies – she had anxiously counted them – and his eyes had assumed that dreamy expression which always came to him with his fourth whisky. He seemed to think himself alone in the room, for he was sitting relaxed in his arm-chair, with his legs stretched far in front of him, in an attitude not altogether correct for a social tea-party with ladies present; from time to time he softly spoke to himself and dilated his fine nostrils.

Having exhausted Amrita's scholarly accomplishments – 'a B.A. she is, a graduate from the Lady Wilmot College' – and her artistic ones – the oil painting of Village Women at the Well – Radha thought it was time to draw attention to her daughter's more practical abilities. Nibbling at a piece of chocolate cake, she innocently addressed herself to Amrita: 'Is not this cake,' she said, 'like the one you baked for me last week?' and when Amrita looked puzzled – it was true, she had once baked a cake but that was at least a year ago and it had not been a success – Radha continued hastily to Lady Ram Prashad: 'I always think that young girls must be taught to cook. We cannot always be dependent on a cook who tomorrow may take it into his worthless head to go back to his village or to one of the Embassies. You must be knowing Mrs Inder Lal Chopra, the wife of the Deputy Secretary Chopra, she had a very good cook and then he left her to go to the Danish Embassy. These foreigners pay too much, they spoil our servants for us, why do they not bring their own servants with them? Mrs Chopra was very unhappy because she could not cook herself and did not know how to train a new servant. That is why I have always been very careful that my Amrita learns how to cook.'

Mira auntie, a tiny white suede handbag, gold-embroidered, dangling from her stout wrist, thought it was time she also made some contribution; 'And always our Amrita is finding new recipes in the magazines, oh, she is such a clever girl, kheer she makes, and barfi she makes, and sooji halwa and rabri and sewain and zarda and firni –' Mira's eyes became soft and misty, and she was beginning to forget her original purpose in this catalogue of her favourite dishes. Amrita sat amazed, while Lady Ram Prashad clicked her tongue in admiration.

But Tarla thought that between them her two sisters were carrying it rather too far, so she attempted to turn the conversation. 'Of course,' she said, 'it is very useful for every girl to know all household tasks. That is why the work at the new Training Centre for Women is so praiseworthy. I hope you will come and inspect our new Centre, Lady Ram Prashad.'

'Certainly I will come,' said Lady Ram Prashad. 'Such good work must be encouraged. Perhaps,' she turned her smile on to Amrita, 'you will care to accompany me?'

Amrita was taken aback. She could think of no reason why Lady Ram Prashad should be wanting her company. Of course Lady Ram Prashad had always been very cordial and charming towards her, but then she was cordial and charming towards everybody: Amrita had never thought that she might want to single her out. Puzzled, she forgot her manners and looked towards her mother instead of answering. This made Radha furious, but she had much presence of mind and cried, 'Oh, but how good of you, Lady Ram Prashad, Amrita will love to come, it will be an education for her!'

'We must,' said Lady Ram Prashad to Amrita, 'get to know one another better.' Under Radha's fierce eye, Amrita smiled gratefully, she hoped – and wondered more than ever. 'I am very fond of the company of young girls,' said Lady Ram Prashad, 'always I have wanted a daughter'; and Amrita looked down at her own toe peeping out from under the sari.

Radha looked fondly at Amrita and said, 'A daughter is a great comfort.'

'It is strange,' Mira said, a crumb of chocolate cake on her upper lip, 'but I have always been happy that my Harish is a son.'

'When a daughter marries,' Radha said, 'one also gets a son.'

'And when a son marries,' said Lady Ram Prashad, 'one gets a daughter.'

Amrita felt very uncomfortable. She knew there was something in the air but she did not dare think what. Her mother's face confirmed her suspicions, for Radha wore that expression of innocence she always assumed when she was up to something. Also, another sure sign, she refused to meet Amrita's eye.

'Perhaps you would care to come to our meetings,' Lady Ram

Prashad suggested, 'and also serve on some of our Committees, there is always so much work to be done. I am sure you take an interest in Social Work?'

Before Amrita could answer, Radha cried, 'Oh yes, she is very interested, always she asks her Tarla auntie, please auntie let me come and help in your wonderful work!'

Lady Ram Prashad smiled and nodded and asked Amrita, 'Do you interest yourself in any particular branch of our work?'

Before Radha could give a satisfactory answer for her, Amrita had said, 'I do not really know, Lady Ram Prashad. Soon I shall be going to England, so I have not very much time to think of other things.'

'Going to England!' cried Lady Ram Prashad; the smile shrunk from her lips, and she threw an offended look towards Tarla.

Radha gave a loud and nervous laugh and said quickly, 'It was what we had at first intended, but now we have changed our plans.'

Tarla said, 'Pappaji had wanted it, but now he also agrees it is not a good idea.'

'It is too far,' Mira explained, 'and what use is there in a girl studying too much?'

Lady Ram Prashad began to look reassured and her smile was almost back to normal, when Amrita said in a loud, clear, innocent voice: 'But of course I am going to England.'

Radha swiftly smiled at Lady Ram Prashad, who was looking disturbed again – these children, said Radha's confidential smile, they are so impetuous – and then she said to Amrita, very sweetly, 'Nonsense, child, you know we had decided no.'

Ignoring the threat behind the honeyed tone, Amrita reasoned, 'But you know I am going, Mamma, it is all decided.'

'We will talk about it some other time,' Tarla auntie said firmly.

'But why?' Amrita protested. 'It is no secret.'

Suddenly Vazir Dayal spoke up from the depth of his armchair. 'Yes it is,' he said in a thick voice, and with his legs still stretched out in front of him. 'It is *our* secret.' And he sniggered, rather indecently. Amrita looked the other way and pretended not to have heard. She was apprehensive as to what he might let out.

Tarla too was apprehensive: she began to fear that he was even more drunk than she had suspected. 'Perhaps a lemon tartlet, Lady Ram Prashad?' she offered.

But Vazir Dayal was not to be overridden. 'You see, Lady Ram Prashad,' he said, without looking at her, 'my niece and I, we are great friends. We have our secrets together, only the two of us and nobody knows about them.' He laid his finger on his lips, then gave another snigger which made shudders run down Tarla's rigid back. 'You have your little plans and we, you see, we have ours. Isn't it?' he shot at Amrita, who desperately tried not to hear.

Lady Ram Prashad had great difficulty in remaining charming; it was only long practice that kept her mouth fixed in the required smile.

'Oh,' Mira said, looking at Vazir Dayal with round eyes and her hand over her mouth, 'I think brother-in-law is not very well today.'

'So many people,' said Lady Ram Prashad, 'have colds nowadays. I think we shall be having a change of weather shortly.'

'Yes, yes,' Radha cried, 'a change of weather we shall surely have!'

'Perhaps you will take one more cup of tea, Lady Ram Prashad,' Tarla pleaded and invitingly lifted the tea-pot.

But Lady Ram Prashad did not wish to expose her social manner to any more strain. She got up, smoothed her sari and said with determination that she thought it was time for her to be going. Radha jumped up, crying, 'No no, it is so early and you have taken nothing!' She snatched a plate and waved it under the other's nose: 'Only one more little cheese pakora!' Tarla still hovered with the tea-pot.

'How I would love to stay,' Lady Ram Prashad said, and continued firmly, 'but unfortunately some ladies are coming to my house, just now they are coming, to discuss the formation of a committee to bring birth control into the rural areas of Assam.'

'How indecent,' said Vazir Dayal quite clearly. So Tarla put the tea-pot down and said, 'Then we must not stop you. We must not interfere with your wonderful work.'

Lady Ram Prashad smiled brilliantly all round – though very tactfully she smiled, not at Vazir Dayal, but over his head – and took her leave. Tarla and a despairing Radha saw her off. 'Ta-ta,' said Vazir Dayal indifferently.

'O Uncle,' said Amrita.

'O Brother,' said Mira.

But before they could say any more, Radha came rushing back into the room, pins falling out of her hair, and swooped down on Amrita: 'Now what is all this?'

'All what?' Amrita said with a feeble attempt at innocence.

Tarla resumed her seat in the middle of the room with dignity and opened the proceedings: 'Please explain yourself,' she called upon her husband.

'I am ill,' he said. 'I have fever.'

Radha had so much to say that she did not know where to start. She sank down on the settee and beat her temples; more hairpins came dropping out. 'You have ruined my life,' she moaned. 'After all the trouble we went to and Lady Ram Prashad so willing . . .'

'So willing for what?' Amrita asked, all her suspicions up again.

'Such a good family,' Radha wailed, 'and now you have ruined it all.'

'Mamma,' Amrita demanded, 'what have you been plotting?'

Radha sank back on the settee, her hand over her eyes: 'Shame and disgrace you have brought into our family.'

'You did not know?' Vazir Dayal said with glee. 'They have been trying to marry you off to the Ram Prashads.'

Radha shot forward again and her hand came down from her eyes. 'We have been working for your good!' she shouted. 'We have been trying to save you from the harm you are doing yourself. One of the best matches in the whole of Delhi we have been arranging for you, and now you have ruined it all . . .'

'Amrita,' Tarla auntie said, 'will you please tell us what it is you and your uncle have been intending?'

'You have your interests,' said Vazir Dayal with another unpleasant snigger, 'and I have mine.'

'What are your interests?' his wife asked patiently.

'At present they are little what-is-her-name here.'

'What?' cried Radha, and jumped up and flapped her arms at him.

'Please do remember that I am ill,' he said and shut his eyes.

'What was that he said, Tarla?' Radha screamed. 'What did he mean?'

'Uncle meant,' Amrita bravely spoke up, 'that he is kindly giving us, that is Hari and me, the money to go to England and be married there.' Her mother let out a scream. 'And I am very grateful to Uncle for helping me when you have all been doing your best to make me unhappy.'

'O no,' Mira protested, 'we all love you.'

'I do not wish to be married to anyone but Hari,' Amrita firmly continued. 'And if Uncle will still give us the money, we will go to England and we will marry there where nobody can hinder us.'

'It is nonsense,' Tarla said. 'Your uncle will not give you one pie even.'

'Yes I will,' Vazir Dayal said, opening his eyes again. 'I will give her all the money she wants.'

'Wait till Pappaji hears of this,' Radha told him.

'That,' he said, 'is what I am looking forward to most'; and he shut his eyes again.

'How I thank God,' said Mira, 'that my Harish is a son. With a son one does not have such troubles.' Discovering that a crumb of chocolate-cake still remained on her upper lip, she flicked it off with her tongue and swallowed it.

22

Radha was in the habit of taking her breakfast in a somewhat haphazard manner. Though it was always a substantial enough breakfast; two or three fried eggs, which she ate out of the pan (mopping up the ghee with a piece of bread), several pieces of toast, a banana or an orange, some sweets and innumerable cups of very milky tea. This breakfast she would carry around the house with her. A bit of it was consumed in the kitchen while she reprimanded the cook; then, munching a piece of toast, she would go and exhort Amrita in her room: after which she made a short trip to the garden to eat a banana and point out to the gardener how he wasted his time and her money; next she would turn to Krishna Sen Gupta, eating his breakfast on the veranda, to draw his attention to several deficiencies in his morals and manners; sipping a cup of tea and from a safe distance, she told the sweeper about dirt and neglect; shouting to the kitchen for another cup of tea, she remembered several points she had omitted to mention to Amrita; and thence back again to the kitchen, where there were still many things which had to be brought to the notice of the cook. In this way, she was fond of observing, she kept her house in order; she was not, she said, one of those ladies who did not know what was going on in their own personal control and if things ran smoothly, they knew whom it was they had to thank. Indeed, she did manage very well to give everybody a good upsetting start to the day; so that there was a general sense of relief when, her breakfast finished, she retired to her bath.

But today she was not her usual self at all. The cook remained undisturbed – and very surprised – in the kitchen, while she sat on the veranda with her frying-pan and her cup of tea and complained to Krishna about the ingratitude of daughters. He was not the audience she could have wished for; he did not seem to be listening very intently, nor did he express the required amount of surprise and horror when she informed him of Amrita's plot with her uncle. Still, she knew that he never did register the expected emotions to the expected degree; it was, she often contemptuously explained to him, his way of showing how much cleverer he was than other people.

She sighed, she moaned, she complained most bitterly, while he remained stolidly eating his breakfast. 'None of you young people has any feelings!' she cried at last; for which he absentmindedly apologized. He was thinking about a letter which he had received that morning from Calcutta. It offered him the Assistant Editorship of what was made out to be a new, but very promising, paper there, and he was seriously thinking the offer over. The salary would probably be lower than his present one, and the work a good deal harder: but he was tempted. For one thing, he was getting tired of students who seemed to be interested in their subject only in so far as it touched on the final examination; for another, he was beginning to get a little homesick: he wanted to see Calcutta, meet his old friends, speak Bengali, eat fish. Then, too, if he went to Calcutta he need not see Amrita any longer, nor be forced to play a part in her affair with Hari.

'But still,' Radha was saying, 'you are quite a sweet boy. Often I wish to myself, why could she not have cared for this one instead of that other?'

He made no comment; he was still thinking how nice it would be to get away.

'At least,' she said, 'you come from a good family and one would not feel disgraced.' She wiped a piece of bread round her frying-pan, swallowed it and licked her fingers.

'You had a letter this morning,' she informed Krishna. 'It was from Calcutta, but it was not from your mother nor from your father. It was written with typewriter.'

'Why did you not open it?' he said.

'What is your opinion of me,' she demanded, 'do you think I have no breeding?'

'Lots of breeding,' he murmured and drank off his cup of tea.

'It is time you had a wife,' she told him. 'Your mother must be asking from Calcutta why do you not bring me home a nice daughter-in-law.'

'No,' he answered with truth. His mother had never spoken to him about such things; he doubted whether she ever thought about them a great deal; she was not like other women.

'I would much like to meet your mother and speak with her,' she said. 'Why do you not ask her to come. I have told you often. My little home is hers.'

The gardener hove into sight and she shouted at him triumphantly: 'I can see you! Now I can see how you waste the time for which I pay you too much money! If I did not watch them,' she told Krishna, 'all day they would lie under the trees and eat my food.'

'Oh, oh,' she began to wail again suddenly, 'but you have not told me what I am to do with my Amrita.'

'Is she my daughter?' he said.

'I will get more sympathy from a dead jackal than from you. You have no heart at all. There is no one to help me, no one even to listen to me with sympathy. A woman is weak, she cannot carry such a burden alone on her own shoulders. He calls this tea, it is like sour coconut water. Not even tea he can make, everything I have to do myself.' She sighed, swallowed a banana in three bites and announced, 'Now I will go and take bath.'

Left alone at last, Krishna drew out his letter and began to read it again; but a few minutes later, Amrita came down, very cautiously, asking, 'She has gone?'

'She is in the bath,' Krishna said and drew out a chair. Amrita sat down; she looked very tired and had circles under her eyes. She wore a white seersucker housecoat which came down to her ankles and made her appear slimmer and slighter than ever. She was looking rather older than her age and very pathetic.

'She has told you?' she asked.

'Yes,' Krishna said wearily; he felt it was too early in the morning to have to endure these confidences.

But she was too intent on her own feelings to notice his. 'So now they know,' she said.

'Yes.' If she had not looked so pathetic, he would have got up and walked away. It struck him that she was really getting rather a bore with her insistent harping on over the same theme. The idea was comforting, for one does not have to love a bore.

'But it makes no difference,' she went on earnestly. 'They may as well know, what does it matter? We shall go. They cannot stop us.'

Suddenly, almost before he realized himself what he was going to say, and seemingly casual, he let out, 'I too shall probably be leaving Delhi.'

It was some time before this sank in. Then she looked at him and said, 'No.'

'What "no"?' he said testily. 'If you can go, surely I can.'

She stared at him with wide-open eyes. 'But why should you ...?'

He shrugged his shoulders and looked annoyed.

'Please do not go,' she pleaded unexpectedly.

'What difference does it make to you?' he asked, with a little laugh. She did not answer but simply continued to look at him with a shocked expression on her face. He played with a tea-spoon, gently clinking it against the cup while he waited, in embarrassment and some suspense, for an answer.

She shook her head. 'I had never thought of it.'

'Never thought of what?'

'That you might one day go from us.'

'You had thought of me as fixed and permanent, like the cistern and the water-tank?'

She smiled wanly and said, 'I have even forgotten how it was before you came. It is only – how long now? – three years, and yet already I have forgotten.'

'After two days,' he said, 'it will be as if I had never been.'

She smiled again and said, 'I do not think so.'

This answer embarrassed him – it looks as if I had been fishing for it, he thought with a slight feeling of shame. He tried to cover it up by saying brusquely, 'And anyway you will not be here; you will be in England.'

'Yes,' she said without conviction and almost absently.

Krishna quite forgot that five minutes ago he had decided that she was a bore and had wished she would stop talking. Now all he wanted was for her to start talking, to answer him fully, completely and at the greatest length. He pressed her, shamelessly, 'If you are not even here, what difference does it make to you if I am here or not?' and waited anxiously for her answer, looking a little away from her and still playing with the tea-spoon.

But whereas before she had been willing to talk in the greatest detail, now, when he wanted her to, she would hardly talk at all. All she said was, 'I had not thought of that,' and got up and moved away, murmuring something about taking a bath.

'Your mother is in the bathroom!' he shouted after her.

Which for some unknown reason made her laugh; but she did not come back.

23

Radha had no difficulty in finding out Hari's address. She borrowed Mira's car and chauffeur, drove up to the radio station, intimidated the officer in the Duty Room, got Hari's address out of him and then drove straight off to his home. She was dressed in her most expensive sari, a metallic-blue Mysore silk with an elaborate border, and wore almost all her jewels: long golden ear-rings set with large stones and dangling nearly to her shoulders, rows of necklaces, her fingers glittering with rings, her arms with bracelets. She looked very splendid, if a trifle barbaric. She leant regally against the pale cream car seat and as they came to Hari's colony wrinkled her nose in disdain at all the evidence of middle-class domestic life, the utility government houses, the children running in the roads, the occasional shops full of cheap household goods, the trunks and charpoys visible through open doors.

When they arrived at Hari's house – one in a row, identical with all the others, and the new distemper already beginning to peel – she waited for the chauffeur to open the door for her and then swept into the house, calling, 'Who is there?'

Only the children came, stared at her, and giggled; and when she commanded them to go and get somebody, went on staring and giggling.

She turned from them and called again, very loudly and sharply, 'Who is there?'

Then Mohini appeared, wringing a wet shirt, and she too stopped and stared, her hands mechanically wringing, the water dripping unheeded down her legs.

Radha said very haughtily, 'I wish to speak with the family of Hari Sahni. I am Mrs Chakravarty,' she added significantly.

Mohini registered no recognition. She went on wringing the shirt, though no more water came out. Suddenly one of the children shot out his hand and pointing at Radha cried, 'Mamma, who is that?'

Radha looked very stern. 'Your children have bad manners,' she informed Mohini, who automatically swung the wet shirt in the direction of the children's ears; they fled, but peeped in from outside.

'Who is it?' came the voice of Hari's mother, and when she got no answer, shouted, 'O Mohini!'

Mohini looked at the visitor and said, 'My mother is praying.'

'She seems to have finished now,' Radha said acidly.

'Yes please,' Mohini said, and turned and ran.

Radha was left alone standing regally in the middle of the room. She tried to ignore the children staring at her, finger in mouth, from the doorway, and looked disdainfully round the room. It was plainly and patchily whitewashed, and the furniture consisted of two charpoys with the strings coming loose, an earthenware water-cooler, two black tin trunks with huge padlocks, and a faded photograph of an old woman, with a garland hung around the frame. 'And such a home my Amrita should marry in,' Radha reflected with disgust.

Hari's mother came waddling in, tugging at her white cotton sari in an attempt to straighten it and, joining her hands in greeting, pleaded, 'Please command me.' Mohini, timid though curious, hovered behind her.

Radha did not return the greeting. She said coldly, 'You are Hari Sahni's mother?'

The old woman bowed her head in assent. 'He is my eldest son,' she said. 'The best son a mother could have.'

Radha drew up sarcastic eyebrows – a finesse she had learnt from Tarla, but one which was lost on her present audience. 'I wish to speak with you about your son and my daughter Amrita.'

The mother and Mohini exchanged glances, puzzled at first but suddenly enlightened, and Mohini began, 'Oh, it is that –' and then stopped herself, clapping her hand before her mouth.

'Please come,' the mother said, and led the way to the other room, the one with the two faded armchairs and the mat on the floor. Radha followed, stepping very carefully and gathering her sari close about her. She did not take her shoes off when she entered the room.

'Send the servant to my daughter's house,' the mother said in an undertone, and Mohini went quickly to chase the servant to Prema's house.

'Please sit,' the mother begged. Radha sat down in one of the armchairs; she sat bolt upright, not touching the sides, and stared at the coloured photograph of Gandhiji on the wall.

'You do us great honour,' the mother said.

Radha ignored this. 'I have come to speak about your son and my daughter,' she announced. 'My car and chauffeur are waiting outside. I have still other places to visit. Lady Ram Prashad Khanna is expecting me for lunch, my time is short.'

'You must not leave my house so soon,' the mother said. 'You must let us honour our guest. Mohini, go prepare with your own hands a sherbet for our guest. Please rest,' she told Radha. 'It is very hot outside and you must sit in comfort.'

'Lady Ram Prashad is expecting me. I must talk with you. It is a very serious business. Your son –'

Mohini handed her a large glass of bright red sherbet. Murmuring that she was not thirsty, Radha took it and began to drink at once; she loved sherbet and this one was very sweet.

'It is to your taste?' the old woman asked anxiously. 'It is sweet enough?' Radha nodded over the rim of the glass. 'Please command us,' the old woman said. 'This is your home. We are only your servants.'

Radha began to relax in her arm-chair. The sherbet had done her good. 'Your house is cool,' she granted graciously, and added, though more softly than before, 'I must speak with you about your son.'

Then Prema arrived. As soon as she saw Radha she was sorry that she had not changed her clothes, but had run across as she was in the old salwar-kamiz she wore at home. But she hoped to make up for the simplicity of her clothes by the dignity of her behaviour. She greeted Radha with joined hands and sat – since both the armchairs were occupied and the mat not quite up to the dignity she hoped to display – on one of the cane stools. Radha returned the greeting with polite condescension.

'My eldest daughter,' the old woman explained. Radha joined her hands again.

'I came running so quickly,' Prema said in her genteelest accent, 'I did not even, please see, change my clothes. I walked here,' she explained to Radha. 'It is very close so I did not need the car.'

Radha said, 'I will take you back in my car if you wish. My chauffeur is with me.' This was unnecessary because Prema had seen both car and chauffeur standing outside.

'Please do not in any way trouble yourself: it is very near and walking is said to be good for the health.'

The old woman nodded her head sagely and remarked, 'Especially for women who have recovered from childbirth. After their forty days they should walk as much as possible.'

'I have even heard,' Radha contributed, 'that they should walk and take exercise before their forty days are finished.'

'It is a modern theory,' Prema said. 'It is my belief that we should follow these modern theories. Our ways are too old-fashioned; they are out of date. Of course one can only be modern if one is educated. Too many of our ladies are not educated.'

'We must go out into the world,' Radha said. 'We ladies have too long been shut up in our homes, now we must go out and work side by side with men. There is much work for us to do. Social work,' she added importantly. 'You are interested in social work?'

Prema nodded. 'It is very suitable for ladies.'

Suddenly Mohini jumped up and ran out. A minute later they heard the sound of hearty, unrestrained vomiting.

'My poor daughter,' the old woman said placidly. 'But it is our lot. She has three already.'

'What month?' Radha asked briskly.

'Only the third. That is why she vomits so much.'

'I was the same with my Amrita,' Radha said. 'Here I would eat, there I would vomit it all out again. It is a difficult time.' And when Mohini came back, looking pleased with herself, she told her, 'You must not lift anything, you must be very careful in this month.'

'She is strong,' said Prema, and Mohini laughed and hid her face in her arm. 'I wish,' Prema went on, 'I had a part of her health. My own health is very weak, always I suffer with my stomach.' She patted it, but did not mention that she spent most of her time lying on the bed eating sweets.

'You are a delicate type,' Radha said, though Prema was as sturdy as her sister, only round instead of square, plumper, softer. 'Like my Amrita, she also is a very delicate type of girl. I worry much about her health.'

'She is very slim,' said Prema.

'You have met her?' Radha took her up at once. 'You have met my child?'

'Once she was at my house. We had tea and conversation together. A very charming girl.'

'A pearl,' said Hari's mother who had not met her.

'I also have seen your son,' Radha said. 'He makes a very good impression. I believe they met at the radio station, isn't it? She met many charming people there; it is a pity that now she must leave from there, but then there are more important things in a girl's life.' She took out a little handkerchief and dabbed it under her nose. 'Yes, a girl grows up, she is educated – my Amrita has had the best education, we sent her to a convent and later to the Lady Wilmot College, she is B.A., a graduate, you must be knowing – perhaps for a little time she does some work only to pass the time away, you understand, and then at last it is time for us to be thinking of a good husband for her.'

'With all daughters it is so,' the old woman said. 'Often it is a great worry.'

'I thank God,' Radha said, 'with my Amrita it is no worry. Of course I should not speak yet, but we are all sisters. One of the first families in Delhi,' she hinted, 'a beautiful fair boy, he has just completed his studies in America, a very highly educated boy, very clever.'

'She deserves all happiness,' the old woman said. 'May she wash the faces of a hundred sons.'

Prema echoed the sentiment and added, sighing, 'When we see our younger brothers and sisters married, then we know our youth has gone. I remember my brother Hari, it seems only yesterday when he was no bigger than Mohini's youngest, and now he too ...'

'A lovely fair girl,' Hari's mother hinted, 'a match worthy of my son.'

Radha's mouth had fallen open and she looked in bewilderment from the mother to the daughter and back again. 'What,' she cried at last, rather forgetting herself, 'you do not mean to say he is being married!'

'We have betrothed him,' Prema said smugly, 'a beautiful fair girl, and from a first-class family.'

'But he has not told you?' cried Radha. 'You do not know? They are wanting to go to England. He has not told you?'

'To England?' Prema said. 'Who is wanting to go to England?'

'But your brother and my Amrita of course, who else!'

'Our Hari cannot go to England, how can he go, he has no money and Suri will not give him. And he is betrothed, how can he go with your daughter, it is not possible.'

'It is true!' Radha cried. 'O, how they deceive us! From my girl's own lips I heard it, they want to go to England and be married there!'

The old woman gave a little scream and called upon her gods and her fathers.

'It is a joke,' Prema said uneasily.

'Joke!' Radha cried. 'Is it a joke when a boy and a girl, both betrothed and from respectable families, want to run away together? Joke? I cannot laugh at such a joke.'

The old woman rocked herself backwards and forwards, her hands clasped over her face. Mohini's eyes had grown quite round and her mouth was open.

'This is how our children repay us,' Radha said. 'All our life we have given for them and now that they no longer need us they trample on our hearts.'

'Ah,' the old woman cried, taking her hands from her face, 'for what sins in our past lives are we so punished?' Her words filled the room, pressed them into silence, and they sat brooding over the ingratitude of children.

At this moment a hawker grinned through the window and offered balloons.

'Get away from here, we have enough troubles!' Prema screamed at him, so vehemently that, contrary to his usual practice, he withdrew at once.

Indignation did her good. She straightened herself up and turning to Radha, said with grim determination: 'You need not worry. Your daughter is safe: she will not go to England with our Hari. You may leave it to us. If an elder sister cannot command her brother, who can? We will marry him, straight away we will marry him, no more delay. At once I will call for the girl's parents and all will be arranged. We will have the wedding next week, finished, he will have a wife and there is an end.'

Radha's eyes brightened, and she asked, 'You can do this?'

'But of course we can do it. We are his family. It is our right to command him.'

'I should have come before,' Radha said. 'These matters can only be arranged when the women of the two families come together. We should have spoken together before.'

'When two families, honourable and respectable, come together,' Prema said, and arranged her dupatta, 'all things will be settled.'

24

And while all this was going on, though poignantly unaware of it, Hari and Amrita sat up in the canteen of the radio station and looked miserable over cold coffee. Hari was looking round towards the door, prepared to pounce with smile and greeting on any acquaintance who might come in. He even kept his hand on the spare chair, ready to draw it out. Only no one came. It was too early for lunch and too late for coffee, and there were only a couple of announcers from the Persian section sitting over in the far corner. They seemed to be talking very wildly and gesticulating a lot; sometimes when he took his eyes off the door, Hari watched them and was fascinated.

Amrita did not notice his abstraction. She was too busy thinking about what she ought to be saying to him; she knew she ought to be urging him about something, but was not quite sure about what. They had to decide on something, she and Hari, on something definite and irrevocable which would – was that what she wanted? – bring them close together and shut their two families out. That, surely, was what she wanted? It was what she had wanted for so long now, and so intensely; this feeling of it-does-not-matter-any-more was probably only due to tiredness: of course it mattered, what else was there if not she and Hari? She looked at him, missed the usual sudden stab of love and thought, how tired I am. Surreptitiously she stroked his little finger with her index finger. He gave a start, then took his eyes off the two Persian announcers and looked at her; it took quite some time before he smiled.

'My poor one,' she smiled back at him. 'We are both so nervous.'

He considered this for a while, then nodded with a grave expression on his face. 'Yes, nervous,' he said. 'My nerves are bad.'

'It is the strain,' she said.

'Strain?'

'Of not knowing what to do or what is to happen next.'

He sighed deeply and said, 'That is true.' He tried not to think of Sushila and the Anand family.

'Please Hari,' she said, 'now we must decide, we cannot go on like this.'

'Yes,' he said vaguely and without hope. *Decide*; always nowadays from all sides it was *decide*; always there was that feeling of unease, preventing him from being happy and comfortable. When all he asked was, to sit with his friends in the coffee-house, to go to the cinema, to lie on his charpoy in the courtyard at home, staring up into the sky and thinking about being in love with Amrita. But . . . 'Yes,' he said, 'we must decide.'

The word 'decide' made her no happier either. It was like spinning a coin and not knowing which side to hope for. In a way it was only the residual impetus of the desire of many weeks before that kept her sitting there talking to him; instead of leaving it all, giving up and going home to, yes, to sleep.

Two more people came in. Hari looked at them eagerly but he did not know them; they were two fat Arabs who sat down and ordered lunch. Now Hari caught the smell of food and knew at once that he was hungry.

Making a great effort to collect herself, Amrita fastened on to the notion 'England' and said, 'We must go to England,' because that was what had once been decided. At least it was something definite, so she said, 'We must make our arrangements to go to England.'

He nodded. He did not think this a suitable moment to announce his hunger, though he wanted very much to eat. The smell of food insidiously wound itself around his appetite; he inhaled deeply as if by smelling more he might begin to taste.

'All we really have to do,' Amrita was saying, 'is book our tickets. What else is there?'

'What else,' he echoed, trying to identify the smell: could it be oven-baked fish, his favourite dish?

'Of course, we must get passports,' she said in a businesslike manner, 'and there are some injections. But I do not think we shall have much trouble with them. They are only' – and she used a phrase of which her grandfather had always been fond – 'a matter of routine.'

'Yes,' he said. As casually as he could, he brought his elbow on to the table so as to steal a quick look at his wrist-watch. Quarter to one! No wonder he was feeling hungry. The Arabs were by this time well away, eating very rapidly and darting with their forks from one subsidiary dish into the other. He could see now that it was oven-baked fish they were eating, with oven-baked bread and spiced vegetables and all the accompanying pickles; he could hear them relish it even from this distance.

'So –' she said, and 'So –' he said, and they looked at one another, thinking of different things.

'My little Amrita,' he said after a while, striking out on a new line, 'are you all right in your health?'

'My health?'

'I am very worried about you,' he said. 'I do not think you are looking after yourself well. Not at all well. I am worried, yes worried.' And he nodded and looked worried.

'O Hari,' she said, quite touched.

'For instance, I notice you are not eating enough. You must eat,' he said firmly. 'I will see to it myself. Just see' – he looked at his wrist-watch – 'it is ten to one and you have not yet eaten your lunch. Now at once I will order for you. I think today there is oven-baked fish, that is very good for the health, it will make you strong almost at once. What will you like to have with it?'

She let him order, which he did in his usual careful, almost anxious, manner. The canteen was quite full by now and he was constantly turning round and greeting his many acquaintances. Amrita was feeling a little more relaxed and she found Hari's solicitude very pleasant, the more pleasant because it was so novel and unexpected; it was good to have him take the initiative, relieved her of some strain. So she leant back a little in her chair and said, 'What do you suggest we do then, Hari?' in a soft yielding voice.

He was turned away from her, waving at somebody, and did not hear. She had to repeat the question in a slightly louder voice. He turned back to her, looking puzzled: 'Do?'

She shut her eyes and said, 'You are thinking only of your oven-baked fish,' and was promptly surprised at herself.

'No no,' he protested, 'it is of you I am thinking.'

And then the food came and he said, 'And now you will eat and at once you will feel happier,' which she did not bother to dispute.

25

Mrs Anand was inclined to be difficult. Mr Anand also looked worried.

'Such a short time,' he murmured, gnawing his lip.

'It is not possible,' his wife said with decision.

But Prema was firm; it must be possible was her answer, implicit in her silence to their interjections. Beneath the softer inflections of politeness, her voice was iron: 'It is better so. We have been speaking about it, and it is better so.'

'But why, why?' Mr Anand pleaded.

'Impossible,' Mrs Anand repeated.

Prema called to her servant: 'Pritam! Bring Coca-Cola quickly!' She turned to her visitors. 'You will take Coca-Cola?'

'It is impossible,' Mrs Anand said. 'We cannot arrange in such a short time. And why should it be necessary? We had agreed – a year they can wait, they are both so young.'

A polite little smile appeared on Prema's lips: it was a smile of patient negation. 'It is better so,' she repeated, and pointedly gave no other reason. Her silence made the position very clear: you, it plainly told the Anands, are from the girl's side, therefore it is your duty to do as we say.

Mrs Anand understood only too well, and it made her furious. She sat with a very straight back in Prema's courtyard, and her eyes glittered. 'It is not better,' she replied. 'We cannot – how can we? – arrange in such a short time celebrations suitable for the marriage of our eldest daughter. We would be shamed everywhere.'

Her husband nodded in gloomy agreement. Prema only rearranged her dupatta in a more becoming fashion.

'It is impossible,' Mrs Anand said.

'Very difficult,' Mr Anand murmured.

'Not very difficult,' Mrs Anand spoke out clearly, 'but impossible.'

Pritam came back with two bottles of Coca-Cola which he presented to the visitors. They both began to suck their straws immediately, Mr Anand humped up and depressed, she upright and very determined.

Prema softened a little. 'It is not good to make young people wait too long,' she said, by way of explanation, though in a rather take-it-or-leave-it manner.

'In our time we waited,' Mrs Anand took her up immediately, 'till our families thought it fit that we should be married and all the arrangements were well completed.'

'In our time,' Prema answered as promptly, 'things were different. We were betrothed as children and there were always many years to wait; a few months did not make any difference then.'

'And what difference do they make now?' Mrs Anand said keenly, leaning forward a little.

But Prema evaded the question. 'We are thinking only of the children. They should not be made to wait too long.' And she called briskly to Pritam to take away the empty Coca-Cola bottles.

Hari's mother came walking into the courtyard, greeting the visitors with joined hands and a wide smile. She sat down, smiling, with her naked feet tucked under her, and fanned herself with a palm-leaf.

'How hot it is,' she said, fanning away. 'Will the cold season never come to us this year?'

But Mrs Anand was by this time in no mood to talk politely about the weather. She turned to the old woman and urged: 'To arrange such an important occasion in such a hurry – it is bad, it will surely not bring good luck to the children.'

The mother sighed and said, 'May the great God protect them and give them all blessing.'

Mrs Anand pressed her point: 'How can we ask God to protect them when we ourselves fail to do our duty by them and do not give them the celebrations of which they are worthy.'

'It is the business of the girl's family,' Prema dropped in, 'to see that the celebrations are worthy. You cannot accuse us if they are unworthy.'

Mr Anand watched his wife apprehensively. But though she turned on Prema with angry eyes, her words were under control: 'Our daughter would never need to be ashamed if the arrangements for her wedding were only in the hands of her own family. To her grandchildren even she could boast of the greatness of the day. But how can we – within a week – what can we do within a week? It is not reasonable, it cannot be asked of us.'

Prema only shrugged her shoulders, but the old woman, still smiling, still fanning, attempted to soothe: 'Of course everything will be done to make the celebrations great and memorable, we know it, we know what to expect of Sushila's family; and even though the time is not so much.'

'It is no time at all,' Mrs Anand took her up. 'A week is nothing when months are wanted.'

'It will be too difficult,' Mr Anand murmured.

'Sometimes,' the old woman said calmly, 'things are done better in a short time than in more time. When we have more time, we say "tomorrow, we will do it tomorrow, there is enough time", but then suddenly the day is upon us and we have done nothing, because always we have been saying "tomorrow". But when there is only a little time, there is no "tomorrow" and every minute of the day the work is done.'

'With us,' Mrs Anand said, all dignity, 'the work would be done every minute even if we have one year for our preparations. We would never neglect our daughter's honour.'

'We know it well!' the old woman cried: 'And because we know it, that is why we can ask you to make all things ready within a shorter time. We know you will never fail us, and because it is necessary to have the wedding earlier –'

'Why!' Mrs Anand then cried, 'but why is it necessary? This you have not told us and this we want to hear!'

The old woman answered smoothly and at once, 'Is it not right for two beautiful young people to be joined and united as quickly as possible? Why make them suffer with delay? I will tell you the truth: our Hari –'

'Yes please?' Mrs Anand said, listening intently.

'– came to us, and tears were in his eyes and he said, "I love Sushila who is to be my wife so much I cannot wait till the time that has been fixed for our marriage; please arrange it for tomorrow." We said, "Tomorrow, how can we do it tomorrow, have you no thought for the girl's family?" but he cried and wept and begged of us so much, we then thought and deliberated and talked among ourselves until we decided as we have told you. That is the reason why we have asked you to change your plans for us, if it is not too much inconvenience, only to save suffering to the poor young people. Pritam!' she called, 'one glass water!'

'One glass water for Mataji!' Prema shouted.

Mrs Anand frankly looked her unbelief. Her husband scratched his head, glanced at his wife, scratched again and said, 'So that is it, that is it.'

'Yes,' the old woman said, without blinking, 'that is our reason,' and she raised the glass of water to her lips.

26

When Hari came to his home in the evening, he found only Mohini and the children there. The children at once clung to his legs and tried to climb on to his shoulders and he automatically patted and pinched them. Mohini was squatting by the water-tap in the courtyard, washing dishes and groaning to herself. 'God, great God,' she said, and made vomiting noises in her throat. Hari did not notice her distress; he only noticed that the place was uncommonly empty and asked, 'Where has everybody gone?' tickling the youngest child under the ribs.

Mohini wiped her arm, bared to the elbow, over her forehead; she held a swab in one hand and with the other grasped a pot. 'I feel so bad,' she groaned, and repeated the vomiting noise. This time Hari noticed and at once turned sympathetic eyes on her. 'You are ill? And they have left you alone?'

'Who cares about me?' she wailed, then immediately afterwards laughed at herself and began vigorously to scrub the pot. 'What can they do? It is nature, no one can help me,' she said laughing.

Hari did not understand but he assumed that she was, after all, all right, so at once he turned to another topic: 'What is for my dinner?'

As he sat eating in the courtyard, Mohini informed him from the kitchen, 'Mataji bought a piece of fish for you this morning. The fishman came, it was the other one, not the one who always comes, and he wanted one rupee for the fish but we soon told him and of course he gave it for fourteen annas. How they try to cheat us, it is good that we know the right price of things.'

'Where is it?' Hari asked, looking up for the first time from his food. The children sat solemnly in a row, watching him eat.

'Mataji gave it to Babla,' Mohini answered placidly.

Hari kept his hand suspended between his bowl and his mouth, vegetable falling out of the piece of chapati he was holding. It was not that he grudged the fish to his younger brother, but it was so unprecedented that Babla should have the extra titbit instead of himself.

'Babla ate the fish!' the children cried. 'How happy he was!'

'How he wiped his mouth after!' Mohini laughed, and laughed again at the recollection of it, as she went back to the tap and dirty dishes.

Hari was still puzzled, but he shrugged his shoulders and said, scooping up more vegetable, 'It is better so. I had fish today, oven-baked fish I had. And Babla needs it more, he is only a boy, he is growing.'

'Do you not want to know why Mataji gave it to him?' Mohini asked from the tap, ready to burst out laughing.

'Why?' Hari asked innocently.

But instead of laughing, she suddenly became very serious and goggled at Hari with round eyes. 'O Brother,' she said in a scared voice, 'they are all so angry with you.'

The children too began to look scared. They stared at Hari with huge black eyes and their front teeth bit into their lower lips.

'Angry with me?' Hari asked incredulously.

'You do not know what has happened,' she said, 'you do not know who was here today –' and she stopped and looked as if she did not know whether to laugh or be scared.

The children jumped up and danced round Hari and cried, 'In a big car she came, with a driver!'

'Who came?' Hari asked looking at Mohini, who only nodded in confirmation.

'And the bangles she wore,' the children cried, 'and all round her neck and in her ears and her sari was real gold and silver! She was a queen, Mamma no? She was a queen, Sita she was, like in the song!' and they began to sing.

'Quiet now,' Mohini shouted, recollecting herself, 'quiet! You will be put in the oven to bake!' But they were so excited, she had to scream louder, 'The oven for you!' and make as if to seize them before they would subside.

'What is it they are saying?' Hari appealed. 'Who was it came today in a gold sari?'

'It was not gold,' Mohini corrected, 'it was blue, only the border was gold and the pallu. Oh, how much money it must have cost, two months' salary it must have been.'

'But who?' Hari insisted.

Mohini goggled at him again and tittered behind her hand. 'O Brother,' she said, tittering.

'Queen Sita!' the children cried, for they could stand it no longer, and began to sing again.

Mohini scrambled to her feet and swung out right and left with her swab. The children dodged skilfully.

'Please sit quiet now,' Hari appealed, 'and tell me who it was came.'

Mohini gave up the pursuit and only shook the swab at the children, who looked out, one behind the other, from the open door of the living-room.

'They are so angry with you,' Mohini said, 'Mataji and sister.'

'But who – ?' Hari implored.

'Your Memsahib –' Mohini began, then stopped to look at him out of the corner of her eye, her mouth twitching.

'Amrita?' Hari cried.

'The Mother,' Mohini said, frankly bursting into laughter. 'She sat in the room and drank sherbet.'

'Two sherbets she drank!' the children cried from behind the door.

'Here?' Hari asked incredulously.

'But what – ?'

'She told us everything,' Mohini said, half mournfully half triumphantly. 'How angry Sister was, and Mataji. And now you are to be married next week, they sent for the Anands, just now they are talking in Sister's house . . .'

Hari got to his feet and cried, 'But what did she tell?'

'Everything,' Mohini replied simply.

'What "everything"?' he cried even louder.

'You and this Memsahib, how you are going to England together . . . she told it, and how angry Sister –'

'She said that? She said . . . ?'

'That you are going to England.'

'I?'

'You and this Memsahib of yours.'

Hari sat down on a charpoy and ran his fingers through his hair. The movement only lifted the oiled strands, then left them as sleek as before. 'It is a lie,' he said, more to himself than to Mohini.

'A lie?' she caught him up at once. 'You are not going? It is all a lie?'

He did not answer; could not answer, for he did not know himself whether it was true or not, whether he meant to go to England or not. He knew he had talked about it with Amrita, or rather had heard her talking to him about it, but whether he had really ever had any serious intentions about it, he did not know. At any rate, it seemed fantastic now that anyone could have taken him seriously and could be taking action against him because of it. It was like being punished for making up an innocent cinema-fantasy.

'It is all a lie then?' Mohini pressed him.

He evaded the question by asking one of his own instead. 'They are all at Sister's house?'

'Yes,' Mohini answered and then remembered: 'You are to go there, an hour ago the servant came to say you are to come when you get home.'

'What, before eating dinner?'

'You have eaten it now,' she pointed out.

Once out in the street, Hari did not turn in the direction of Prema's house. He told himself that he wanted to eat a pan first, and though there was a panwala just opposite the house, he made straight for the main bazaar; there I will get a better pan, he explained to himself.

He walked along, absent-mindedly picking bits of vegetable out of his teeth. He was thinking as hard as he could, trying to draw some definite strand out of the tangled skein of thoughts lodged in his head. But the trouble was, as always, that he did not know what strand it was he wanted to pull out. Prema angry, his mother angry, everybody angry – that was the worst; he thought about that first, that was what made him most unhappy. But then he remembered that Mohini had said he was to be married next week: that also was very bad. Amrita, what would she say? He passed P. L. Shastri's Private College, Girls and Boys Separate, Preparation for B.A. (Final), and looked automatically at the little group of girl-students gathered outside. They were all very plain, with thick waists and pigtails; only one drew his attention, a smiling girl, healthy and well-developed, wavy strands of hair escaping from her pigtail. She reminded him of – yes, of course, of Sushila; only Sushila was prettier. Suddenly all his body flushed as he thought, Sushila, next week, and at once he looked back at the girl – she too was slyly looking after him, but when he turned she swung away abruptly and laughed and talked the loudest among her companions – he looked back to remind himself once more of rounded breasts and strong hips. Next week, he thought, and his heart leapt and his body ached with anticipation.

He was walking in the middle of the road, and a boy wobbling on a bicycle with his little brother at the back and his little sister in front nearly ran into him, but he did not even notice. He could think of nothing except of next week and sturdy, shapely legs outlined against a silken salwar. And it was only when he turned into the street of the bazaar that he remembered Amrita, and his family sitting angrily in Prema's house.

He stopped at a panwala's and gloomily asked for a pan with

cardamoms and aniseed. It was the conjunction of the two thoughts, his family and Amrita, that was so unpleasant. The anger of his family could be wiped out and converted into love and tears and forgiveness by a simple submission and confession of error; all then would be well and the marriage would take place smoothly, happily and amid rejoicing. It was only – he shifted his pan from the left cheek to the right – only when he thought of Amrita that the scene became clouded over. Was he to go to her and say, forgive me, I cannot go with you to England, next week I am to be married? He could imagine the scene – not as between himself and Amrita, but between two plump shadowy figures with garlands round their necks sitting in a jasmine-bower; his head was bowed, she stared dry-eyed into the distance; there was silence except for his heavy sighs; then she began to sing, very low and sad, a song of sorrow and separation.

His eyes now were moist with tears, and he walked along chewing his pan and thinking of the inevitable, the fate-ordained ending to his great love. He framed the sentences – our souls are as one – the cruel world tears us asunder – and stepped out of the way of two pariah-dogs snuffling around the Muslim meat-stall. He was to be sacrificed in marriage and the day that should have been full of rejoicing would be the unhappiest of his life, for he would think of nothing but Amrita, the lost ... But suddenly he visualized thick black lashes lowered over coy eyes, a surge of hair falling forward over a rounded cheek ... how thin Amrita was getting, it occurred to him, she looked so thin and weak always, not like a fresh young girl should look, not like – the strength of her, the youth of her, the bursting bud, the promise; next week, and weakness flowed into his thighs as he turned the corner by the huge poster advertising a cure for impotency, with a picture of the advertiser in rimless spectacles.

He was going towards his own house, not Prema's, but when he let himself notice this he explained to himself that he was tired now and wanted to sleep. And anyway, what was the point of talking now, it was all settled, he would sacrifice himself to the wishes of his family.

When he got home Mohini, serving dinner to her husband, shouted, 'Again Sister has sent the servant to ask for you, where have you been?' and her husband threw him a look of pity.

But Hari only lay down on his charpoy, face downwards. Soon he was fast asleep.

27

A curious feeling of calm hovered about the house. At first Amrita could not understand the cause of it until suddenly she realized that, of course, it was her mother. Radha had become smooth and content. She no longer rushed about the house in a flurry of rebuke nor, every time she looked at Amrita, did she burst out into a diatribe on the ingratitude of daughters. Instead she sat on the sofa in the living-room, reading the newspaper with her shoes off and quietly smiling to herself. It seemed to Amrita almost sinister, this sudden change; from time to time she crept to the door of the living-room and apprehensively peeped inside at her smiling mother.

During one of these peeps Radha looked up and caught Amrita's eye; she smiled a bit more and patted the sofa, saying, 'You come and sit here with me, my pet, it is cooler here.'

Amrita advanced slowly, as if fascinated in spite of herself. 'Come,' Radha said, moving over a little, and then, 'Shall Gian bring you some tea or a sherbet, my love?'

Amrita shook her head and kept quite still when Radha stroked the hair back from her forehead.

'My little one,' said the mother, stroking, 'how pretty you are,' and Amrita felt like a small girl again, dependent on her mother and secure near to her. She edged closer and put her head on Radha's shoulder. 'My little star,' Radha said, 'my bird,' playing with Amrita's hair. Amrita gave a little sigh; she sensed danger in the sudden change, but for the moment ignored it and let herself feel secure and comfortable.

'Shall I read to you from the newspaper, my little heart?' Radha asked. 'Would you like it? What shall I do for you?'

'Only let me sit here with you, Mamma, and rest,' Amrita murmured.

'Rest, my beauty. Rest, rest, rest,' she crooned, her arm about Amrita, softly rocking. Amrita shut her eyes and let herself be rocked. After a while she said with her eyes still shut, 'Mamma . . .'

'My beauty, my star, my life,' Radha crooned.

'Mamma, you are not – ?' and she opened her eyes to look up at her mother. Radha's cheek was close above her, wrinkled and darkened with age and very soft.

'Not what, my only one?' Radha said comfortably.

'You are not,' Amrita went on, looking very intently up at her mother, 'making any arrangements – ?'

'Arrangements, my sweetest?'

'With Lady Ram Prashad or anybody?'

Radha went right on rocking, crooning under her breath, 'My child, God's gift to me,' and then answered smoothly, 'No, my love, I will do nothing that displeases you.'

Amrita lifted her head from her mother's shoulder and said, 'Because, you see, Mamma, even if you do, it will be no good, because I am going to marry Hari. We will go away to England together.'

'Rest now, sweetest,' Radha murmured; and then Krishna Sen Gupta appeared in the doorway and stood there looking at them both.

'How charming,' he said, 'Mother and Daughter.'

'Go away,' Radha cried, 'why must you always come between us? Can you not leave us alone together for one moment?'

He stepped into the room, saying, 'But you have no secrets from me.' Amrita disengaged herself from her mother's encircling arm and tidied her hair.

'I went to the kitchen to find Gian,' Krishna said, 'and do you think he was there?'

'Naturally not,' Radha answered with dignity, 'he has gone to bazaar. He has other work except only to wait on you.'

Krishna sat down in an arm-chair and said, 'Then when he comes back, please tell him to go and get my laundry back.'

'Why do you want your laundry early?' Radha asked; and promptly supplied her own answer: 'Only so as to cause trouble to others.'

'That too,' he said. 'But also because I am going away on Saturday.

'Oh,' said Radha, taking it in, 'so you are going away.' Amrita said nothing, only looked down at her toe while she edged it in a circle round the floor.

'You need not be too apprehensive,' said Krishna, 'I shall be back.'

'You think it matters to me if you come back or not?' Radha said, throwing back her head. 'Tomorrow you can go if you wish, what am I saying, today even; with my own hands I will pack for you your two or three miserable little pieces of shirt.'

'Is it,' Amrita suddenly asked in a small voice, 'something to do with this work you were speaking of in Calcutta?'

'I am going to see about it.'

'Going to see about what?' Radha asked.

'Krishna has had work on a magazine offered to him in Calcutta,' Amrita answered.

Radha sat bolt upright on the sofa and cried, 'What, you are leaving us for ever?' Amrita again drew her toe round in circles and looked at it.

'If I find on this visit that the work suits me, then yes.'

There was a short pause, during which Amrita looked at her toe and Krishna, after giving her a quick curious glance, looked intently away from her. The first sound to be heard was Radha sniffling. Both looked at her in some surprise; which made her sniffle more loudly and bring out her handkerchief from the pocket of her pink morning-gown and dab it against her eyes.

'What is the matter, Mamma?'

'That he should leave us,' she said wetly, dabbing, 'now after he has lived with us so long ...'

'Oh,' said Krishna, 'you will soon find another lodger.'

'Do not speak like that,' she said, but without spirit. 'You have become like a son to me; like a son ...'

Krishna looked embarrassed; he cleared his throat and began to rummage about in his pockets as if he were searching for something.

'Even the way you tease me I shall miss,' she elaborated. 'I know you never mean anything bad. O, how lonely we shall be without you!'

'Yes,' Amrita said in a very low voice, 'we shall miss you.'

'Thank you,' he said, hoping to sound elegantly amused, but merely sounding hoarse.

Radha heaved a shattering sigh and said, 'It will be like a tomb here without you, only we two – the thought of it is terrible. You are my son, how can I bear to lose my son? Gian!' she shouted. 'Gian!' and explained, 'Let him bring tea. I must drink a cup of tea else I cannot support this news.'

Gian appeared and Radha insisted that they all drink tea. 'And you can bring those jalebis I bought yesterday, we will eat them now.'

'You are celebrating?' Krishna asked her, and Amrita gave a little laugh and said, 'Yes, Mamma, it really looks as if you are celebrating Krishna going away.'

'I am doing him honour,' Radha replied sharply. 'If the idiot had any breeding or manners he would realize it. Only you have no breeding and no manners,' she told him, 'so what can I do for you?'

'Now I feel better,' he said; 'now you are yourself again.'

'You have written to this magazine to accept?' Amrita asked.

'I have written to say that I will come and speak with them,' he answered. 'I shall go just for a few days –'

'Just for a few days!' Radha cried. 'You are spending so much money for your ticket to Calcutta only for a few days?'

'It cannot be helped,' he said, stirring his tea and lifting with his spoon the sugar at the bottom, 'and naturally I am going third class, so it will not come too expensive.'

Radha put down the jalebi into which she had been about to bite, and there was a short pause. Then she said, a little uncomfortably, 'You are joking.'

'How joking?'

'You cannot go third class.'

'Why can I not go third class?'

She made a vague gesture, picked up the jalebi and put it down again. 'It is not right for a gentleman to go third class. For a professor at a College. What will you do if any of your students see you, can you tell me that?'

'Die of shame,' Krishna gravely answered.

'Oh,' she said, 'there is no use in talking with you. You will never understand what it means to be a gentleman and what are the duties of a gentleman. Now I am really happy you are going; let your mother see what she can do with you. This I know: she will often ask herself, is it for this we have spent so much money on his education? Can it be that this boy with his bad manners is England-returned?'

'How perfectly you understand my mother,' he said.

'What is so bad about going third class?' Amrita asked.

'It is like going in the 1/4 seats in the cinema,' her mother answered decisively.

'Well,' Amrita said, throwing down the challenge out of habit, 'when Hari and I go to England we too will be going in the cheapest class.'

'Do not,' Radha told Krishna, 'expect us to see you off at the station if you are really going by third class.'

Krishna was surprised; so was Amrita, and she felt rather foolish, having so audaciously thrown down her challenge only to see her mother politely walking round it. Krishna looked at her and when their eyes met, they both hastily drank tea.

'I have eaten so many jalebis,' Radha said, 'now I will have no appetite for my lunch. Amrita, you will be out for lunch?'

Again Krishna was surprised. Something had happened to Radha; or, more likely, had been made to happen by her.

'No,' Amrita said, 'today I have no duty.'

Radha frowned, almost imperceptibly: perceptible, though, to Amrita and Krishna, who knew her too well. 'What is the matter?' Amrita asked, a little hurt. 'I shall be in your way?'

Radha pretended to be hurt in her turn: 'That is not a question to ask your mother.'

'Yes it is if the mother pulls faces when she hears her daughter will be home for lunch. Well,' she sulked, 'I *am* going out then. I will go and see Mira auntie, she at least will be happy to have me.'

This plan obviously suited Radha, for she looked smug and content; though she made a point of protesting, 'Why should you go out, where is the sense in it? Can you not stay one day with your mother?' But Amrita now was set on going.

When she and Krishna had both gone, Radha went to her room to change. She put on a plum-coloured sari, making it fit tightly over her burgeoning hips and fastening it at the shoulder with a large brooch in the shape of a sitar. She looked at herself in the full-length mirror, front and as much as she could of the back, and having looked, hummed a religious tune very gaily to herself. On her way out, she stopped at the dressing-table and dabbed a little scent behind her ears. Then she made her way to the kitchen to lift the lids from the pots and sniff inside; what she smelt was very pleasing to her, but nevertheless she did not neglect to rebuke Gian. 'A hundred times I have shown you how to make kofta curry and still you do not know! You have forgotten, I am sure, the lime?' But he had not forgotten and she knew he had not.

Soon a car drew up and Tarla stepped out of it. She carried a briefcase under her arm; very important papers, she explained, she needed them for a meeting of the All India Advancement of Literacy for Married Women Committee in the afternoon. The chauffeur quietly disappeared into the kitchen, to sit with Gian and drink warmed-up tea-leaves.

'Where is Amrita?' Tarla asked briskly, settling herself on the sofa in the living-room.

'I have sent her to Mira,' Radha said. 'Was it not clever of me? I wanted to talk with you alone.'

'Why?' demanded Tarla shortly; she sat very upright and one hand was laid on her briefcase.

'I have such news for you,' Radha said, and giggled and clasped her hands before her. 'Wait till you hear!'

'Well?'

'No, wait, first we will have lunch, I will tell you when we are having lunch. We are having fried rice and kofta curry and black dal –'

Tarla made a wry face and said, 'I had hoped you would make only a little salad and buttermilk. How to eat so much in this heat? It is bad enough that I have to go through Husband's lunches at home, I had hoped that when I come to you . . .'

Radha looked very disappointed. 'But kofta curry, your favourite – whatever one does for you,' she sulked, 'always it is wrong. Always you have something to grumble over, really I will never again try to please you.'

Tarla put a withered hand to her brow and said wearily, 'Please, if you could avoid a quarrel, I have such a headache.'

Radha pouted and played with her bracelets; Tarla shut her eyes, still sitting upright and her hand on the briefcase.

In the end Radha relented. 'You want to lie down?' she asked. To this her sister assented, and they went to Radha's bedroom.

The bed was covered with a white counterpane which had been washed too often, so that only half the embroidery was left. Pairs of shoes were ranged very neatly side by side under the bed, and three saris folded over one hanger were hung high up on the side of the wardrobe. On the little table next to the bed lay a copy of the *Gita* and on top of the wardrobe several issues of *True Story*.

Radha turned down the counterpane and Tarla stretched herself out on the bed, with her briefcase still next to her and her legs and toes stretched out very straight in front of her. Having positively refused to have her temples rubbed with eau-de-cologne, she said, 'What was it you wished to tell me?'

'Please do not disturb yourself now over such matters. You must take complete rest.'

A very straight vertical frown became grooved above Tarla's thin nose. 'Do not make an unnecessary fuss,' she said. 'If you have something to tell me, then tell it.'

Radha smiled and said, 'I did not know, Tarla, that you could be so curious.' But as she was more anxious to tell than Tarla to hear, she went on again immediately, 'Everything is all right now. It is all settled. Nothing more can happen between my Amrita and this boy. Only think, Tarla, he is betrothed, he has been betrothed all this time that we have been worrying ourselves, and now his family will make his marriage without delay. They promised it to me.'

'You have met them?'

'I went to see them. They were as much distressed by this connection as we were. They are really very respectable people, simple people of course, not our class, but really very respectable. They realize fully that a connection with our family would be quite out of the question; they are very well aware of their place in life. They treated me with great respect. How are you feeling now?'

'Better.'

'Shall I tell Gian to bring lunch in here on a tray?'

'No,' said Tarla, 'really I do not feel any hunger at all. But will the boy do as his family tell him?'

'Of course,' Radha replied without hesitation. 'You know how it is among these people; their family ties are very strong, stronger than among us, the educated ...'

'It is a great tragedy,' Tarla said, opening her eyes. 'When I think of all the suffering within these narrow family circles; the women are like slaves –'

'The women I saw,' Radha interrupted, 'did not seem like slaves.'

'It is these family ties,' Tarla said, 'that we have principally to fight against. It is they who retard all our progress.'

'Nonsense!' Radha cried vigorously; Tarla winced and brought her hand up to her head, a gesture which her sister ignored. 'Nonsense!' she cried again. 'I think they do a lot of good. How else would we have settled this affair? You see how we had to rely on the boy's family to end it; we ourselves, I am ashamed to say it, were powerless; yes powerless. Even I, the mother, even Pappaji himself, what could we do? But you see, the boy's family had only to come and all was well. I think such a system is very good, and I am only sorry that it is lost among us.'

'Your words show,' Tarla said in a very quiet, patient, suffering voice, 'how short-sighted and selfish you are in your views. Because it settles your own particular difficulty, you recommend this evil; you give no thought to the suffering and privation it brings on the individual members of this tight tyrannical group –'

'Oh!' shouted Radha, 'now I should start thinking of the sufferings of that boy because he has lost my Amrita?'

'Always the selfish view,' Tarla repeated in the same tone as before, 'always it is only your own problem you can think of.'

'I should think of this boy, is it, and his problem? I should go to him and tell him, here, please take my Amrita, please take her away and marry her!'

'As always you miss the point,' Tarla said wearily.

'I miss the point!' Radha said with spirit. 'It is I who miss the point! I am tired of you, always you know better than everybody else, always you call everybody else fool, and when you have lost an argument you say the other person has missed the point!'

'Pappaji is quite right,' Tarla said. 'It is doubtful if you are an adult at all.'

'Those are your words!' Radha cried. 'Pappaji would never say such a thing of me. He has a very high regard for me.'

Tarla only gave a sarcastic laugh and kept her eyes shut.

'I know he has!' Radha cried. 'It is only you who are malicious and try to turn his thoughts against me. Well, I will tell you, you will never succeed, because he loves me too much, both me and my daughter Amrita. He is very proud of my Amrita, and he is very glad that I have given him this grandchild. Not *all* his daughters have given him such a gift.'

'Always you come back to the same thing,' Tarla said. 'It is the only thing you know to bring up against me.'

'There are many other things I could bring up against you if I cared to, but I am too good-natured to say them and that is fortunate for you. And now,' she said, getting up from the bed on which she had been sitting, 'I will eat my lunch, I do not care what you will do. This is my house and I can do what I like in it.' And she marched out and told Gian that Memsahib was sick and would not eat, but to take out lunch for herself.

She sat down at the table in the dining-room; she was very upset, and her bosom heaved up and down. Angrily she thrust aside the fork and spoon which had been laid for Tarla, and shouted to Gian, what was he doing, would she have to wait till sunset for her lunch? He came hurrying in with the dishes, and she piled her plate with rice and flooded it with curry. She began to eat, heartily but with some absence of mind, for she was alert to sounds from the bedroom. She was expecting angry footsteps, the chauffeur summoned, then the sound of the car starting; but nothing happened: Tarla did not stir. She ate a few more spoonfuls of rice, stopped, and let the spoon rest on the plate; with resolution then, she went to the bedroom and looked in, to see Tarla still stretched out as before, very stiff and rigid on the bed, with her eyes shut.

'Your headache is better?' she demanded, almost commanded.

'Do you think my head has been cured by your shouting?'

'You will eat something at least,' Radha said, frowning, and stepped further into the room.

'Something light,' Tarla conceded, and at once Gian was shouted for.

While Tarla lay sipping buttermilk on the bed, Radha sat at its foot and very heartily tucked into her plate of rice and curry. 'It is a pity,' she said, 'you are not well. This is really excellent kofta. Gian does very well when I watch over him every minute.'

'So you believe it is all settled?' Tarla asked after a while.

Radha had her mouth full just then, but she answered as soon as she could. 'I have his mother's and his elder sister's word for it; I do not think we need worry any further. And Lady Ram Prashad's son is, I understand, coming home next month ...'

'You are still thinking of that?' Tarla was surprised.

'Why not?' Radha demanded. 'Lady Ram Prashad knows very well a daughter-in-law like my Amrita she cannot find every day.'

'I should have thought that if everything is settled, as you say, and there is no danger from this boy, then there is no need any more to marry the poor girl off in such a hurry.'

Radha put her empty plate on the dressing-table and said complacently, 'It is always safer. And such an excellent match also – it is a very good chance for us.'

'Pappaji still wishes her to go to England.'

Radha shrugged her shoulders. 'You understand how it is. Pappaji wants our Amrita to have the very best education, that is why he wants to send her to England. She has always been his favourite grandchild – poor Mira's Harish has been, right from the beginning, the greatest disappointment to him, and he the only boy in the family, really it is a great pity – that is why he wants Amrita to have all this expensive education. But he forgets she is only a girl, what use will so much learning be for her? Of course a girl must also be educated – a B.A. for instance, like my Amrita – but too much education is also not good.'

'Why are you telling me all this?' Tarla asked. 'You must speak with Pappaji.'

Radha felt righteously irritated: Tarla was being stupid on purpose. 'Because I want you to explain to him,' she said bluntly.

'Why?' Tarla cruelly asked. Her headache had almost quite gone.

'Gian!' Radha shouted. 'What is he doing? Why does he not come to clear the plates away, are they to stay here all day for the ants to eat up? Gian!'

'I should have thought,' Tarla went on, 'that it was your business, not mine, to tell Pappaji that you want Amrita to be married.'

Radha was forced to voice the explanation that Tarla wanted to hear. 'Pappaji will listen to you most,' she admitted; and tried to tone it down with, 'It is I think because you are the eldest; and also you are more – more like a man than a woman, so he thinks you are very clever.' This pleased her. 'I am too feminine,' she elaborated. 'It is only in you that Pappaji can see the son he wanted. That is why he will listen to you more.'

'I must go,' Tarla said brusquely, sitting upright.

'But your headache – ?'

'It is better. And I have a meeting to attend.'

'Oh,' Radha said deprecatingly, 'you always have a meeting.'

28

The porters, in uniforms dyed a patchy red, squatted in a long line in front of the station. Every time a car or tonga drove into the yard, a cluster of them leapt up and seized the baggage. When Suri's big car came in, there was an eager scuffling: and a disgruntled retreat when the car disgorged only one passenger after the other, Suri and Prema, the mother and Hari, Mohini and her three children, and not a piece of baggage.

They had all come to call for the mother's sister and her family, who, informed by telegram of the wedding, were hastening to Delhi to be in on whatever preliminary feasting there might be. The whole family was already impregnated by that holiday spirit – the sense of unlimited sweets and Coca-Colas and singing at night in the courtyard – which would last right through the marriage celebrations. Even Hari felt it, the same elation he felt about other people's weddings. And this one was especially good, for they were on the boy's side and so had no responsibilities; they could feast, enjoy themselves and send for their relations, all at the expense of the bride's family.

They made their way into the station hall and Suri bought the platform tickets. The children insisted on being weighed, and they got little cards which told them not only their weight but also their characters and fortunes in English and Hindi. The station hall was very crowded, and they had to keep close together for fear of losing one another. Clusters of passengers squatted by the pillars, surrounded by tall baskets and parcels tied with string. They looked prepared to wait for ever, the women with their heads decorously covered, the men bovine, expressionless and ready to move off if anyone with a badge or a piece of uniform told them to. A turbaned policeman swaggered with thumbs in the belt of his shorts and a truncheon swinging against his naked thigh. Piles of luggage, unguarded, unattended and belonging apparently to no one, stood piled up in obstructive places. An old man or two slept peacefully on the stone floor. Boy porters snatched pieces of luggage, quarrelled and were driven off by older porters. Village women swung along in bright blue skirts with yellow waistcoats, thick silver hoops around their ankles, and babies, fast asleep, slung over their shoulders. The man behind the information desk calmly repeated over and over again, that trains would be three, four, five hours late, had been cancelled, had never started, would not arrrive till tomorrow.

The porters were not very interested when Krishna Sen Gupta came into the station-yard with Radha and Amrita accompanying him. He carried only one small attaché case, and he alighted neither from car nor taxi nor tonga. He had, as a matter of fact, come very soberly by bus. Radha had protested – who had ever heard of going to the station in a bus? – had offered to get Mira's car, Tarla's car, if Krishna was too mean to spend money on a taxi, even offered to pay herself, but was met only by a silent smiling negative: the bus, Krishna thought, would be all right. The argument had reminded her very forcibly of a thousand arguments she had had, just so, with her husband; but she quickly ignored the reminder, for she did not care to think of any differences of opinion between herself and Nirad. Now that he was dead, she had transformed the memory of their marriage into one long flowered path of pleasing accord.

She became indignant again when Krishna refused to give his little case up to a porter. No gentleman, she considered, should be seen carrying anything; with which Krishna heartily agreed.

'If I had known you would behave so badly and put me so to shame,' she said, 'we would not have come with you.'

Krishna and Amrita smiled at one another, for which they were promptly scolded; and when Krishna went off to get their platform tickets, Radha asked her daughter, 'Why do you not help me to persuade him to behave more like a gentleman? He would be a very nice boy if only he would learn to behave like a gentleman.' To which Amrita answered with more warmth than her mother had expected: did he not behave just as Nirad, her own father, had behaved and had wanted others to behave? And Radha, not easily put out, replied swiftly that 'those times were different. The English were here then': an argument to which Amrita had no answer.

On the platform there were little barrows piled high with Indian film magazines and American pocket editions – 'The Answer to Your Sex Problems' and Plato's Dialogues, abridged – and cheap editions of Russian classics. Prema threw a quick look over the magazines; the man stopped his barrow for her and pressed her to buy Marx and Engels, Selected Works – 'Two volumes,' he said, 'please see what big books and how cheap.' 'Buy me that,' Prema told Suri, pointing to a magazine with a cover of two portly lovers in jewels. The man pulled it out at once, with two others, and held them out while Suri said, 'What for do you want it? You are not going on a train,' but Prema insisted.

The children got more and more excited and wanted everything bought for them. All the barrows stopped for them, barrows piled with fruits, with cigarettes and coloured drinks in bottles, with plaster-of-Paris figurines of Krishna playing the flute, with wilting biscuits and flecked cream-horns in glass cases; and hawkers came running, their trays bulging with hairpins and buttons and combs and plastic toys, with coloured pictures of the Taj Mahal and the interior of Agra Fort, with safety-pins on cards and sticks of incense and potato-chips in plastic bags; the children wanted everything. And after the hawkers came the beggars: old women with borrowed babies, appealing and threatening, an old man winding himself round a long stick and holding out a withered arm, and children with gay faces and tangled hair, shouting joyously that they had no mother and no father and were hungry.

Hari's mother cursed them all, the hawkers and beggars. 'Hath!' she cried, trying to shoo them away, but they only laughed and plied all the more. And it was not till Suri turned round on them and spoke his curses in a way they understood, that the wave receded and they were left in peace. Mohini scolded the children; but all the same she thought some hard thoughts about Prema, who had bought a magazine for herself and nothing for the children: as if she could not afford it, and anyway, were they not also her children?

Krishna said, 'Please do not wait; it is still half an hour before the train will go.' But Radha answered irritably, what was the use of seeing someone off at the station if you did not wait to wave to them. It was some relief to see Krishna going by Inter class instead of third; true, it was still embarrassing – what if someone should see them? – and that was why she had suggested they should stand on the platform (if he had gone by second or air-conditioned class she would have made herself comfortable in the carriage, for she loved sitting in a train), but Inter at least was better than third. She remembered very vividly the embarrassment she had undergone every time she had seen her husband off on a train; for Nirad had gone third class, always and inevitably, and on the strictest principle; whereas Krishna only went by that class which he could most easily afford.

'How hot it is,' Radha said, as they walked up and down on the platform. It was evening, but the day's heat remained stored and concentrated in the stone pavement and in the heaps of old baggage piled up, in the barrows and the coloured bottles and the flecked cream-horns, in the bodies of hawkers and beggars and porters and passengers patiently waiting.

'Why do you not go home?' Krishna urged again.

'You wish to be rid of us?' Radha asked.

They passed the third-class compartments, packed to choking point and bursting out of the windows. The people who had waited such endless hours by the pillars in the station hall, now too sat and waited, as if for ever, for the train to start and carry them away through a night and a day and another night, wedged and hemmed in, silent and patient, anxious eyes fixed on their little bundles and baskets.

'See how full it is,' Radha said with satisfaction. 'Now are you not glad that you did not go by third class?'

The Inter class also was quite full; in Krishna's compartment there were already two thin, frightened women in spectacles and Madrasi-style saris, a young man who hurriedly announced that he was B.A. and was going to Calcutta, where his uncle had found him a job, a very clean old man being seen off by four sturdy sons, and a loud raucous woman speaking in Sindi, with three children, innumerable baskets of provisions for the way and a huge earthenware pot of drinking-water. The Sindi woman was already spreading bedding for the night along the narrow benches, while her children ate bananas.

'I hope you will be comfortable in the night,' said Radha, not sounding as if she hoped so at all. 'A few rupees more and you could have gone second class and spent the night sleeping on a berth like a gentleman.'

'Perhaps, Mamma, Krishna is right; it would be better to go home.' Amrita was hot and she hated the noise and disorder of the station; and she did not want to see the train carry Krishna away, herself waving an ineffective handkerchief.

'Nonsense,' Radha said sharply. 'I am here in the place of his mother.'

'He might wish us to go,' Amrita murmured.

Krishna was sad that she should wish it.

'Do you wish it?' Radha turned on him.

He looked at Amrita, who looked away. 'Let us sit down,' he said, leading them to a bench. A man sat at one end of the bench, holding on to a little bundle. Under Radha's fierce glance he quietly removed himself.

'He was doing you harm?' Krishna asked her.

Radha said indignantly, 'I did not say anything. He went himself.' And added: 'The man knows his place.'

The train they were expecting was three hours late already – they had telephoned from home, for they had known it would be, but now on further inquiry, Suri discovered that it was to be at least another half-hour late. Prema sighed and groaned and said, why had she come; and the mother thought of her poor sister stuck in the hot train trailing, three and a half hours late, through the desert.

'We will go and come back later,' Suri suggested, but Prema said, 'Now we are here, we will stay.'

'You yourself said you wanted to go,' her husband pointed out.

'Now we have bought the platform tickets,' she said. 'There is no sense in wasting money.'

Hari did not mind whether they went or stayed. He hardly noticed where they were, for, hovering a little apart from the family group, he was intent on his own thoughts. These were, for the most part, pleasant – for were there not days of celebration ahead of him, of music and eating and singing and communal rejoicing; and beyond that happiness there was – but about that he did not let himself think too much; he was not so sure about that, did not quite feel it to be real. He had consented, yes, he had told his family with tears in his eyes that he had erred, and he had begged their forgiveness and had promised to do just as they directed him; but even while he was promising, he was making mental reservations because, after all, there was still Amrita and his great love for her. So he kept off the thought of Sushila because it was complicated with other thoughts: kept off it, but with some regret. Nor did he find himself much inclined to dwell on thoughts of Amrita; here too there were complications which it was better not to think about. But the wedding celebrations, these it was all right to think about, they made wholly pleasant thoughts; and he did manage to think about them in a quite detached manner, divorcing them from anything they might mean to him and dwelling only on the pleasant anticipation of habitual jokes and habitual songs, the men laughing together, the women busy over a hundred special dishes, the coloured lights, the hot marquee with the sweets piled up and the good wishes and jocular references, the band, the strangers staring outside, the bright orange flower-garlands.

'You want, Kaka?' Prema nudged him, and he looked up and became aware that Suri was buying cold drinks for everybody. The children could not make up their minds which they wanted, till their mother settled the problem for them by deciding they would all have the green – mango flavour – or nothing at all. They were standing in front of a little makeshift stall, and one man was opening the bottles while another washed glasses in a bucket. Hari chose yellow – pineapple flavour – and he was about to ask Prema whether after all the red, the rose flavour, would not have been a better choice, when he saw that she was greeting somebody. He turned to see who it was, and nearly dropped his glass when he recognized Amrita's mother. Looking even more formidable than when he had first seen her, in a dark grey sari, her black umbrella held tight under her arm, Amrita's mother was returning Prema's greeting. Both looked very stately with their heads slightly bowed over their hands joined together in respectful greeting. There was someone with her, Hari saw, it was – yes of course it was that what-was-his-name, the one who had come one night to the house, and again to the coffee-house and upset him so. Hari always thought of him as a very uncomfortable man, and was no more pleased to see him than he was to see Amrita's mother. And so put out was he by these two, that he noticed Amrita last of all; and having noticed her, did not know what to do about her except look the other way.

There was nothing for it, Radha saw, they would have to pass that family group; and passing it, would have to stop and talk. Two anxieties posed themselves to her in the few seconds before the actual coming together. The first was how to explain to Amrita her acquaintance with Hari's family; though this was not a very acute anxiety, since Amrita could always be overriden – was she not her own daughter, with no right to question her mother's actions? The second anxiety, however, was more serious, for it was this: how to prevent Hari's family, and especially Prema, from finding out that they were seeing someone off who was going by Inter class.

Prema, as she smiled and greeted with joined hands, suffered a similar anxiety. She feared lest the train they were expecting should come in and Radha should see their relations, fresh from the village, with earthy hands and earthy faces, shouting their greetings in earthy voices from out of the window of a third-class carriage. Prema could only hope, as she smiled more and greeted with joined hands, that the train would be later still.

Hari's mother, as the other party descended upon them, smiled and smiled at Radha, greeted and greeted, what a pleasure it was, she said, what an honour. Radha, though rather apprehensive that they might find out about Krishna going by Inter, managed to be condescending to the correct degree. The children cried to their mother, 'Is that – ? Is it – ?' and had to be silenced with some very sharp pinches; but they could not stop looking at Radha, with mouths hanging open in disappointment because it was the same lady, but where was her golden sari, where her jewels and rings? An ordinary lady with an umbrella was all she was now, no more a queen, and they turned away in what was almost contempt to drink their green drinks.

Suri at once recognized Krishna. 'Ah,' he said, clapping him between thin shoulder-blades, 'our Bengali friend.' And Radha, startled into crying, 'You know him?' only just recollected herself to say 'of course' in the same breath.

'Of course,' Hari's mother took her up, beaming at her, beaming at Krishna, 'our Hari's friend is also our own friend.'

Krishna beamed back at her and then at Radha, who gave him as furious a look as she dared under the circumstances and tried to piece things together.

Amrita also was busy piecing things together. She did not have to think long before arriving at some idea of how Radha had become acquainted with Hari's family; and after that she also very quickly connected that acquaintance with the curious calm which had settled on the house during the last few days. She gave her mother a quick look from under lowered lids and, by the studied way in which Radha was expecting and avoiding her glance, knew that her suspicions were not wrong. She would find out, she promised herself, as she shyly greeted Prema; and then retreated as much as possible behind the back of Krishna Sen Gupta, thus foiling Mohini, who dodged backwards and forwards to get a good look at her. Hari meanwhile had sheltered himself behind Suri. Neither of them, neither Hari nor Amrita, had any desire to recognize or speak to the other.

Because there was nothing to say – or at least nothing they found it convenient to say under the circumstances – Radha and Prema only smiled at one another, smiles of perfect accord and goodwill. The old woman also smiled, even more broadly than the other two, and kept telling Radha that today was indeed a happy day, such a meeting they could not hope for every day. Hari was surprised by so much cordiality. However, he thought it safer, as far as he himself was concerned, to keep as much as possible in the background. One could never tell with a lady of Radha's temperament: his recollection of their last meeting was still sharp and agitating.

Amrita could not altogether keep her mind on the scene. She was looking at the back of Krishna Sen Gupta's neck – as scraggy as the rest of him and the hair needed cutting – and was surprised when she realized that for the next week she would not be seeing him every day and as a matter of course.

They were all very uncomfortable standing there. Whistles were indiscriminately blown, chopped-off portions of announcement came blurting intermittently from a loudspeaker which was out of order, porters quarrelled, passengers asked questions without any hope of an adequate reply, hawkers pushed their barrows and trays relentlessly through the crowd, beggars attached themselves wherever they could; at the end of the platform someone was relieving himself on to the line. It was not the place for conversation, and especially not for the kind of delicately balanced conversation which they had to conduct.

Radha was longing to ask in some roundabout way whether the arrangements for the wedding were being made according to plan. Prema was longing to inform her in some roundabout way that they were. But all they could do was to smile at one another, and then smile again.

At last Krishna said it was time for him to be going. A guard was already practising to wave flags and the conductor was hopelessly checking up on a long list of reservations.

'You are going on the train?' Prema asked. 'You have a comfortable compartment?'

Krishna caught Radha's eye: it was definitely imploring. 'Yes,' he said to Prema, 'it is very comfortable.'

'Air-conditioned of course,' Prema said. 'I do not know how people can travel in a compartment that is not air-conditioned. I would die.'

Krishna said he would die too; and Radha thought it wiser to say goodbye before he carried it too far. Hari's mother, in parting, put her hand on Radha's and pressed it warmly. 'I hope you will come to honour us,' she managed to whisper, 'it is to be next week.'

Radha whispered back, very sincerely, how happy she was in their happiness.

They moved away at last, and Radha now began to worry lest they might be seen ushering Krishna into his Inter carriage. Amrita was so busy realizing that Krishna was going away, that she forgot all about Hari skulking behind his brother-in-law; and Hari's only feeling, when they had gone, was one of relief.

Just then, the train came in carrying Hari's relations. As it came by, the relations were seen and recognized peering through the bars of a third-class carriage. Led by Suri, the family pushed their way through the crowd, pointed and waved, shouted and laughed, and Hari's mother cried a few tears; only Prema was somewhat distracted, and looked back to make sure that Radha did not see.

Radha was also looking back, to make sure that Prema did not see.

Krishna boarded his carriage and Radha hardly had time to send her best greetings to his mother, and to recommend once again the jar of mango-pickle which she was sending by him, before the train moved off and Amrita waved her handkerchief.

29

Lately the Rai Bahadur had been experiencing a curious sense of unreality. Though the things around him were real enough: there were his law books and the dusty upholstery in his study; and outside the study door the house was kept in silence and in order by the butler who had been with him for over forty years. In the cookhouse the cook prepared his vegetables; the coachman sat in the stable and polished his carriage. The gardener watered his garden. In the garden there was a white sun and it was hot; in the house it was cool, fans turned silently, curtains were drawn. After lunch – boiled vegetables and a few chapatis, which he ate alone at the big table in the dining-room – he came back to his study and shut his eyes, sitting upright in an armchair with ear-flaps. Once a week his three daughters came to lunch or dinner, and then rice was sifted in the cookhouse and spices pounded, and the butler carried a dish full of chicken pilau, a smell sweet and pungent as incense, into the dining-room. These things were; they were life, reality. It was only when his thoughts strayed outside the house that he became confused and was no longer sure what was life and reality. The Law Court, he supposed, though he never went there now, was still as it had been. He could with an effort recall it, and see in his mind's eye the pleaders sitting with a clerk and a typewriter under a tree. But somehow he could not believe it to be real: or if it was real, then this house, his books, his butler, his cook, his coachman were not real. That it should exist, should carry on as it always had done and he no longer there, and not only he but all those he had associated with it, who in his time *were* the Court – Andrew Goleby, John Seymour, P. N. Dutt – without them how could it exist? Yet he knew that Andrew Goleby was in England, he had letters from him from 'Koh-i-Noor', Wormsbury, nr. Marlow, and John Seymour had died four years ago of coronary thrombosis in a Hampstead nursing-home, and P. N. Dutt had a house in Simla where he shivered in winter and was cool in the summer, and wrote to the Rai Bahadur, why did he not come to stay with him.

And the men who had taken their places; who now held the positions of respect and eminence that they had held: it was incredible, unthinkable, that it should be men like his son-in-law Nirad Chakravarty; men whom in his days of power he had often tried to help, though he had believed them to be beyond help; over whom he had shaken his head, regretful at seeing them so wilfully bent on ruining their own careers. For that was how it had looked then: young lawyers refusing to serve in the Courts, making illegal speeches at illegal meetings, going to prison – who could guess that these same young lawyers would one day succeed to his own position of eminence, would become as respected and as respectable as he himself. They had no love, he knew, for P. N. Dutt and himself; and though now all that was over and there was no more ill will, still it seemed strange and not fitting that it should be these people who had taken their place. It was like a stranger stepping into one's property instead of one's own son; a stranger whose way of life and way of thought were alien, so that, having left it behind, one could no longer imagine one's property, could no longer think of it as being real because it was being perverted into strange ways by a stranger. No, life as he knew it was no longer out there but here, here in this house, in this room, locked up and locked away from the strong sun outside; here and in 'Koh-i-Noor', Wormsbury, nr. Marlow, and in a spacious bungalow in Simla; and a bit of it had died four years ago in a Hampstead nursing-home.

Within the limits of his house, guarded by the servants whose life had been his, he felt safe. Here he was still what he always had been: a man of importance. Within the limits of his immediate family circle he had also, up till recently, felt safe: Tarla, Mira and Harish, Radha and Amrita, they believed in his judgement and followed it. His son-in-law Vazir Dayal, it was true, had always done his best to undermine his position; but then, the man was a fool and all he could put in his way were petty annoyances which the Rai Bahadur had enough dignity and self-respect, so he believed, both to despise and ignore. But Amrita's defiance – and he could only call it that – was different; that struck home deeper, penetrated right through the servants, the law books and notes, and lunch in the dining-room. He began to doubt whether these things were the sole reality which he had for the last ten years assumed them to be: or whether there was not something beyond them which he had forgotten. The thought troubled him greatly: and then sometimes it seemed to him that all these things, everything around him, all his reality, were as thin and flat as a paper-knife, and his importance no more solid than a silhouette. And he saw, or perhaps only guessed at, disturbing visions of a life outside his house, of real round figures agitating black and solid in a rhythm which he did not understand; and with Amrita among them, accepting this strange rhythm, denying his own. It was an intolerable vision, and with an effort of will he shut it out. He read his law books, he made his notes, he thought of his English furniture and the silver knives and forks laid out on the dining-table: there was life, then, real, unalterable, fixed for ever in a mould of dust and silence. And because things were so; because this was life and the Rai Bahadur a man of importance; because things were so, Amrita had to accept his decision and go to England. It became something of an issue with him, a kind of assertion of his own importance; a justification of his reality.

Tarla realized this better than Radha did. She knew they could not change his mind for him; they could only point out to him that the situation was no longer the same, and hope that in view of the new facts he could be persuaded to change his mind, authoritatively, by himself. 'You must tell Pappaji,' she told Radha, 'that you have been to see the boy's family, and that the danger is over.'

'Of course I will tell him, I have sense in my head,' Radha said; she resented such obvious advice.

They were sitting in the drawing-room of their father's house, she and Tarla and Mira, waiting for lunch. Amrita was on duty at the radio station, which was useful, because today Radha had decided to settle the issue with her father.

Mira said, 'How brave of you to go there, to these people,' and Radha turned to snap at her, 'They did not eat me.'

'No,' Mira said, suggesting though that they might have done. Bathed and powdered, and dressed in a white georgette sari with red pagodas on it, she looked very fresh and even, in her large soft way, dainty. One had to admit it, Mira – though of course much too fat – kept herself well. Not, Radha mentally added to depreciate the compliment that had been forced upon her, that she had anything else to do or think about all day except bathing and dressing.

'You and Tarla are always doing such brave things,' Mira said.

She had a good heart, Mira had, thought her sister; no one could deny it; and she really could not help being so stupid and having no other interests except her food and her toilette. 'That is a very nice sari,' she said aloud, and Mira was pleased. 'I bought it at Varma Brothers –' she began, when Tarla cut in with, 'So what will you tell Pappaji?'

'*You* will tell him,' Radha said, and settled herself against the cushions, crossing her feet and folding her hands over her stomach.

'Oh?' said Tarla, drawing up plucked eyebrows.

'Yes, it is what we have agreed.'

Tarla thrust her head forward in a challenging manner and said, 'I did not know.'

Mira looked anxious: she hoped there would not be a quarrel. 'Lunch is late today,' she murmured.

'Of course,' Radha said, 'when you came to my house – I will speak with Pappaji, these were your words. Why do you pretend you have forgotten?'

'I never spoke such words and you know I did not,' Tarla said. 'Why should I undertake to do your work for you?'

Mira said, 'Or is my watch so fast?'

'*My* work!' Radha cried, unclasping her hands and sitting upright. 'Amrita then is nothing to you?'

But before she had finished the sentence, Mohan Lal, the butler, came to announce lunch, and Mira was up at once, saying, 'We must not keep Pappaji waiting.'

'I often wonder,' Radha said as they went into the dining-room, 'if you have a heart at all, Tarla.'

The old man came in, in his fine white shirt and his dhoti falling in folds, and the first thing he said, after he had sat down and looked round at them over the top of his steel-rimmed spectacles was: 'Where is Amrita?'

'O Pappaji,' Radha said, a little breathless, she was in such a hurry to answer him, 'today she has duty at the radio station, she is so sorry she could not come. And also so very disappointed.'

He made no comment as he helped himself, very sparsely, from the dish of rice which Mohan Lal held out for him. Radha looked significantly at Tarla, for Amrita having been mentioned, this was an opportune moment; but Tarla was ostentatiously intent on helping herself to salad.

'But I think,' Radha had to go on by herself, 'all that will soon stop.'

'All what?' her father, who hated vagueness, asked at once.

'This radio,' Radha said. 'I think she will soon not go there any more. And I am glad.'

'There was no harm in it,' the Rai Bahadur said acidly; his daughter Radha always managed to irritate him with every innocent word she spoke. 'The girl had to have some occupation while she waited. Though now of course there is no further need of it, since she will shortly be going to England.'

Radha assumed what was almost an ingratiating smile and began, hesitatingly and as nervous as a young girl, 'Do you think, Pappaji – ?'

and found herself cutting across Tarla who was also speaking. She stopped at once.

'You still intend, Pappaji,' Tarla was saying in her crisp voice, and *she* did not stop when she found herself speaking together with Radha, 'you still intend that Amrita should go to England?'

Very sharply the old man answered, 'I was not aware of any change of plan.'

'We were thinking –' Radha began breathlessly, but again Tarla took precedence of her. 'Of course not, Pappaji,' Tarla said, 'there has been no talk of any change of plan.' Radha thought, now what is this fool saying? She will surely not agree with him, though one can never know what she will not do, in spite.

'Only,' Tarla went on, talking to her father and taking no notice whatsoever of her sister, 'there has been some change in the situation.'

'Yes, Pappaji,' Radha rushed in, 'I have wanted to tell you ...'

'Change in situation?' the Rai Bahadur said to Tarla.

'The connection between Amrita and this boy has been broken off,' she answered promptly. 'The boy's family have arranged a marriage for him next week.'

'So soon,' Mira murmured. It was her first contribution to the conversation and came deep out of a preoccupation with fried rice and mutton curry.

The Rai Bahadur said calmly, 'Then she will go to England without repining.'

'Oh!' cried Radha involuntarily and then looked, biting her lip, at Tarla.

Tarla said, quite on her own and acknowledging no alliance with Radha at all, 'Yes, Pappaji, if it is still your wish that she should go.'

'If it is your wish of course,' Radha rushed in with heaving bosom, 'of course'; and then could not stop herself but kept saying, 'of course, of course, of course' in a distracted manner. Neither her father nor Tarla took any notice of her; only Mira echoed out of sympathy, 'of course' as she helped herself to more rice.

'But we had thought,' Tarla began tactfully, ignoring both her sisters, 'that, now that the danger is over, you might care to reconsider your decision; perhaps after all Amrita could stay here with us; if you think it might be better.' She was respectfully quiet and let him think it over.

Only Radha would not let him; she thought it better to reinforce Tarla's words, so she cried. 'Yes, Pappaji, if you think so, we thought that if you – you see, now that it is all finished, we thought a young girl like my Amrita is it right for her to be without her mother and so far away ... ?'

She trailed off, having, she thought, made her point and being rather anxious as to how it would be received. Tarla looked disgusted and drummed her skinny fingers on the table.

After a moment's silence, the Rai Bahadur addressed himself to Tarla: 'What do you suggest the girl should do then? You have perhaps thought of other plans for her?'

Now is the moment, Radha thought, and could only hope that Tarla would not be such a fool as to miss it. She wanted to signal to her, tried desperately to catch her eye, even tried to press her foot under the table; she managed to press something but was not sure that it was Tarla's foot.

But Tarla said, 'Of course we wait only for your suggestion, Pappaji.'

'We had thought,' Radha spoke up very boldly: 'Yes?' the old man said, cupping his ear in his hand; 'that we would consult you first,' Tarla carried on for her, 'as to your opinion.'

'About what?' he said, and suddenly shot out at Mira, who was again helping herself to rice, 'You eat too much.'

'I know,' she said sadly but placidly. Leisure, independence, good food, good clothes had given her a placid calm which destroyed all stronger emotions; once she had felt very nervous before her father, but now even he could not disturb her. 'It is why I am so fat,' she added.

He turned from her in silent disapproval and asked again of Tarla, 'About what?'

Tarla was about to answer in her own discreet way, but Radha rushed in before her: she could not bear to be thus overruled and overlooked – who after all was the mother, she or Tarla? 'An excellent match has been proposed,' she said, 'such a match we cannot hope for every day. A beautiful boy, very fair and of course very highly educated –'

Her father interrupted her by asking his elder daughter, 'What is this?'

Tarla was furious. To blurt it out like this, in the most tactless manner imaginable – she would have liked to disown all knowledge of the scheme. She knew very well how strongly her father disapproved of arranged marriages, for he still held on to the emancipation of women as a very new and therefore very high and rigid ideal.

'You must be knowing Lady Ram Prashad Khanna,' Radha went on, recklessly now. 'The widow of Sir Ram Prashad Khanna, the industrialist, it is her son, who is now coming home from studying in America. An alliance with such a family cannot disgrace us. And such a beautiful boy and so clever –'

'Does the girl herself know of this?' the old man thundered from the top of the table, so loudly that Mira dropped her spoon on to the plate and said, 'Oh, Oh' at the noise it made.

'Amrita? She will be very happy, which girl would not be happy with such a –'

'Does she know of it? Does she consent to it? Is it her own choice?'

Radha could not exactly say that it was her own choice, nor really that she consented to it. But she could not help feeling that her father was approaching the question from the wrong angle: surely his first consideration should be the family of the Ram Prashad Khannas, not the, at present, irrelevant question of Amrita's feelings. Feelings could come afterwards, after marriage; and with a little inward sigh she recalled that feelings before and after marriage were inclined to be very different. Not, as she always very hastily answered herself when such thoughts came up, that her own marriage with Nirad Chakravarty had not been a happy one; but, nevertheless, it could not be denied that her feelings about him before marriage were very different from those that came after. And this always prompted the thought that supposing her parents had chosen for her instead of allowing her to have her own choice: supposing that they had chosen somebody of the same community and with the same social background as her own, someone who could have given her the kind of life to which she had been brought up; even if she had not at first been able to love the man they had chosen, would it not have been possible for her feelings to have changed after marriage and for love to have awakened, just as with Nirad it had – well not died then, but changed, yes love had changed – ?

'Is it her own choice?' the old man said again and beat the flat of his hand on the table.

'Of course the boy is in America now,' Radha circumlocuted.

'She has not even seen him?' And when his daughter did not answer, probed deeper. 'None of you have seen him?'

'It is shameful,' he said after a short pause, 'that you do not allow your child the liberty which your parents allowed you; that you should revert to the – the primitive custom that I took pains to eradicate from our family.' And he got up, walked out, scorned to say more.

After an uncomfortable silence, Mira said, 'Pappaji is very angry.'

'You expected him perhaps,' Tarla said to Radha, 'to be happy at your proposition?'

'*My* proposition! May I know, who was it started the talk with Lady Ram Prashad?'

Mira, beckoning to Mohan Lal to bring the bowl of kheer to her again, sighed, 'Pappaji is so advanced.' She herself, as far as she ever thought about it, was in perfect agreement with the principle of arranged marriages. She considered that it was the parents' duty to find suitable mates for their children; the young people, poor things, could not be expected to do it for themselves. It was all very well for Pappaji to say that he had not arranged his daughters' marriages: but Mataji had been there and all the aunts, and they had seen to it that suitable husbands were found. How else could she have married Harish's father? She could not have gone out to *look* for him. And Tarla too – Vazir Dayal had not just walked into the house; various aunts had seen to it that he got there. That was the way things were done; the way they had to be done. Just see what had happened to Radha, who had chosen her own husband and in consequence did not even possess a motorcar.

Tarla said, 'Now you can stop thinking about Lady Ram Prashad. Pappaji will never consent to it.'

Radha answered, 'When Amrita agrees, Pappaji also will,' rather ominously.

30

When her mother told her that Hari was going to be married Amrita said quite wearily, 'How can you tell such lies, Mamma?'

Radha had not meant to tell her; she had thought it would be both more effective and less disturbing if Amrita found out for herself. But when Amrita had begun to question her as to how she had become so friendly with Hari's family, what was behind it all; and after she had tried to evade the question and Amrita would not let her, but had pressed her closer and closer, then she had burst it out, the truth, the final answer. It was an anti-climax that Amrita quite genuinely did not believe her.

Radha tossed her head and virtuously folded her hands in her lap, saying, very well then, let us wait and see who is telling lies and who is not. This righteous indignation made Amrita turn round and think again, and scrutinize her mother to find in her quite definite signs of outraged truth. She thought she knew all her mother's expressions and what lay behind them, and this one looked sincere enough to her. But surely it could not be true, whatever Mamma's facial expression; she must have made a mistake somewhere, misunderstood perhaps by wishful thinking. Why, she herself had talked to Hari only the day before yesterday, and then there had been no suspicion of anything like that at all, they had been as they always were, they had – yes of course – they had talked about going to England together. They had discussed it quite thoroughly, they had even made plans about passports and inoculations, so how could what Mamma said be true? Hari was the simplest, sweetest, most guileless of souls, he did not even know the meaning of deception.

'We will see,' Radha was saying, 'we will see.' And although she was persuading herself that there was no cause for suspicion at all, Amrita felt uneasy. She would be seeing Hari today at the radio station, that at least was some consolation; he would be able to explain everything quite to her satisfaction, she would not have to remain in doubt for long. But all the same, even though she was going to be reassured so soon, she could not help feeling disturbed. She wished she had someone to talk to about it, and when she thought 'someone' she knew she meant Krishna Sen Gupta. It was not the first time she had missed him since his departure.

Radha also thought about Krishna; she had already said three times that they had not heard from him yet. Amrita pointed out that they could hardly have heard from him when he had only just arrived. He could have sent a telegram, Radha sulked, he knows we are anxious; 'he has become like a son to me, like a son,' she said several times, looking meaningfully, even reproachfully at Amrita. And when Amrita gave no reaction, she hinted broadly at last, 'Krishna is a gentleman, he is of our own class, it is a pity you could not –' She trailed off, because Amrita had run out of the room.

Hari did not come to keep her company while she was announcing, as he usually did. She knew he was free and could not understand what had happened to him. While she put on records of Ustad Sayyid Khan playing the sitar, the morning's suspicions deepened and she had to tell herself very firmly that her mother, even if she had not deliberately invented the story, must have misunderstood. The last record played – how she resented just then the imaginative flights that soared and fell and soared again, turned and twisted, wound and darted, the endless elaborations of Ustad Sayyid Khan's art – the last record then at last played, she made the final announcement and got out as quickly as she could. She made straight for the canteen at the top of the building, quite sure that he must be there waiting for her. But he was not. She sat down by herself at a table, quite sure now that he had meant to be there but had been delayed. After fifteen minutes she began to feel conspicuous, but did not want to leave because at any minute he was sure to come in. It was lunch-time and the place was crowded; people sat together in groups and laughed and talked. After another ten minutes she ordered coffee for herself, to give herself an air of occupation. It took quite a long time for the coffee to come, but even after it had come and she had drunk it, there was still no Hari.

She got up, walked out and down the stairs. The only thing now, she thought, was to go home; and even as she was thinking it, she was walking directly towards the office in which Hari usually reported for duty. But only the typist was there, a thickset young man who stared at her with complete blankness over his typewriter. She turned away, and thought again, I must go home. But she tried all the studios first, and though she saw many people who knew him, she could not ask them anything. On her way out, for now indeed there was nothing for it but to go home, she passed through the External Services division, and coming from a little room at the end of the corridor she heard much happy shouting and laughter; and immediately recognized Hari's voice. She wanted to hurry past, for she had not the courage to pluck him from out of a roomful of people. But she hesitated for a moment as she walked past, and in that moment Vaidya saw her and called, 'Ah, our friend, the negative lady!'

She was too confused to see the distress and embarrassment which came into Hari's face and instantly wiped out his happy smiles. 'Come in, come in,' Vaidya called, but she said hastily that she was just going home.

'"No" again!' Vaidya spluttered. 'With this lady it is always "no".'

The others laughed good-humouredly – Hari too – and the one girl who was in the room – a lively sturdy girl in coloured salwar-kamiz, who announced the Punjabi programmes – looked her up and down. Amrita wished fervently that she had gone straight home after she left the canteen.

'Please Amrita,' Hari said, recollecting himself, 'come in.' She saw now that there were several trays on the office tables, and used plates and cups piled up. 'Ha ha,' Hari laughed uneasily as he followed her glance, 'we thought today we would have our food down here. It is more comfortable.'

Amrita turned and walked out, with Hari hurrying behind. Vaidya shouted after her – he meant no harm but prided himself on much humour – 'We would have asked you to join us had we not known you would say no!' and the Punjabi girl tittered.

'I did not know,' Hari was saying, 'that today you had duty.'

'No,' Amrita replied, 'only for six months we have met on this day.'

'I had forgotten,' he said miserably.

They stood at the top of the steps by the main entrance. When he said he had forgotten, she walked straight down.

'Where are you going?' he asked, running after her; and when she did not answer, pleaded, 'Please do not run away from me, Amrita. Come up and sit with me in the canteen; I have eaten my lunch but we will drink coffee.'

When he mentioned canteen, her heart really hardened towards him and she walked a bit faster. She did not stop until she reached the bus stand, and saw the bus just turning the corner and coming towards her. She would soon be home now. But she had to make sure, and because there was no time for anything except the direct question, she turned to look Hari full in the face and asked him, 'Hari, is it true that you are going to be married?'

He shot out at once, 'Who told you?' and she answered as promptly, 'My mother. Is it true?'

After a short pause, during which he did a lot of confused thinking, his face fell into the deepest misery and he murmured, his eyes downcast, 'It is true.'

The bus drew up at the stop. Amrita did not get on. She stood looking at Hari and waited for him to say more.

'What can I do?' he said finally. 'My family – they have arranged it all.'

'And you of course say "yes" to everything they arrange,' she said bitterly, though she had not meant to be involved at all.

'What can I do?' he said again, even more plaintively. And when she did not answer went on, 'You do not know how unhappy I am, I cannot sleep at night and I have no proper appetite because I am so unhappy. I lie in the night and I think, what can I do to stop this marriage, and when I think of you and of our beautiful love I cry because I cannot bear that we should be torn apart.' His eyes were wet; she looked up at him and saw them glisten. He was very, very moved. 'Amrita,' he said, out there by the bus stand, with three tongas waiting for passengers under a tree, and bicycles dawdling along the track, 'Amrita,' he said, 'you know that my heart is only for you, how can I even think of marriage? The idea only is very hateful to me, to be joined with another woman when all the time my thoughts, my heart, my whole soul are yearning for you.'

Another bus drew up; again Amrita did not get on. 'But why, Hari,' she said gently, 'did you not tell me about this marriage they are arranging for you?'

'Is it not enough,' he said with passion, 'that I should not sleep nor eat but I must make you suffer too?'

'My dearest,' she answered, 'how good you are.' Her hand crept towards his and met it. Surreptitiously they pressed one another's hands, and then quickly let go lest anyone should see. Amrita felt suddenly light-hearted and almost happy, because they were once again close to one another; lately all they seemed to have been doing was misunderstanding one another.

For a few moments they stood together, silent and blissful. Then Amrita, feeling that they must above all be practical, rallied and said in her most practical tones, 'Now of course we must *act*.'

He was tumbled out of charming abstract thoughts of love to agree, 'Yes', in a somewhat weak and deflated voice.

Still being very practical – and unconsciously imitating her mother, for her own nature could not so well stand the strain of being practical – she said, in words that might have been Radha's, 'Now the time for talk is over.'

'Yes,' Hari sadly agreed, 'it is over.'

'Now we really must go away to England together as soon as possible, it is the only way.'

'Yes,' Hari agreed again, and then pointed out, 'Your bus is coming.'

'I am not taking it,' she said with decision. 'I am not going home. I am going instead to my uncle: I shall tell him, please give me the money to go away to England because now the time for talk is over. Is not that the best plan, Hari?'

He nodded, and tried very hard not to think of Prema and his mother and the Anands, and all the relations who were already gathering together.

'And you will come with me please, Hari,' Amrita was saying.

'To see your uncle?' he cried. If thoughts of his own relations were at that moment unpleasant, thoughts of Amrita's were more so. 'You think he will like to see me?'

'Yes,' Amrita said in Radha's voice, 'I am sure he will like very much.'

Tarla auntie, though, who received them, did not like it a bit. She was sitting with Lady Ram Prashad at the desk and they were going over some papers together. Both wore horn-rimmed spectacles at the end of their noses, and they both looked very busy and important and not at all happy to be interrupted. Tarla auntie was rather brusque, telling them to sit down and wait, and Lady Ram Prashad was charming only very perfunctorily.

Amrita and Hari sat down side by side on the huge soft divan with the black and gold upholstery and crimson cushions. Hari looked round with awe: he had never been in such an elegant room before; it was just like being in a film. He at once thought of Prema and how impressed she would be by this room. It was, he had to admit it, really very much more elegant than her drawing-room, even though that had also cost a lot of money. A lakh, he estimated for Vazir Dayal's room, looking round it, it must have cost at least a lakh to furnish.

'Tut-tut-tut,' Lady Ram Prashad was saying, 'this must be seen to. To arrange a social evening with refreshments and then to cancel it one hour before, that must not happen in *our* organization.'

Amrita whispered to Hari that Tarla auntie did a lot of good work for various Ladies' Organizations. Hari was impressed, but hoped that Amrita would not become as ugly as her aunt when she grew old.

'And please see this,' Tarla auntie pointed out to her companion. 'Again subscriptions are behindhand in this branch.'

'Tut-tut-tut.'

Amrita fidgeted on the divan, even very gently coughed, but Tarla auntie was too busy. Hari kept looking round him and did not mind how long he had to wait. In the end Amrita piped up, 'Tarla auntie, please.'

'We are very busy, Amrita. Kindly see these figures, Lady Ram Prashad, they have just been sent to me by Mrs Subramanya four months late.'

Amrita grew quite bold and interrupted again, 'Please excuse me, auntie, but it is Uncle we have come to see.' Hari stared primly ahead of him; he looked as if all this were no concern of his, as if indeed he thought it very rude of Amrita to keep interrupting.

'Your uncle is not here,' Tarla auntie replied shortly, taking out a new sheaf of papers with an impressive, 'Now, Lady Ram Prashad.'

'When will he be home again please, Auntie?'

'Really, Amrita,' Tarla auntie said, 'how am I to know? I expect as soon as it becomes a little cooler he will come back; till then he will stay there in Simla.'

'In Simla!' cried Amrita. 'He has gone to Simla?'

'What else?' said Tarla auntie tartly, and turned all her attention back to her papers and Lady Ram Prashad.

Amrita would have liked to ask many more questions – when did he go, did he leave no message for me, did he not even mention me? – but she knew they were futile questions, and anyway she had not the courage to ask any more. So she said sadly to Hari, 'Come, we must go, Uncle has gone to Simla,' and he, implicitly obedient, got up and preceded her to the door.

'You are going?' Tarla auntie said, pausing with a sheet of paper held in her hand and glaring at them over her spectacles. Lady Ram Prashad took out her most charming smile and wished to be remembered very specially to Amrita's mother. Amrita thanked her and took her leave, without introducing Hari at all; while he, fearing questions as to who he was and why, had already slipped out of the French windows and could be seen contemplating the garden. Tarla auntie threw a derogatory look at the back view of him and nodded Amrita's dismissal.

'Such a charming girl,' commented Lady Ram Prashad when she had gone; 'who was the young man with her?'

'A cousin from her father's side,' said Tarla auntie.

'Also very charming,' said Lady Ram Prashad.

31

The Anands' house had begun to fill up. Relations, determined to be in on everything connected with the wedding, came and settled down, whole families of them, on the floors of the Anands' three rooms, on the veranda they shared with the other tenants and up on the roof-terrace. The kitchen, a very small square room leading off the veranda, was always crammed with women busy cooking; and up on the roof there were several other makeshift kitchens, consisting of battered buckets filled with hot coals. Some of the people were very strict and would, for instance, eat only root vegetables cooked in mustard oil, or only food prepared by their daughters-in-law with their own hands and in pots brought from home. Mealtimes also varied greatly – mostly depending on what time the old people happened to say their prayers or take their baths – so that all day long some one of the family parties would be preparing a meal. The old women prayed, the young women cooked, the children screeched, the men sat on the floor talking of business and religion. In the evenings there was usually some singing, bursting spontaneously from one little group and spreading to the others till they were all sitting in one big circle, taking turns at beating the dholak and clapping their hands in accompaniment. Sometimes quarrels flared up – between the old women as to the particular time and mode of their particular prayers, between the young women as to whose turn it was at the tandoor, as to ghee, sugar, masala and the best way of preparing dal. The men attempted to soothe, were drawn in and then tried to extricate themselves by means of philosophical generalities and half-expressed parables. The quarrels, having reached their highest pitch – by which time the original issue was usually forgotten – subsided of their own accord and for a while there was calm, till the children started.

There was nothing new in all this to Prema. Her own house, as well as her mother's, was crammed with relations, cooking, praying, singing and quarrelling just so. They were the heralds of the coming celebrations, of every celebration Prema could remember, betrothal, wedding, name-giving, initiation; without their presence well in advance of the actual days fixed for the ceremony, the whole spirit of festivity would have failed. As it was, the smell of their cooking, the sound of their prayers, the singing at night, the gossip, the quarrels, created the right, the indispensable atmosphere of family festiveness.

Some of the relations gathered at the Anands' were already known to Prema, for they were the same people, distant branches of her own family, whom she had met over and over again at all the family functions. Others – and these she could not help feeling to be rather vulgar and not at all the sort of people with whom she was accustomed to mix – were unknown to her, being either members of Mrs Anand's family or other branches of Mr Anand's, too distant from her own to have appeared at previous functions. She herself was treated with great respect by everybody; as was fitting, since she was the prospective bridegroom's elder sister. However, she was not at all proud; she behaved with great politeness and condescension, greeting everybody – even Mrs Anand's second sister who was a widow – almost as if they were on an equal footing. She felt gratified by the good impression she was sure she was making. Sushila came running to meet her and touched her feet, and then pressed her hands with great happiness; and that was even more gratifying, for not every young girl showed such love for her future husband's sister. Already she heard whispers about herself – 'she is a very rich man's wife, two lakhs they have got together and they ride about in a big car' – and to confirm the good impression, she made Sushila sit next to her on a strip of carpet, and stroked the hair out of her face very tenderly. Sushila's lips were slightly parted, the shadow of a dimple played on her cheek, her eyes shone with happiness; and Prema sighed, thinking how soon that happiness, that expectancy, must fade and give way to the disillusionment of the wife. Not, of course, that her brother Hari would not, within the limits of husbands, make a good husband, but he could not help being a man and men – even if they were not Suri – could never understand the gentle yearning of a woman's soul. She sighed more deeply at the thought, feeling her own soul gently yearning, and murmured, 'My sweet little Sushila' as she stroked the girl's hair more tenderly than ever.

Mrs Anand came up to the roof-terrace and greeted Prema with an ill grace she hardly bothered to disguise. Prema greeted back at her most charming, feeling confident and superior. She was wearing a new kamiz, the best silk, bought from the best shop, orange with a design of dark red petunias: so that she could defy Mrs Anand's fine bosom encased in a kamiz of an artificial silk which could be bought at 2/4 a yard at every refugee-stall in town. Mrs Anand curtly asked her daughter if she had no work to do, was this the way she prepared for marriage, by idling the time away and letting her elders wait upon her. Regretfully and a little shamefacedly, Sushila got up and went downstairs into the little kitchen, where her sisters sat on the floor and pounded spices.

Kicking off her shoes, Mrs Anand sat herself down next to Prema on the strip of carpet. 'Of work there is enough,' she commented, wiping the perspiration off her face with her dupatta. Prema laid a sympathetic hand on the other's knee and soothed, 'In our house too there is so much work for us women; but it is part of our happiness'; Mrs Anand looked down at Prema's hand, then lightly moved her knee from under it. Prema went right on smiling; she knew that all the other women were looking at her and was giving of her best. She laid the rejected hand, plump and smooth, on her dupatta and said, 'Weddings are always so busy for us ladies.'

'Especially,' Mrs Anand added forcefully, 'if they have to be arranged in a hurry.'

Prema now smiled at the widowed sister, who was so overcome that she did not know where to look. Brusquely Mrs Anand ordered her to go prepare chutney in the kitchen, and meekly she went. Prema went on smiling, indiscriminately, though very charmingly, at the other female relations, and was very glad that she was wearing that expensive new kamiz.

The last of the sunset, incredibly orange, lingered behind the ragged line of roofs. Already shadowed and half-silhouetted by evening light, the women began to prepare for the night meal, lighting the tandoor and filling the bruised buckets with hot coal. They glided and bent in that evening light like figures in a mime. One old woman mumbled fierce prayers from out of her sari. An old man washed himself by the pump, then turned and prayed with folded hands. Big black kites curved and swooped over the roof.

Purified by bath and prayer, the Anand grandmother came up the stairs. She sat down near Prema but did not greet her; she even ignored Prema's own respectful greeting and angrily drew her feet away. A grim little smile played about Mrs Anand's mouth as she watched Prema's face slipping out of self-assured charm. The old woman began to mumble to herself, and under cover of this, Prema turned to some of the others and commented, 'Soon my husband will come to call for me in the car.'

'Suri is coming?' Mrs Anand said casually.

'Suri Sahib is coming,' Prema confirmed and corrected. The other women looked properly impressed by the mention of the car.

The grandmother's mumbling began to get louder, even in places comprehensible. 'Sin,' they could pick out, 'it is sin before God.' They all looked uncomfortable now, except Mrs Anand, who remained unmoved and at her ease.

'He will soon be here,' Prema said rather desperately, 'we have arranged it, when your business is finished, I said, you will come, with the car to fetch me from Mrs Anand's . . .'

Suddenly the old woman said quite loudly, and as distinctly as her lack of teeth would allow, 'It is not a marriage, it is a sin; a sin before God.'

'. . . I will be there waiting for you,' Prema lamely concluded.

There was a pause. Mrs Anand calmly looked at her nails, which were long and red.

'Sin!' the old woman shouted. 'There has been no betrothal ceremony, no ceremonial letter has been sent, the bridegroom's people dare to show themselves in our house, and it is called marriage? It is called sin!'

A murmur of sympathy came from some of the other old women. Indeed this was not the way things should be done, not how they were always done. She was right, let her speak out; if they, the old women, did not see to it that things were done in the old, in the correct manner, what would become of their community? So they nodded their old heads and shifted their pans from one corner of their mouths to the other, murmuring, indeed this was not the right way.

'Never will they be blessed,' the old grandmother prophesied, 'God will never gladden them with a son, even all prayers will be unavailing, because the proper rites and ceremonies have been neglected. That such a disgrace should fall on my son's family, after all the prayers and all the good deeds that have been stored up, Oh, Oh!'

And 'Oh, Oh!' the other old women echoed, and rocked their heads from side to side, one hand laid on the cheek, 'Oh, Oh!'

The young women who were busy cooking listened sharply, although they had their heads turned away and their hands worked ceaselessly. Those who were not busy sat by, outwardly passive, awaiting events.

Prema shifted uneasily; she felt as if they were all expecting her to say something, but how could she dare speak against these religious old women? She looked to Mrs Anand for support, but that lady avoided her glance.

'But we are not to be blamed,' said Mrs Anand, 'this has been forced upon us.'

Now they were all looking directly at Prema, all except the old grandmother herself, who concentrated on her daughter-in-law; whose acquiescence with her sentiments did not please her.

Prema really had to say something; so she murmured, hoping not to be heard too distinctly, 'Sometimes there are circumstances . . .'

Attention at once shifted from her to the other protagonist; but the old woman was still too engrossed with her daughter-in-law's surprising attitude to seize upon the central fight and carry it through. So she only repeated, 'It is a sin before God, a shame to my son's family,' and narrowly watched her daughter-in-law.

But again Mrs Anand disappointed her. 'What right have we to speak,' she said, and turned fully on Prema as she said it, drawing the others' attention with her, 'when the bridegroom's family wishes it so.'

The old women began to click their tongues and to mutter imprecations against those who hindered the proper observance of customary ceremonies; but when their guiding spirit did not join in, their disapproval trailed off and died upon the air. The grandmother's heart was set on other things; she could never participate in a quarrel in which she and her daughter-in-law were on the same side; so she did not even consider Prema, but speaking only for Mrs Anand, said, 'There is not such another mother who will ruin her daughter's life by giving her away in sin.'

But again Mrs Anand only said, 'Of what use is all our talk? We may break our hearts, but we are powerless,' and once more turned attention towards Prema.

Just then Mr Anand came stepping up on to the roof, home from his day's business, the clean white shirt with which he had set out in the morning crumpled and stained with patches of perspiration. Seeing Prema, he at once joined his hands and lowered his head over them in deferential greeting. She was so relieved by his appearance at this critical moment that she greeted him with a quite unwonted cordiality, such as she usually kept for more important people; which so surprised him that he joined his hands again and tried to look even more deferential.

But neither his wife nor his mother had any intention of breaking up the scene because of his arrival. Mrs Anand repeated, 'We are powerless, we cannot even speak,' while the grandmother said, 'It is the mother's duty to see that every detail of her daughter's marriage ceremony is correct.'

Mr Anand wished that he had not come home; but being there, he took refuge in Prema and said, 'Good, good, good, and Suri Sahib is not honouring us today?'

Prema, as desperately, took refuge in him. 'Soon he will be here,' she answered eagerly, 'any minute I am expecting him, we had arranged –'

'Thank God,' the old woman exclaimed, 'that I did my duty by my daughters in their time!' And the other old women said, 'Ah', and nodded and rapped the side of their noses.

Mrs Anand said, 'It is a great pain in a mother's heart to be hindered from doing her duty for her daughter.'

'But here he is!' Prema cried, and indeed there was Suri at the top of the stairs, well-fed and self-assured in a silk bush-shirt and a gold wrist-watch. Never had she been so pleased to see her husband.

Mr Anand also was very pleased, and he stepped forward saying, 'Ah Suri Sahib, we have been waiting for you, it is an honour for us,' and Mrs Anand pushed up her dupatta and laid a hand to her hair.

Suri grinned, greeted, and slapped Mr Anand heartily on the back. Already Prema's relief at seeing him was giving way to annoyance: if only, she thought, he had a little more sense of his own dignity, and would learn to behave to these people with the reticence which befitted his position among them. He was, after all, not only the brother-in-law of the bride-groom, but also the rich man in the family, of whom they spoke proudly to outsiders, whose gold wrist-watch and big American car were part of their own security in life and claim to respect. It was all very well being cordial – there he was, still slapping the delighted Mr Anand and guffawing at the other men – she herself, she hoped, had behaved with a certain amount of cordiality, but she had known how to temper it with a touch of condescension; as was necessary if one was to retain the respect to which one's position entitled one.

Mrs Anand got up and said, 'So, Suri Sahib, you have come,' just as if there were some secret understanding between them and she had been the only one to know that he was coming.

Suri directed his guffaw at her, very hearty and friendly, and tried to keep his eyes from straying too overtly to her bosom. He succeeded, but still Prema was furious. That he should communicate in so cordial a fashion with this woman, who not a minute before had tried to insult and draw ignominy on his wife, his own wife – but what did he care about her? When had he ever protected her or avenged the insults directed at her? He had no heart for her, no eyes for her, he thought only of other women, her marriage was a failure, her husband did not even think about her, she was utterly alone – the familiar thoughts and sensations came back in a flood of grievance, and automatically her eyes became wet and she dabbed at them with her dupatta.

'It is all going well, Anand Sahib?' Suri was saying, still slapping away, and Mr Anand said, 'Tee-hee, we will see when the day comes, when the day comes.'

'Such a marriage shall never be!' the grandmother suddenly shouted, 'not in our family!'

Suri turned his polite attention towards her, for she was old and had sons, and so must be honoured above other women. But Mrs Anand said curtly, 'Enough now,' words for which Prema had before waited in vain.

The old woman too had waited for them and now pounced: 'Sin!' she screamed, 'it is sin, not marriage, it is destroying all the good and all the prayers stored in our family, never will they be happy, never blessed ...' but she was so excited that she spoke quite indistinctly and the impact of her words was lost. Mr Anand only asked soothingly, 'Mataji, have you had your food?' and Suri said, 'It is fate,' in an easy conversational tone of voice. Even the old women deserted her, neither nodded nor shook their heads nor called on God, but merely sat huddled together discussing how many lakhs Suri was the owner of. Though she still sat muttering, cursing, complaining, her moment was past; and when, a little later, one of her grand-daughters came up from the kitchen and gave her vegetables, she retired into a corner, with her back to the company, and huddled herself over her bowl. Her vegetables were well curried, her chapatis piping hot; she resigned herself to the inevitable and found consolation in the fact that at least she was free from sin, having always performed, in the correct manner, all the prayers and ceremonies required of her.

32

Amrita had written to her uncle at Simla, telling him – how shameless she had become, she reflected after she had sent the letter safely off – that, please would he let her have the money, now, at once, to go to England, for it was very, very urgent for them to go almost immediately. When she received no answer to this letter (sent by express post and marked 'Urgent' in very big capitals) she despatched a telegram, 'Please Send Money Vital Amrita', but so far even that was unacknowledged. Meanwhile she drew out all the money she had in her savings book; it was only eighty rupees, but at least it was enough to pay the doctor for their inoculations and the fee for their passports. Hari unfortunately had no money at all as he gave all he earned to his mother, keeping only thirty rupees a month for his own expenses.

Amrita had gone to a travel agency, and though at first she was assured that all berths had been booked months ago, in the end two cancellations were, by great good luck, found for her on a ship called *Jal Jawahar*, which was due to sail from Bombay on 11 October. She was very happy about this and took it for a good omen that from now on everything would go quite smoothly. She was so sure that within a matter of hours Uncle would wire her the money that she arranged with the travel agency to come within three days to pay for her booking; and blithely agreed that, of course, if she had not brought the money within the three days, they would sell the tickets.

Meanwhile she and Hari went to a doctor and had their anti-cholera and yellow fever injections, and arranged to come back for their smallpox vaccination a few days later. Hari was quite placid and complaisant about it; he had at first tried to argue that, what was the need for all these injections, but when she pointed out that if they did not have them they would not be able to go to England, and was quite firm about it, he said 'All right' in a fatalistic manner.

When the doctor grasped his arm, he shut his eyes tight, but with the needle entering his flesh tears pricked the closed lids, and suddenly behind this veil of tears there appeared to him, as clear as if he were looking at a calendar, the date 3 October in red letters. It was the date for which his marriage had been fixed, the date which he had shuffled over with vague thoughts of postponements; for were there not always postponements in all arrangements, was not the actual date fixed always the earliest and most optimistic one, which everybody knew could not possibly be kept to? So he managed to reconcile 3 October with the date of *Jal Jawahar*, 11 October, and had no qualms. Later, when Amrita asked him, had his family fixed the date for the wedding yet, he said he was not sure but – taking her hand and murmuring, 'My little one, my Amrita – it could not possibly be before November, and by that time – my Amrita, my goddess.'

When they went for their passports, they were told that they must produce either their birth certificates or their horoscopes testified before an attorney. So they went home to find them.

Hari doubted very much whether he had ever possessed such a thing as a birth certificate; and as for his horoscope, he had never seen it, though he knew that some time ago it had been taken out of its secret place and sent to the Anands' house, there to be pondered over by the astrologer and compared with Sushila's, to make sure that their stars were not in opposition. As soon as he had left Amrita, he decided that after all he did not want to go home just now, not with all the relations there, talking about marriage; so he got off the bus and turned back, and spent a very pleasant two hours in the coffee-house, during which he forgot all the things which were troubling him, 3 October as well as *Jal Jawahar*.

Amrita could not forget, though she would have liked to. The thought of *Jal Jawahar* was not pleasant or easy for her either. To leave everyone and everything she knew behind, to embark like this on a long and secret expedition, she who had never had any inclinations for adventure or, if it came to that, for travel, none whatsoever – it was not an easy thing. And when she considered what she was doing it for, and the only answer was for Hari, she failed now to get that sudden rush of emotion which had lifted her above all other considerations and had made it all quite undeniably worthwhile; she just failed to get it the way she had only a week or so ago. Strain, she told herself, worry; when once we are safely on the ship, it will all come back, and being with him will be all that matters. So she told herself, and ignored the small peculiar doubts nibbling at the back of her mind, the reluctant vision of Hari intent on oven-baked fish or skulking behind his brother-in-law on the station platform.

The first thing she did when she got home was to ask for post. She was quite sure that Gian would hand her a letter or wire from her uncle, but all Gian said was, 'No please, nothing.'

'Nothing?' she repeated, and quite suddenly realized that she was almost as disappointed that there was nothing from Krishna Sen Gupta as that there was nothing from her uncle.

'Nothing please,' Gian confirmed, and she thought, well, what is there for him to write except I have arrived safely, I am well, are you well, I shall come home in four days; though he could have written that, she thought, if he had cared to. But Uncle – she should have heard from Uncle by this time. What could have gone wrong? If she did not hear from him by the day after tomorrow, she realized, she would lose the berths on *Jal Jawahar*, she would not be able to go to England, they would be trapped here and then Hari would have to be married. Strangely enough, she was not seized by panic at the thought; as a matter of fact, she found herself considering it quite calmly. Realizing this, she felt very guilty and tried to atone by rushing out at once to the Post Office round the corner and sending off another telegram: Very Anxious Kindly Send Money Immediately Amrita.

When she got back again, she walked into her mother's bedroom. Radha was fast asleep on the bed – resting after lunch, she called it – with that look of dissoluteness about her which always seemed to accompany her midday sleep; probably because she did not take her sari off, nor plaited her hair, so that she looked as if she had fallen down in a stupor rather than laid herself respectably to sleep.

Her keys were tied to the petticoat string at her waist, and Amrita quite calmly took them off. She knew about the tin box in the wardrobe, in which her mother kept all important documents and old letters; so she went straight to it, to get her birth certificate out. As she fitted the key to the lock, she was quite certain that Radha was going to wake up now and see her, and sure enough, she had no sooner put up the lid than her mother gave a little cry and sat up wildly in bed, saying, 'Who is it, who?'

Amrita quite calmly announced herself and did not even try to hide the opened box with the keys stuck in it.

'O you,' her mother said, sinking back again, her hand – an instinctive gesture on waking – feeling for her keys. She shot up again at once. 'I have been robbed!' she cried, wide awake.

'Your keys are with me,' Amrita said.

'What has happened? What are you doing with my keys?'

'I wanted to get something out of the tin box.'

'You are mad perhaps.'

'No. I only wanted to get something out of the tin box.'

With great dignity, though her sari had slipped from her shoulder and her hair out of its pins, Radha sat on her bed and said, 'So it is now your right to take keys from your sleeping mother and open her boxes.'

'But some of my things are in there too.'

'My things, she says!' her mother flashed. 'My things! And may I know, what are your things? Perhaps you will tell me, has a daughter any right to say my things to her mother?'

'Why not?' Amrita asked, quite irritated by what she considered unnecessary drama. She began to look through the papers for her birth certificate, lifting piles of faded letters; many of them, she saw, written on yellow prison-forms.

'Take your hands out!' her mother cried. 'Take your hands out of what is sacred to me!'

Amrita said, 'O Mamma,' in a deprecating manner, because Radha was really getting far more excited than the occasion warranted. 'I am only –'

'Bring that box here!' Radha screamed. 'Here to me!'

With a little sigh Amrita brought it. Her mother seized it, clutched it close to her and glared at Amrita with eyes of fire; they were a little dimmed now, for she was nearly fifty, but she could still flash them very effectively – though only in the service of indignation, no longer in that of passion. Amrita's eyes – it was the fundamental difference between mother and daughter – had never learnt to flash; they were soft eyes, melting and timid, and a little dreamy – or was it only absent-minded? – pleading eyes always.

'How dare you,' Radha hissed.

'But Mamma,' Amrita said uneasily, 'what have I done?'

Radha opened the box and fluttered her fingers through the contents. 'Your father's letters,' she said. 'Written in prison. And you say my things.'

Amrita hung her head and said nothing; and that was exactly the way her mother wanted her.

'That you have no respect for me, that I know, that is bad enough,' Radha pressed home. 'But your father, your dear dead father ...' She stopped, but as she was incapable of not overdoing an effect, went on again immediately, 'Your mother, we know it, is nothing to you, you treat her like a bazaar pariah; if you trample on her heart what does it matter to you, her tears do not bring you pain ...' Amrita lifted her head again and felt better ... 'she is the one who feeds you, clothes you; when you are sick she tends you day and night and strips herself of all her jewels and trinkets to send offerings for your recovery, but when you are well again you have not even a thought for her ...'

'Mamma,' Amrita interrupted, 'have I got a birth certificate?'

'Certainly you have,' Radha promptly replied. 'When you were born, at once your grandfather said we must get a birth certificate. Look!' she said, thrusting her hand under the pile of letters and drawing out the certificate, 'here it is.'

Amrita took it, looked at it, held on to it.

'And here,' Radha said, drawing out the long blue scroll, here is your horoscope. O my darling,' she suddenly said, leaning forward to grasp Amrita's head between her hands, 'does it not say that you will be married at the age of twenty, does it not say so?' and she kissed her face all over.

'It says so in the horoscope?' Amrita asked, also quite excited.

'Yes, my sweetest pet, it says your ascendant is in Aries and your – but I do not understand that, only the Pandit understands; a very holy man I went to for my darling's horoscope, the holiest and the most learned, it cost a lot of money, but it was only for building an ashram that he took so much money, for himself he wanted nothing, imagine, my beauty, he ate only little, little raw vegetable each day and only water he drank, he was so holy.'

'And he said this year I would be married?'

'Yes, my nightingale, when you are twenty, and a beautiful fair boy and from the best family.'

'Did he say where I am to be married?'

'Where? Here of course, where else, where you were born and your family is known and respected.'

After a little pause, Amrita said, 'I do not believe in horoscopes. I do not think they are very often correct.'

'You do not believe, you do not think!' Radha said. 'That is because you are very young and stupid and know nothing of the world.'

'Krishna! who is Krishna? He is perhaps not young and stupid? And not one line we have had from him, we do not even know that he has not fallen under the train. But wait till he comes home, I will soon speak with him.'

'He is home,' Amrita pointed out, a trifle sadly.

Radha too grew sad – though more flamboyantly – at the reminder. 'I have taken him so to my heart. I cannot think of any other home for him but ours.' She missed Krishna even more than she had anticipated; she found him very stimulating company, more so than either Amrita or the cook or the gardener. He was the only one to deliberately fan the fire of her indignation, and she found this a relief from always having to fan it herself. 'How we shall live if he leaves us for ever, I do not know,' she said, sighing heavily. 'But it is Life. All that is dear to us will go from us. That is why it says in the Gita that we must not let anything become too dear to us. We must live only in prayer.' She began to kiss Amrita's face again and said in a very gentle, melting voice, 'My sweet child, I am preparing such happiness for you, O such happiness.'

At once suspicious, Amrita drew her face away to ask, 'How, Mamma? What are you doing for me?'

Radha became evasive and pretended to look through the pile of letters. 'My only one,' she murmured as she did so, 'how beautiful she is, my child.'

'But how are you going to make me so happy?' Amrita persisted.

Radha now noticed that both her sari and her hair had slipped down. As she hitched up the one and pinned up the other she said, 'Even in the home, one must not neglect one's person, especially after marriage. If one wants to keep husband's love, one must always be as fresh and pretty as a bride.'

'Why are you telling me this?'

'One day you will marry, isn't it? And you have heard me tell,' she added roguishly, 'what your horoscope says: one day is perhaps not so far off.'

'Are you still trying to arrange?' Amrita asked wearily.

Radha did not answer. What might almost be described as a smirk played about her mouth.

'Not still Lady Ram Prashad's son?'

'And why not still Lady Ram Prashad's son?' Radha asked with a tolerant little smile.

'Mamma, but I told you –'

'It is all different now. Now at least we no longer have to worry about – please do not think I am scolding you again, I have forgiven now, I know it was only because you are so young and you were misguided and also there are many things you do not understand. But thank God you have a mother who can make all well again, so it is all finished and you do not have to suffer by your mistake. Please, my only one, give me the comb for my hair.' Amrita silently gave it to her and waited to hear more. 'Yes,' Radha said, taking the pins out of her hair, 'that is how it is and I shall make an offering to thank God for letting me save you.' Here she stuck the hairpins into her mouth and began to comb her hair; this gave her an opportunity to think out what she was going to say next.

When she had finished thinking she stopped combing, and then said in her special important-occasion voice, 'Yes, my darling, in marriage the most important thing is that husband and wife should come from the same social class. Of course we are very modern in our family and are not so strict about community and caste: but the class, my loveliest, is still very important, and you cannot be happy if you marry into a family that is not so good as yours.'

'Why?' Amrita brusquely asked.

'It is so, my only one, my sweet. When you are older, you will understand.'

'Were you and Pappa not happy?' For Nirad Chakravarty had come from a family of peasant landholders, and he himself had been only the first generation to be city-educated.

Radha, finding the question awkward, took up her comb, but put it down immediately, because she did not care to take the pins out of her hair again. 'It was different,' she said. 'Your father was such a clever man, so of course,' and she grew irritable, for she herself did not see that it was 'of course' at all, 'it was different.'

'Why?' Amrita asked, as was to be expected.

Which made her mother more irritated: 'Why, why, why! Can you not listen to me quietly one moment without always why, why, why!'

'Speak then,' Amrita said.

'There is no use speaking with you. You are only an obstinate, disobedient girl, and I waste breath when I talk sensible things to you. With daughters like you one makes the marriage first and talks afterwards.'

Penetrating straight to the hub of her mother's problem, Amrita said, 'Grandfather would never allow it.'

'Out!' Radha cried, really furious now. 'You dare speak like that?'

'Is it not true?'

'True! Shameless girl! Your grandfather not allow what your mother commands? We think with one head and we feel with one heart, your grandfather and I, and when I say she shall be married, will he not say so too?'

'No,' Amrita said ruthlessly, 'if I say that I do not wish to be married, Grandfather will never allow it. I know it, because I have often heard him say that girls must choose their own husbands and that it is criminal, that is what he said, to force them into marriage.'

Radha considered for a while. Amrita had hit the truth far too exactly for her liking, but she saw that she would not get far by merely raging; and she did want to get to at least a certain point. So she said rather ruefully and as if taking Amrita into her confidence: 'Yes, child, your grandfather does sometimes think a little differently from other people. Of course he is very wise and very clever and very learned, and he has held very high position and everybody respects him and we are all very proud of him but – you see, my darling, he is not young any more and his ideas are also sometimes not quite modern.'

'Oh Mamma!' Amrita pointed out. 'You want to tell me that Grandfather, who does not want to have arranged marriage, is not modern, and you, who want to have it, you are modern? Oh Mamma!'

'Do not "Oh Mamma" me,' Radha said. 'It is quite true. In the last generation it was sometimes thought that it is better to let marriages come by themselves. It was thought that we ladies would not be emancipated if we did not choose husbands ourselves. But it is not true: look at your Tarla auntie, it was Mataji and Parbati auntie and Shantidevi auntie who brought your Vazir uncle into our house, and yet see how emancipated your Tarla auntie is, even though her family chose her husband for her.'

'But you –' Amrita began, only to be brushed aside, for Radha had anticipated the objection. 'That was quite different. It was an exception, because your father was an exception, such a man you will not find in the whole world again.' And then she switched hastily on to, 'Now in the modern world it is thought that arranged marriages are after all the best, and you see the best families arranging matches, some even call in the broker or put advertisements in the newspaper, but of course the very best families only arrange with one another. You remember only two months ago Judge S. K. Mathur's family of Asoka Road married with the P. N. Mathur's, the Deputy minister's family ...'

'What do I care,' Amrita cried with unusual warmth, 'about the S. K. Mathurs and the P. N. Mathurs? A hundred times they can marry but still I will not marry Lady Ram Prashad's son!'

Radha shut her eyes and said in a pained, patient voice, 'Do not speak like that, child. You do not know what you are saying. You are very young, and you do not realize what a fine thing it is to be married into a family like the Ram Prashad Khannas –'

Amrita got to her feet and announced in tones more dramatic than she normally used, 'If I live to be one hundred years old, never will I realize it.'

Radha shut her eyes again and sighed. It was going to be more difficult than she had anticipated. 'Very well, child,' she said with great restraint, 'we will see. When you are a little older you will understand, and then perhaps you will know how to thank your mother for all she does and plans for you.' And as Amrita made for the door, she added, 'Please give me back the birth certificate.'

Amrita was holding on to it rather self-consciously. 'Why can I not keep it myself?'

'Because you cannot. Please give it here.'

'Why?' Amrita prevaricated, but Radha had swiftly leant forward and deftly snatched it back.

'Oh,' said Amrita, but her mother was already very firmly locking the box.

33

The morning after the inoculation Hari woke up with a terrible headache. He opened his eyes and knew at once that he was very sick. He moaned, but no one heard. It was still very early, about half past four, and everybody asleep. The courtyard was crammed with sleepers, two or three to every charpoy and some painfully bundled on the floor. Hari's younger brother slept next to him, on his stomach with his face squashed flat on the bed. Hari moaned again, a bit louder and gave his brother a push, but Babla only grunted and tossed himself on to his side. Hari lay quite still and very much afraid. He tried to lift his legs slightly to find out whether they too were hurting him; and, just as he had feared, he could hardly move them, they were so heavy and painful. Paralysis was his first thought, and he remembered his father's elder sister, who had lain paralysed for five years and had had to be fed by her daughters-in-law with a little spoon. He remembered very distinctly the food dribbling out of the corner of her mouth. He wanted to scream out loud then, but his voice stuck in his throat; perhaps he had lost that too and would never be able to speak again. O God, he prayed, make me die now, at once, do not let me be fed with a little spoon.

There was a sound of coughing and then more coughing, one starting after the other. The bundled figures stirred, groaned, sat up, coughed and spat and called on God. Crows cawed throatily, fluttered over the courtyard fearlessly near and settled on the wall to peck with bad-tempered beaks. A bullock-cart rumbled by outside. Someone crossly called to the little servant-boy, who at once stumbled up from the kitchen threshold, rubbed his eyes and got busy lighting the fire. The cow began to moo and stir in its shed and Mohini, yawning loudly and stretching herself, went in to milk it.

Hari lay quite still because he could not move nor speak. From time to time he moaned, but no one heard, for they were all concentrating on their own innumerable pains. Babla was the only one still fast asleep. Mohini walked past, carrying a jug frothing with warm milk, but she did not even glance at Hari. She was making vomiting noises in her throat and a minute later she came running past again to be sick in the bathroom. The women clicked their tongues – 'poor girl' – and looked reproachfully at her husband, who was sitting rubbing his hair, too tired to care. As soon as Mohini came out, there was a rush for the bathroom. An old man spat in a corner and cleaned his teeth with a little twig. The old women were drinking their first cups of tea with audible relish, and the little servant-boy staggered under a load of bedding. Someone was furiously tugging at the lavatory chain, but it had already been flushed too often and there was no more water left.

Hari let out another groan, a very loud one, for he was determined to be heard. His mother hurried round to him – 'Son?' she inquired – and he whispered, his eyes luxuriously shut, 'I am sick'; and realized that, thank God, he could speak. At once she began to lament, her hands clasped; and the other women came running, 'What is it? What has happened?' – and their first thought was that if Hari were sick there could be no wedding, they would have to go home without having been feasted.

Babla was pushed off the bed, the women clustered round, felt Hari's forehead, his wrist, his hands; someone began to massage his legs, someone else his temples, and all the time his mother cried, 'My son!' One old woman climbed, with surprising agility, on to the end of the bed and began to pray, spreading her hands over Hari and looking up to Heaven. 'And he to be married!' the mother cried. Mohini came with a wet cloth, which she slapped on to his forehead – the water trickled down his nose, making him feel uncomfortable, so he raised his hand to take the cloth off. It is not paralysis, he realized then, for he could move his arm. But there was no doubt about it, he was very sick, otherwise why should they be crowding round him like this, crying and advising and contradicting one another's advice and praying over him. The sun was coming out, quite hot already; it touched his legs making him pull them up, and he realized that they too could move. Not paralysis: but what could it be then? One comfort, at least it could not be cholera, only yesterday he had had an injection – and then he remembered that the doctor had said he might get some unpleasant after-effects from the drug. But this was not merely after-effects, it was a real sickness, something very bad, why else should his head be hurting so – Oh his head, his head, and he groaned again. His mother wailed, the old aunt prayed more fervently. Then someone noticed that the sun was touching him and they carried his charpoy indoors, shouting at one another to be careful not to jolt him.

Just as they were carrying him in, Prema came running with her hair undone and a frantic look in her eyes, for the news had already spread to her house. She was followed by Suri and a crowd of relatives who were staying at her house. Everyone crammed into the little room with the family trunks and stood clustered round Hari's bed; the air was thick with anxious talk. Suri at once asked, had they called the doctor; but no one wanted the doctor: 'Doctor? And he will perhaps take him away to the hospital!' And at that word they all groaned aloud and began to tell of things that had happened in hospitals. Suri shrugged and said, anyway it was probably nothing, Hari had only eaten too much or perhaps (with a laugh) he was trying to shirk his wedding-day. At that Prema could not restrain herself, but screamed at Suri – everyone fell silent out of respect for a husband-and-wife scene – how dare he suggest such a thing about his wife's brother? she screamed, and burst into tears. So Suri thought it best to get out and go to work. Mohini's husband had already quietly slipped away, without any breakfast.

Suri's half-humorous suggestion made Hari realize for the first time that if he were really so ill as they were all saying, the marriage could not take place. His first reaction was one of disappointment: no sweets, no music, no garlands, no jokes, and he had been so looking forward to it all. And worst of all – it took him by surprise, the intense surge of disappointment – no Sushila. Her eyes, her breasts, her hair like a black flame: no, he quickly told himself, his illness was nothing, just the after-effects of the drug, as the doctor had said, it could not be anything else: it must not be. One of the old women brought medicine for him, some green herbs with which she said she had cured many illnesses – a rupture, dysentery, diphtheria, smallpox – a wonderful medicine; but to Hari it was only a horrible taste in his mouth. The old woman was telling how once in the village a man lay dying of cancer, a doctor had come and said he could do nothing, the man must die, and then she had given this medicine ... Hari remembered Amrita, and then it seemed to him that this illness of his was God's intervention on behalf of their love. He resisted thoughts of Sushila and persuaded himself that it was a very bad illness indeed, which God had sent to prevent the marriage. Though he could not help wondering whether God could not have thought of a better way of preventing it: for what was the use of making him lie here miserable, unable to marry Sushila and barred from seeing Amrita?

The news of his illness spread quickly, and soon Mrs Anand arrived, looking suspicious and determined, like one who suspects a trick which has to be got to the bottom of. As soon as she came in, they all fell silent and looked anxious, except his mother, who wailed, 'My son', and the old aunt at the end of the bed, who prayed with new fervour. Prema began to massage Hari's legs very vigorously. Mrs Anand gave him a pretty shrewd look, but she spoke with sympathy. 'What is this we have to hear,' she said, and was answered from all sides of the room about God's will.

'Indeed,' she said very significantly, 'it is God's will.'

Prema stopped massaging instantly to say, 'He will be well on the day of his wedding,' to which all the others assiduously assented: he must be well, what else; they could not go home without having been feasted.

'And if not?' Mrs Anand said, sitting down on the edge of Hari's charpoy, facing Prema, who sat massaging on the other edge. 'If not? Then it is all to go to waste, all the arrangements we are making? This risk we cannot take,' and she started to massage Hari's other leg. He lay quite still. 'The wedding must be postponed,' she said. 'By at least three months. We must be quite safe.'

'Three months!' all the women cried. Hari shut his eyes and hoped he looked asleep.

'Three months,' Mrs Anand said firmly, and arranged her dupatta in a decorous and matronly manner.

Hari's mother stopped crying and gave a sign to the old aunt to leave off praying. 'Ah no, dear sister,' she told Mrs Anand, 'God has been merciful this time, it is only a very little sickness He has sent. On the day of the wedding, what am I saying – tomorrow even, he will be well again,' and she stroked the prostrate Hari's brow.

Hari wanted to say, 'Even now I am already well,' but did not think it would be, under the circumstances, fitting. So he kept his eyes shut and his body rigid, letting anyone who cared stroke or massage him.

But Mrs Anand clung fast to her point: the wedding must be postponed; they could not go ahead with the preparations if they were not sure the bridegroom would be there; who knows, tomorrow, God forbid, he might be worse; and tomorrow the electrician would be coming to fix all the lights – the bright revolving circles and the flashing 'Welcome' and what if they had to take it all down again, what of the expense, was it a little thing? No, it must be postponed by at least three months.

'And the poor children?' Hari's mother demanded, clasping her hands and with tears in her eyes. 'My poor son, here already he is sick with longing for his bride, and now he must wait three more months?'

Her eyes, her breasts, her hair like a black flame; and Hari felt that indeed it would be a hard thing to have to wait three more months.

'They are young,' Mrs Anand said. 'Three months are nothing in the many years they will have together.'

But Amrita: this sickness had probably been sent as a special intervention. Many things could happen in three months, and perhaps they were after all meant to go to England. Perhaps after all he was not meant to marry Sushila. He kept his eyes tight shut, wishing he could go to sleep and only wake up when they had ultimately decided whether the wedding was to be or not.

All his relations were fast resolved that it was to be, had to be. They all started talking at once – Mrs Anand might be thinking of the expense of the preparations, but they could think only of their pleasant anticipations, and the bitterness of having to go away with no wedding celebrated, their preparations, expectations all gone to waste: and they told her the sickness was nothing, perhaps it was only the excitement and his terrible longing for his bride; and then the medicine which had never failed, could they not rely on that? But Mrs Anand remained adamant, sitting there on the edge of Hari's bed with her head flung back.

'I will tell you,' Hari's mother said desperately, 'yesterday in the night we had korma, my son is very fond of korma, three times I filled his plate and so today his health is not so good.'

But Prema took up a new attitude. Across Hari, she looked at the other woman, and though her eyes were not as fine, as glittering, as skilled as her antagonist's, yet she knew how to charge them with sufficient expression. Her mouth smiled as she said, 'Of course, if you really wish it, then there must be no wedding. Your wishes are our commands.'

All the women fell silent; they knew there was something more behind this, and waited. Mrs Anand also knew; she faced Prema across the bed, eye met eye in optical combat.

'The risk for you is great,' Prema said, still smiling. 'It is too great, therefore the wedding must not be.'

The other women shifted uneasily. They hoped Prema knew what she was doing, and would not in the end merely give way: the thought of having to return home unfeasted and with nothing to talk and reflect over in the coming months was terrible to them.

'What are two-three months,' Mrs Anand said, her eyes still battling with Prema's, though they were a little screwed up at the corners now, intense with concentration, 'when they are both so young?'

And then Prema said it. 'Two-three months,' she said, 'who can tell what will not be in two-three months?' and she dropped her eyes away from Mrs Anand's.

The women almost gasped. So this was it, she was risking all – though what risk was there, they silently asked themselves, were young men like

Hari in such abundance today that the mother of three daughters could afford to sacrifice him on a point of pride? They looked at Mrs Anand: yes, she was proud, sitting there with her bosom sticking out and her hard black eyes; they measured her from top to toe, contemptuously now, now it was their turn, she was proud, but she had three daughters, and they had Hari. They took Prema up, 'Who can tell, two-three months is a long time,' and some of the less subtle ones even murmured, 'So many offers, so many beautiful girls with good dowries.'

Hari opened his eyes abruptly. He even sat up a little way, he was so startled, but his mother pushed him back immediately – 'Rest, son, rest' – and rubbed his temples. His heart was beating fiercely, all thoughts of Amrita and divine intervention were drowned in the surge of fear that came over him, for were they not threatening to take Sushila away from him? He looked from Mrs Anand to Prema and back again to Mrs Anand, and stayed there, his eyes wide open and fixed on her, trying to penetrate through the face, trying to sway her thoughts to be kind to him. But she did not even look at him; like all the others, she had forgotten his presence.

She was smiling; she was defeated and knew they all knew it; so she smiled and said, 'Perhaps for the children two-three months will be very long.'

'Our Hari,' Prema said, and remembered to massage his shin again, 'will wish only as his family wish.'

But Mrs Anand, having had to accept defeat, was not inclined to stay and allow Prema to press her victory home. She got up, arranged her dupatta in a dignified manner, and said to Hari, 'Please do not eat any more korma before your wedding day.' She was still smiling.

Hari also smiled, for he was happy. He felt light with relief and entirely well again – until he remembered his love for Amrita. And then his conscience told him that perhaps he should have made more of this morning's sickness, which had been sent to him so opportunely. But thoughts of Sushila pressed close upon him, and his conscience lay, for the moment, quiet.

34

Krishna Sen Gupta did not have a very happy time in Calcutta. For one thing, the job about which he had come to inquire was not all it had been made out to be. In the letter he had received, the magazine whose Assistant Editorship he had been offered was represented as an accomplished fact, a flourishing weekly with a reliable body of subscribers. The letter-head had indeed been very impressive. But when he got to Calcutta, he found that the paper was still in the coffee-house stage. The organizers, who had written to him, were in a ferment of enthusiasm about it. They sat all day in the coffee-house, drank coffee, smoked cigarettes and made schemes. They could afford to make schemes, for they had financial backing.

This came from a young man, the son of a multi-millionaire government contractor, aged twenty-three and just back from America, with an American accent, a pink nylon shirt and a lot of ideas. Looking healthy, well-fed and well-dressed, he tapped the marble top of the coffee-house table with his signet ring and said that it was their job to educate the educated: a phrase which apparently pleased him, for he brought it in several times. He said he had been shocked on his return to India by the ignorance he found among the so-called intelligentsia; they were, he said, completely out of touch with modern ideas and trends in Art and Literature. His magazine was intended to stir up this pool of intellectual stagnation. The educated, he said, tapping his signet ring, were going to be educated; they were going to be taught a thing or two about Modern Art and Literature. He had gathered about him a large and ever-growing group of young men – M.A. students, most of them, from modest homes – all very keen about Modern Art and Literature. They listened to him eagerly, admired his American accent, his advanced ideas and his father's money, and wished that their parents, too, could have sent them to a foreign University instead of only to the Calcutta colleges. The magazine, they thought, was the best thing that could happen to the Indian intelligentsia.

It had not yet actually materialized, but they had everything ready. They had a Circulation Manager who spent his time copying names out of the Directories. They had a printer, a young man whose father had bought him a printing-press, with which he was going to do great things. They had not got an office yet, but the cousin of the America-returned young man had agreed to put a room in his flat at their disposal, with use of telephone. They had a telegraphic address – LITART. They had a dramatic critic, a very gifted man closely connected with Calcutta amateur theatricals. They had an art critic, himself a painter just passed out of Art School. A young College lecturer in Poona had already sent them an 8,000-word article on The Conception of Form in Modern Literature; and Professor Hoch of Delhi had consented to contribute a series of articles on The Influence of the Paris School on Modern Indian Painting. They had one agent in New York and another in London – both graduates of Calcutta University whose families had sent them abroad for further studies – and were in correspondence with an Indian painter in Paris; and they hoped eventually to enlist a substantial body of overseas subscribers. It was all very exciting and cosmopolitan, and some consolation for having to live in Calcutta.

Krishna blamed only himself. Lying at home on the bed in his own room, smoking cigarette after cigarette till his mouth became thick with the taste of them, he laughed at himself for imagining anything else but this. And he to be caught by it, who had himself started several schemes like this, years ago when he frequented coffee-houses and was for ever discerning genius in himself and those around him. He laughed again, with his head in the pillow, and then thought only of going back to Delhi as soon as it was decently possible. For home was hardly home any more. Strange, for when he was in Delhi he thought of himself as belonging to Calcutta, but now that he was here, he was a stranger and belonged only to Delhi. Many of his old friends had gone, were scattered in government posts in different parts of India; they were all respectable now, earning a good salary, being good Civil Servants with pensionable posts and fertile wives. Those who had stayed in Calcutta had also settled down, and instead of sitting in the coffee-houses railing against the society they lived in, they sat in their offices or clubs or homes and were themselves content to be a solid part of that society. They were very pleased to see Krishna when he walked into their offices the first day – 'it is Krishna Sen Gupta, how long it has been, come and have lunch' – and pleased too the second time, but after that – who was Krishna Sen Gupta, a friend once, but that had been years ago and everything was different now, they had wives, jobs, their own little circle in which they moved.

Worse than disappointment over friends was disappointment over his parents. Certainly they were happy to see him, he was after all their only child; and scattered about the house, interspersed among photographs of leading Congress personalities, were others of little Krishna in a lace-frock or bigger Krishna grinning outside Agra Fort. But they had got so used to being without him that there was really no proper place for him in their lives. They were disappointed people, his parents, for political reality had turned out to be rather different from the ideal, and Congress was no longer the Congress which had been themselves and those like them. But they were too intelligent to be fundamentally embittered by what was, under any circumstances, inevitable, and they realized that disappointment such as theirs was a natural consequence to the fulfilment of a life ambition. There was a quiet sadness about them now, a kind of resignation made sweet by their perfect affection for one another. They were restful people to be with, but not forthcoming; finding all the human contact they needed in one another, it was difficult for them to adjust themselves to any outsider, even when that outsider was their son. They would have liked to get nearer to him but they could not, they had got out of the habit. Once or twice his father had tried to talk with him about – neither Krishna nor his father himself was quite sure what about, but assumed it must be about fundamentals, about important things; but all the father managed to get out were some platitudes concerning the future and a conscious habit of life, which so embarrassed both of them that they parted as quickly as possible. After that they just contented themselves with cordial surface relations, his father making little jokes and puns over the dinner table at which his mother painfully smiled.

His mother had become even more withdrawn than he remembered her. It was as if nothing interested her any more. Krishna found her apathy very disconcerting, for it was to her he wanted to speak more than to anybody else. He knew that once penetrate that barrier of apparent indifference and one would draw from her wise and impartial advice and, if at all possible, helpful action too. But he could not penetrate. Several times he tried; he went downstairs, found her in her room, and then could not even come near the subject about which he wished to talk to her. She sat there, bundled up in an indeterminate cotton sari, apparently willing to give him all her time, listen to him if need be all morning, and yet also apparently quite indifferent to anything he might say to her. So all he could do was tell her the latest jokes about the Government, draw a faint painful smile from her, but no further response. He found himself, in the middle of such an interview, longing for Radha; for she at least would rush at one with all the response and more that one might ask for; and if one did not ask, still she would rush; and however irritating her forthcomingness might be, it was at any rate, he felt now, more relaxing than his mother's attitude of complete withdrawal.

When he had run out of jokes, he left her – she as indifferent, or as easy, about his going as about his coming – and went upstairs again, there to sit on his bed and think what to do about Amrita. Sometimes, when he was feeling very resolute, he seized a writing-pad and wrote 'My dear Amrita' or 'dearest Amrita' or 'Amrita', but after that he did not know what to say. And yet he realized that it would be easier now, when she was far away and more of an idea than a person, than it would be later, when he was with her again in Delhi and would feel too shy or too proud or too awkward to speak, with her there before him, her hands moving and the changes of expression on her face visible to him.

35

Next time Amrita tried to find the tin box in which her birth certificate was kept, she discovered that it had disappeared. Radha, ever cautious in her suspicions even when she did not know the true cause of them, had found another, safer hiding place for it. But that was not Amrita's only worry; her worst one was that, despite her letter and two telegrams, she still had no news, let alone money, from her uncle in Simla. Today was the last day left for her to redeem her two bookings on *Jal Jawahar*, and if she did not hear from her uncle by some post today, she would have to give them up. She had seen Hari for a few moments in the morning – just before they had had to go their separate ways to announce their separate programmes – and he had told her, when she asked him, that no, he had not found his birth certificate, nor his horoscope (he did not tell her that he had gone to the coffee-house after they had parted, and had, in that relaxing atmosphere, forgotten all about his birth certificate as well as all about his other worries). And when she got home there was her mother talking about Lady Ram Prashad's son; she now presented him to Amrita as an accomplished fact, and pretended to regard the actual marriage as quite fixed and only a matter of time. And meanwhile there had also been no news of Krishna Sen Gupta.

Amrita decided to go and see her grandfather. It was the first time, as far as she could remember, that she had gone to see him like this of her own accord, without having been summoned, and unaccompanied by her mother. The servants were surprised to see her, and rather put out, because they were afraid that she might want lunch or tea or dinner and they did not care to have their day's routine so unexpectedly upset.

But she was far from thinking about lunch or tea or dinner, walking up the stairs and along the passage to her grandfather's room. Nothing stirred in the house, all was silence and old age; young and slim and enfolded in her pale green sari as in a petal, she felt shy and out of place, and an intruder; though her light step could not do much to disturb the settled silence of that house. She thought about what she wanted to say to her grandfather, but nothing occurred to her; she hardly knew why she had come, except that Mamma would not stop talking about Lady Ram Prashad's son, and Vazir uncle gave no sign of fulfilling his promise, and Krishna had not written. Perhaps Grandfather could help her, though how or in what way she wanted to be helped she was not sure.

'May I come in, Grandfather?' she called through the curtain, and he, sitting upright in his chair after lunch, opened his eyes as soon as she called and clearing his throat said, 'Come in.'

He was sitting at his desk. His papers were arranged in a neat sheaf before him, the fountain-pen closed, lying on top. His spectacles peered emptily from the desk. He picked them up and put them on and looked at her over the top of them. If he was surprised to see her, or glad, he did not show it; he only said, 'Yes, Amrita? Where is your mother?' To which she replied, 'At Tarla auntie's.'

He waited, and she did not know how to begin, or on what to begin. It was as she had feared, coming up the stairs and along the passage; she really had nothing to say. But still he waited, so in the end, for want of anything better, she burst it out – 'Grandfather, is it true I have to marry Lady Ram Prashad's son?' and even as she was asking, she was sorry about it, because she knew she was being disloyal to her mother.

It was only by the short, breathless pause before he replied, and by the way he did not look at her, that she knew he was very angry. All he said was, 'You are going to England.'

'When please, Grandfather?' she humbly asked.

'As soon as possible,' he pronounced. 'You will go as soon as possible. There is no talk whatsoever of any marriage for you. You are going to England for your studies, please understand me.'

'Yes Grandfather,' she said. She felt doubly disloyal now, not only to her mother but also to her grandfather, for was she not planning to elope – that was the word – at the same time as she was asking him for help, which he was giving?

'You will go as soon as it can be arranged,' he said again. His lips, always thin, had disappeared almost entirely, they were set so tightly. He looked at her over his spectacles as if she were the cause of his displeasure and said very sternly, 'You may set your mind at rest, you will not, now or ever, have to submit to any marriage that is not of your own choice.' And he nodded her dismissal, because he wanted to be alone.

She was glad to get away, feeling more unhappy and more perplexed than when she had come; and the servants were glad to see her go, though they said politely, 'Enough? Is that all? You are not staying to eat in our house?'

The Rai Bahadur's anger soon became mixed with what was almost triumph. His daughter might try to defy him, but then, he felt, he could deal with his daughter; Radha was no problem; she presented no threat. The threat had been in Amrita: it was her defiance he had felt, even perhaps feared, and now here she had been, seeking his help and the shelter of his authority. With vigour and determination he unscrewed his fountain-pen and wrote a few pungent lines to his daughter Radha, to summon her into his presence. As he wrote, he thought of his servants going about their work, his silver gleaming in cabinets, his orange-tasselled lampshades and symbolical statues, the huge heavy dining-table at which he had feasted Andrew Goleby and John Seymour and P. N. Dutt. All these things seemed very real and solid and important to him. Remembering their importance, and his own, he cleared his throat and looked authoritatively over his spectacles, though there was no one to see him.

Radha meanwhile was at Tarla's house. It was after lunch and they were sitting in armchairs in the drawing-room. Radha was feeling distinctly unsatisfied, for meals in that household, now that Vazir Dayal was not there, were of a strictly utilitarian order. 'It is no wonder you are so thin,' she grumbled, and Tarla asked brusquely, 'You are still hungry?'

'Idiot,' said Radha, turning her face away, but Tarla, straightforward woman that she was, said, 'If you are, please say so and the cook will easily make you an omelette.'

'Omelette!' Radha said contemptuously, but on a sudden notion her eyes lit up. 'Send to *Ragko Mull's* for pastries.'

Tarla gave the order without comment. A few minutes later they heard the car start up outside. A disgruntled driver sat at the wheel, rudely forced out of his afternoon sleep; he had not even had time to button up his uniform jacket, and a soiled vest looked out from underneath.

'That I am so thin is not the only wonder,' Tarla said caustically, but Radha was too happy anticipating the pastries to wish to take offence. She kicked off her shoes and stretched her feet in the air, luxuriously waggling the toes. 'And Amrita?' Tarla asked.

'What about my Amrita?'

'Has she yet consented to Lady Ram Prashad's son? Because you know, without her consent Pappaji will never –'

'My Amrita is a good girl,' Radha cut her short. 'She will always do what her mother wishes.'

'Hm,' said Tarla; Radha contentedly contemplated her waggling toes.

'Really,' Radha said after a while, 'we must do something about Mira.

She is getting so fat and slothful, she thinks of nothing but her food and her clothes. Sometimes when we are in company I feel quite ashamed because she does not know at all how to take part in intelligent conversation. I think you ought to take her more to your meetings, it will perhaps broaden her outlook a little. Of course, poor Mira can never really become intelligent but I think we ought to help her to become at least a little more up to date. She does not know anything, even when people talk about Pakistan she looks stupid. I do not think it is very good for our position in society to have such a sister.'

Tarla struggled with herself for a bit but could not hold it back. 'My dear Radha,' she said, 'I am sure no one knows better than I how one can suffer from stupid sisters.'

'I know,' Radha replied cheerfully, 'what do you think I have been saying? We must seriously speak with Mira, she must improve herself if only for our sake. But it is very much your fault too.'

'Mine?'

'Yes yours, who else? You are so selfish, you never wish to take poor Mira anywhere. Always it is I who have to take her out to people. We hear so much of your committee-shommittees, but I have not yet heard that you have done anything useful for your own family.'

Tarla drummed her fingers on the side of her chair and looked wry; both expressions were either lost on, or ignored by, her sister.

'When it comes to your own family,' Radha, with her passion for elaborating, went on, 'then we do not see so much of all your good actions. Only when it is Committees and Lady Ram Prashad and reception with tea at Rashtrapati Bhavan, then we hear spoken the name of Mrs Tarla Mathur.'

Tarla could see no point in encouraging her sister by a reply, so she asked abruptly, 'When is Krishna Sen Gupta coming back?'

'There is another one!' Radha cried, successfully deflected. 'You will perhaps not believe me when I tell you that not one word we have heard from him, and it is nearly one week now that he has gone away!'

'It is nearly two weeks that Husband has gone away,' Tarla said drily, 'and I have not yet heard one word from him.'

'Oh,' Radha waved her away, 'you know very well Vazir never writes letters.'

'Never home, no,' Tarla agreed.

'But this Krishna Sen Gupta now – would you think it is the behaviour of a gentleman, England-returned, not to write to those who are anxious even "I have arrived safely" on a postcard?'

'You would have heard very quickly if he had not arrived safely.'

'At least a picture-postcard of Calcutta he could have sent,' Radha complained. 'It is so long since I have been to Calcutta, I would like very much to receive a picture-postcard of the Victoria Memorial.'

'If he leaves you, you will find it hard to replace him with such another paying guest.'

'I will find it impossible to replace him,' Radha dramatically declared. 'You do not know what a place he has found in my heart. Ah Tarla,' she said, leaning forward to lay her hand on the other's knee, 'you do not know how often I have wished – he a Bengali, the son of a lawyer, how suitable it would have been, how happy would have been her poor dead father!'

'It is not yet too late,' Tarla said, but Radha sadly shook her head. 'Lady Ram Prashad,' she said, 'we have almost promised her, and then of course it is such a very good match, such a good family, and America-returned –'

The telephone rang.

'The telephone,' Radha pointed out; Tarla picked up the receiver and said, 'Hallo,' and, 'Ah yes, Lady Ram Prashad, how are you?'

'What a coincidence!' Radha marvelled. She idly looked at her hand against the dark background of the chair while she listened to Tarla saying, 'No, Lady Ram Prashad, I have not yet had time to copy the minutes of that meeting, you know there has been so much . . .' and again thanked God that Amrita had inherited her father's fine slim hands.

The bearer came in with a cardboard box tied daintily with lilac ribbon; he had placed it ceremoniously on a silver tray. 'And plates?' Radha whispered fiercely. 'We have to eat from the floor?' Already she was picking at the lilac string.

'I cannot help feeling,' Tarla was saying, 'that in spite of the vote taken at the General Meeting we ought to set up a separate sub-committee.'

'And tea!' Radha cried *sotto voce* after the bearer. 'We will have tea too.' The box was open: eight little cakes nestled inside, chocolate éclair, white meringue, green marzipan, pink coconut with blobs of cream: Radha's tongue protruded slightly from between her lips.

'Exactly, I quite agree with you, Lady Ram Prashad. And if you could spare the time to act as President . . .'

Such a pity Amrita was not here, a pastry would have done her good, and the poor child so thin and weak-looking. If there were any left, she would take them home and Amrita would have them with a glass of milk in the evening.

'Oh,' said Tarla. Her tone made Radha look up.

'Then we must I think congratulate you,' Tarla said; and Radha – 'What for? She has given birth to twins perhaps?' This seemed to her very funny and kept her laughing to the end of the telephone conversation.

Tarla put down the receiver and said, 'That was Lady Ram Prashad.'

'I have ears,' Radha placidly remarked. She was taking the pastries out of the box and reverently placing them on a plate with a lace doily on it. After each one she licked her fingers.

'She said –'

'You will take tea?' Radha asked, poising the pot over one of the Limoges cups.

'How can I take tea so soon after my lunch?'

Radha, pouring, said, 'You call those few little crumbs of vegetable lunch? Even the servants, I could see it in their eyes, despised us for taking such food.'

'If perhaps you will let me tell you what Lady Ram Prashad said . . . ?'

'What is it to me what she said? I care nothing about your committees here, committees there, I have more important things to think over.'

'Oh?' Tarla inquired, and with distaste watched her sister hover undecided over the pastries. 'Now you have decided that our work is not important?'

'Oh no,' Radha said. 'At least it gives something to do to women who have nothing else to do. Women who have no children, for instance, no daughters to worry their heads and their hearts over.' She decided finally to start on a chocolate éclair.

Tarla said abruptly, 'Lady Ram Prashad told me that she had just received a letter from her son.'

Radha looked up from her plate. 'Could you not have said so from the beginning? You know it is very interesting to me.' She bit into her éclair; cream came oozing out.

'Yes,' Tarla went on with relish, 'he has written to her that he has just married an American girl.'

Cream stained Radha's mouth; she held the half-bitten éclair in mid-air. Tarla studied her own nails, feigning indifference. But to her annoyance Radha began to laugh.

'An American girl!' she cried. 'How angry Lady Ram Prashad must be!'

'Not at all,' Tarla said. 'Lady Ram Prashad is an educated and broad-minded woman, and I am sure she will welcome the girl into her family just as much as if she had been a Hindu girl.'

'Yes,' Radha laughed, 'what else can she do now, poor woman? She will even pretend to be happy. Like Mrs R. K. Mehta, the wife of the Deputy Minister, when her son brought her home from London an English daughter-in-law. I know very well that she was eating her heart out and she was so ashamed, but before everybody she said how happy she was and what a nice girl her daughter-in-law was, no different at all from a Hindu girl, she said at least a hundred times. You will see, Lady Ram Prashad will say just like that. But in her heart I know she will be longing for my Amrita!' and she very complacently popped the remains of her éclair into her mouth with one hand, while the other she stretched out for a green marzipan apple.

'And also,' she went on after a while, 'I do not think that the Ram Prashad Khannas are such a first-class family. Who are they, the Ram Prashad Khannas? If they had not made money in business in the first war, they would still be sitting on their few miserable little acres in the U.P. No,' she declared proudly, 'such people are not good enough for the grand-daughter of Rai Bahadur Tara Chand.'

'Or the daughter of Nirad Chakravarty,' Tarla could not refrain from adding.

But Radha refused to be provoked. 'Of course,' she agreed blandly, 'the daughter of Nirad Chakravarty.' And that set her thinking to such purpose that a little smile began to flicker on her face. Tarla looked at her suspiciously.

'Do you know, my sister,' Radha said, a trifle roguishly, 'what I would like very much?'

'How should I know?' said Tarla churlishly; it irritated her to see Radha in such a good mood after this blow which she had just delivered to her hopes.

'I should like very much,' Radha said, the smile deepening, 'to see my Amrita marrying a Bengali; and what I would like more than anything is the son of a Bengali lawyer, what could be more fitting for my child?'

'Why do you not leave the poor girl alone now? Can you not stop for one moment thinking about marriage?'

'Now I have got into the habit of it,' Radha said, smiling broadly. 'And also, you know what it says in her horoscope, that she will be married at the age of twenty.'

'Tcha!' said Tarla in disgust.

36

No word from Vazir uncle. The three days were up, she did not even dare go to the travel agency. She felt too weary for further effort: perhaps Hari would suggest something now, though she felt rather doubtful about that. She lay on the sofa in the living-room, trying to read a book which Krishna had given her. It was a novel about India, written by an English lady: well-written too, Amrita could see that, all the proper accoutrements of style and sensibility, but Amrita could not understand why the lady had given Indian names to her characters.

She found it hard to concentrate, burdened as she was with various worries. Half an hour ago her grandfather's bearer, in brilliant white uniform and huge turban, had brought a note for Radha: it was lying on the table now, sealed, and Amrita felt rather guilty about it because she could guess what was in it, and when and why Grandfather had written it.

The postman too had been and gone, leaving only the electricity bill and a letter from Hyderabad for her mother. She had given up hope of hearing from Vazir uncle and was trying hard to persuade herself that there was really no reason why Krishna should write. He would be home soon, anyway, a few more days and he would be here. She felt much relieved at the thought; though she would not have been able to say why, since his homecoming could bring no solution to what she thought were her problems. She explained to herself that it would at least be a comfort to have someone with whom to talk about it all; and then, too, Krishna might be able to think of something they could do, which Hari – well, she had to admit it – never would. Krishna would not write to let them know when he would be coming home: he would just come walking in, in two, three days perhaps; she might be lying just like this on the living-room sofa, trying to read a book, and she would look up and there he would be. She looked up and there was her mother with a little cardboard box from *Ragho Mull's*.

'Just see,' she cried, holding it up, 'what I have brought for you!'

She sat down on the edge of the sofa on which Amrita was lying. 'Pastries,' she said, 'I was at your Tarla auntie's and there were these two pastries – fresh from *Ragho Mull's* – and I said I will take them home to my little one, they will do her good with one glass of milk. You are resting, my darling?'

'I am reading.'

'Rest, rest, child, please do not strain your eyes. You will eat them now?'

'What?'

'The pastries I have brought for you, what else.'

'There is a note for you from Grandfather,' Amrita said uneasily. 'On the table.'

Radha got up and opened it. The expression on her face as she read it revealed nothing. Amrita pretended to be intent on her book.

Radha folded the note close and pushed it carefully into her bosom. 'From your grandfather,' she said unnecessarily.

Amrita asked casually, 'What does Grandfather say?'

'Only he wants me to visit him. Poor Pappaji, how lonely he must be without us all, it is no wonder he sends for me. Oh, how well I can imagine it, how his heart is longing for his daughter! I shall feel the same when my own sweet child has gone from my house.'

Amrita sat up and turned her face away to look out of the window. Through the anti-burglar bars she saw the papaya tree, and the sky already streaked with orange. She could not repress it: 'Grandfather is not angry with you?'

Radha's hand groped instinctively for the note in her bosom; but no, she remembered, it had been sealed. She dropped her hand and looked sharply at Amrita. Amrita was studying the pattern on her sari, blue chrysanthemums and green sprigs on a white background.

'Your grandfather angry with me? How dare you even think such a thing!' and when Amrita gave no answer, she worked herself into a greater passion: 'There can be no anger between us, one head we have, one heart we have – have you no shame, no respect, to speak such things to your mother?'

So Amrita was stung into blurting it out: 'I know Grandfather is angry with you, because I went to see him today.'

Radha stood stock still in the centre of the room: 'You went to see your Grandfather?'

'Yes,' Amrita went on, close to tears, 'I went to see him and I told him how you torture me –'

'I torture you!'

'You do!' Amrita cried, her lips trembling. 'Always with your talk of marriage and Lady Ram Prashad's son, I could not bear it, that is why I went to see Grandfather and I asked him to please make you stop it, that is why I went, and Grandfather said nobody can make me marry if I do not want to and he is very angry with you, I know he is, so please do not tell me lies!'

Radha, still standing in the middle of the room, rapidly calculated her next step, while Amrita tried hard not to burst outright into tears.

'My darling,' Radha said, in a voice soft as honey, 'my darling,' and she sat down by Amrita on the sofa, 'do you not know that I live only for you?'

Amrita turned her head away and withdrew the hand which Radha had begun to fondle.

'My only one,' Radha said, softly, softly, laying her hand on Amrita's knee and fondling that instead, 'do you not know that all I do, I do only for you, to please you and make you happy?'

'But you do not please me and you do not make me happy!' Amrita cried.

Radha, undeterred, replied as sweetly as before, 'Why could you not tell me so? If you had told me so, I would not have spoken with Lady Ram Prashad one moment longer.'

'But I did tell you, what else have I been telling you every day!'

'No, my sweetest,' Radha murmured, 'you did not tell me even once.' Amrita looked at her quite incredulously but she carried on, 'Not once you said to me "Mamma, I do not want, please do not arrange this thing for me." One word from you and it would all have been finished, do you not know that? You are too shy, my little one, my child, always it is so, I know you do not like to speak out and perhaps displease your mother. Is not that what you were afraid of, to displease me?'

She stopped and waited, but Amrita refused to lend herself to the game; so Radha went on playing it by herself. 'I know it was,' she said and kissed Amrita on the forehead, 'I know all that goes on in my sweet child's heart. But Oh, my darling, how could I be displeased at anything my love wishes! All my pleasure, all my happiness, is only in your happiness, I have no life apart from you.'

Amrita looked out of the window. The orange had gone from the sky and the papaya tree was fading into silhouette.

'And now of course,' Radha was saying, 'now that I know your wishes, there will be no more talk of Lady Ram Prashad.'

Amrita turned her head and looked at her mother, hopefully if somewhat suspiciously. 'Really Mamma?' It was almost dark in the room and Radha's features appeared blurred.

'What "really Mamma"?' Radha said in mock indignation. 'There is no question. Now that I know that my only one, my love, my nightingale, that she does not wish it, I will tell Lady Ram Prashad, go away from us, go find another wife for your son, our Amrita is not for you.'

Amrita gave a sigh of relief and let her head sink on to her mother's shoulder. 'My beauty, my star,' Radha murmured into Amrita's hair. 'Just like that I will tell her, our Amrita is not for you, go find another. My charm, my little bird.' The room was so dark, only Amrita's white sari stood out.

'Go find another,' Radha repeated over and over in a sing-song voice, till Amrita said very quietly, 'Mamma, I did wrong to go to Grandfather, please forgive me.' Her mother smothered her face in kisses, saying, 'And does a mother have to be asked for forgiveness? Does not a mother's heart always forgive?' And then they sat for a long time without speaking.

Finally Radha, who had been busily thinking, said, 'We will go to Grandfather, and we will tell him that it was all a mistake, that you had misunderstood me, that is what we will go and tell him, isn't it, my darling?'

'Yes,' Amrita docilely answered. She had her eyes shut.

It was hot in the room, so they went to sit in cane chairs outside on the veranda. Out in the street people were coming home from work on bicycles, and some of them were singing. They could hear the singing quite close. Radha yawned, 'How tired I am,' and casually, 'I wonder will this Krishna be home soon.'

Amrita stared out into the distance. Though night had not quite come yet, the moon already hung between land and sky, belonging to neither, a bold and incongruous globe.

'How we miss him,' Radha sighed. 'If he leaves my house for ever, how my heart will break.'

Amrita was listening, but she did not say anything. The smell of ratki rani rose and spread like a wave, then disappeared again.

'Such a sweet boy,' Radha said. 'You also like him, isn't it child?'

'Yes,' Amrita said, so faintly she did not know whether she could be heard.

'Very much?' Radha inquired. Amrita, at once suspicious, listened more intently, but her mother did not speak again for some time.

At last she said, 'You were right, my sweet, I have to say it. Lady Ram

Prashad's son, who is he, finally, that he should dare think of my Amrita?' And after another pause: 'There is a better one for my child.'

Amrita became so excited, she got up from her chair and said in a low, but very intense, voice, 'Mamma, please, you are not thinking of Krishna now?'

'I have not said one word of him.' But Amrita ignored the protest – 'Please Mamma,' she said, very agitated, 'this you must promise me – you must never think of Krishna like that and you must never, please, I beg of you, never, never speak to him about – about anything like that.' She burned with shame at the thought. 'Please Mamma!' she cried, 'please promise me never even to hint to him!'

Radha was puzzled. She could not understand why Amrita should be feeling so strongly about it. 'What is the matter?' she asked. 'He has not been bad to you?' Amrita was still crying, 'Please promise me, promise me!'

Radha said, 'If my love wishes it, have I ever done anything against my love's wishes.' And a new suspicion began to grow, very hopefully, in her ever-fertile mind.

37

Meanwhile Krishna was still lying in his room and writing, 'My dear Amrita' or 'Dearest Amrita' or 'Amrita', and still not getting any further. He had nothing to do, he was very bored, and wanted most of all to go back to Delhi. But to go back when there was nothing settled, and the letter still unwritten – so he put it off a few days more, hoping always, tomorrow I will write it.

As he lay there on his bed, smoking cigarettes, with nothing to do and no one to talk to, his mother downstairs in her own room, more remote than Delhi, he became then, sometimes, very cynical about himself; and he thought, so I want to be like all the others, like all my former friends, with a steady job and pension, a little house, a wife, two servants. And he wondered where it had all gone to, his rebellion, his ambition, his fierce determination to lead a different, a better, life. He remembered how he had been four years ago when he came back from England, talking Communism in the coffee-house and shocking the servants by making tea for himself in the kitchen. Now he lay under the fan, with the curtains tight shut against the hot street – the dhobi on his bicycle with a big bundle of washing tied up in a sheet, an old man pulling a barrow uphill, three servants at the corner gossiping about their employers – he had drawn the curtains against them and lay there, waiting for lunch. Thinking, who can change it, and even perhaps wanting it so, because it was home and what he was used to.

He remembered England now only as a brown place, where one could not sit under the stars, and the grass was pale and the flowers, and everybody looked the same. The years he had spent there were as nothing and the ideas he had brought from there were forgotten. Forgotten, he told himself, because they do not belong here and they do not belong to me. He vaguely regretted his fervour, even his bitterness, but he shrugged off the regret. I am getting lazy, placid, older, he told himself. Perhaps it was true, but he was not capable of really despising himself for it. They do not belong here and they do not belong to me, he kept repeating; and when he asked himself what does belong to me, he was capable only of a vague mental gesture which somehow included everything – heat, flies and air-conditioned restaurants, coolies, mud huts and Vazir Dayal Mathur. And often he thought of Amrita; and then sometimes he saw her – not close up, not clear, but as he had seen her walking towards him one night across the moon-flooded lawn, enfolded in her sari, silver-lighted, sharply shadowed.

It was then that he took up his writing-pad again and wrote, 'My dear Amrita' or 'Dearest Amrita', or simply 'Amrita'; and no longer thought of himself as only wanting to be like the others, with a little house, a wife and two servants.

38

The day of the wedding was so near now that it was tomorrow, and even Hari could no longer feel vague about it. His clothes lay all ready in the big trunk – the long golden coat which Suri had worn on his wedding-day and which had now been altered to fit Hari, the fine white silken leggings, the cummerbund, the turban, the red and gold slippers with pointed toes. Every now and again the mother put her hand on the trunk and sighed.

In the same room sat Mohini, feverishly turning the handle of the little sewing-machine, shreds of material scattered over the floor. The children were wildly excited, playing at wedding with the innumerable little cousins who were staying with them, and getting in everyone's way. They were all of them indiscriminately slapped from time to time, but they hardly noticed. One of the women stood behind Mohini, desperately clutching a half-finished satin blouse, tearfully asking, would Mohini never finish with the machine? And Mohini cried, 'Wait then, wait,' and burst out crying, though she went on sewing, sewing, the tears rolling down on to the piece of cloth under the needle.

Suri came, and said he was having trouble with the band because they were asking too much money and threatening to go and play at another wedding. But he had got the mare, that was all fixed, a beautiful white mare that had done service at all the best weddings in town. The owner had told him that only last month it had been hired to the house of Shri Ram Seighal the cotton millionaire, for his son, and repeating this, Suri said, 'At the house of Shri Ram Seighal, is that a trifle?' And they all looked at one another, whispering, 'Shri Ram Seighal, and we have the same mare.'

Mohini came darting out of the room, seized one of her children and, liberally pinching and slapping, fitted a little orange suit on him, her mouth full of pins.

Then Prema came, and behind her two bearers carefully carrying four huge cardboard boxes. At once all the women came running, and gathered round the boxes, eagerly straining forward while Prema opened them.

Prema enjoyed herself very much, and was as slow and dignified as possible. 'This is for Kamladevi,' she announced, as she drew out one salwar-kamiz after the other, the clothes presented by Hari to his female relations, paid for by Suri, 'this for Rampyari', 'this for Parmeshwari'. They snatched the clothes and critically held them in front of themselves, admired themselves, while at the same time they kept a sharp look-out as to what the others were getting. Already murmurs were heard – 'why blue, when everybody knew she did not like blue, it did not suit her at all' and 'why should Rampyari get a better suit than her, was she then a better sister to Hari?' Prema's clothes were in a separate box and she allowed them a glimpse – a dark lilac satin suit glittering with sequins, which drew exclamations from them as envious as anyone could wish. 'Nine hundred rupees,' Prema was saying as the women dispersed, 'nine hundred rupees was spent on the clothes.' But they all knew that it was not more than five hundred.

Hari went to the radio. It was his last day there, for after the wedding Suri was going to take him into his business. Everybody at the radio knew he was getting married and leaving; everybody, except Amrita. Sitting in the bus, looking with dreamy eyes out of the window, Hari began to realize that what he had put off for so long was inevitably before him: he would have to tell Amrita that tomorrow he was to be married and that they must part now for ever. Perhaps she had already found out, people at the radio were bound to talk. He fidgeted in his seat: supposing she had found out and was sitting there waiting for him with accusing eyes, what was he to say to her, how was he to justify himself? And supposing, on the other hand, she had not found out; supposing she would meet him in all trustfulness and innocence, sitting in the canteen, her face lighting up as she saw him; how then to tell her of what had to be?

He turned his face and diverted all his attention out of the window. But as the bus stopped outside the *Palace* cinema and he saw next to the *Palace* the elaborate inlaid portals of the *Cavalier* restaurant, he remembered that afternoon he had spent there with Amrita and Vaidya not so long ago, when they had talked about England; and then he remembered other times they had spent together, all the meals they had in the radio canteen, the shami kebabs and parathas and oven-baked fish they had consumed in one another's company; and he remembered how they had sat together in the control-room while one of them announced, and how they had stood together by the bus-stop so many dozens of times and how they had sat side by side on the bus and how they had strolled down the corridors of the radio and how sometimes, when no one was looking, they had held hands. But most of all he remembered himself lying on a charpoy in the courtyard at home, staring up into the soft night sky, thinking about Amrita and his great love for her. And then he thought what a cruel bitter thing it was that they should be thus torn asunder, that the flood of fate should come rushing between them and carry them away, two helpless lovers, to drift their separate ways. By the time he walked up the steps to the radio, his eyes were full of tears.

She was sitting in the canteen waiting for him. He did not see her at first and half hoped that she was not there: what a relief if she was not there, and he would not have to go through an explanation with her, would just go off tomorrow and be married and never perhaps ... But there she was, he saw her, sitting alone with her head bent and drawing invisible circles on the table with her finger. He walked towards her, uneasily smiling, wondering, does she know, has anybody told her; she looked up and her face hardly altered as she saw him, she only said with a wan smile, 'Today you are almost on time.'

At once he began to make excuses – the bus, he had had to wait for it so long and then it came so slowly, so much traffic on the roads; and while he was talking, he tried to read from her face, does she know, does she? She cut him short: 'My uncle has not sent the money.' Which decided him that she did not know.

Someone called to him from the other side of the canteen; he looked round and saw Vaidya and some others waving to him and laughing; one of them made some remark and then they all laughed more, and Hari guessed that they were talking about his wedding. Now he felt that he must get Amrita away before she could gather anything from their hints; though, a little regretfully, he thought that it would have been rather pleasant to have joined them, and to have let himself be teased about getting married.

'Let us go from here,' he said to Amrita, while hastily – though still very cordially – laughing and waving back at the other table.

'Your friends are here,' she pointed out.

'No,' he said, and this surprised her very much, 'I want to be alone with you; can we never be alone?'

So they went; and walking down the stairs with her, he wondered where they could go. He had not had his lunch, but he hesitated to suggest going to a restaurant. He did not like to be seen – and he was sure to be seen – with another girl the day before his wedding. Then he remembered that this was a sad occasion, and at once he looked sad and began to think how to tell her that today they must part for ever. They were walking down the corridor-veranda of the first floor, past the air-conditioned offices of high-ranking officials. It was very quiet and empty, only a few peons in khaki uniforms sat nodding on stools.

'Where are we going?' she asked, but he did not care. They stood still and looked out over the garden down below; it was deserted, left to brood alone under white noonday heat. Over in the corner a new wing was being added to the External Services division, but work had stopped now, and odd bricks, planks of wood and white-splashed buckets lay abandoned. Three workmen sat in the shade under the big banyan tree and ate chapatis.

'So what now?' Amrita said, and he answered, tenderly and inappropriately, 'Let us only stand here together.'

'I mean,' she explained, 'what are we to do now that Uncle has not sent the money and we cannot go to England?'

He nodded as though considering, but all that seemed so remote to him now, so very finished and done with, that he could not understand why she was still talking about it.

'We must think about some other plan,' she went on. This, he decided suddenly, was the moment to tell her.

'Amrita ...' he said. But when she looked at him inquiringly, he only repeated, 'Amrita' and left it at that.

She frowned slightly and said, 'Please let us be practical now.' This chilled him, and they were both silent, looking out at the three workmen eating chapatis and the kites hovering above them. He was still thinking vaguely, I must tell her, but he could not find the words, nor the right tone; so he postponed it, and let himself stand there, for the moment, quite detached, only looking out and telling himself that the sun was hot and that it would not be pleasant to go out now.

'It is very difficult,' she sighed after a while; 'if we had money ...' but really she did not know any longer what they could do, what she would want to do, if they had money.

One of the workmen wore a solid white turban and Hari was concentrating on that, thinking how it would be if a kite were to alight on it and start pecking at the man's head. But then he felt ashamed of himself. This was their great parting scene, the end of their love, they would never see one another again, fate was cruelly tearing them apart, and here he was thinking about kites pecking. At once he looked away from the turban and assumed an expression of such deep sorrow that she, noticing it, was sorry for him and consoled, 'Never mind, we will think of something, the date of your wedding is not yet so close that we cannot think of something in the meantime.'

He looked more sorrowful than ever but did not speak. Where to start, he thought, how to tell her, and wished more than anything that she knew already: so that he could only tell her how he would love her and remember her for ever, even though he was forced to be another's. He longed to say those words and to look at her with tears in his eyes; the tears actually came into his eyes as he thought what he would say, but he looked away from her, down into the garden, where a man in a loin-cloth was walking across the lawn with a sackful of mown grass on his head.

'We will think of something tomorrow,' she went on consoling him. 'Tomorrow I will come and we will speak about it. Only today, you see, I cannot stay, I have to go home.' Because the postman would be coming at half past two, and she wanted to know quickly if there was a letter from Calcutta. Though there would not be, he would not write, one day – soon now – he would just come walking in.

'Tomorrow,' he echoed, and recollecting himself, added quickly, 'yes yes, tomorrow.'

They went walking back across the empty corridor – the peons did not stir – and down the stairs. Someone was walking upstairs and as they crossed, Hari said, 'Hallo-hallo-hallo' very cordially, though he could not remember the man's name. Walking just behind Amrita, he could see her small head with the black hair piled heavily on top, and the nape of her neck; and as he looked at her he thought, I shall not see her again, it is all finished now; but his only feeling was one of guilt because he had not told her.

Several people were standing in the main doorway, smoking cigarettes and idly looking at everyone who passed. So Amrita only said in a low voice, 'Tomorrow then,' and he said, 'Yes, tomorrow,' and they did not look at one another. Then he turned and walked away, his head bent, upstairs to his lunch, and to Vaidya who would chaff him about getting married.

It was only when she reached the bottom of the entrance steps that she remembered: tomorrow she had no duty and would not be coming. She looked back to tell him but he had gone. She shrugged a little – the day after tomorrow then – and putting up her parasol, she almost ran to the bus stop, she was in such a hurry to get home.

39

Hari felt as if he had been sitting on the mare for ever. Though the night was almost cool, with a sweet breeze blowing, he felt very hot in his golden coat buttoned right up to the neck, in his cummerbund, in his heavily garlanded turban. They had come from his own district through dense shop-lined streets and ragged lanes with straw-roofed huts, under railway bridges, past sewers, past temples, the steps clustered with people and chanting within, past bullocks grazing sparse tufts of grass from the pavements, past down-at-heel workshops and makeshift restaurants with rows of coloured bottles, past tailor-shops and silk shops with gaudy saris fluttering on hangers, past crumbling tombs of the Lodi period and flashy little red and white petrol pumps, and yellow ice-cream vans and coloured balloons bobbing on long sticks, and barrows with slices of flecked coconut on green paper and fruit-shops with polished pomegranates piled in triangles; past a furniture auction, an X-ray clinic, an open air prayer-meeting. And everywhere people stopped to look at them, and accompany them a little way, so that they drew with them a crowd of spectators and children skipping beside the band. The band – Suri had finally settled with them – played incessantly, two different tunes over and over again; and sometimes they stopped and blew the trumpet, first to one side of the street then to the other, inviting everybody to the wedding. Men with naked legs and ragged shirts walked in front of the band, and beside Hari on his mare, carrying tall lights in wooden frames on their heads so that wherever they went they brought with them a glare of bright white light. Behind Hari, very slowly, came Suri's car, containing Suri himself and Prema, Hari's mother and younger brother, Mohini, her husband and two of the children. Behind them came two other cars, hired, and behind these three tongas all overloaded with relatives. The cars and the tongas were garlanded, and the tonga-ponies rang with bells and bunches of flowers nodded on their foreheads. They had to stop several times. Once because the road was up, though there was no board or barrier, they had to turn back, the whole procession cumbrously, and go by a different way.

Another time they came to a railway crossing, and they had to wait till the little engine had puffed past and someone had found the guard to unlock the gate again. A third time they stopped respectfully for a funeral – 'a bad omen!' cried Hari's mother and looked hastily the other way – the body pitifully shrunken under a cloth and a ragged little band of followers wailing, 'Ram Ram You are the Truth' consistently on one note.

Hari felt all the time that it was someone else sitting up on the mare, being stared at, and he felt very strange and somehow far away; only the discomfort of his coat and turban brought him any sense of here-and-now, that and his little nephew sitting behind him in an orange satin suit plucking at him and urgently whispering that he had to go to the bathroom. Strings of flowers dangled from his turban over his face, so that he saw everything through a frame of flowers: he stared fixedly to the side of him, and only now and again did anything intrude itself into his mind – a shopman unfurling a roll of bright green silk, a tailor threading a needle under a kerosene lamp, an odd face here and there staring up at him. Once he saw a girl walking slowly down a side street with an earthenware pot on her head, and her narrow hips and long slender neck made him think of Amrita: and he wondered whether she had waited for him at the radio, and whether they had told her, but his thoughts were remote and unreal and did not touch his feelings, like words overheard from a stranger. Another time he caught sight of someone he knew in the crowd, a boy who had been to school with him, whom he had not seen since; and for the first time he was touched, for he remembered how it had been then, at school, sitting on a little bench under the trees, secretly eating jambuls and throwing the stones at his friends when the teacher was not looking. And then he remembered how they had shaved his head when he was four years old, and how once he had been very ill, tossing days and nights between blankets while his mother and his aunts touched his forehead and murmured prayers over him; and once he had gone with his father, there was a big crowd and his father had held him up on his shoulder to see Gandhiji, just out of prison, smiling. It was all long ago, he felt it as having been long ago, but still it was as near to him as this now, this riding on a mare to the house of his bride.

They sat in the garden after dinner, sunk in deck-chairs; only the Rai Bahadur sat stiffly upright on a green garden-chair. A cool breeze rippled through the trees and over the lawn, bringing the smell – remote as yet, perhaps only a memory – of fallen leaves, of winter not so far away. They breathed it in deeply and with pleasure, and from time to time Radha said 'aah' with great satisfaction. Mira murmured, half-asleep, she must go to

Rayner's and get a new coat made for the winter, which drew from Radha a disapproving snort, did she not have enough good coats already? Yes, said Mira, but this year the fashions are different, coats are long and loose, she saw it in an English magazine, very suitable for ladies with stouter figures.

The butler came with a little table and a lamp, and when the lamp was switched on it cast a little pool of red light from under its shade. The Rai Bahadur did not like to sit in the dark, it made him feel uncomfortable.

'Husband will be home from Simla soon, I think,' said Tarla, but it was not possible to tell from her voice whether she was pleased or not.

'And Krishna Sen Gupta from Calcutta,' Radha said, sounding a little smug.

Beyond the pool of red light everything was a dark, almost a black, green, for they were surrounded only by their own garden. The sound of traffic, a car hooting, the rattle of an old bus, came to them distantly from the main road two blocks away.

'We will send Amrita to England next March,' the Rai Bahadur announced. He sounded very pontifical, and had every right to do so. In the afternoon Amrita had come with her mother and they had both declared that it had all been a misunderstanding, and that of course they would be guided only by the Rai Bahadur's own decisions.

'Yes Pappaji,' Radha said demurely.

'She will need many warm clothes,' Mira said, 'for I hear it is always cold there. I will take her to Rayner's with me and they will make a beautiful coat for her.' After reflection she added, 'In beige.'

Suddenly they heard from the main road the sound of a band. It came to them filtered through still night-air, a blatant joy very remote from their own dark garden with the old trees.

'Another wedding,' Radha commented, and thought with satisfaction of Hari.

Mira sighed and said, 'And I thought perhaps this year our Amrita ... Beautiful saris I have all ready for her, and jewellery, is she not our only daughter?'

'We will have no more talk of that,' the Rai Bahadur said without turning his head, so that he spoke out into the dark garden.

'Of course not, Pappaji,' Radha said, aiming disapproval at Mira. 'Not until the child herself wishes it. I have never approved of these arranged marriages myself; they are very backward and not suitable to modern times.'

The music from the wedding had faded away into the far distance, still insistently gleeful.

'When the girl herself comes with reasonable wishes,' the Rai Bahadur pronounced after a while, 'then of course we shall put nothing in the way of her happiness.' The platitude rolled smoothly and weightily from his lips.

'Yes Pappaji,' Radha assented, so cheerfully that Tarla threw a sharp look in her direction. But the light from the little red lamp was too dim to reveal facial expressions.

At last they reached the bride's house, where the whole roadway was blocked by the big red-and-white striped wedding-marquee and a ragged crowd of spectators. Two bands struck up, a gramophone played, coloured lights revolved and flashed, and the bride's party cried, 'They have come!' and stood on chairs to get a better look at the bridegroom.

Hari was helped off his horse and hustled inside; people pressed him close, laughing, slapping him on the shoulders, stroking his neck, his cheeks, and someone gave him a garland which he held in his hands; a passage was cleared, and then Sushila was brought to him, in red salwar-kamiz with gold and silver ribbons stitched on, her face veiled by her dupatta. She stretched up and hung a garland round his neck, and he, looking intensely over her head, slung the garland which they had given to him round her neck, as he might sling a worn shirt over a bedpost. Sushila's grandmother shouted out loud that they were standing in the wrong way, that he had to face East and she West, that now everything was lost and they would have to start all over again. But the others said, no, never mind, it was a good omen, and they cleared a passage for the photographer, who came bustling forward while Hari and Sushila were placed side by side to blink foolishly into the flashlight.

And then the introductions were effected, the bridegroom's uncle met the bride's, his cousin her cousin, his nephew her nephew, though for the most part they had already known one another all their lives. But before the introductions were finished, the women – the bride's aunts, sisters, cousins – carried off Hari, out of the marquee up into the house, and they all sat down on the floor in one of the rooms, with Hari and Sushila in the middle, and they began to sing, clapping their hands and laughing and making fun of the bridegroom. Hari grinned sheepishly all the way through; he felt lost and stupid among all these teasing women and, not knowing where to look, he kept his eyes fixed on his big toe. He did not think of Sushila, never looked at her, but her presence there so near to him was a discomfort and an embarrassment to him. It was worse still when they threw a rupee into a bowl of water and he and Sushila had to compete in getting it out: he could make no effort to win the coin, could only concentrate intensely on not coming into contact with her hand there under the water. Oh, but how they mocked him, taunted him, teased him, all these girls and women, what fun they had at his expense; he did not notice, did not care, was only concerned with not touching Sushila's hand.

At last Suri and others from his party came to rescue him, good-humouredly bantered and bargained for him with the women, who refused to give him up, had indeed hidden his slippers so that he could not leave. One of Sushila's sisters was pushed forward. She giggled, she hid her face in her dupatta, she could not speak; till Mrs Anand pinched her arm and said, 'Hurry now, hurry,' and then the girl said, choking with laughter, that she would return Hari's shoes and let him go if she was paid ten rupees. There was great laughter and applause, Suri pressed ten rupees into the girl's hand, saying she knew how to drive a bargain – which amused Mr Anand so much that he flapped his arms up and down crowing, 'her father's daughter!' – the slippers were produced and Hari was released. The sister held out the ten rupees. She did not know what to do with them, so she offered them to her mother, who gave her a push and told her to get away and leave her alone. Hari's feet were tight and uncomfortable in his golden slippers, and it was painful for him to walk down the stairs.

Amrita paced up and down the lawn, too excited to stay still. She held Krishna's letter in her hand, six pages of it beginning, 'Amrita'; she had been holding it ever since it had come by the evening post, and from time to time she ran into the room and read it again under the lamp, from beginning to end. After which she walked into the garden again, round and round, clutching the letter, and sometimes she laughed and hid her face in her hands. The servant kept asking, would she not come and eat her dinner, but she could not eat; Gian looked worried and said, what would her mother say when she came home and found that Amrita had not eaten her dinner. Amrita too wondered what her mother would say, though not about the neglected dinner; she thought about how she would tell her – she did not want to show her the letter, and see Radha put on her spectacles and solemnly, self-importantly, go through it, line by line – no, she would tell her, she would say, 'Mamma ...' But she could not keep her thoughts fixed, nor think out rationally just how to tell her or in what words; she had to move about around the garden, feel the breeze flutter her sari, stop by the plantain tree, pluck a flower from the hedge and, inwardly bubbling over with laughter, stick in into her hair. Only sometimes she thought, 'poor Hari' and wondered how she would be able to tell him; but the thought did not disturb her nearly as much as she felt it ought to, and she soon glided away from it, walking round and round the garden with the white flower gleaming in her hair and the servant calling from the veranda, please to come and eat her dinner, or what would her mother say.

The auspicious hour for the ceremony was at half past one in the morning. The bridegroom's party has been feasted: there had been kebabs and mountains of white rice and meat curries and gram and curds, but to Hari everything was tasteless, and he even found it difficult to move his jaws for chewing. They kept piling his plate higher and higher shouting, he must eat, would he not soon need all his strength? And there was much laughter and further suggestive jokes, so that Hari thought it best to keep on smiling, though he was not really listening. And now he was sitting cross-legged under the canopy in front of the sacred fire, with Sushila next to him. The pandit sat opposite and droned ceaseless prayers; from time to time he was interrupted by some of the old people, mostly by Sushila's grandmother, who protested that he was saying the prayers in the wrong order, that it was all unorthodox and unfitting, but he always managed to settle the dispute very quickly, for he was used to dealing with religious old women. The fire was very hot and the pandit kept moving back a few more inches, and twice he called for a glass of water. Hari's foot had gone to sleep and perspiration was running down his nose; he also felt his turban coming loose, and all the time he was aware of Sushila's knee, clad in red. It was all he saw of her and he could not get away from it. Just behind him his mother was sobbing, and sometimes he felt her hand stroking his back and heard her pronounce God's name. Prema was also crying, looking at Sushila, still and veiled, and remembering her own wedding and contrasting the happiness of that day with the bitter years which followed; and then she was reminded to look at Suri and saw him looking at Mrs Anand, which made her cry more. Most of the children were asleep, sprawled over their mothers' knees, while the pandit chanted his stream of prayers. The old grandmother sat with her eyes tight shut and prayed incessantly; only sometimes she looked round, and whoever met that sharp black eye instantly looked devout. But at last – after many hours, or so it seemed to Hari, though really it was only two – at last the pandit stopped, and they helped Hari to his feet and adjusted his turban, and then they tied the end of his cummerbund to Sushila's dupatta. And so he led her round the fire, though he hardly realized that he was leading her; he walked and walked in a circle, never looking up, the fire so hot and people pressing round and the pandit chanting again, he just walked, losing count, so that he did not know how many times he had already been round, prepared if they wanted him to walk thus for ever. His cheeks became wet, then his neck, right inside the collar, but it took him some time to realize that he was crying. He went on walking, aware only of the heat of the fire and the wetness of tears, though he could hear women sobbing and one cracked old voice shouting that the dupatta was tied in the wrong way. And then suddenly they began to throw flowers over him, from all sides they came, the petals, a sweet and sickly shower falling over his head and face and shoulders. It was all over, a high-pitched voice sang a hymn, the sobbing was near to him now, he felt himself surrounded, his mother, his sisters, more flowers came falling down on him: he had led her round the fire seven times and now she was his, and though he still could not see her, hardly even thought of her, he was suddenly so happy, he felt he had never been so happy in all his life.

MORE ABOUT PENGUINS, PELICANS AND PUFFINS

Ruth Prawer Jhabvala

'One questions whether any western writer has had a keener, cooler understanding of the temperament of urban India' – *Guardian*

'A writer of genius ... a writer of world class – a master storyteller' – *Sunday Times*

'Someone once said that the definition of the highest art is that one should feel that life is this and not otherwise. I do not know of a writer living who gives that feeling with more unqualified certainty than Mrs Jhabvala' – C. P. Snow

GET READY FOR BATTLE

In a series of wittily observed scenes Ruth Jhabvala draws a sharp and perceptive, yet always compassionate, portrait of middle-class family life in contemporary Delhi, though a group of people who are all ready for battle – with each other and themselves. But beneath the ironies, the personal problems and conflicts, we catch a glimpse of India's terrifying social problems, and also of the deep moral consciousness which may prove her salvation.

A BACKWARD PLACE

The trouble with Bal was not his lack of ideas but the fact that they tended to be rather grand long-term visions whereas his life was organized on a decidedly short-term basis. And for Judy his English wife, Etta the ageing sophisticate, Clarissa the upper middle-class drop-out from the English establishment, the worthy Hochstadts on a two-year exchange visit, and all the other characters who figure in this enchanting novel, India always poses a host of contradictions.

and

ESMOND IN INDIA

THE HOUSEHOLDER

HOW I BECAME A HOLY MOTHER

IN SEARCH OF LOVE AND BEAUTY